A TALE OF TWO COLORS

# STORM of TERROR

VOLUME VI

A TALE OF TWO COLORS

# STORM of TERROR

VOLUME VI

## ANTHONY WOOD

WILL ROGERS MEDALLION WINNER

HAT CREEK

## HAT CREEK

An Imprint of Roan & Weatherford Publishing Associates, LLC
Bentonville, Arkansas
www.roanweatherford.com

Copyright © 2024 by Anthony Wood

**Library of Congress Cataloging-in-Publication Data**
Names: Wood, Anthony, author.
Title: Storm of Terror/Anthony Wood | A Tale of Two Colors #6
Description: First Edition. | Bentonville: Hat Creek, 2024.
Identifiers: LCCN: 2024939219 | ISBN: 978-1-63373-949-9 (hardcover) |
ISBN: 978-1-63373-950-5 (trade paperback) | ISBN: 978-1-63373-951-2 (eBook) |
Subjects: | BISAC: FICTION/Historical/Civil War Era |
FICTION/War and Military | FICTION/Action/Adventure |
LC record available at: https://lccn.loc.gov/2024939219

Hat Creek trade paperback edition November, 2024

Cover & Interior Design by Casey W. Cowan
Cover art by W. Herbert Dunton (1878-1936)
*Night Riders,* 1915, Oil on canvas
Editing by Amy Cowan & Lisa Lindsey

*For my brother, Larry,*
*whose faithful friendship planted the seed*
*for the character of Lummy's brother, Elihu.*
*I'm the better man for you being in my life.*

# ACKNOWLEDGEMENTS

WHERE WOULD HISTORICAL fiction writers be without those who so willingly give of their time and energy to ensure accurate history is made available to researchers and authors who desire to write the most authentic historical fiction scenes as possible? There is not enough room here to list all of the museum curators, park rangers, librarians, living history reenactors, and others who have so willingly helped me in my research efforts. I thank you all for the blessing you are to my writing.

One historian's work rose to the top as I spent many hours trying to understand the life and times of the legendary West-Kimbrell Gang and their eventual execution by local residents.

The late Jack Peebles's *The Legend of the Nightriders,* proved to be invaluable and without his fine work, I could not have written this novel. Special thanks goes to his wife, Nydia Peebles, and her son, Scott, for helping me obtain a copy of Mr. Peebles latest revised edition, which includes additional research essential to understanding the events that happened in Winn Parish, Louisiana so long ago.

Much of the dialogue in the scenes surrounding the demise of the West-Kimbrell Gang is as Mr. Peebles recorded it from various primary and secondary sources referenced in his fine volume. I made little to no variation as I crafted the scenes and give Mr. Peebles full credit for his invaluable work to preserve these historical events, descriptions, and conversations. What a treasure it is to have the actual dialogue included in this work of historical fiction.

# AUTHOR'S NOTE

R ARE IS IT indeed that an ancestor encounters such a notorious outlaw as John West. Being two of only one hundred or so privates who served with Company F of the 27th Louisiana Volunteer Infantry would have put Lummy Tullos in daily contact and close proximity with John West during the siege of Vicksburg, according to Terry G. Scriber's *Twenty-seventh Louisiana Volunteer Infantry,*

While it is unknown if Lummy Tullos took part the demise of the West-Kimbrell gang, he certainly must've shouldered a weapon alongside John West or shared a meal together in a rifle pit in the 27th Louisiana Lunette in the great Civil War contest for Vicksburg. One thing is for certain, though. Lummy Tullos knew John West.

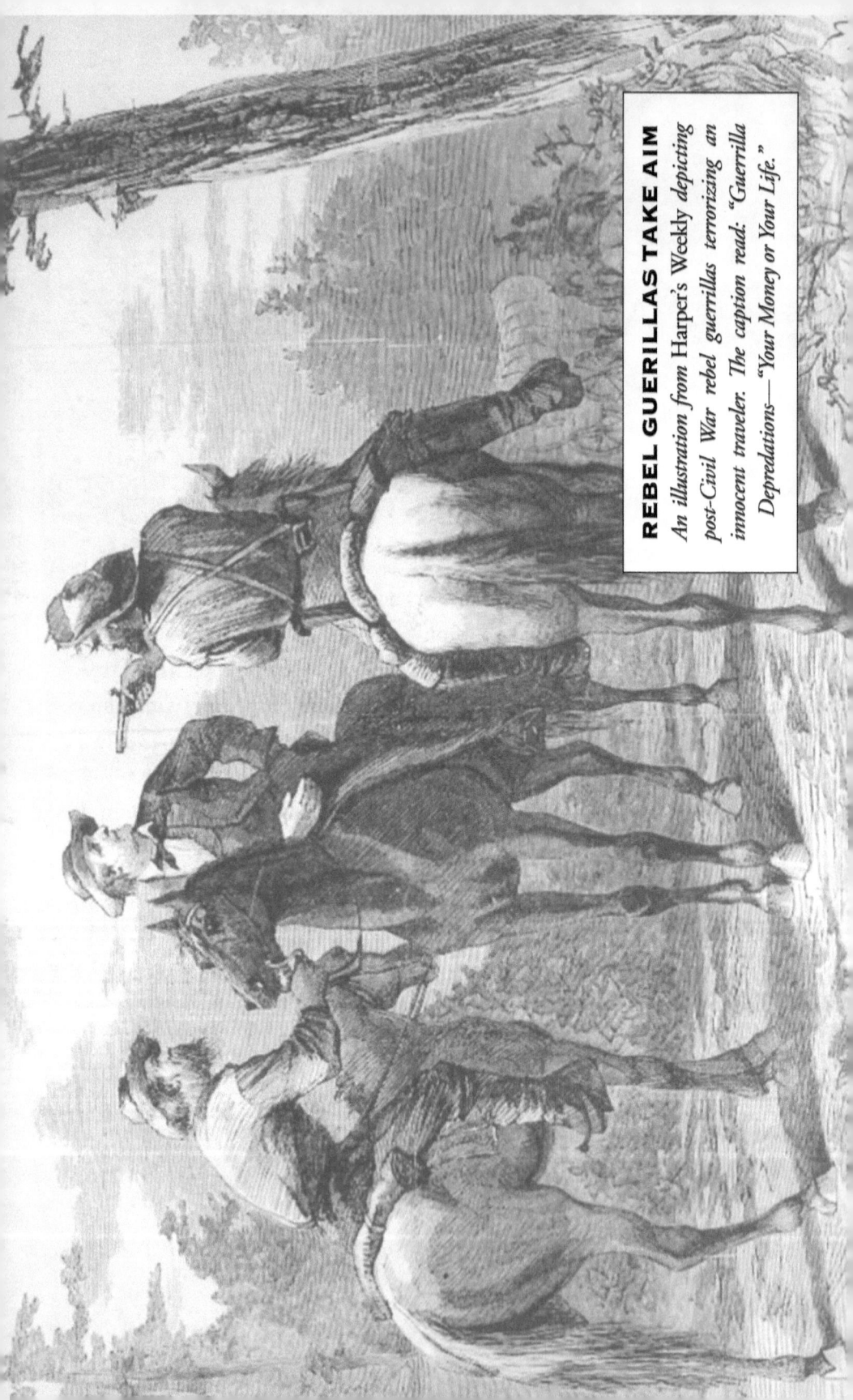

**REBEL GUERILLAS TAKE AIM**

An illustration from Harper's Weekly depicting post–Civil War rebel guerrillas terrorizing an innocent traveler. The caption read: "Guerrilla Depredations—"Your Money or Your Life.""

# DRAMATIS PERSONAE

ANNIE "FANNY" HANDERSON: Lummy's sassy and frisky snuff-dipping friend who patched up his shoulder injury suffered during a ferry crossing the Mississippi River from Vicksburg, Mississippi to Desoto, Louisiana, in search of Susannah. She was a mess. Lummy crossed paths with Annie at Desoto on his way to enlist in the Confederate Army, and when he returned to Vicksburg to enlist in the Union Army, he found her married to Beau, the owner of Handerson's Café. Annie introduced Lummy to her widowed sister, Martha. Lummy's heart is captured, and he and Martha marry after the war. Lummy settles into a peaceful life with Martha and her children on the Tullos farm. Annie Fanny is still a mess.

COLUMBUS "LUMMY" NATHAN TULLOS: Archibald and Mary Tullos's sixth child, born in 1834. As the main character, Lummy leaves his home in Choctaw County, Mississippi to begin an adventurous journey to find his love, a young slave woman named Susannah, who was taken by a gambler in a card game. He finds her in Winn Parish, and they eventually marry, but nearly a year into Lummy's service with the Confederate Army in Vicksburg, he receives news of Susannah's death. He joins the Union Army to help end the war and finds new love in the process. He returns home to the Tullos farm in search of peace and quiet and finds it. But not for long.

**DAN CREEKWATER:** Lummy's Choctaw friend whom he first met on the road to Winn Parish back in 1859. Dan's wisdom of the Universe helped Lummy sort out his recent war experiences and make his decision to join the 1st Mississippi Mounted Rifles. Lummy shared a camp with Dan in the haunts of McCurtain Creek Swamp after killing Lester, who tried to rape and kill Lummy's family. Dan helped Lummy find his soul again. He's always around, ready to help Lummy in any way.

**ELIHU TULLOS:** Lummy's eccentric older brother who stayed home to care for the family and farm in Choctaw County during the war. Elihu became Lummy's greatest ally as he made his decision to join the Union Army. Elihu was the first to experience Lummy's trauma due to his war experiences. He is a faithful brother to a fault.

**ELZEY BURK TULLOS:** Lummy and Susannah's son who was unknown to him until he traveled to Winn Parish after Vicksburg surrendered. Because of his less-than-stable state of mind and the possibility of re-entering the war, Lummy decided to leave Elzey with a good family in Winn Parish until such time that he might return, which he hopes to do one day.

**JASPER NEWTON AND JAMES A. TULLOS:** Lummy's two younger brothers who served with the 1st Mississippi Light Artillery, Company C during the Siege of Vicksburg, near where Lummy was stationed. They returned to the Tullos farm after the war and enjoy family and farming.

**MARTHA BROCK TULLOS:** Lummy's wife and Annie Fanny's sister. They marry in Vicksburg and move to Choctaw County with Martha's four children. It's not long before they have a daughter together, Delaware.

**RAINY MILLS:** Lummy first met Rainy while running into his camp being chased by coyotes on his search for Susannah. They quickly became friends, and Rainy came with others to help end Captain Tom Ford's evil reign in Choctaw County.

SERGEANT "SARGE" McGUGARTY: Lummy met Sarge at the parole after the surrender of Vicksburg. He encouraged Lummy to join the 1st Mississippi Mounted Rifles, the only white Union regiment from Mississippi in the Civil War, which he did. He served under Sarge when Lummy and Tom Poole led Union cavalry to burn the manufactories in Bankston, Lummy's hometown, and until the end of the war. Sarge came to Lummy's aid as he and a small band of friends took down Captain Tom Ford's outlaw gang.

SETH: A young runaway slave Lummy took under his wing on his way home to the Tullos farm from Winn Parish after ending Dawg Smith and his outlaw gang's reign of terror. Seth became a member of the family. In helping Seth, Lummy realizes the good influence that the late Mr. James T. Gilmore had in his life. Seth is murdered by Captain Tom Ford and his men.

SUSANNAH: A young slave woman and Lummy's first love taken from Choctaw County, Mississippi to Winn Parish, Louisiana by James T. Gilmore, who won her in a card game. Lummy left home to find Susannah in Winn Parish and eventually marries her. He learned while stationed in Vicksburg a year later that Susannah died of measles. Lummy returned to Winn Parish after the surrender of Vicksburg to find that Susannah did not die of the measles, but rather was brutally raped and murdered by Dawg Smith and his outlaw gang. Lummy made things right by ending Smith's life. Susannah will always have a place in Lummy's heart. She visits him on occasion still.

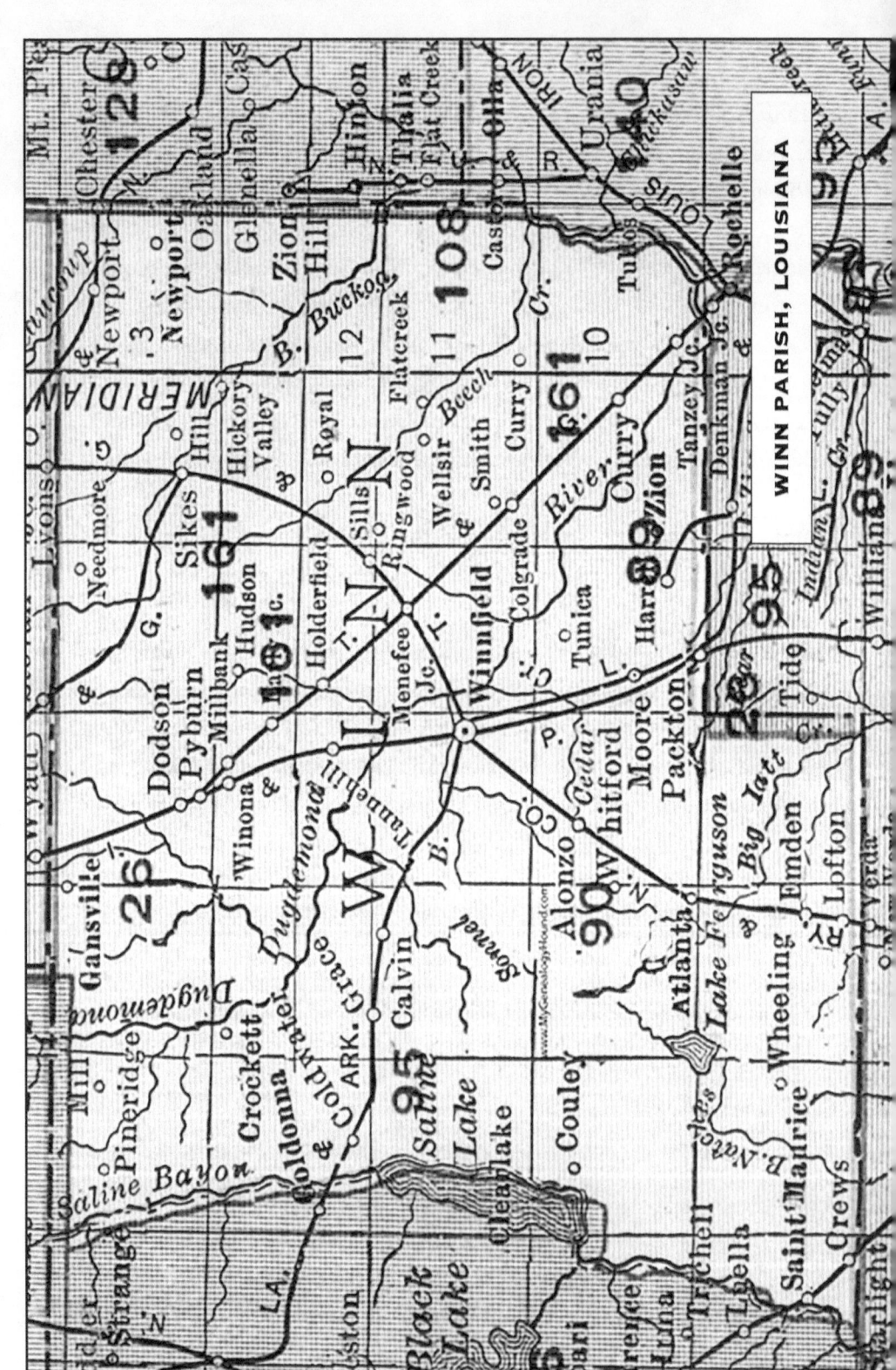

WINN PARISH, LOUISIANA

# SCAENA

**CHOCTAW COUNTY, MISSISSIPPI:** Founded and created in 1833 from lands ceded by the Choctaw Indians and named for them. Lummy's parents, Archibald and Mary Tullos, settled there as pioneers in 1835. Lummy grew up in Choctaw County, and his family helped start one of the county's first Baptist Churches, New Zion, in 1842. With the war over, he desperately wants to find a peaceful life with his family on the farm there only to find Captain Tom Ford and his gang terrorizing the county. Lummy, with a band of friends, ends Ford's reign of destruction.

**VICKSBURG, MISSISSIPPI:** An important river port and railroad town that linked the east and west of the growing United States. Lummy boarded a ferry there in search of Susannah and later saw Vicksburg again from across the river as he boarded a steamer to travel south to enlist in the Confederate Army. Returning to the city after training at Camp Moore in early May 1862, he survived the Siege of Vicksburg and was paroled in July of 1863. He passed through Vicksburg on his way to Choctaw County from Winn Parish after taking down the Dawg Smith gang. He returned once again to the city to enlist in the 1st Mississippi Mounted Rifles and meets Martha, who becomes his new bride. He and his band of friends gather at Annie Fanny Handerson's café in Vicksburg to make a plan to destroy Captain Tom Ford and his gang.

WINN PARISH, LOUISIANA: Lummy traveled to Winn Parish in search of Susannah and finds her with James T. Gilmore, a gambler who won slaves to set them free. Lummy joined his long lost brother and family to work on the Gilmore farm where Ben is foreman. Lummy married Susannah just before he left to enlist in the Confederate Army. Lummy's plan was to return to the farm after the war where he and Susannah could build a life together. Returning to Winn Parish after the surrender of Vicksburg, Lummy learned the truth of Susannah's death and found out they had a son, Elzey. Life with Susannah no longer possible, Lummy went home to Choctaw County after settling his affairs in Winn Parish. Given his state of mind, he believed it best to leave Elzey in Winn Parish with a good family until such time as he was fit to return for his son.

A TALE OF TWO COLORS

# STORM of TERROR

VOLUME VI

# CHAPTER 1

# WHEN THINGS DON'T GO AS PLANNED

## MARCH 2, 1870

*Some wars never end.*

"**D**AMN IT ALL to hell! Am I not *DONE* with all of this?" The young, blue-uniformed private cringes, daring not to look me in the eye. "Sir?"

"You want me to come with you?"

"Yes, sir. That's what I was told to say when I found you."

"By whose authority?"

He salutes. "President Grant himself, sir."

I stand up, working the lever on my Henry Rifle, and push my son to the side. "Stand back just a bit." My son by marriage, John A., backs away from our chess game.

The messenger, too young to even shave, trembles, standing at attention at the bottom of the steps of our dogtrot home. He awaits my response.

I say nothing.

His voice squeaks like a newborn kitten. "I don't want any trouble, sir. I'm just following orders." His skin is pale as fresh cream, his face as smooth as a baby's behind, and he looks to be twice as innocent.

I try to soften a bit. I can't get there. "When'd you enlist, son?"

He straightens his belt and repositions his hat. "June twenty-sixth of this year, sir."

"Ain't that the damnedest thing—" I catch myself. "The same day I mustered out of the Mounted Rifles back in '65, five years ago."

I crumple the official piece of paper and sit back down in Pa's old rocking chair. I want to tear the message to shreds and burn it. I ease the hammer on my rifle back into the safe position.

"Martha, dear, would you come out here, please? I need you." Martha, my rock and savior.

"Be right there, Lummy."

I squint at the private. "What's your name, son?"

He throws up another salute. "Private Sam Reed, at your service, sir."

"You don't need to do anything for me, and stop calling me sir. And enough of the salutin'."

Private Reed drops his hand. "Yes, sir. Just trying to be a good soldier, sir."

"And a fine soldier you'll make, I'm sure. At ease, son, you'll find no trouble here."

Private Reed puts one foot forward and relaxes on his right hip with hands folded in front. He breathes a long sigh of relief. "Thank you, sir. So, you'll be coming with me?"

"I didn't say that." I hand the message to Martha.

Martha pats John A. on the shoulder. "Son, you and Mary go inside, please."

John A. starts to scoop up the chess pieces.

"Hold it, son. We'll finish our game in a minute."

John A. drops the pieces on the porch. They look like so many soldiers fallen on a battlefield. He squats to scoop them up.

I stare at the soldier, and young Granville's face appears. Granville died at seventeen in the Vicksburg trenches. I touch the playing board. "A young man named Granville made this chess set for me, John A." I'm looking right at John A., but I don't see him. "He was killed."

I grip the rocking chair arm to the point of white knuckles. Cannons blast, and men scream. I want to scream with them. I come to for a moment. The young soldier turns away. Things are spinning out of control. The war is seizing my soul, and I can't stop it. I need to do something to stop this. Right now.

"Mary stays," I bark. "Somebody needs to remember what's happening here."

Mary pulls a pencil and paper from her apron pocket.

"And John A., too, Martha. He's a man now."

Martha squeezes my shoulder. "Okay, dear. John A., bring this young man a cup of cool water, please. He'll be thirsty from ridin' with news I'm sure none of us want to hear."

"Yes, 'um."

Private Reed doesn't know how to respond to my silence or Martha's reddening face as she unfolds the wadded up piece of paper. He tips his hat. "Fine children, ma'am."

Martha doesn't smile. A soldier's message can't be good news. "What's it say, Lummy?"

"Read it for yourself." Though it's not about her, I can't help snapping at somebody.

Martha stiffens.

I catch my thoughts. What am I saying? This message has everything to do with her. I touch Martha's arm and stroke her smooth skin. "Sorry, dear. I didn't mean to be so rough."

Martha's eyes forgive me without her speaking a word. She flattens out the wrinkled paper wad against a porch post and compliments me in my emotional storm. "I haven't heard you cuss like that in a long time."

"Yeah, it's been a year since I said any bad words out loud, but I still think 'em when I used to say 'em." I wink at John A., who hands the soldier a tin cup of water. "It takes a while to undo things practiced for a long time."

John A. pats me on the shoulder. "It's okay, Pop."

Martha takes a deep breath. "I still say you've made good progress, dear. I'm proud my boys are growin' up with a man who loves his Creator more than himself and is willing to change when he needs to. Now, what's this about?"

I scratch my stubble beard. "You won't be happy about it. Some things don't change."

Martha covers her mouth with the wrinkled message and grabs a porch post, steadying herself. She squeezes her eyes shut tight as the full weight of the truth sinks in. Tears appear in the corners of her eyes. She stares back at the paper, her frown betraying a heavy heart. She looks to the clouds. "The possibilities attached to this message could affect all of our lives." She comes back to herself and reads the note again.

Her words spill from her heart like a cow kicking over a milking bucket. "Dear God. Not again." She crumples the paper and throws it at the soldier's feet. "No, suh. My husband's done his bit for God and family, for gray and blue, and right here in Choctaw County. I don't care what President Grant or anybody else wants. My husband stays home."

Mary picks the message up and stuffs that piece of family history into her apron pocket.

Martha has every right to be upset. I clench the rocking chair arms hard enough to break them. It's coming. I can't stop it.

A shot rings out down the creek behind the house. I dive for the porch floor, covering my head, grasping for my pistol that's not there. "Where are they? Have they made it to the pit? Where's my gun? Where's J.A.? I need J.A.!"

All I can see are hundreds of bluecoats charging and screaming as they claw their way up the hill in front of the 27th Louisiana Lunette in Vicksburg when we rise as one man to pour devastating fire into their ranks. Blood showers the ground in every direction like a cloud burst. A cannon shell explodes overhead, and a minie ball splits the man's skull next to me like a ripe melon. Granville is balled up like a roly-poly, crying, and Hog Fart has his back against the earthworks wall, his pants wet all down the front.

"Get your head down, Hog Fart!" Warm blood and brains splatter on my face as I line my musket up on the brass button of a scared Yankee soldier. I pull the trigger and... hands shake my shoulders.

"Lummy, come back. It's all right. It's me, Elihu."

I don't know where I am or who I'm looking at for a moment.

He splashes a bit of water in my face. Elihu's face becomes clear. "Martha's here, too, little brother."

Martha takes the knife Pa made me from my hand and gives it to Elihu. "It's all right, dear. You're safe, and everyone here is fine. Come back to me, my sweet husband."

I wipe my eyes. "I'm okay." I rub my neck. "It's just another one of those crazy daytime dreams I've been havin'."

Elihu strokes the back of my head. "I'm sorry, Brother. I shot us a big swamp rabbit for supper in that cane patch down by Phoenix Creek. I'll hunt farther out next time."

"Wasn't your fault. These crazy feelin's come with no warning. It's like I'm reliving the war all over again. When they come on me, I can't tell if I'm here or there. It's too real. And I can't stop it when it starts."

Private Reed sneaks back out from behind his horse where he's been hiding. "I've never seen anything like that before."

Elihu barks, "That's because you ain't never gone through anythin' like that before."

Martha smiles sadly. "Rest yourself, soldier. This may take a minute."

He nods and removes his hat. "Thanks for the water, ma'am."

Mary fills a blank page in her little book. She pulls the message from her apron and scribbles down the words written there. She catches Private Reed eyeing her and sneaks him a grin.

Martha kisses my forehead. "They're comin' a little more often these days, aren't they, dear?" She caresses my neck and cheeks. "Maybe you should see the doc?"

"I don't know what he can do for me, but after this one, I suppose I should."

"I wish you would. You do a pretty good job of hidin' it, but—"

"I'm too dangerous when they take hold."

"So, maybe soon?"

"The pain on the outside is never as deep as on the inside." I stroke her arm. "Yes, soon."

James steps out on the porch, nursing a cup of Elihu's cool muscadine wine. "What's all the damned commotion?"

Martha gives her youngest brother-in-law the evil eye for cursing and motions to Mary to hand James the paper.

Mary glances at Private Reed.

He grins, and she blushes.

I want to say something, but it's not the right time. Besides, she is a beautiful young woman to be admired by young men.

James snickers. "Pa always said that sometimes the only word that'll work is damn." I know what's coming, and it won't be good.

Martha cuts her eyes at me, then at James. "Not in this house, mind you, James Tullos. You, too, Lummy. Save it for when you boys go huntin' and moonshine sippin'." I love her strength and fire.

Gently, James helps me back into my rocking chair. "You have another attack, Brother?"

"Yeah, but it was much stronger this time. I could see right into the eyes of them Yanks."

He hands me his half-finished cup of wine. "How often is this happenin'?"

"More'n I want, that's for sure." I take a long drink.

Martha turns to face the messenger. "And now they want to peel off a little more of his hide."

Private Reed doesn't dare look up.

James opens the folded paper. "What do you mean?"

"Read it and see," Martha whispers, wringing her hands.

The young soldier shifts one foot to the other, hoping Martha won't bring her wrath down on him. He offers what he hopes is a peaceful compromise that will remove him from her path.

"Sir, I'm sorry, but I have to ask... are you coming now, or should I say you will report in the morning?"

James finishes the message and throws the paper down. "Son of a bitch!"

Martha slaps his shoulder. "James, the children!"

James reels from the blow. "I'm sorry but not half as much as I am for what's on that paper." He picks the message back up and shakes it at the young soldier, who steps back.

Mary reaches for the message. "Uncle James, I need that."

He hands it to her. "This is goin' over like bad wind let out in the school-house. We should kick his ass—uh, I mean, backside—back up the road. Sorry, Martha." James steps toward the young soldier who takes another step back. "Why him?"

"That, I can't tell you, sir. I'm just delivering the message my lieutenant ordered me to deliver."

I stand up. "And just who would that lieutenant be, Private?"

"Lieutenant McGugarty, sir."

"Lieutenant Michael McGugarty, my old sergeant from Company C of the First Mississippi Mounted Rifles?"

Private Reed nods.

I cringe. "I don't believe it, and stop callin' me sir. If you want to call someone sir, go up that hill there and talk to my pa. He's the only sir around here. And he's dead. And you will be, too, if—"

Martha slides a comforting arm around my shoulder. "Calm down, dear. He's just doing what he's been told."

James rubs his forehead. "Lummy, did you read the entire message?"

"More bad news?"

"You could say that, but Private Reed is right. He has to call you sir."

I grab the piece of paper. "Let me see that. A sergeant? What in the hell?"

Private Reed salutes. "Yes, sir, Sergeant Columbus Nathan Tullos, sir."

## CHAPTER 2

# PEACE LIES ON THE FAR SIDE OF TROUBLE

### NEAR MIDNIGHT, MARCH 2, 1870

*Peace always lies on the other side of trouble, if you can make it there.*

THE ONLY COMFORT I allow myself tonight is an occasional sip of the Wood brothers' moonshine. The sting in my throat reminds me of worse pains, especially at the center of my soul. Against it, the moonshine's no more than a cool sip of water from Aaron Wood's Spring.

How unexpectedly things change. Just when I thought I'd be free to work the farm, raise the kids, have a few of my own, and love up on Martha, the "gods," as they say, seem to favor a different plan. Gods are just another way of saying demons—demons who believe they control the world. Sometimes they do. Sometimes I let them. I'll have to do that now.

My only consolation, besides Martha, is that Creator is in my corner. I'll listen for his voice, if I can hear it. It'll come by the word of the woman who brought love back into my heart. Martha. What a blessing.

SLEEP DOESN'T COME easy, and I'm up before the rooster crows. A red sun peeks over the ridge, bleeding all over creation. Martha is waiting with a cup of coffee fixed just the way I like it—fresh cream with a little honey. And hot.

She puts her arm around me. "What time are you supposed to meet Sarge?"

"Ten o'clock." I blow on my steaming cup. "He's a lieutenant now. That'll take some gettin' used to."

"Can I go with you? I need to pick up a few things."

That cheers my heart. "Good company makes a bumpy wagon ride smoother." In truth, I know she wants to go along in case I have an attack like yesterday.

"When do you want to leave?"

"As soon as I can get the wagon hitched."

"Good. I'll put on a nice dress and fix my hair."

"You might wear a bonnet. It's windy out."

"Thanks, I will."

"I'll bring a tarp. It could rain."

"I'll look a fright if it does."

I glance out the window. "Pa used to say when he woke up to a morning like this, 'Red sky at night, sailor's delight. Red sky in the morning, sailor's warning.'"

Pa said that old saying was passed down from our ancestor, Cloud Tullos, after he survived a great storm when he crossed the big water from Scotland to Virginia back in 1661. I'm sure he learned early how to know when a storm was brewing.

A storm is brewing right before my eyes, and I don't even know from what direction it will hit. If Sarge is part of it, it will be of the worst kind—a storm of terror.

# CHAPTER 3

# A TWENTIETH STAR
# FOR ALL

*The best of old friends sometimes deliver the worst news.*

I HELP MARTHA out of the wagon in front of Wesson's Mercantile. She kisses my cheek. "I won't be long. Meet back here in an hour?"

I straighten my jacket. "Sure."

"Tell Sarge I said hello. Invite him to supper and to stay the night."

"I'll ask him." I start to cross the street to the Bankston Hotel and notice a couple of middle-aged women gawking and covering their mouths with gloved hands as they whisper.

Martha squeezes my hand. "Never mind those old bitty-cluckers. They got nothing better to do than chatter like squirrels lookin' for nuts when they are the nuts."

"Why, Martha Tullos, I—"

"They act friendly at church, but when your back is turned, they talk bad about you."

"I didn't know you had such words in you."

"Your mother's a good teacher. I'm grateful for it. Not a fearful bone in that woman's body."

"Nor yours." I give her a peck on the lips. "See you in a bit."

The short, squatty one glares. "That's the one I told you about. He helped the Yankees burn Wesson's mills. What a terrible night that was."

Martha tugs on my coat. "Lummy, be nice."

"As only I know how, dear." I can't resist. I walk right up to them and tip my hat. "It's a beautiful morning for good and tasty gossip, wouldn't you say, ladies?"

"Young man, what did you say?"

"King David said it best. 'Mine enemies speak evil of me…. And if he comes to see me, speaketh vanity. His heart gathereth iniquity to itself. When he goeth abroad, he telleth it.'"

The short squatty woman cries out, "Well, I never."

"Oh, yes, you have, ma'am, too many times."

Her skinny, hawk-billed nosed friend gasps. "Why—"

"I expect to see you two down on your knees come Sunday morning at church, beggin' forgiveness. You two do go to church, don't you?"

The hawk-billed one juts her chin into the air. "We're charter members of the Bankston Baptist Church, front and center every Sunday morning."

"Good, the altar will be a short walk when you confess your sin and repent. Bein' members held in such high regard, I suspect Jesus ain't so pleased with your words about me and my wife. Think about that come Sunday morning as you iron starch into your skirts and try to let the Lord remove it from your hearts. Good day, ladies."

"At least my son wasn't no yella dawg swallowin' Yankee turncoat who burnt down Wesson's mills."

"Pray tell, ma'am, where is your son?"

"Proud that he's buried with his fellow soldiers at Franklin, Tennessee."

I wince but continue. "Yes, ma'am. I'm very sorry for your loss. But had the Yankees burned Wesson's mills sooner, your son might be walking you to church this Sunday rather than lying cold in the grave. Wesson was supplyin' General Hood and the Fifteenth Mississippi Infantry with boots, uniform wool, flour, and… my brother is buried there."

She stiffens. "Then he died for the right cause."

"For a lost cause. Wouldn't you rather have your son home, safe and sound?"

She sniffles. "Yes, I just wanted my dear son to come home."

I put my arm around her shoulders. "Me, too, ma'am."

She bawls like a baby and shouts, "Now I'll never have grandchildren playing at my feet like your momma." She buries her head into my shoulder.

I am sad for her loss and for George lying in some unmarked grave in Tennessee. I turn and tip my hat at Martha, who's smiling.

The ladies straighten and poke out their chests. "We're still proud mothers of the Confederacy!" They hustle away like scared rabbits.

Martha points at the Bankston Hotel and mouths, Go!

I let my eyes adjust as I close the door behind me. A graying man sits in the corner. He dons clothing any respectable farmer would wear to church. I expected a blue uniform.

I'm happy and angry at the same time. "My goodness, Sarge, how in the hell are you?"

Sarge grasps my hand with the strength of two men and pulls me close for a hug. "Better now that I'm seeing you, old friend. How's the family?"

"Fine, doin' fine."

"And the children?"

"Growin' like weeds and can't keep 'em fed or in clothes."

"Martha?"

"Pretty and sweet as ever. And your children?"

"Growin' up and doing well."

I chance the question. "You have no ring on your finger?"

Sarge fidgets a bit. "I'm still not ready for that, but I am seeing a nice lady. Maybe someday. I don't know. We'll see."

With the small talk done, the silence grows loud and awkward for a moment. We're just recounting memories. Sarge and I have come a long way together since we met at the parole after Vicksburg surrendered. He helped me take the new oath, which was the one I started with before the war—to the stars and stripes.

I don't want to know why I'm being ordered back into the army, but I'm not one to beat around the bush either. "Did you notice the flag at the Post Office, Lieutenant?"

Sarge smiles. "The messenger mentioned my promotion, did he?"

I nod, grinning. "Comin' up in the world, Lieutenant Michael McGugarty."

"Just a lot more responsibility but not a whole lot more pay. It's the army. Hell, what can a man expect? Just call me Sarge. I'm more comfortable with that." Sarge straightens his shirt. "But yes, the twentieth star is permanently stitched into the flag. It looks damn good, too."

"I'm glad Mississippi is finally fully back in the fold for good."

"That's why I'm here, Lummy. Some don't have the freedom that comes with that."

"They don't? That's why I switched from gray to blue and fought for Choctaw County. Good men died so everyone could have what Creator wants for every human bein'." I'm stewing and trying not to at the same time. I lean in. "I've fought bullies, I've fought for the Rebs, I fought Dawg Smith, I fought against Lester, I fought for the Yanks, and I fought against Captain Tom Ford. Why are you houndin' me to fight again? All I want is peace and to be left alone."

Sarge scratches his ear. "It takes the man of peace to fight so that others may have it."

I stand up, shaking. "I don't know if I can—"

Sarge pulls me back down. "The war is over, but the battle's still going. Don't make this about me, son." He stares right through me. "You wanted Mississippi's star back on the right flag. As much as anybody I've ever known."

"I still live by it. The twentieth star for Mississippi is back on the right flag, and I fought with the blue to get it there. What more do I need to do?"

"Make it a twentieth star for everybody, everywhere."

"Didn't I do that? Besides, I'm gettin' older now and have responsibilities—a wife and children, my aging mother, and the farm."

Sarge stretches out his leg, and his knee pops like a stick snapping. "Son, I wouldn't be here myself if wasn't for a direct order from the president. I've got a home and family, too."

"I thought this was all done when Captain Tom Ford was hanged."

"It was. For Choctaw County. But there's more trouble around the state now than right after the war. Other places, too."

"I've heard, but don't you think the Tullos's have given enough? The war took my brothers, and when it was over, I buried some of the best friends I ever had. I'm damn tired of killin' and sufferin'. I want to be left alone and lead a quiet life. Is that too much to ask?"

"No, it's not. I mean no harm, but remind me of their names, the ones who died. Let's drink to their memory before we go any further." Sarge waves at the barkeep. "Two whiskeys. Make 'em strong."

The barkeep pours two glasses three fingers high and sets them on our table. "If you don't mind me sayin', sir, I know you. You're Lummy Tullos, my uncle's friend."

I don't want the conversation, but I do want to know his uncle's name. "And who would that uncle be?" I snap.

"Tom Poole."

I didn't expect to hear that name. I hold back the tears. I nod to Sarge and take my glass in hand. "I need this now, before we honor my brothers and friends." We hold up our glasses. I choke out, "We drink to the memory and bravery of Private Tom Poole, Company C, First Mississippi Mounted Rifles and defender of his beloved Choctaw County."

Sarge swallows it in one gulp. "Here, here."

I take mine in several sips, letting the memories of two young boys fishing, cutting up in church, and chasing pretty girls flood my mind.

The young barkeep offers his hand, and I take it. "Thank you, sir. I'm Matthew Poole. Friends just call me Matt. My uncle said you were the best friend a man could ever have, even closer to him than a brother, like the Good Book says."

I want to curse and ask what the Good Book ever did to save Poole's life. I hold my tongue and point at our glasses for a refill.

Sarge quotes a Scripture. "Somewhere in the Good Book, it says, 'A friend loveth at all times, and a brother is born for adversity.'"

Matt furrows his brow. "What do you mean? Kinfolks can cause more trouble than friends?"

Sarge squints. "No, son, a brother is born for times of trouble. He's there when you need him the most."

"My uncle did say that for a man who is as close to his Creator as you are, Mistuh Lummy, you could be hard as woodpecker lips."

I chuckle. "Sounds like somethin' Poole'd say. Good to meet you, Matt. They don't make 'em like your uncle no more."

Matt fetches another bottle.

"Dang, Sarge, when did you go to quotin' the Bible?"

"When I got back home and started going to church with my kids. Back to honoring those who've already crossed over the Jordan."

As I rub my finger around the top edge of the whiskey glass, old memories fill my head. "Ben was murdered by that low down scoundrel Dawg Smith in Winn Parish, and Mister Gilmore with him. Amariah died of an unknown disease while serving with the same artillery company as my brothers Jasper and James. Hog Fart—I mean Edrow—and Granville, were two boys who just wanted to survive the Vicksburg siege and go home. All my friends in gray who died at Vicksburg come to me at night. All the Yanks I killed when I was a Reb haunt me still. My brother, George Washington Tullos, killed at the Battle of Franklin in Tennessee, was probably dumped in an unmarked grave. Old Bart and Poole died to save me and my family. Dawg Smith and Lester... I almost couldn't hold back killin' that Captain Tom Ford. Now you want me to do more killin'?"

Sarge doesn't move.

My heart races, and my head pounds like it will explode any second. It hits me. "I can't forget Old Bart, Seth, Mister Allrice, Missus Sophie, and my dear Susannah." My fists clench, my eyes narrow, and my face burns hot. I want to fight.

Sarge lays a hand on my forearm. "All right, calm down, son. They all died so you could have the life you have now."

"So, why would you and President Grant want to take it from me?"

"We don't, but it's possible, with what we're asking you to do once again. But to answer your question, the home you men fought so hard for must be defended for others. The people you just mentioned are one of the main reasons I'm here—your black family, especially your son."

I'd forgotten that I told Sarge about Elzey. "Why me?"

"You have the skills and knowledge, but also the wisdom to help me lead this mission."

"Mission? What mission?"

"I'll get to that. I've never known a man who could keep his promise not to kill again in the middle of a war. But you did. And that's what's needed. Men who can keep their heads in the worst of times and lead other men to do the same."

I touch the knife Pa made me, the one I removed Dawg Smith's head with. I don't want to go back there. Reliving those days births new anger and resurrects old sorrow. The rage that still hides deep within is too overpowering and too dangerous. The sorrow in my heart saps my soul. I realize I'm talking out loud.

"I know you're tired, son. But how could your soul be at rest when evil men bring a storm of terror on good folks, white and black, trying to make good lives for themselves?"

"Damn you, Sarge." I look out the window at what used to be Wesson's Manufactories that Poole and I helped burn. That took a lot out me, and this will, too.

Sarge leans in and whispers, "A man named Frederick Douglass once said, 'A man's rights rest in three boxes—the ballot box, the jury box, and the cartridge box.' The folks we'll be helping are afraid to vote other than how they're told. They live where court cases are decided by the dollar or at the point of a gun, and they can't take on these bastards by themselves."

"Damn, Sarge, aren't you the scholar?"

"Yeah, I try to keep up by reading the papers when I get a chance."

"Callin' you Lieutenant is gonna take some gettin' used to."

"It'll come, but for where we're going and for what we have to do? Sarge will be good enough. Use Lieutenant if we get somewhere official."

"So, it's that kind of mission?"

"Yes, like when Sergeant Parr's men called you Handerson as you ate breakfast in this same hotel after they set fire to Wesson's factories."

I straighten up in my chair. "I understand."

A sweet, familiar voice captures my heart from the kitchen doorway. "If it ain't my dear brother-in-law."

# CHAPTER 4

# A GENTLE REMINDER NOT TO BE GENTLE

## 11:30 A.M., MARCH 3, 1870

*A sweet memory from the past can make for a sorrowful moment in the present.*

I STAND UP, knocking over my chair. "Susannah?" I stare dumbfounded. I'm dizzy from the bourbon and the surprise.

Before I can sit, a beautiful dark lady throws her arms around me. "It's me, Ruth. Your sister-in-law."

I hug her back. "Sorry, Ruthie, I had some strange feelin's just now."

A scruffy-looking customer at the bar throws me a sordid glance and whispers something under his breath.

I ask, "You need to say somethin'?"

Sarge whispers, "Calm yourself, son. Not anything worth getting riled up about."

I settle into my chair. "I'm sorry I called you Susannah, Ruth, it's just—"

Ruth smiles just like Susannah. "That I look too much like my sister?"

I look at Sarge. "I'll never get over any of this."

Ruth smiles. "I hear you're doing good."

I manage a grin. "Ruth, how's Miss Rachel?"

"Doin' poorly, I'm sad to say. Old age creeps up on the best of folks. I'll tell her you asked about her. Y'all need anythin'?"

Sarge shrugs. "Maybe a couple of biscuits with ham, if you've got them?"

"Lummy?" Ruth squeezes my shoulder, and I wince. The pain reminds me of the tree that fell on my shoulder when I ferry-crossed the Mississippi, chasing after Susannah.

"Maybe some coffee and somethin' sweet. I might as well get somethin' out of this."

Sarge chuckles. "It's on me. The government, that is."

Ruth kisses my cheek. "Be back in a bit."

Sarge leans in. "There goes another reason we need you."

"What do you mean?"

"So your brother James won't have to hide his love for a black woman like you did."

"It'll be a cold day in Hell when Mississippi lets black and white folks marry."

"Yeah, but just because the government doesn't have the guts to make it right doesn't make James and Ruth living together wrong in God's eyes."

"Why, Lieutenant McGugarty, I didn't know you felt that way."

"I didn't until I listened to you go on and on about it while we were riding with the Rifles."

"No way. You sweet on a black lady?"

Sarge blushes. "Remember what I told you at the parole?"

"You said, 'I won't judge a man for the color of the flower he picks for his bride.'"

"We both want the same thing, Lummy."

"All right. What's so important that President Grant himself wants me?"

## CHAPTER 5

# THE MISSION

12:15 P.M., MARCH 3, 1870

*A mission ain't always a calling. But it has to be answered, anyway.*

**M**Y SHOULDER ACHES. "You know I don't want to go on this mission, whatever it is."

"I do, but this is special work for a man with certain talents."

"You'd think as much of this horsesh—" I catch myself—"as much of this kind of work I've done, God would've made it my calling. It ain't."

"I understand." Sarge waits.

I fidget air like a kid who knows he's about to get a whipping for cutting up in church. "I'm listening." I want to walk out.

"President Grant called for men just like you who proved an uncommon devotion to their state during the war. Your devotion to put Mississippi's star back on the Union flag, to switch sides, wasn't too common. You may not know, but of the six hundred or so men who enlisted in the First Mississippi Mounted Rifles, one hundred and sixty took the bounty and equipment and ran off. They deserted. That's what gave our regiment a bad reputation with some officers. With the others who got sick and died or killed in action, only three hundred and fifty of you boys were left when you mustered out. You enlisted and saw it through to the end. That's admirable in anybody's book, I say."

I don't hold back this time. "You're not tryin' to butter me up with sweet horseshit, are you, Sarge? Put a bow on a hawg, you still got an ugly-ass critter."

"You did what had to be done to get the war over."

"Weren't we the only white Mississippi regiment to fight for the Union?"

"Yes, but here's the reason I came for you. President Grant asked General Grierson for a list of men in this area who could be trusted. Nobody knew the State of Mississippi during the war better than Grierson—except for General Forrest."

"So, Poole and me leadin' the raid on the Bankston factories got me on this list?"

"At the top of the list when I made my choices. The four other groups—"

I bristle. "Made your choices?"

"Let me finish, and I'll explain everything."

"I haven't said yes yet."

"I know that. The four other groups like ours will be led by a lieutenant, a sergeant, and three corporals—men like you who've proven themselves. They have assignments in other states."

"Do I know any of them?"

"You remember the scout, Chickasaw? Being from Mississippi, he'll lead a group to Alabama."

"You're askin' me to go to another state?"

"Yes, so you'll be where people won't know who you are. Well, in your case, mostly."

"Why?"

"So no harm can come to your family."

It hits me. "Just five men for each mission? I don't like the sound of this, but do go on."

"Yeah, we can sneak in and out, making ourselves scarce as hen's teeth when the job's done. We won't wear uniforms. We'll go about as civilians. It's not our job to lead the locals but help them lead themselves. That way the government won't be blamed for what happens."

"Sounds risky. We had twelve when we fought here in Choctaw County and still lost good men."

"Twelve of the finest ever to shoulder a rifle to protect home and family."

"With Henry Repeaters at that."

"Do you still have yours?"

"I do."

"We'll provide you with a short double-barreled shotgun, the newest Colt pistol, fresh mounts, and supply ammunition, food, and the gear you'll need."

"I've got a shotgun."

"The barrel on that shoulder Napoleon is too long."

"I can fix that. Ben wouldn't mind. Ain't no duck shootin' around here no ways."

"Wasn't Ben your brother who died trying to save Susannah?"

"Yeah, Ben and Mistuh Gilmore were too late to save her." Pain squeezes my heart like a woodworker's clamp. "Let's get back to talkin' about what you want me to do. Why did you say 'mostly' when you talked about where I'd be goin'?"

Sarge calls Matt back over. "We need coffee."

I draw in a deep breath. "So, where will we go?"

"You may not like it."

"I'm gonna find out sometime."

"Winn Parish."

"Damn, I knew it."

# CHAPTER 6

# A FIVE MAN ARMY

### 12:30 P.M., MARCH 3, 1870

*Jesus had twelve disciples for his mission. We don't get that many.*

"THE PLAN IS simple. I lead a group of four handpicked men to bring a storm of terror on the cowards who befriend travelers on their way west only to rob and murder them. They intimidate good black and white folks just trying to make a living, too. They work up and down the Natchez Trace that goes from Vidalia on the river across from Natchez to Winn Parish and then on to where it becomes the El Camino Road in Texas. They have a network of stations and men all along the road with a communication system better than the Army. They've brought hellfire down on good people for too long."

"Who are these outlaws?"

"Ex-Confederate soldiers, a drifter or two, but it's a family and neighbor enterprise."

"But who are they?"

"Nightriders who call themselves the West-Kimbrell Gang. They're not the hooded cowards who frighten former slaves. This family's tighter than a bull's ass at fly time."

"West? That sounds familiar. Is it the—"

"Yes, the same John West you fought alongside at Vicksburg when you were in the Twenty-Seventh Louisiana Infantry."

"We were in Company F together. I'll be damned."

"You will be if you don't come with me. I know you, Lummy. You can't stand a bully, and this one is too close to home for your best friend there. West operates near Atlanta—"

"Atlanta, that's where—"

"Yes, where J.A. lives. Let me get to that in a minute. West finished out the war but went back to his farm near Atlanta in Winn Parish. He hooked up with a family named Kimbrell who've been terrorizing travelers for some time, robbing and murdering. West's the worst of the lot, and now he's their leader."

I go back to the march out of Vicksburg just before J.A. and I left the Confederate Army. "West said he'd get back at everybody after the war. Guess he's gettin' rich doing it."

"That's not the worst of it. The things these outlaws have done are too horrible to speak out loud."

"Tell me."

"You can handle it?"

"Stop stallin' and tell me. No sugar coatin' it."

"They invite weary families moving west into their homes and offer them a hot meal and place to stay. When all are sleep, the outlaws sneak in and murder them. They've learned the fine art of using knives on their victims so they can't even let out a yelp as they lay dying."

"I do know how that's done, I'm sad to say. What do they do with the stolen goods?"

"They repaint the wagons, switch around parts to make them less recognizable, and sell the horses and all the goods in Texas or Mexico where no one knows the difference."

"Crafty bastards, ain't they? West always bragged how he was the best carpenter in Winn Parish and could fix anything."

"He fixes things all right. They have men all along the road to Texas and special hunters horn bugle calls to communicate. They can send a message up the road and summon men for a night of murder and thievery in just a few hours' time. It's criminal organization at its worst."

"They've figured out how to make easy money and get away with it."

"There's no law in Winn Parish to speak of, or anywhere over there for that matter. If there is, it's been bought and paid for by the outlaws. Hell, they are the law. Most people in Winn Parish believe them to be fine, upstanding, church-going people. But more than a few have figured out that it's West who's played the Devil these past years. And they want it to end."

"What about Sheriff Barnett? He was doin' a good job when—"

"Son, that was over five years ago. Barnett lost in a rigged election, and now the West-Kimbrell Gang is the law."

I rub my beard. "Okay, give me the worst of it."

"The men murder the men and children. The old matriarch of the clan, Aunt Polly, kills the women. I mean, damn, she makes them get down on all fours and slits their throats so the blood will drain into a dishpan. It's horrible, son."

I breathe deep to ward off the anger creeping into my heart. "It's demons that do the Devil's work."

"They say that John West dashed an infant's brains out on a barn post because the child wouldn't stop crying."

I grab a spittoon and puke.

"Lummy, do I need to stop?"

I wave him off. "Go on, I need to hear it."

"They dispose of the bodies in cisterns around the countryside where no one will look." Sarge leans up and whispers, "These bastards have murdered hundreds, maybe even a couple of thousand men, women, and children."

"And no one, not even the government, has done anythin' about it?"

"No one went after them with the war going. Now they're too afraid."

"My goodness, I thought I'd seen it all fightin' Dawg Smith, Lester, and Captain Tom Ford. Damn the meanness of some human beings. So, why go after them now?"

"First, as I said, the law in that part of Louisiana ain't worth shit, and the Federal government has had bigger problems. But they've been watching the situation."

"Watching what?"

"It started back in '66 when West and a couple of his men robbed and killed Lieutenant Simeon G. Butts. He was on his way to deliver two saddlebags full of currency destined to be distributed by the Freedman's Bureau post in Vernon, Louisiana. He had to go through Winn Parish to get there."

"I bet the hatred of even the sight of a blue uniform was thick like it was in Choctaw County in those days."

"It was, but West was more interested in the twenty-seven hundred dollars. He couldn't care less who was carrying it."

"Didn't they know that somebody would come looking for Butts?"

"Yeah, but they stripped him of anything identifying him as a Union soldier and went home by different routes. A witness who overhead old lady Kimbrell talking said the Kimbrell boys did it. We believe West was there, too."

"Did they ever find Butts's body?"

"A farmer found him when the buzzards flew up. Between them and the scavengers, there was nothing left but a tuft of hair and the skeleton wrapped in a bloodstained undershirt."

The weight of this evil presses down on my head. "My goodness."

"Investigators found some sleeve buttons and part of a necktie that would've been his. A pistol ball hole had passed through his skull. The locals call the place 'Yankee Springs' now."

"So, why didn't the Federal government do anything?"

"They tried, but there was too much bad blood. With all the chaos going on and the local law worthless, justice became elusive at best. The sheriff at the time told the Kimbrells to leave the parish. They hid in Texas. Ain't that a kick to the head?"

"What about West?"

"They knew he and some fellow named Shumate were involved, but they couldn't prove it. While the Kimbrells were in Texas, West became even more dangerous."

"West believes the law can't touch him."

"Exactly. The Kimbrells came back from Texas. General McLaughlin, on behalf of the government, pursued them for killing two Negroes. He caught up with Billy, who lit out for John West's place. They had a running gun battle until Billy got thrown from his horse. McLaughlin shot him twice with bird-shot, but Billy fled. McLaughlin finally caught up with him and shot him off his horse as they raced through the forest. Billy died there. Your Sheriff Barnett had to arrest McLaughlin as a formality, but the judge ruled Billy's death as a justifiable homicide. It wasn't long after that Barnett was voted out of office."

I rub my forehead. "These men hate the Federal government for the South losing the war and giving aid to former slaves. They take it out on people headin' west."

"That's about it. These men are demons destined for death." Sarge waits for my response.

I'm nauseated again—not in my stomach, but in my soul.

# CHAPTER 7

# FAMILIAR MEMORIES DON'T MAKE DOIN' THIS ANY EASIER

## 12:45 P.M., MARCH 3, 1870

*A blurry line separates the righteous and the unrighteous.*

DEPRESSION PRESSES HEAVY on me like a cold wet blanket. "Who am I to judge West and his gang? I ain't that much different than them." Sarge pounds the table. "Damn you, Lummy Tullos. Can't you get it through that thick skull of yours that you made the right choices? Yes, you did some pretty bad things. We all did. But you've done a whole lot more good than you ever did bad. It's time to answer that call one more time so Louisiana can be free again. Do it for the Davises, for Mister Gilmore and Ben who gave their lives to set people free. Do it for Susannah's memory and for your son, Elzey."

I raise my hand to backhand his face. "Enough!" I lower my hand. "Sorry, Sarge, I got a bit riled there."

Ruth rushes from the kitchen. "Everything all right?"

Sarge pats his hands in the air. "I apologize. We're good. Matt, bring us another round of whiskey. We need it." He whispers, "You're doing good, Lummy. I needed to rile you up. You forget I know you."

"You do. So, we're to terrorize the terrorists, that it?"

"That's part of it. We must end their reign of terror and show no mercy."

"You know I do understand what that means."

"Yes, you do."

I squint. "Only a demon can defeat the Devil's work. I've gotten pretty good at that."

Sarge sighs. "I'm sorry, son. I don't know what else to tell you."

"I know what to tell you, Sarge."

"And what's that?"

"Let's get it done so I can get back home."

"Do you want more details about the West-Kimbrell Gang?"

"Save it for when we get there, Sarge. That's the stuff I'll need to dig up the rage necessary to see this through."

"With your war dreams, do you think you can handle it?"

"You wouldn't be here unless you thought I could."

"You've got me there." Sarge studies me. "You'll report to me, I report to General Grierson, and Grierson only to President Grant. Nobody knows the government is behind this secret mission except those who need to know."

It hits me. "Atlanta. You were going to tell me about—" The heat in my face flashes quicker than a red hot poker slapped on a festering wound. "Tell me he hasn't hurt J.A. and his family."

"No, but West's place isn't far from J.A.'s farm. I made a reconnaissance trip to Winn Parish. I started to pose as a cattle buyer but figured that was too dangerous. I didn't want to get killed before I got started, so I dressed like a farmhand looking for work. West wouldn't be interested in a poor farm laborer passing through."

"That was smart."

"I stayed in J.A.'s home a couple of nights, and he gave me the details."

My heart leaps. "What'd he say? How's he doin'? What about Mary Jane and the boy, Aaron?"

Sarge laughs. "You and J.A. had some times, didn't you?"

"I miss that boy."

"He said to make sure you knew he and his family were all right and that he missed your sorry ass."

"That's J.A. all right."

"West doesn't bother people close to home. It creates too much suspicion."

I tuck my chin into my chest. "What'd J.A. say?"

"He says he can't do it without you."

"That's what I said to him just before we went after Dawg Smith."

Sarge sits back, folding his arms. "So, there it is."

A thousand memories of Ben, Mr. Gilmore, and Susannah flash through my mind. Martha and the kids and the danger my son Elzey could be in push those thoughts to the side. I slap the table to stop them from taking over my soul.

Sarge leans in. "You good?"

"Yeah, I was just countin' the cost like the Good Book says."

"And...?"

"When do we leave?"

# CHAPTER 8

# THE DECISION THAT IS NO DECISION

### 1:00 P.M., MARCH 3, 1870

*When nothin' needs decidin', you can call that a callin'.*

"WHO ARE THE other three men?"

Sarge throws back the last of his whiskey. "Hand-picked for just such an undertaking."

"Huh, sounds like we'll be callin' on an undertaker soon."

"Could be, but hopefully not for any of us."

I fold my hands. "If somethin' does happen to me, would you—"

Sarge's jaw drops. "For a man who made it through the big war and a smaller one here in Choctaw County, you sure can turn mushy quick."

"If I'm killed, bury me in the Tullos Cemetery above our house."

"I won't let that happen, son, even if it kills me."

"Same here, Sarge. You have children to go home to, and maybe a wife."

"We'll just have to get each other home."

I lift my glass. "That's good enough for me."

"We'll gather mid-morning tomorrow at Mount Pisgah Baptist Church. I've already spoken with Pastor Dobbs."

"That preacher never ceases to amaze me. He may be mild and gentle, but he's got the heart of a warrior when it comes to plannin' and prayin'."

"He wants to send us off on the angels' wings of a mighty prayer."

"We need Saint Michael to go before us."

"He will. We have you, Sergeant Tullos."

"I don't need any title or praise for what we're about to do."

"I made you a sergeant so the others will follow your lead. You're really the one leading this mission. You know the land, the people, and will carry the most authority amongst the men in Winn Parish we'll need to rid the earth of the West-Kimbrell Gang. I'm just going along to support you and make sure it's done legal."

"I can do that. I want Martha and the kids taken care of while I'm gone."

"Not a problem."

"The Army will take care of everything?"

"That's right."

"Have a courier deliver all of my pay to Pastor Dobbs. He'll see that Martha gets it."

"Good decision. No one will ever know who was behind this mission, so don't worry, you won't receive any recognition for doing this. When the mission's over, you'll never be able to speak of it again, understand?"

"Yes, Lieutenant McGugarty, sir," I say with a slight grin. "Forgive me if I forget and call you Sarge out on the road."

"Keep it Sarge. That way you boys can tell strangers I was your sergeant in the Reb army. That should keep down suspicions."

"What about that Yankee mouth sound you've got?"

"You mean my accent? How's this?" In the slowest molasses-in-wintertime drawl that sounds just like one of my brothers talking, Sarge says, "I'd lak summa dem butter'd up cathead biskits wid sum 'ah dat good soppin' gravy, pleaz ma'am."

I nearly fall out of my chair laughing. "All right, I'm convinced. You speak ridge runnin,' swamp cat, Missip talk better'n I do."

Sarge squeezes my arm. "All funning aside, there's one more thing. You're not going to like it. It's the worst part of what you'll have to do."

"I might have to kill again?"

"Yes."

"Who's going with us?"

"Handpicked and the best. I've got two already. Anybody you want to come along?"

"Rainy Mills, if I can find him."

"He was the very first person I contacted. He'll be here in time for to-morrow's meeting."

"Imagine that, Rainy Mills, a corporal in the United States Army."

Sarge laughs. "The age of miracles will never cease."

"Ain't that the damned truth?"

CHAPTER 9

# THE REMINDER

1:15 P.M., MARCH 3, 1870

*A man's soul sometimes needs to be stirred to do right.*

"I DON'T WANT to be some kind of slick-haired, hired government agent like them Pinkertons. They done good savin' President Lincoln from being assassinated that one time, but they get away with murder in the name of the law, too."

Sarge assures me. "You won't be."

"Don't get me wrong. I got nothin' against them trackin' down outlaws and bank robbers. Heck, I felt like one myself when we hid out at Big Sand Rock whilst we were chasin' Captain Tom Ford."

Sarge taps his finger on the table. "You know all outlaws eventually get caught or killed."

"Some are still fightin' the war like them James boys. It can't be all bad, what they're doin'. Some call 'em heroes. I might do the same thing if I'd gone through what they did. In some ways, I did, didn't I?"

"You did but on the right side, I believe."

"Yeah, but bein' on the right side is often decided by who wins and writes the history."

Sarge shrugs. "I still have to believe right will win in the end, or I might as well go on home."

"Maybe you should, Sarge, before you ain't alive to go home."

"I don't have a choice, not if I stay true to who I am. Do you even want a choice when it comes to doin' right?"

I have no answer. Yes, I do. "You're right. There's no choice when it comes to doin' right."

Sarge raises his glass to get one last drop of whiskey.

I wave at the barkeep for another round. "Tell me, Sarge, what do I have to do?"

"Not just yet. Let's honor the good men and women who allowed us to sit here together. Barkeep! Whiskey."

Matt is standing behind Sarge with a bottle and an extra glass. "Sir, Lummy's ahead of you. If y'all don't mind, may I lift a glass with you to my uncle and the others you honor today."

Sarge asks, "Okay with you, Lummy?"

I nod. "Sure, Matt." We lift our glasses. "To Thomas Poole, my brothers, friends, fellow soldiers, and my black family. You know all their names, Lord. God rest their immortal and blessed souls."

We throw back our drinks, and the man at the bar growls, "Ain't drinking with no niggah lovers huggin' up on black whores."

I whisper, "That's one too many words." I set my glass down and lay my hands on the table, palms down. "You, at the bar, as I see it, you've got two choices. Leave now, or I throw you out."

Sarge doesn't say anything this time.

The man quickly reaches into his coat, but I have the knife Pa made me at his throat with a thin red line of blood trickling down his neck.

"Drop it!"

The man slides a derringer from inside his coat and pitches it to the floor.

"Matt, pick up the pea shooter and give it to Sarge."

Matt hustles over, never taking his eyes off my knife at the man's throat. "You gonna kill him?"

The man at the bar grimaces, the razor sharp knife blade stinging his throat. Dawg Smith's eyes flash before mine. I'm angry and weak at the same time. I see the blade slicing into Dawg's neck as his eyes bulged in disbelief. I shake my head to lose the memory.

The man closes his eyes tight, expecting any second to have his throat sliced. "I'm sorry, mister, didn't mean no harm."

I snap back to where I am. "You did harm, and I want to know that you're sorry."

"Tell me what I got to do to make this right." The man touches his neck and pulls blood back on his fingertips. "I'm bleedin'! Please take the knife away."

"This knife took the head of a man twice as bad as you, and the blade's sharper now than it was then."

Sarge stands. "Lummy, don't go any further, son."

I yell, "Ruth! Come in here, please."

Ruth walks out of the kitchen with a tray. "I'm sorry it took so long, but—" She drops our food tray on the closest table.

I flip my knife over so the sharp part of the blade faces away from the man's neck, but he doesn't know that. I pull the dull side of the knife tighter against the man's throat. "Apologize to this lady for ever thinking she could be anything less than the best of who Creator put on this earth." I pull the knife ever so slightly like I'm slicing his throat.

The man pisses himself, and I move my feet back. He shakes like a new-born calf trying to stand up for the first time. "I'll do it! Please don't cut me."

I relax the knife just a bit.

"Ma'am, I am sorry that I even suggested you were a black whore. Please forgive me."

Ruth stiffens. "Sir, I accept your apology, and will expect you not do that again."

"No, ma'am, I won't."

Ruth puts her hands on her hips like Susannah did so many times. "You should go to the church up the street and get down on your knees, ask the Lord to forgive you, and give thanks that this gentleman has not removed your head."

I push him toward the door.

He turns to retrieve his pocket pistol.

I re-sheath my knife. "Leave it. It's the cost of your sin."

"I'm sorry, sir. I really am." I believe him, for now. He eases the door shut behind him.

Sarge hands me the derringer, and I stuff it in my coat pocket. Now I'm reminded of why I'm here.

Sarge chuckles. "That part of you I hope you'll never lose."

"Which part, Sarge?"

"Hating bullies."

"It'll probably get me killed someday."

"Not if I can help it, son."

I have to ask. "Ruth, where did you pick up such a fine command of the English language?"

In a sweet, though sarcastic voice, Ruth lays it on thick. "Whys I do attends school, Massuh Lummy, don't ya knows?"

"You better stop, or I'll—"

Ruth smiles and sashays over with our food. "You'll do what?"

"Tell James on you."

She winks. "Honey, don't you worry none. I can handle my man."

Ruth reminds me of Annie Fanny's sassy ways. "James has good taste in women."

Sarge grins. "He does, and that's why I'm here."

I sip my coffee. "I ain't been called Massuh in a long time. I'm glad that day's over, for everybody."

Ruth lays our food out and kisses me on the cheek. "This is on the house, you good men of God." She goes back to the kitchen.

Sarge doesn't say it, so I do. "God's got nothin' to do with this."

# CHAPTER 10

# OLD FRIEND, BITTERSWEET REUNION

## 1:30 P.M., MARCH 3, 1870

*Some reunions lead to the bitter of bittersweet memories.*

THE SUN SLIPS from behind the clouds to create a silhouette of a man standing in the hotel doorway. He doesn't move. He just taps his finger on his holstered pistol. "You're not a hard man to find, Lummy Tullos—taller than Goliath and twice as hard on bullies, giving them hell beyond what they can bear."

I upset the last bit of coffee in our cups racing to the door. I bear hug the man who saved my life and protected my family. "Rainy Mills, how in the hell are you?"

He laughs. "You ain't changed a bit, you old coyote."

"Not since you scared 'em off my ass back in Louisiana."

He whispers in my ear. "Keep a sharp eye out for the coyote you just shamed. He mumbled about how he'd get back at you, one way or the other."

Damn, I hate to hear that. I'll warn Elihu and Jasper to keep James out of harm.

Sarge grabs Rainy's hand. "You're a day early. Glad you made it."

"Yeah, I boarded a steamer called *The Dime* from Vicksburg up the Yazoo River. An old deckhand told the passengers about some fool who was almost eaten by a gator when he swam out to remove a log jam ten years or so ago. You know anybody like that?"

I laugh. "Heard somethin' about that. Some fools never learn." I slap Rainy's shoulder. "I still have the gator tooth necklace in a box back at the farm."

Rainy takes off his coat. "I caught a hack up Big Sand Creek to Carrollton with some fellow you knew a long time ago, Lummy. Said his name was...."

"Dale, that old river rat, how's he doin'?"

"A bit older than when you saw him last. He limps a bit. He said the same stump-tail moccasin that slid over your shoulder back in '59 got his leg. Nearly lost it and says it hasn't been right since. You never told me about that."

"That story's best told by a warm fire with a cup of cool moonshine. How does Dale work his business with a gimped up leg?"

"His two sons work the boat while he rides along to do talk business."

"Sons? He wasn't even married when I last saw him."

"He married a sweet war widow like you and got two hardworking river hands in the deal. He said tell you hello and to come see him. He also sent you a gift." Rainy hands me a pouch.

I have no idea what it could be. "I should get over there sometime. That man taught me a lot in the short time I was with him." I untie the leather string and pull away the cloth. It's the ivory horsehead pipe Dale's father carved. I have no words.

Rainy sits and motions to Matt for a drink. "He said you were like a son to him in those few short days, and neither of his two stepsons smoke. Do you smoke?"

"On rare occasion."

"Good, we'll try her out tonight. That is, if I can invite myself out to the Tullos farm for some of Martha's good cooking. I bought some fresh tobacco that'll go well with a little of Elihu's fine red muscadine wine."

"You don't need an invite, Rainy. You're family. You comin', Sarge?"

"You boys go ahead. As much as I'd like to, I've got business to take care of before we leave. You two report at Mount Pisgah Baptist Church by ten in the morning."

We stand and salute. "Yes sir, Lieutenant McGugarty, sir."

Sarge turns to walk away. "Good, come with me. There's something we have to do before we go any further."

I have to ask, "Why are you doin' this, Rainy?"

"Hell, I can't sing, and I can't dance. I might as well do this." We laugh.

Rainy throws back his whiskey and flips Matt a dollar. "As Mark Twain once put it, 'Travel is fatal to prejudice, bigotry, and narrow-mindedness, and many of our people need it sorely on these accounts. Broad, wholesome, charitable views of men and things cannot be acquired by vegetation in one little corner of the earth all one's lifetime.'"

"Dang, Rainy, you have become quite the philosopher."

He stands to stretch his back. "I did receive a good classical education growing up in the orphanage in Natchez. And while you boys were loving up on your wives and raising children, I was improving my intellectual prowess. I've been studying wisdom of the ancient sages, and a few contemporary ones, too."

"Your Mark Twain also said, 'I was educated once. It took me years to get over it.'"

"Where'd you hear that?"

"Read it in the newspaper."

"So, you'll appreciate me sharing the wisdom of the ages with you swamp-water drinkers."

"Dang, we've got a long ride, and you're gonna tell us everything you know."

"Not everything. Just enough to help you farm boys know more than how to slop a hog."

I grin. "You'll appreciate that hawg sloppin' when you sink your teeth into a piece of that fine farm fresh bacon in the morning. C'mon, boy, let's go."

We walk to the town square where a United States flag stands straight out in the steady wind at the Post Office.

Rainy elbows me. "A storm's coming up. It'll be here tonight."

"From what Sarge says, the storm that's comin' for us has been goin' on for years, and we're runnin' straight at it."

Sarge points us into the bushes where Wesson's wool factory used to be. "No one needs to see this."

Rainy whispers, "Is this one of the buildings the Yankees burned down?"

I shield my eyes from the sun's glare. "Yeah, I'm still not proud of helpin' do that."

Rainy squeezes my shoulder. "A necessary thing often carries no joy in the doing."

"Ain't that the damn truth?" I find the twentieth star and fix my gaze there.

Sarge clears his throat. "Throw up your right hands and repeat after me."

We recite the oath of allegiance. We promise to serve to the best of our abilities in the United States Army and hold to the secrecy of our mission.

The postmaster, who once hid the books Seth had ordered for his new school for black children, peeks through the blinds. I wish I could've seen the look on his face when Elihu took them out of the back room that day and loaded them into the wagon. That was a Federal offense Elihu never got charged with. The postmaster knew better than to press it. Damn, I miss Seth.

Sarge gives us our stripes—me three and Rainy two. "Though you will never wear those, you have them and this paper to prove who you are and what you're doing. Have Martha sew them into a pocket on the inside of your hats. Only use them if you get challenged. We don't know how deep into the West-Kimbrell Gang we'll have to go to bring them down. One or more of you may have to infiltrate the gang if needed."

I shake my head. "Infil—what?"

Rainy squints. "Damn, Sarge, I didn't know we'd have to go that far." He whispers to me, "It means join the gang to get close in with them."

Sarge straightens his jacket. "I wanted you, Rainy, because of your dealings with guns. It's the perfect cover for outlaws who are always looking to buy new weapons in secret. You want a different assignment?"

"No, no, that's the one I would've chosen. I just thought we'd just ride in, capture the sons of bitches, and let the locals deal with the hangings."

"It won't be that easy. They own the law and buy the juries. We'll talk more on that later."

I backhand Rainy's chest. "You good?"

He grins. "Hell, this'll be fun."

Sarge finishes his speech. "Good enough. Rainy, you'll hold the rank of corporal, and Lummy, as you already know, your rank is sergeant. You two men are now duly sworn in and must do your duty even to the cost of your lives, if necessary."

The last part hits hard. I know the meaning and the sacrifice that comes with taking an oath.

Sarge motions for us to leave. "You boys head on out, and I'll see you in the morning. My first business is with the Bankston Postmaster." The shades close.

Rainy stares at the flag. "I've made enough money roaming this country that I ought to serve that flag. Imagine that, me a corporal in the United States Army."

I pop Rainy on the shoulder. "As your first order, Corporal Mills, follow me to get the best supper you'll have in a while. Martha's cookin', and Elihu's pourin' the muscadine. We may even scare up a jug of that good ole Wood brothers' moonshine to top it off."

Rainy chuckles, "You don't have to twist my arm. Let's go, brother. But know this. I ain't saluting your ass." We laugh.

Sarge opens the Post Office door. "You boys better not show up in the morning with bloodshot eyes and headaches."

We fall over each other saluting like a couple of schoolboys wrestling. We have to find a little humor in what will not be so funny soon.

Martha steps out of a store near where I slammed Kneehigh down on the hardpan street back in '59. I regret doing that, but there was no other way at the time. I do hope he's all right. It set a string of happenings into motion that still follow me today.

Martha hands me her packages and hugs Rainy. "I watched you boys take the oath. I hope those words are strong enough to bring you back home."

Rainy helps her up into the wagon as I load the packages in the back. "They are, Missus Martha, they surely are."

Martha sits down hard and folds her arms, making her opinion known.

Rainy kisses her hand. "Missus Martha, have no fear. I will do everything within my power to see Lummy home, at the cost of my life."

Martha wipes her nose with a lacy handkerchief. She sits up straight and fusses with her hair a bit. "You better see to it, Rainy Mills, that Columbus comes home all in one piece. Or else, I will have your hide."

"Yes, ma'am." Rainy mounts his horse and whispers to me, "Maybe we should take her along. She'd certainly give the West-Kimbrell boys a damn good whipping."

Martha turns. "I heard that, Rainy Mills. If you keep on cussin', I'll put lye soap gravy on your biscuits tonight."

I pop the reins lightly, and we start for home.

Rainy trots his horse alongside, talking more than I've ever heard him. He's nervous, and I don't know why. Yes, I do. He figures maybe his time is up, and he wants to leave this world having done something more for others than himself. He must think fighting with us here in Choctaw County wasn't enough. It was enough for me, but like him, I can't turn away from what needs doing for folks treated wrongly.

The sun sets behind the ridge as we turn onto the road that leads to the Tullos farm.

Rainy sniffs the air. "I can already smell fried chicken and biscuits."

Martha smiles. "You should. Ma and Mary'll have supper on the table when we get there."

I hand Martha the reins. I hop off the wagon and start running. "Beat you to the cabin, boy."

Rainy slaps his mount's rump. "The hell you say!"

# CHAPTER 11

# LAST OF THE
# LAST SUPPERS

## SUNSET, MARCH 3, 1870

*A good parting is only as good as the eating together before it's time to go.*

EVEN WITH MY head start, we get to the house at the same time, me huffing and puffing.

Rainy hops off his horse. "Ain't what you used to be, are you, old man?"

I whisper, "You should know, you worn out, crotchety old bastard."

Martha ties the reins to the wagon brake. "I heard that. Leave your cussin' out in the yard." She covers her mouth to hide her laugh. "Old man is right, dear. You did run a little crooked."

Rainy laughs. "He's an old fart that's weaker than a popcorn poot."

Martha shakes her finger at us. "Go wash up and get in the house, both of you boys."

We say together, "Yes 'um."

Rainy washes up while John A. and I lead the horses to the barn.

Martha's oldest, John A., has become quite the young man. He takes my horse's reins. "Go on and wash up, Pop. I got this. They're putting supper on the table now."

I join Rainy at the well to wash and discuss the mission.

Rainy sighs. "Where we headed, do you know?"

"Yeah, I know."

"You don't seem too happy about it."

"Hell, why should I be happy? I've got a good life here. Why risk losin' it just to revisit old memories that still burn blisters on my heart?"

"Winn Parish?"

I give him a scowl. Words would be too harsh.

Martha walks out on the porch, looking prettier than the first time I saw her cooking in Annie Handerson's Café—rubbing her forehead with dough on her hands and baking flour on her nose and cheeks. "I just put a blackberry cobbler in the oven. Tell John A. to bring in a pitcher of cream from the springhouse."

I wave. I still marvel at her beauty. "How can I leave her, Rainy?"

Rainy lays his arm on my shoulder. "C'mon, boy, it'll be all right."

Martha puts her hands on her hips. "Rainy Mills, you corruptin' my husband already? Y'all ain't nothin' but a couple of wild and crazy boys who ain't never growed up. My Lord, racing a man ridin' a horse. I just knew you'd both land on your heads the way y'all skidded up to the house. Y'all should know better."

Rainy waltzes up to the porch steps and bows like an actor as a play ends. "We don't know better, sweet and beautiful bride of my very best friend, and we never will." He kisses Martha's hand.

I enjoy the show. Mr. Gilmore and his play acting ways flash through my mind.

"You and Lummy's boyish ways are no secret, Rainy Mills, and I—"

"Would have us be no other way, is that not true?"

Martha laughs and whispers, "Hell, no. That's why I married that stinker over there and the reason I like you, Rainy Mills."

"My day is complete. Observing such unimaginable beauty and sweetness of voice is enough to fill the hungriest of famished souls, my dear. The finest of cuisines await our veracious appetites if I understand correctly?"

Martha winks at me, then checks Rainy's hands. "You are correct, sir, but not before you clean under those fingernails. I ain't havin' those hawg hooves at my table."

Rainy bows and starts back to the well.

Martha grabs his hands again. "Bring my beloved home, Rainy Mills, promise me."

"I—"

"Promise me!"

"At the cost of my life, dear sister."

Martha wipes her tears and smiles. "Now get over there and get those hands clean, mistuh."

"She's a tough one, brother."

"That's why I married her." Martha is just trying to keep her feet on solid ground when our world is spinning out of control.

"Her firmness complements her Aphrodite-like beauty that could charm the hardest of hearts." Rainy chuckles.

"Damn straight, brother. She charmed mine. You best hurry or all the biscuits'll be gone."

John A. lugs a heavy stone jug to the house. "Is this how men act, Pop?"

Martha taps her foot and gives me a wink. "Only when they want to act like little boys."

John A. laughs. "So, I don't have to grow up?"

I take the jug. "I wish that were true, son. But it don't hurt to have a little fun every once in a while, especially when an old friend visits."

I ease up the porch steps and kiss Martha. She wraps her arm around my waist. "C'mon in dear, supper's gettin' cold."

# CHAPTER 12

# SEEING TRUTH IN THE DARKEST LIGHT

## 12:30 A.M., MARCH 4, 1870

*The deepest darkness reveals the brightest light.*

THE MOON AND stars shine full and bright on this less than peaceful night. My body sits calm and still, but my soul races here and there. It takes most of my dwindling energy to capture and manage my thoughts. I can't afford another outburst like the other day. I catch myself rubbing my hands together like I'm washing up for a meal. I don't know what to do, so I look to the sky.

The steadiness of a full moon gives me strength for what's coming. Stars fixed in the blackness anchor my spirit. The greenish tail of a shooting star disappears into the eastern sky, offering hope that my path may be long, but this fight will be over soon—for good. A warm breeze kicks up, and storm clouds roll in from the west, blocking the clear sky. Lightning strikes some far off tree in the distance. Muffled thunder tells me rain will be here soon. It smells good.

I scoot my rocker back against the dogtrot wall. A view from the shadows makes the light of truth brighter this night. Flashes of lightning and peals of thunder signal that Creator is still Master, and His will is as perfect as when the first raindrop splatters on the roof. We need the rain to make ground-breaking easier. But I don't need another storm in my life.

The worst of the storm passes, and rain pitter-patters on the porch steps, making me drowsy. I can't sleep. It's dark. No moon, no stars. I'm brooding. I slide my rocking chair to the far end of the porch away from the dogtrot. It's darker there—almost as dark as my soul.

A door hinge creaks. Martha strains to see in the dark. Her eyes finally adjust. She tiptoes my way. With the light behind her, I can see through her thin nightgown. Her form stirs my soul and body.

"What are you doin' over there? It's darker than dark in that corner, dear."

"I'm better sittin' here."

"In the shadows?"

"I can see the light of truth better from the shadows. It stands out brighter."

"That's more about your soul, I think."

"It is, sweet wife. Come sit with me, dear."

Martha sits on my lap, a rare event with so many children running around. She lays her neck against mine, rubbing her cheek across my nose, and kisses me.

I stroke her silky hair. "This will be the worst kind of soldierin' I'll ever have to do. And I've done some of the worst."

"Even worse than seein' Captain Tom Ford through to gettin' hanged?"

I nod. "And ending Dawg Smith's life and killin' Lester, too. There's only one way to defeat demons."

Martha whimpers. "You have to fight worse than they do."

"You have to think and fight like them, and the worst part is, become one of them."

"You'll have to let the old ways return, at least for a time."

"If I'm to survive, yes, and I'm hatin' it already." I hug her. I'm through talking. I stop so she can talk it out.

It's like she's giving the world a piece of her mind. I've done that many times, but now I just listen.

Martha tightens her hand around the back of my neck. "It may be the worst kind of soldierin', but there's nothing more important than keepin' people who've been set free, free, and end the lives of men who steal other people's lives."

"I appreciate you sayin' that, Martha."

"Don't let it change you back. You've come far with your wakin' dreams and sweaty nightmares." Martha wraps her arms around my head and shoulders, pulling me close to her chest. Her warm breasts remind me of the love and peace I don't want to leave or ever lose. Stroking her smooth hips reminds me of the joys we have as husband and wife. How can I leave this life? It's what I always wanted—what I fought and killed for.

"I just don't understand it. Why me? Why is the Lord puttin' me through this again? Doesn't He know I've had enough?"

"Yes, but He also knows—"

"Knows what?" Hot blood rushes to my face. "That I'm good at killin'?"

Martha lovingly strokes my beard. "No, dear. That you will survive when others won't."

"How do you know that?"

"How do you know the special things you know?"

"I'm sorry, Martha, it's just...."

She presses her cheek to mine. "Let's just enjoy the quiet."

The stars come out, and the moon finds a break in the clouds. Martha leads my hand to the barn where my loving wife brings me all the joy a man's body could ever want, and more. I return the favor.

When we lie back in the hay in each other's arms, Martha caresses my cheek. "When you start to have one of your war dreams, let the memory of this night chase the bad ones away." She stands before me uncovered in the moonlight. Martha never looked so good.

Truth just got a little brighter. But it's still not clear.

# CHAPTER 13

# TULLOS CEMETERY HILL

## 1:30 A.M., MARCH 4, 1870

*To survive in this life, sometimes you have to talk to someone in the next.*

"I'LL BE BACK in a bit, Martha."

"Goin' up on the hill?"

"I have to. Call it a comfort. Call it seekin' wisdom. Whatever it is, I need some time."

"I'll wait up."

"I may be in the cemetery for a while."

"Wake me when you come to bed. I want us to fall asleep together."

I hug her close and kiss her neck.

The well-worn path to where Pa is buried is easily followed in the moonlight. The storm has passed us by, for tonight.

Night creatures seeking their evening suppers scamper away into hollows and over ridges. A winged forest angel sweeps past my head, knocking my hat off. It lands on a limb not far away and hoots. I reposition my hat and thank the owl for the company.

The cypress grave markers I carved when I lived with Dan Creekwater in McCurtain Creek Swamp stand as firm as the day they were set in the ground. Cypress. Tall, steady, and lives a long time. Like Dan, who helped me find my soul again.

"I get it, Lord, wisdom of the owl and strength of a bald cypress tree."

The owl hoots again. I still talk out loud. Too much. Maybe not. I'm certain Creator gets a little weary of humans asking him to give, give, and give. I'd never claim to know Creator's mind by any stretch, but I kind of understand his soulfulness. I bet Creator would enjoy a simple conversation with no strings attached, no requests. If Creator already knows what I need, why should I bore him with what he already knows? Polite conversation is what I seek tonight. The rest is in Creator's capable hands.

Yesterday at breakfast, little Margaret wanted to thank God for the food. She's shy, but she knows something's in the air. Ma and Martha were so proud when she volunteered to say grace. After a few stumbling words about the farm, her home, she called everyone by name while looking at them to make sure she didn't miss anyone. But it was the way she ended her prayer that has me thinking about who I am in life with my Creator. She ended with, "And God, I hope you have a great day." She spoke to him as a friend like folks in the Bible did.

She finished, and as the boys reached for the biscuits, Ma leaned over and whispered in my ear, "That girl is a thinker, just like you. 'Blood ain't the only thing that makes kin,' Granny Thankful used to say. People can be put together because they have the same spirit."

That's why I'm here—Granny Thankful. I pull out the multi-colored agate she gave me in Vicksburg and roll it between my fingers. Its smoothness calms my troubled spirit. A moonbeam sneaks through the pines to land on the rock. It glows like I'm holding it up to sun. I lay the rock on the top of Pa's grave marker. I chase away all thoughts to empty my soul for the wisdom Creator may share.

A slight breeze wafts through the thicket to my left, and a long flowing robe roams the graves. I'm not frightened, but I am nervous about what I may learn. I confess that I did ask for this when I told Martha I could see truth better from the shadows.

Granny Thankful appears on a stump a few feet away. *"There's my boy. All grown up and still searching for a home."*

"Will I ever have peace, Granny?"

*"Peace springs from within the heart, not from without."*

"I can't seem to find it."

*"There's a certain kind of calm that can only be found after the worst of storms."*

"I've had the storms. When do I get the calm?"

*"The calm, Grandson, is in accepting what Creator blesses you with once the winds stop blowing."*

"When will the winds stop?"

*"For some, they never do."*

"That's not very comforting, Granny."

*"It is when you realize what your sacrifice means to others."*

"The painful memories keep coming back, Granny. They won't stop. The war, losin' Susannah, Ben, Mister Gilmore, Poole, Old Bart. What am I saying? You know all of them."

*"I do, and they watch over you. Talk to them when times get hard, when you think your mind has left you. They are never far away."*

"When will the visions stop? When they come, it's like I'm back in the earthworks at Vicksburg or rollin' around on the ground fightin' Lester."

Granny hangs her head. *"They won't stop. They will only get worse, Grandson."*

"Why me?"

*"You know the answer."*

"What is the answer?"

*"Your dearest love has already spoken that truth."*

The words Martha spoke. "I will survive when others won't."

Granny fades into the night but not before reassuring me. *"Hold tight to the love in your heart and the stone in your hand. Both will bring you home. I will ask Michael, the Protector of God's People, to come when you need him most. Michael will always be able to find you if in your hand the agate you possess."*

The hint of first light peeks over the far ridge. Two owls in the trees above my head give long comforting calls and are answered from far away.

Elihu and Dan Creekwater step out from behind a clump of bushes.

Dan reaches for my shoulder. "Crazy Deer Dancer, you will survive, but you have given much of your soul to other people. And so, they live. And now, you must give even more."

Elihu squats on his heels, chewing a twig. "Lummy, keep a clear head and sharp eye."

"I always do."

"I'm not talkin' about the fight you have comin'. I'm talkin' about tendin' to your soul. Know when your mind is goin' places it don't need to go. Do somethin' to stay in the moment so you don't lose your head when you need it most."

Dan holds out his hand. "Put this on your wrist." It's a leather bracelet with a single owl claw attached. "When the dreams come, press the talon into your wrist. The pain will keep you in the now and give you the wisdom of Brother Owl."

Elihu sings a familiar old hymn. Dan dances in rhythm. I hold the top of Pa's grave marker with both hands and contemplate what's coming. I touch the knife he made me when I was just a kid—the knife that saved life. And took it.

Pa's here, holding up his pointing finger. *"One last time, son, and it will all be done. You must return the favor the Lord has blessed you with."*

"I'm not sure if I have it in me. But what favor?"

Granny whispers through the pine boughs, *"That you have never had to be alone in what you have been called to do. There is one who needs your help. To him you owe a favor. To you he will give his life. Now build a fire and dance."*

# CHAPTER 14

# DANCING WITH PICTS

## JUST BEFORE DAWN, MARCH 4, 1870

*Rousing ancestors brings an army of hope.*

I WANDER AROUND in the dark, looking for sticks, pines cones, and anything that will burn. "Who needs my help? Who do I owe a favor? Why would he need to give me his life?"

Dan drops a load of sticks, and Elihu goes to stacking them for a fire.

Dan brushes off his shirt. "That, Crazy Deer Dancer, will be revealed in time, as was your name the first time we met."

I take a small piece of fat pine from my pocket and pitch it to Elihu. I chuckle. "What about the blue paint? We gonna do that, too?"

From the shadows, Dan says, "I believe this will do, Crazy Deer Dancer." He stalks out of the thicket quiet as a deer wearing only his moccasins. "Now become one with the universe as Creator brought you into this world. Elihu, light the fire."

I rub my shoulders. "Ain't it a bit chilly to do this?"

Dan cuts his eyes at me. He's serious, and I know better than to argue.

I strip down to nothing but my brogans.

Dan paints me with a dark color made from berries that looks to be more purple than blue. He fashions designs on my skin I've never seen before. Elihu paints Dan. Then, I paint Elihu with the same ancient symbols Dan drew on me. The fire is roaring now.

Dan shares a strong sweet drink that burns like fire but relaxes my body quicker than any moonshine I've ever had. The early spring chill in the air turns warm. My head swims, and my body sways as Dan starts an old chant that summons a vision of blue painted warriors gathered around a fire hundreds of years ago. Families marked with ancient symbols have come to support husbands and fathers, knowing it might be the last time they see them. The entire clan is there, old and young. Granny Thankful nods, and I understand the markings painted on my body.

I sway in the breeze with the pines. We dance in a perfect circle. It's as though I'm floating. Maybe I am. All the people dear to me, dead and gone, join the dance. They, too, are naked and painted blue. No one notices. No one cares. Bare and free, pure and holy. The universe at its best. It's who they are. It's who I am. A presence greater than all present fills the place.

In one voice, they all shout chants to Creator. *"Who was, Who is, and Who will be."*

We circle the fire, humming and dancing.

I shout with them. "All life and all glory belong to Creator!"

The fire flashes brilliant blue. Their eyes match the flames. They stop and point at me. *"Go!"* They fade into the forest and become trees in the waltzing shadows of the pines.

Granny steps into the fire, her eyes blazing blue. *"Grandson, you must go tomorrow."*

I search my body. "I'm missing something." Then I remember. "I'm wearing nothing but the shoes on my feet. Should I take the gator necklace? Or the button that stopped the bullet and saved my life at Vicksburg? Maybe the cross Poole carved from cedar?"

*"Carry just one and the rest in your heart. The gator necklace will protect another."*

"Protect who? Sarge, J.A., Rainy?"

*"It will be revealed in the moment you see Susannah's eyes in the place where she rests."*

I search my soul for the answer of who that might be. It escapes me.

Granny's flowing robes change from blue to red, gray, then purple, orange, green, then in a flash becomes a rainbow. *"You need but two things to carry you through all things as you go into battle, for it is into battle you go."*

"Tell me, what are they?"

*"First, the sword of your father, which wields justice."*

"The knife Pa made me. And the other?"

Granny holds out a glowing stone. *"It is by the wisdom of the agate that you will survive. Be prepared. You will lose a part of you that reasons to see into what holds you steady—the gift of sight into the other side."* She drops the rock, and I scramble on hands and knees to grab it.

I look up, and she's gone. The fire becomes it's brightest, and I stare at the multi-colored agate in my hand. It's the same multi-colored agate I held in my hand the day I found out Susannah had died in a letter from Mr. Gilmore. The same day my brothers, Jasper and James, showed up alive. Death and life in the same moment—the circle of the universe. I glance at Pa's grave marker. The stone I'd left there is gone. It's in my hand.

A splash of water wakes me. "Lummy, are you all right?" Dan wipes my face with his shirt.

Elihu pours me a cup of cold muscadine wine. Dan and Elihu put their clothes back on.

I find my mine lying on a log. "I don't know if I had a dream, a vision, or what. Elihu? Dan? It was real, wasn't it?"

Elihu looks at Dan, who nods, and then to me. "It was, brother. What did they say to you?"

"Just one word—*go!*"

# CHAPTER 15

# SO OTHERS
# CAN HAVE A HOME

## SUNRISE, MARCH 4, 1870

*Ancestors will lead the way to home.*

RAINY SOPS GRAVY with his last biscuit. "What a feast, Martha. You are as excellent a cook as you are a beauty to behold."

I'm getting impatient. Why, I don't know. "Okay, lover boy, finish up, and let's go. Sarge said to meet him and the others at Mount Pisgah Baptist Church by ten o'clock."

Elihu pushes back his plate. "Your horses are saddled and ready to go. I threw a sack of grain on each."

Rainy swishes the last of his coffee around in his cup. "In a minute, Lummy. Let me finish my coffee first."

Mary asks, "Uncle Rainy, where did you go to school? You have a very good command of the English language."

Rainy squints. "Down in Natchez. That was a long time ago." I can see pain mixed with joy in the faraway look in his eyes. "A kind old preacher who ran the orphanage where I grew up made sure I received a good classical education and learned a profitable trade. I work with guns and read. Always have."

Mary is too inquisitive. "Who were your parents?"

Rainy's eyes tear up. "Sweet niece, please forgive me. Let that be a story for another time."

Mary tucks her chin into her chest. "I'd like to hear it someday."

"Someday you will."

Mary announces like she's making a point in a schoolroom, "The stories of our lives must be written down for our grandchildren. How else will they know us if no one takes the time?"

"Mary, dear child, you are wise beyond your years." Rainy lays his palm on his chest and speaks like an actor in a play. He reminds me of Mr. Gilmore in Winn Parish and Gunnard at Vicksburg. "A wise man once wrote, 'To be ignorant of what occurred before you were born is to remain always a child. For what is the worth of human life, unless it is woven into the life of our ancestors by the records of history?'"

Mary shivers. "Sounds like some ancient Greek philosopher."

"Actually, a Roman lawyer and philosopher, but you are correct, he *is* one of the ancients."

Mary writes furiously. "What was his name?"

Rainy grins at me. "Why, maybe one of your ancestors, Lummy, or at least he had your name."

Mary squirms.

I ask, "So, wiseass, what *was* his name?"

Martha elbows me in the side.

Rainy stands to throw out his arm in true thespian form.

I sigh. "Dang. You just know we're gonna have to put up with this all the way to Winn Parish."

Rainy speaks like a preacher. "The great Marcus Tullius Cicero."

Mary jumps up, she's so excited. "I've heard of him. He was a great statesman, writer, and orator, but didn't Mark Antony cut off his—"

Rainy shakes his head. "We won't mention that part."

I have to know. "What part?"

Mary hangs her head. "He tried to overthrow the government, and they…."

Martha barks, "Go on, child, might as well tell it."

"They cut off his head and hands and displayed them in the town square."

Elihu mumbles, "Guess he shoulda kept his mouth shut."

The memory of lifting Dawg Smith's head from his body haunts me and sends me places I don't want to go in my head. I have to break this chain of thought before the old feelings jump on my back. I press the owl talon into my wrist. It works. "Let's talk about somethin' else. More coffee, please, Martha?"

Martha clears her throat and pours the dark steaming liquid into my cup. "You both will do well to use some of your Roman grandpa's wisdom and get yourselves back here quick, or there'll be hell to pay." She throws her chin into the air. "Lummy, you best—"

"Yes, my sweet wife, I heard you."

Martha starts clearing the table. "It wouldn't hurt to have Pastor Dobbs say a prayer over you and the rest of your band."

I take her hand. "I'd rather have your prayers."

Martha softens. "Those, you always have."

I kiss her hand.

We walk out onto the porch, and I sit with Martha for just a minute more.

Rainy and Elihu go to the barn to get our horses. Elihu takes a cigar Rainy offers him, and he sniffs its fine aroma. He lights his smoke on Rainy's cigar, and they stop to enjoy the moment. They walk the horses up to the house, and Elihu goes into the room where he sleeps, across the dogtrot from the kitchen where the girls, Martha, and I sleep.

Elihu holds out my double-barreled ten-gauge shot gun with a flour sack full of shot, wadding, and powder. "Here, little brother, this'll keep the two-legged wolves away."

Rainy grins. "I can take care of the wolves. It's the coyotes he needs to worry about."

Elihu sawed the double-barrel off to a foot and a half-length and polished the ends. You'd never know it had been altered.

I take it outside into the yard to see how she handles. It's much lighter and throws up good against my shoulder. I shake his hand. "This'll work just fine. Thank you, brother."

Elihu spits a stream of tobacco. "It'll do the job when the fightin' gets too close."

"That it'll do." I thumb the end of the barrels. "You even put a new aiming bead at the end."

Elihu rolls his cigar from one side of his mouth to the other with his teeth, smiling. "That's because you can't shoot worth a shit. For the life of me I don't how you survived—" He covers his mouth.

Mary giggles. Martha's face reddens. Rainy is laughing so hard his shoulders bounce up and down, but he makes no sound.

Elihu holds up his hands. "Martha, I am sorry."

Martha nods. "I'll break you Tullos boys of cussin' one of these days."

Mary snickers. "But Aunt Martha, it was funny."

Martha covers her mouth and bursts out laughing. "It was, wasn't it?"

I kiss Martha on the cheek. "You're the best."

Elihu clears his throat. "But back to the shotgun, you don't need a bead. Shoulder cannons don't need aiming. That thing'll knock the leaves off a tree at twenty feet. The bead just makes it look better." He pitches me a leather saddle sheath he made for the shotgun.

Rainy takes the sheath from my hands. "Fine piece of leatherwork, Elihu. May I call on you should I need one, or more?"

Elihu nods.

Rainy ties it to my saddle.

I slide the shotgun into the sheath. "Thanks, brother."

Elihu steps down from the porch. "Make sure you hold on tight. With most of the barrel gone, she's gonna kick like a mule."

"I will." I give him a firm handshake and hug. "Always takin' care of me, ain't you, big brother?"

"It's what I do." Elihu holds out a jug of muscadine wine.

Rainy steps up. "I'll take that. He's got the extra weight of that shotgun."

I try to laugh but can't with what we're headed to do and what I'm leaving behind.

Martha stands at the edge of the porch, biting her lip. The children are quiet. Little Margaret cries.

I take little Delaware from Martha and hold her high in the air. I kiss her on the forehead and hand her to Ma. "My daughter, what a blessin'."

Ma sits down in Pa's old rocking chair. "Just keepin' it warm 'til you get back, son. Take good care of yourself. The Lord and your brothers will protect your family here. Go on now and get back quick as you can."

Martha rushes down the steps and falls into my arms. "You be careful, Columbus Nathan Tullos. I want you back home." She cries, and I hold her.

There's nothing more I can say. She wipes her tears and straightens her dress. "Get goin', Lummy, my love. Like you always say, the sooner you leave, the sooner you'll be back."

Rainy kicks the dirt. "I'll get him home, Martha, I promise."

"You and the Good Lord, Rainy Mills."

I wrap my arms around her one last time. The children gather around, and I kiss each one. John A. marches up and sticks out his hand. I take it and pull him close for a hug. "You're the man of the family, John A. I know you'll make me proud."

He whimpers, trying not to cry. "You get on back home quick, Pop. We never finished our chess game."

I squeeze the back of his neck and turn for my horse.

Jasper and James offer firm handshakes, reassuring me they will watch over my family.

Elihu walks his horse out of the barn. "I'll go as far as the church house with you."

We trot our horses down the road that leads away from the Tullos farm. We stop and turn before the last bend to wave.

I take one last look. Martha waves big, wearing the same blue skirt she wore the day I left for Memphis with the 1st Mississippi Mounted Rifles. That image will bring me home—alive.

I give my horse a gentle prod and cry like a baby. Rainy pats me on the back. Elihu sings a familiar old hymn. I wipe my face. The hoot of an old owl wafts down from the piney hill where Pa is buried.

Dan Creekwater throws his right fist into the air. "My spirit is with you, Crazy Deer Dancer."

Elihu backhands my shoulder.

I wince from the old injury from when I crossed the Mississippi back in '59.

"Sorry, brother, but me and Ole Dan will stand guard over Ma and the girls day and night from cemetery hill."

"I know, and Jasper and James aren't far away."

Elihu grins. "Yeah, and neither are the Wood boys. They ain't scared."

"That I do know."

As we turn onto the Old Natchez Trace, we slow our mounts to a walk. We have a long road ahead, and we'll get there soon enough. But the first stop is Mt. Pisgah Baptist Church where we'll plan the Devil's work.

It seems like a hundred years since I left this farm in search of Susannah. Here I go again—leaving so others can have what I leave behind.

Tears fall like warm rain. Rainy squeezes my shoulder.

Elihu leans over and pops me on the back. "It'll be all right, boy."

I pull down my hat. "Let's go get this done, dammit."

# CHAPTER 16

# MT. PISGAH BAPTIST CHURCH

## MID-MORNING, MARCH 4, 1870

*This ain't the first time Satan called a meeting in a church house.*

WE TIE OUR horses to the hitching post in front of the white-washed house of worship.

Sarge walks around the corner of the building, fastening his belt buckle. "Stomach ain't too good this morning, boys. You might hold off going to the outhouse for a bit."

That's usually funny. Not today. I witnessed too many men die of dysentery and too many men shit their britches before a fight like the one we're headed to. It's not funny. Not at all.

As I open the church house door, a grayhaired old lady bursts out, flailing her arms and kicking up her heels like a showgirl. "Missus Bessie, you all right today?"

"Better'n a bullfrog with a belly full of flies!"

"I don't believe I've ever seen you move so good."

"Don't 'cha know, son? Just this morning, when I went to get a chicken to make y'alls dumplin's, I got stung by three bumblebees. And praise the Lord, my arthritis ain't givin' me a lick of trouble. Hallelujah!"

"Gettin' stung makes you better?"

"Better'n a jaybird eatin' fermented crabapples. Come Sunday, I'll be dancing and praisin' in worship like a young girl." She pats her bottom. "That is, if I don't get my rump out of joint."

Rainy bows over laughing. "Now that's one I've never heard."

Mrs. Bessie winks at Rainy, and she pats me on the bottom. "But don't you worry, son. I won't get too happy."

"Now we can't be havin' your rump gettin' all crooked, Missus Bessie."

"Heck, naw." She laughed. "I wouldn't be fit to bed my old buzzard of a husband if that happened."

My face steams hot with embarrassment. "That's more'n I needed to know."

"Maybe so, but you and that pretty wife of yours best keep the fire goin', or else. You don't miss the water 'til the well runs dry. Oops, gotta go. My husband will starve to death if I don't get his food on the table when he gets back from checking his fish traps."

Rainy pulls the door open, shaking his head the whole time. "You certainly grew up with some interesting people."

"Ain't it so?"

Pastor Dobbs waits inside, hands folded. "Lummy Tullos, it's always good to see you. Just wish you'd come around a little more on Sundays."

My anger flares at being called out for a belief I no longer hold, but I love this man. He cares for my soul. "I go to church every Sunday, Pastor. I just don't believe you can lock Creator up in four walls on Sunday mornin' and say that's the only place you can find him."

Rainy clears his throat. "Here, here."

Pastor Dobb smiles. "I agree, but in a different way. C'mon in. Coffee's hot, and I have a surprise for you."

We shake the chill from our jackets. It takes a second for my eyes to adjust to the dark room. The shape of a man clears into my view.

"Lummy, how are you, son?"

"H.P. Dotson, how in the h— I mean, the *heck* are you?" I cut my eyes at Pastor Dobbs, who pats his foot, smiling.

"Better than where you're headed today, old friend."

I remove my hat. "Always the man who gets to the point in a hurry."

H.P. chuckles and offers his hand. "My wife says that, too, but only about things I want to discuss."

Pastor Dobbs holds out his hand. "Rainy, how's the world treating you these days?"

Rainy shrugs. "About the same, Pastor, I reckon. Buying, selling, and trading guns. Not much more, except reading and studying a bit."

Pastor Dobbs motions us to sit close to the big pot-bellied stove.

H.P. lays his hand on Rainy's shoulder. "I want to talk to you about getting a good squirrel gun for my boy before you leave. He'll turn ten soon, and he's ready to hunt by himself."

"Not a problem. I'll order it when we get on the road, have it sent to you."

H.P. offers his hand. "How are you doing these days, Sarge?"

Sarge takes off his coat and lays it on a pew. "As good as the Good Lord desires, I'd say."

H.P. sits. "No uniform this time?"

Sarge sits by the stove and rubs his hands, grinning. "For your information, Mister H.P. Dotson, defender of the stars and stripes, that'll be Lieutenant McGugarty to you, sir."

H.P. laughs. "Yeah, Pastor Dobbs told me. They must've plum run out of qualified men to serve as officers. Congratulations, Lieutenant."

McGugarty grabs H.P.'s hand. "Good to see you. Just call me Sarge, H.P."

Pastor Dobbs smiles. "You going cloak and dagger this time, Sarge?"

"Yes, sir. Orders."

"It's always better to go in truth of the Lord."

I laugh. "Yeah, but what about that righteous deception you used to talk about? You said the Bible's full of it."

Pastor grins. "You are full of yourself this morning, Lummy Tullos."

Elihu slaps his knee, laughing. "He's full of somethin', that's for sure."

Pastor Dobbs points at Elihu with a grin. "Careful, son, you're in the Lord's house. But I do miss our spiritual sparring sessions, Lummy. I'll get the coffee."

Pastor Dobbs returns with a tray of cups and sets the coffee pot on the stove to keep it warm. "I have honey and fresh cream if you need it." We all take it black. "I want to say a short prayer over you men and another before you leave. Let me talk to the Lord, and I'll retreat to my study. What I don't know, I can't tell." He asks Creator to give us wisdom and strength to plan well and to bring us all home safely. He walks to his study, shaking his finger in the air. "Don't leave before I pray over you good men again."

I kick Elihu's foot. "Ain't you got somewhere else to be besides here?"

Elihu stands and stretches. "Think I'll see if Pastor Dobbs has figured out a way to save my soul."

Rainy blows on his coffee to cool it. "That's what you call a foregone conclusion. He can't."

Elihu laughs and sticks his tongue out at me.

H.P. smiles and yells to Pastor Dobbs. "Hey, Pastor, before you try to save Elihu's reprobate soul, don't you have a surprise for Lummy?"

Pastor Dobbs snaps his fingers. "Yes, I almost forgot. Old age is creeping up on me. Isaiah, would you come out here, please?"

I turn to Sarge. "Who's Isaiah?"

"See if you can figure it out."

A young, well-built black man walks out of Pastor Dobb's study and stands in front of me with a slight grin.

I look around at everyone, and it hits me. I see her in his eyes. "You're Susannah's brother."

"Do I look that much like her?"

I grab his hand. "Yes, and you're the better for it. Good to meet you, Isaiah."

"You, too, suh. I've heard a lot about you,"—he grins and winks—"and I see it's all true."

I laugh. "I'm not sure how to take that, brother-in-law."

Isaiah squints. "In the very best way possible, brother. Sarge has told me all about you. I'm glad my sister married you. I'm happy about my sister Ruth and your brother James takin' up with each other. I met him yesterday in Bankston."

"That dawg. Why didn't he tell me?"

Isaiah stretches his palms out in front of the stove to warm them. "I wanted it to be a surprise."

"A good surprise it is, brother."

Sarge motions for Isaiah to have a seat and hands him a cup of coffee.

Isaiah blows the steam off. "Mistuh Lummy, we saw each other once durin' the war."

"When and where would that have been?"

"Not far from here, where we whipped the britches off the Rebs at Franklin Church. Do you remember?"

"Do I? That's when me and forty First Mississippi Mounted Rifles ran into General Wirt Adams and damn near the whole Rebel cavalry." Everyone laughs. "It sure wasn't funny then. We came around a bend, and the Rebs looked like Yankee cavalry. We were ridin' hard and ran headlong right into 'em, our horses slippin' and slidin' across the muddy road all up in and amongst 'em. We turned and skedaddled with them Rebs hard on our heels. I never rode so hard in all my life. Truth is we led them straight to the fightin'. What I saw at the Battle of Franklin Church, though, was a dream come true—black soldiers fightin' with honor to set their own people free. Y'all showed Gen'l Wirt Adams what for."

Isaiah's chest swells with a good pride. "General Grierson said we men of the Third U.S. Colored Cavalry fought admirably."

"You did. I was there when we raised the Ebenezer."

Isaiah smiles. "I was the one who carved the letters in the millstone."

"Then we did see each other. I was the one Colonel Osband asked to read from the Bible."

Isaiah stands and gives me a strong hug. "Everythin' these men said about you is true, and more. Again, I'm glad my sister married you. I'm just sorry I never knew her. When massuh sold off our family, he kept me. That was the worst day of my life. Will you tell me about her sometime?"

"It'd be a pleasure, Isaiah."

Isaiah sips his coffee. "I'm proud of my name, Isaiah, but just call me Ise."

Sarge leans up. "Ise it is. Okay, boys, let's get down to business."

I wave my hand. "Just a minute, Sarge. I've got one question for Ise."

Ise sits up straight like he's been called to attention. "Go ahead, brother."

"Why are you here?"

Ise rubs his chin. "I fought to set my people free, and they are. We still have a long way to go in these United States, but now I go to help set everybody free."

"You could get killed."

Ise stares into my eyes. "I do this because… what was it Thomas Jefferson once said?"

Rainy whispers, "I prefer dangerous freedom over peaceful slavery."

Ise taps his foot. "There's your answer, brother."

I top off everyone's coffee. "I'm encouraged, Ise." I fill Sarge's cup last. "Sorry I butted in. I needed to hear that."

Sarge waves off my apology and leans in. "Let me explain a few things here at the beginning. For years, slave-owners kept their slaves under control through fear of the whip, but also by stirring up rumors of haints, night doctors, and body snatchers. They even went around wearing bedsheets, masquerading as ghosts to keep slaves in their beds at night. They called themselves county patrollers. Blacks say patterollers."

Elihu slurps his coffee. "Patterollin' bunch of damn cowards if you ask me."

Ise turns his head, hiding a tear. "My father was killed by patterollers."

I shift in my seat. "Susannah said he was killed loggin' timber in McCurtain swamp when a cypress tree fell on him."

"That's what they told everybody, but I found out the truth. Patterollers came through one Sunday night when we were all at church, except Father, who stayed home sick. They lured him out sayin' they were government men tryin' to help black folk."

Elihu sets his cup on the potbelly stove. "Men like Captain Tom Ford?"

Ise shakes his head. "Not from what Sarge tells me. These men were far worse. The ones who killed my daddy were passing through on their way somewhere across the Mississippi River." The look on Ise's face turns from sadness to a growing rage. "They hanged him from a tree limb upside down. You can imagine the rest."

I chance it. "No, we can't. Tell us."

Sarge grabs my shoulder. "You sure about this? It could trigger one of your war dreams."

I push his hand away. "I need to prepare myself so that it doesn't."

Ise opens the potbelly stove door and stares into the flames. "They opened him up like I just opened the door on that stove right there." We sit still. "They gutted him like a hawg and strung his insides from one tree to another. They left him there to bleed out. I was there when they found him. Scavengers got to him before we did."

I remove the cover lid on the stove and puke into the fire. Sarge stands to help me. I wave him off. "No need. I'm all right. It's not just breakfast I puked up. Old memories came with it. It's my way of dealin' with it, I reckon." I put the cover lid back and shut the stove door.

Sarge sets his cup on the stove. "Could they have come from south of Jackson? There was plenty of activity around Natchez before the war."

"I'm not sure. They worked the Trace for a bit and then went on to Louisiana after the war."

Sarge sighs. "Sounds like the men we're hunting. They never stopped harassing Negroes after the war. In fact, they've gotten worse."

Elihu stomps his foot. "Nothin' more than a bunch of murderous thievin' night patrollers like Dawg Smith, huh, Lummy?"

I summon the memory of taking Dawg Smith's head off with the knife Pa made me. "Yeah, worthless nothin's terrorizing good and decent folk."

Sarge leans back in his chair. "That's the mission. Catch and kill the West-Kimbrell Gang, who now carry out their evil deeds in central Louisiana." He stares at the ceiling, waiting for me to say it.

I need to say it. "In Winn Parish."

Sarge squints. "Yep, Winn Parish, Louisiana, is where we're going. These men make Dawg Smith's gang look like a bunch of sissy schoolboys."

I need to talk this out for the others. "So, that's it. Take out John West and his ruffians."

Sarge sips his coffee. "That's the mission. General Grierson remembered hearing about your encounter with Captain Ford just before we hit Bankston. He did some investigating and found out enough to recommend that you serve as our scout since you know the territory."

"Last time I was asked to be a scout, I helped burn down the manufactories in my home town and barely kept the Greensborough courthouse standing."

"That's why they picked you, old friend, and made you a sergeant."

I sigh with belabored acceptance. "All right, Sarge, when do we leave?"

Pastor Dobbs steps out. "Before you go, come eat the dumplin's Missus Bessie made. I want to send you men off with a prayer and full bellies as you go do the Lord's work."

Sarge stands to stretch. "Good enough."

Pastor Dobbs drops to his knees and prays a prayer the apostles would be proud of. "And thank you, Lord, for good women like my wife, Missus Bessie, and Lummy's Martha, and Sarge's wife to be, who hold steady when men go about doing Your will. Thank you for the food that we know comes only from You, as do all good blessings. Amen."

We say "amen" together and look up just as Pastor Dobb's wife brings in the dumplings.

Pastor laughs. "God does have his timing."

Elihu jumps up to help.

Sister Dobbs asks, "Elihu, would you please bring the basket in Pastor's study? I hope the cornbread is still warm."

He tips his hat. "Yes, ma'am, Sister Dobbs. That cornbread'll be good hot or cold if it was you who made it."

"Thank you, brother." She sets the large cast iron pot on the stove.

Sister Dobbs offers Sarge a bowl, who hands it to H.P. "H.P., will you take care of any messages between Lummy and his family, by mail or telegraph?"

H.P. turns to me. "Be glad to, Lummy."

Sarge takes a bowl. "Just to be clear, Lummy, send all letters or messages to him. Put no return address on them. He'll get them to Martha and your family. You might consider masking your handwriting. If anybody asks you, H.P., just say that they're letters from Lummy's sister-in-law, Annie Handerson. That damn postmaster is a damn nosey son of a—" We all look up at Sarge. "Sorry, but that man irritates me something fierce."

Pastor Dobbs laughs. "I did hear Archibald Tullos say that the only word that works sometimes is damn."

Elihu elbows me as he spoons dumplings into his mouth.

I laugh. "Pastor, my pay will be sent here. Please have H.P. deliver that along with my letters if I write any."

"Done."

I shake H.P.'s hand. "Thanks for your help."

"It's the least I can do. Where should I have Martha's letters sent to in Winn Parish?"

"Not gonna chance it. If there's an emergency, I instructed her to send a telegram to Mistuh Davis in Winnfield."

We finish our meal in silence.

# CHAPTER 17

# REMEMBERING WHY I LEFT HOME

## NEAR BIG BLACK RIVER, FIRST LIGHT, MARCH 8, 1870

*Sometimes you gotta leave home to remember why home is so important.*

F AINT RED LIGHT paints naked limbs covered with tiny budding leaves as a squawking blue jay wakes up the world.

"Red sky in the morning, sailor's warning," Sarge grumbles. "We'll ride in the rain today."

Funny, I said that to Martha just a few days ago.

I'm not too excited about that prospect, but Vicksburg's not too far away, and my sister-in-law Annie and her husband Beau will be glad to see us. "I best get the coffee goin' before it soaks everything."

Thunder claps with the deafening report of a cannon boom just above our heads. I drop to the ground like I did at Vicksburg when a shell exploded overhead. I roll over next to a tree, shaking. The sounds of men screaming confuse my mind. I don't remember anything after that.

I come to with Sarge shaking me. "Lummy, it's all right, son. I'm here."

I realize my pistol is cocked and stuck in his gut.

Ise pulls the barrel away from Sarge's belly, and the gun slips from my hand into his. The clicking sounds of the hammer being released calm my shakiness.

"I'm all right. Just give me a minute."

Ise hands back my pistol. "Rest a minute, Mistuh Lummy. I'll get the coffee goin'."

"Just Lummy, if you don't mind, Ise." I lean back against a sweetgum tree, pulling a gumball out from under my backside. I pitch it into the fire and laugh. "Such a small irritation under my butt sure brings a man back to what's real."

Realizing where I am and who I'm with doesn't set in until Ise hands me a steaming cup of coffee. The cup warms my chilly hands. The care of my brothers-in-arms warms my soul.

The light touch of feet in the leaves not thirty yards away in the shadowy bushes makes me think of a deer slipping past us to bed up for the day—except deer have four feet, not two.

I wheel around with my pistol cocked, using the sweetgum tree as a shield.

A frightened black girl, wearing a torn nightshirt, grabs the nearest tree and squeezes her eyes tight, waiting for the pain of the bullet. I can't imagine the trouble she's gone through, dressed the way she is.

"It's all right, don't be scared," I whisper.

"Thank you, kind suh."

"Ise, Sarge, get over here. Bring a blanket." I holster my pistol. "No one's gonna hurt you." I walk, hands in the air, to her tree. I peel her fingers from the bark as I hum "Amazing Grace."

She faints, but I catch her and lay her beside the fire.

She comes to and smiles. "You know that Good Book song?"

"I do. What's your name, sweetheart?"

"Jenny."

Ise asks, "Just Jenny?"

"Yassuh, that's all I know. My poppa didn't want us called by the massuh's name. So, I ain't got no other name."

Ise whispers, "Might just have to do somethin' 'bout that."

I backhand Ise on the shoulder, who's grinning bigger than a possum chewing corn. "All right, Miss Jenny, how about some hot food and somethin' better to wear? Then, you can tell me and my friends how we can help you this morning. How's that sound?" I learned that bit of kindness from Mistuh Wiley in Winnfield back in '59.

"Jest fine. Thank you, suh."

Sarge brings a plate of food and a cup of coffee as Ise wraps a blanket around Jenny.

Ise rubs her shoulder. "Just like the Good Samaritan, huh Lummy?"

"Yeah, I can't help it. I had good teachers. No passin' by on the other side for me."

Rainy cleans Jenny's swollen and bloody feet. "Let me see if I can find you something better to wear, little dear."

Jenny hadn't noticed the big tear in her nightshirt that exposed her from belly button to thigh. She snatches the cloth to cover herself. "I'm so sorry, suhs. I never run around lookin' like this. I was so scared, bein' out in them woods after dark. I just knew the haints ridin' them horses were gonna ketch me any minute. Couldn't go nowheres else. Black folks at them other plantations wouldn't hide me. I was all alone, hopin' no night doctor would find me and cut me up."

Ise pats her on the shoulder. "Nothing to fear here, Jenny. These are good white folk."

I'm curious. "Haints, what are you talkin' about?"

Sarge explains. "Remember what I told you? Masters and overseers instilled such a fear of ghosts and witches, these people learned to fear the dark and hate each other in the process."

"But what in the hell is a night doctor?"

Sarge shakes his head as he hands Jenny a damp cloth to wash her face. "It's just another way to scare these people from moving around at night."

Jenny shuffles her feet, shaking from the cold. "If them body snatchin' night doctors catch you, they'll skin your head and sell it to rich white folk so they can make leather for their collars and shoulder wraps like a coon fur."

Rainy comes back with a shirt that will cover Jenny at least to the knees. She holds it up. "Thank you, suh." She then waits.

It hits me. "Yes, yes, of course, sorry." We turn our backs.

"Thank you, kind suhs." She slips off the ragged nightshirt. The starched cloth of Rainy's shirt ruffles when she puts her head through the neck hole and pulls it down over her.

I catch Ise looking her way from the corner of my eye. I can't resist. "You know squirrel-eyein' somethin' you ain't supposed to be gawkin' at can get your eyeball shot out."

Embarrassed, he snaps his head forward like he's been called to attention. "I do, but it's—"

"It's what?"

"It's just, she's so dang pretty."

I can't help but grin. "Ain't it so." Jenny brings sweet memories of Susannah's beauty and shape. "It ain't never right to take advantage of a lady, especially if you're interested in her."

"I am, Lummy."

"Then get about showin' it the right and proper way, startin' right now."

Satisfied Jenny is covered, we turn to find her sitting on a log next to the fire, eating her food like it's the last she'll ever get.

Rainy squats to put socks on her feet. "They're a little big, but your feet will stay warm."

Ise fills his plate and walks her way. "Mind if I sit?"

Jenny smiles, taking no time to answer for eating so fast.

Sarge calms her. "It's okay, Jenny, you can slow down. We're in no hurry, and we have plenty of food."

Ise takes the blanket away and helps her put on his heavy coat.

She takes a drink of water. "Thank all you suhs. I didn't know what I was gonna do when them men killed my momma and poppa. I jest runned off into the night." She covers her ears. "I can still hear my folks screamin', bein' burnt alive in their own home." She cries uncontrollably. "Them mean ole men caught me and wanted to do bad things to me."

Ise puts his arm around her. "It's all right, little sister. We'll take care of you."

Rainy balls up his fists. "We've got to get her somewhere safe."

Sarge grins. "That's second on our list of things to do today. I do believe the first thing is coming down the road right now."

I crane my neck to see riders coming. Here again, I'm reminded of why I had to come on this mission.

# CHAPTER 18

# WHEN A LIE MEETS THE TRUTH

## 6:45 A.M., MARCH 8, 1870

*Give it just a little longer, and the lie will be revealed.*

T HE SPLASHY CLIP-clop of shoed horse hooves in the mud rounds the bend of the road.

Jenny tries to bolt.

I pull her back down. "You're safe with us."

Sarge whispers, "Sit still. It'll be all right, little dear. If it's them, better to face it now than keep runnin', don't you think?"

Jenny whispers, "Yassuh. I hopes so." She shakes so hard, she drops her plate of food and balls up like a squirrel on a tree limb trying to get warm in the early morning winter sunshine.

Sarge whispers, "Y'all play dumb."

Rainy laughs. "That won't be difficult for us."

We all laugh in good spirits for show but pull our weapons close.

Three men dressed like farmers wearing worn Rebel hats trot up as the second round of salt pork is just about done in the skillet.

Jenny curls up even tighter, covering her legs down to her ankles with Rainy's shirt. Nursing her coffee, she never looks up. I can't imagine the helplessness she feels with these ruffians on her trail and having to trust men she met just minutes ago. What does it mean to be a poor ex-slave girl depending on white men to protect her? She cowers like a whipped dog. My face is hot.

The short, wiry one laughs. "Damn, I could smell Momma's cookin' half a mile back down the road. Mind if we join you?"

Sarge answers, "There's enough. Hot coffee and a fire can take the chill out of your bones."

The wiry one doesn't notice that I see him cut his eyes at Jenny as he dismounts. The other two stomp their feet to get the blood circulating for having been in the saddle all night. When they tie up their horses, I cock my pistol under my coat.

Laying back on a log by the fire, Rainy doesn't look up from his whittling. He looks disgusted and says nothing. The unsnapped flap on his army holster speaks for itself.

I ask, "Y'all out huntin' this mornin'? It surely was a coon's night."

A big man with a long scar down his neck chuckles. "You could say that."

I realize what I said. *Coon*—a disrespectful word to use for former slaves, or any black person for that matter.

Sarge pokes the fire. "Raccoon fur'll be thick this year and sell for a good price. Any luck?"

The wiry one nods. "Bringin' top dollah. We'll catch us another good'n any time now."

The big one with the scar laughs.

The younger turns his head to hide his face.

Sarge nods to Ise, who knows his part in this charade. "Boy, get those horses saddled and ready to go."

Ise plays along. "Yassuh, right now, Massuh."

I go sit by Jenny. She's trembling.

The scarred man laughs. "Now that's it right there, keepin' them niggahs in their place."

Rainy chuckles. "Takes a niggah to know a niggah, fat boy. It's never been about a person's skin color."

"What did you say?"

"That scar must've damaged your hearing as well as added to your ugliness. You lose your bedsheet, too, you sister boy hawg's ass?"

He starts to stand. "Ain't no uppity niggah lovin' educated smart ass tellin' me nothin'. I'm proud to patrol these parts. Can't have no niggahs runnin' loose here and there."

Rainy pats the air. "Why don't you calm down before you choke on those free biscuits, friend."

The scarred man reaches for a piece of salt pork, growling like a mad dog under his breath, "Call me a fat hawg's ass, will you?"

The wiry one elbows the quiet one and nods at me. "Hey, look at ole string bean over there, cozin' up with a damn ape. Wonder what it's like takin' a roll in the hay with a she gorilla?"

The young quiet man kicks the dirt. "You ought to know, Uncle."

Quick as lightning, the wiry one backhands the young man. "Say somethin' else, bitchy boy. I'll cut your stones off and hang 'em in a tree for a possum."

The young man cowers but grits his teeth. He's bigger than his uncle and could take him in a fight, but the wiry one has power over him because he's young. It's clear the boy doesn't want to be here. That's in our favor for the coming fight. And it's coming.

I figure it's time to bring this gathering to a close. "As far as having sexual relations with a fine young black lady, given the young man has properly courted and married her, it's a helluva lot better than you three treetop monkeys corn holin' each other every night."

The wiry man sets his plate down and starts for the log Jenny and I sit on. "Just for that, I'll try me some of that she ape this mornin'. You got a problem with that?"

"Try it, and see what happens." I pull the knife Pa made me, thumb the blade, and touch the bit of blood to my tongue.

He stops short.

"Hmm, my blood's a bit salty right now. I do believe yours will taste a little sweeter on those cathead biscuits, sister boy."

The scarred man reaches for his pistol.

Rainy draws his quicker than a cottonmouth. "Don't. This old girl has a mind of her own, and she doesn't always obey very well."

The scarred one stands. "I don't like what your inferrin', you carpetbaggin' bastards."

I sit up straight, looking around. "Carpetbag? Rainy, have you got a carpetbag? Sarge?"

They shake their heads, never blinking, but poised ready to strike.

Rainy reaches for a biscuit and gives them a wink and grin.

The wiry one throws his coffee cup down. "You smart-mouthed, coon lovin', son of a bitch!"

I lay back the rabbit ears on my ten gauge shotgun. The clicks are unmistakable. "I'm sure the buzzards and crows will thank me while they're pecking your guts."

Ise laughs. "Ain't the string bean you thought he was, huh?"

The wiry one stiffens up. "I came for that girl, and I mean to have her."

I stand. "You get to feelin' froggy, boy, you leap."

The wiry one reaches for his pistol, and I blow him half in two, firing both barrels of my shotgun.

Rainy shoots the scarred one in the back of the head, blowing teeth out of his mouth in every direction.

The quiet man turns to run, but Ise throws a knife that catches him in the buttocks, bringing him down.

We hold still for a moment, making sure it's over.

Rainy yells to Ise, "Dang, son, good throw. Where'd you learn to hurl a blade like that?"

"Our plantation butcher back in Alabamy," Ise says, wiping the blood on the quiet one's pants after yanking it from his butt.

Rainy laughs. "That's a neat trick. I'll have to show you my throwing knife."

The young man cries. "Don't kill me, please. I didn't want to come with 'em."

Ise pulls the man's head back by the hair to expose his neck. "But you did. I don't think you shaved this mornin'. Think I'll give you a close one now." He lays his knife blade against the boy's throat.

"I'm sorry!"

Ise starts to pull the blade across his throat.

Sarge barks, "Ise, stop. We need what he can tell us and decide if we'll lock him up."

The quiet one coughs and chokes. "I'll tell you anything. Just don't kill me."

# CHAPTER 19

# TRUTH LEADS TO A PATH LESS FOLLOWED

## 7:30 A.M., MARCH 8, 1870

*To the noblest of us all.*

ISE SHEATHS HIS knife and jerks out a handful of hair as he pitches the young man's head forward. "If I was an Injun, I'd scalp your ass right here and now."

Sarge pulls Ise back. "That's enough, Corporal."

Ise pitches the long stringy hair into the fire. "Yes, sir."

Sarge still holds his cocked pistol.

I ask, "Why didn't you fire, Sarge?"

"There were only three of them. I wanted to see how you boys worked together. This will get worse, you know."

Jenny cries, hiding behind the log we were sitting on.

I'd forgotten all about her in the confusion. "You okay?"

Jenny reaches her hand out, and there's blood. We scramble to get to her as she sits up. "It ain't too bad. I just need a little—" She collapses.

Sarge stuffs a handkerchief in the bleeding shoulder wound and picks her up.

Ise spreads a blanket on the ground next to the fire.

Rainy gets his sewing needle and thread. "Somebody get whiskey."

I pitch him my bottle of Wood brothers' moonshine. "That ought'a get it clean."

Rainy sighs after examining the wound. "Good, it's just a flesh wound. Bullet went straight through, no bones touched."

Sarge squats beside Rainy. "Get to sewing while she's still out. It'll be better for everybody."

"Right." Rainy dowses the wound with moonshine and closes the wound in a few minutes.

Ise guards the quiet one. "What's your name, boy?"

Sarge squeezes his shoulder—hard. "Settle down, boy, you're shaking like a field mouse shittin' a cocklebur."

"Timothy, like in the Bible."

Ise barks, "You should've stayed home and read more about Timothy in that Bible instead of bein' out here hurtin' folks."

Sarge asks, "How old are you?"

"I turned fifteen a month ago."

"Pretty young to be night ridin', don't you think?"

"I done told you, suh, I ain't no Nightrider. I hate 'em." He points at the body of the dead wiry one. "My uncle made me come along. Said it was the final act to make me a full-fledged Nightrider and a man."

I ask, "What do you mean, the final act?"

"We beat up niggahs, stole their stuff when they was away workin', and the last thing was what we did a couple nights ago. They blinded-folded us boys who'd turned fifteen in a shack deep in the woods where they had a bunch of young black girls tied up naked. Those girls were so scared. I felt bad for them. They told us to strip down to nothin' but our shoes. I yelled at my uncle to let them go, but he slapped me so hard I fell on the ground. He told me if I didn't do what he said, he'd kill me right there in front of everybody and let the buzzards have me."

Sarge leans up. "What happened next?"

"They walked them naked girls past us like livestock at an auction. The boys fidgeted like they had ants in their britches. I felt nothin'." Timothy cries for a minute. "They turned the girls loose, and they ran like scared rabbits in every direction. My uncle counted to ten and shot his pistol into the air. He said, 'Go get 'em, boys!' I asked my uncle, 'What are we supposed to do?'"

Ise asks, "What'd he say?"

"Nothin'. A crotchedy old man, who looked to be a hundred years old, stepped out from the shadows and said, 'Do what we've been doin' here since we pioneered this land. It's time to go and get you some, boys. Pick out one of these fine black bitches and chase her down. You'll figure out the rest, heh, heh.' The other boys ran like wild animals after the girls, fightin' and pushin' each other out of the way, sayin', 'This one's mine! Stay away from that one!' Stuff like that. Them girls screamed as they was bein' raped. I'm so ashamed."

I ask, "They made you do it?"

Rainy growls and butts in. "It's a ritual. It's some folk's idea of what it takes to become a man in the South."

Timothy whimpers, "I didn't want to do it."

Rainy spits. "My father made me do the same thing back home. It's the worst thing I've ever done in my life. I've been trying to make up for it ever since." The shame on his face bespeaks a man doing penance—lifelong penance. He glares at me with the fiery eyes of a catamount. "Why in the hell do you think I'm here?"

What a mix of misfit miscreants we are.

Jenny comes to and reaches for her aching shoulder. I stop her and wash her tear-stained cheeks with a damp rag.

She smiles weakly. "I'm all right, thank you."

"So, why were you chasing this girl when you came to our camp?" Sarge asks.

The boy hangs his head. "When I didn't run off with the rest of the boys after one of the girls, my uncle kicked me so hard up my ass I could barely walk, much less run. But I did."

"What happened when they found you with the girl?"

Timothy points at Jenny. "I was just sittin' there." He shudders. "But I didn't rape her, I promise. I didn't even touch her. I couldn't. It was just wrong."

I turn to Jenny. "Is that true?"

"He's tellin' the truth. He never touched me."

The boy sighs in relief.

Sarge barks, "That still doesn't answer my question."

Timothy cries. "My uncle was gonna make me give her a poke, come hell or high water. I didn't want to, but I'd taken too many of his beatin's already. I was gonna do it just to get it over with but couldn't. I helped her escape."

I ask, "Jenny, is that true?"

She sips her coffee. "He did. When they got liquored up, he untied me, and I runned off like a chicken escapin' Sunday dinner."

"That's the truth. Y'all gonna kill me, too?"

Ise breaks in. "Not just yet, boy."

"Please don't kill me. I'll do anythin' you ask. I'll tell you where the gang went. It's across the big river from Vicksburg. I've been there once visitin' my Kimbrell cousins. I'll take you there if you want."

Sarge stares into his eyes. "No need. You tell me where, or I'll turn Ise loose on you with his carving knife."

Timothy shakes like a leaf in a storm. "Said they was goin' to someplace called Atlanta."

Ise perks up. "Atlanta, Gawgia?"

Timothy rubs his hands together. "No, suh, Atlanta in Louisiana near—"

I sigh. "Winnfield, in Winn Parish."

Sarge shoves the last bite of a biscuit in his mouth and starts saddling his horse. "Good, that confirms the telegraph I received. Let's get going."

Ise asks, "What about this boy?"

Sarge pulls his pistol. "I'm gonna say this once, Timothy, before God and these witnesses. Promise me that you'll go home and never speak of what happened here, about who we are, or where we're going." Timothy nods, but Sarge wants more. "Promise, damn you."

Timothy stands up like he's being a man for the first time. "I will never speak of this again. But what do I tell the folks back home?"

"That their friends who went to Louisiana killed them for their horses, money, and weapons. And you escaped."

Timothy hangs his head. "Okay."

Sarge pats his shoulder. "It ought to make the folks back home think twice about supporting Nightriders, you think?"

"Yes, suh, I do."

"Take nothing but the clothes on your back and be gone."

Timothy just stands there like a deer with a lantern shining in its eyes at night.

Sarge barks, "Go, before I change my mind."

Rainy sits up. "Hold on, Sarge. I don't want this kid leaving without learning something."

Sarge pours himself more coffee. "All right, make it quick."

Rainy points at the dead men. "As long as you need their approval, you'll always be their slave."

Timothy stands still. "I didn't think I had a choice."

Ise whispers, "Solomon said, 'He that walketh with wise men shall be wise, but a companion of fools shall be destroyed.'"

Rainy squints. "You always had a choice. Your mind said you didn't, but your soul said you did."

"How's that?"

"'The content of your character is your choice. Day by day, what you choose, what you think, and what you do is who you become,' Heraclitus wrote."

Timothy scratches his neck. "I ain't never heard anything like that."

Rainy stands. "Son, why didn't you rape this poor girl?"

Timothy kicks the dirt. "It was the noble thing not to do. You know, like in the storybooks."

Rainy's face burns red. "Now tell me, just what is noble?"

The boy ducks his head in shame. "Not real sure, but I think it means doin' good things?"

Rainy scowls. "Anybody can do a good thing, but not everyone can do the *right* thing—the thing that is beyond us."

The boy straightens up to recieve his instruction. "Tell me, suh. I want to know."

Rainy snickers. "A wise man once said, 'I cannot teach anybody anything. I can only make them think.' Socrates, I believe it was."

"Please, suh. Nobody's teached me like this."

Rainy rubs his chin. "Noble is rising above yourself to reach down and help the lowliest."

I throw a stick into the fire. "It's doin' the right thing even when it hurts."

Rainy snickers. "Even when it humiliates you in front of others."

I drop my head. "Even if it kills you, or worse, takes the life of a friend."

Rainy pours each man a sip of whiskey and holds his flask up. "To Poole, Old Bart, Mister Gilmore, and Susannah, God rest their eternal souls."

I lift my tin cup. "To the noblest of us all."

The fire crackles, and no one says a word. Sometimes the best of memories are savored in silence rather than weakened in the retelling.

Rainy pitches Timothy a small sack of food and the boy's hunting knife. "Go, but hear this first. Life is not a matter of holding good cards but of playing a poor hand well."

I reach for the coffee pot. "Mister Gilmore used to say that. Son, you better get goin'."

Timothy tips his hat. "I'll remember that." He disappears into the brush.

I have to ask Rainy. "Did you do the ritual and rape a black girl?"

Rainy spits. "Oh, hell no. I just told him that to leave him with some wisdom. I didn't meet my blood father until not long before I met you near the tracks that night back in '59."

"So, how'd you know the ritual actually happens?"

"A boy in the orphanage where I grew up in Natchez told me his father made him do it."

"Why was he in the orphanage?"

"His father was killed in the Mexican War, and his mother drank poison. She couldn't live without him, I reckon. You just never know what lies in another person's past."

I rub my hands together. "Sometimes Creator lets bad things happen to get us where we need to be. It's on us to go do the right thing."

Rainy drains his flask. "Ain't that the damn truth."

"Tell us about you livin' in the children's home in Natchez."

Rainy turns his head away. "That story isn't easy to tell."

I leave it alone and check Jenny's wound. "Let's get you home."

"Oh, please, suh, don't send me back there. Them men you killed? They gots lots of family back there. You take me there, they'll just kill me."

Sarge shrugs. "Do what you think best, Lummy. We're going through Vicksburg anyway."

"All right, Jenny, I know just where we can take you."

# CHAPTER 20

# OLD BATTLES, NEW BATTLES

## 1:30 P.M., MARCH 8, 1870

*Familiar places, sounds, and smells bring bittersweet memories.*

SARGE WHIPS HIS head around at a noise in a thicket. I turn, but no one's there. "Sarge, you sense it, too?"

"The back of my neck itches."

Jenny tightens her grip around my waist. "It's them haints. They's followin' us, I just know it. They'll come tonight and snatch us all away."

Rainy chuckles. "Only if they can get past the hail of fire from our arsenal."

Still, I check the vines and cane breaks for any bedsheets with eyeholes cut in them.

We water our horses at Four Mile Bridge, a place I never can seem to escape. Throwing Negroes out of their homes to take their shacks for the winter back in '62 didn't sit well with me. Many cold rainy winter nights standing guard at this railroad bridge gave me time to sort out my thoughts. The seeds of switching sides from Reb to Yank were planted in this place. The growth since that acorn was dropped in the ground has produced a strong and mighty oak of wisdom and courage in my soul. But I still have a long way to go and hate that I have to learn most of my lessons the hard way. I've had good people, seen and unseen, to guide me. Now, if I can just find that strength once more for the sake of a scared little woman like Jenny and others, maybe Creator will decide that I've done enough.

"Sarge, I need to do something. Let's cut over to Graveyard Road and go in town from there."

"The Twenty-Seventh Louisiana Lunette?"

I let Jenny down, and Rainy pulls up one of the Nightrider's horses who didn't happen to need it anymore.

Ise is all too happy to help her up on the horse. He's so gentle with her.

"I won't be long. Just want to give them boys who didn't make it out of the lunette a nod of respect as we ride by." I take off in a trot. I trust Sarge will explain things to Ise. I need a few moments alone.

The earthworks have eroded, but I can still make out my spot in the rifle pit. I breathe in as I scan the hills I watched for forty-seven days during the siege. Lots to remember at Vicksburg. Too much. But the battle I race toward now starts here for me. I need to summon what I hate the most—the worst part of me that can rival a demon in all ways known to human beings.

I ride up on what was once the parapet. The stones J.A. and I laid in honor of the men who died here are covered with dirt. Much like their memory. Here we raised an Ebenezer for the men of the 27th Louisiana Volunteer Infantry. I'm not breathing. I let out the air in my lungs and close my eyes. Everything goes silent until familiar sounds emerge—muskets firing, cannon shells exploding, men screaming, and my own heavy breathing. My head aches. My heart pounds. It's like the entire forty-seven day siege flashes by in one moment—men shooting and men dying, bugles blaring and buzzards flying, muskets silent and a march to the city in surrender. I grab my chest where the bullet struck the brass uniform button. A Yank gets blown to bits by a grenade he caught, thinking he could throw it back over at us in time. His body from the waist down stands for at least a half minute, quivering.

I blink twice to stare into the eyes of a Yank pressed against me. I'm there. It's real. I can't escape the moment—sweat burning my eyes, his foul breath choking me, and the fear of what I'm about to do. Kill. Brave Confederates scream the Rebel yell and shove the wad of blue demons over the edge into the pit in front of the lunette. With bloody hands, I claw at my friends who grab at me as I slide into the pit. The Yank's breath smells of bad coffee and burnt beans. A minie ball splits his head just above the eyebrows, splattering brains all over my face.

"Lummy, wake up. Lummy!" Water splashes my face. Rainy bends over me.

I reach to get up with my right hand but sit right back down. Pain shoots through my shoulder like someone struck me with an ax handle. I shake my head. "What the hell happened?"

Rainy hands me his handkerchief. "You sat on your horse for at least five minutes, then flailed your arms around and fell off."

I should've used the owl talon Dan Creekwater gave me.

Sarge helps me up. "You hit hard on that right shoulder. War memories?"

"Yeah, that and a tree slamming down on my shoulder when I took a ferry across the Missip from Vicksburg to Desoto back in '59."

Rainy dusts me off and hands me my horse's reins. "Some memories just won't fade away."

I wipe my face. "Some aren't meant to, I reckon." I walk to the line where I killed more than my share of Yankee soldiers.

I can still see the blue wave across the field. They're all saluting. I look from left to right. The men in gray, who didn't make it out of these trenches, lean on their muskets, waiting for the next attack, laughing and talking. Granville and Hog Fart smile as they share a rat blackened by the cook fire. Hard as those days were, there were some good times. Only because we were alive and believed we might make it out of this hellhole. Those two boys didn't.

I swing up into the saddle, and Ise asks, "You fought here, Lummy?"

"I did."

"Why? I thought—"

"That I only fought for the Union? In my heart I did. I had to walk through a briar thicket to get to the ripened field of corn, you might say."

Rainy chimes in. "It's like hunting. You walk through the wrong woods to get to the right forest to find game."

I pull up my reins. "Yeah, somethin' like that."

Sarge eases his mount up beside me and salutes. "To brave men, gray and blue. May they never be forgotten."

I join in his salute. "Amen, Sarge."

We jog our horses down Graveyard Road into the city.

# CHAPTER 21

# VICKSBURG, AGAIN

## 3:30 P.M., MARCH 8, 1870

*The best memories are better savored in silence than weakened in retelling.*

AS I TOP the hill, memories surge through my mind like the Mississippi River flooding in springtime. "Let's stop here a minute if you boys don't mind."

Ise shields his eyes. "Dang, I can almost see forever from here. What's this place called?"

Sarge leans up. "Sky Parlor Hill. On a clear day, you can see fifty miles over into Louisiana, right, Lummy?"

"Yeah, but this time I could see a thousand miles back into my old life."

Rainy whispers, "Ain't it so? You've come a long way from being chased into my camp by a pack of coyotes that night."

I wink and grin. "A helluva long ways, Rainy Mills. Didn't you spend a bit of time here?"

"I did, working with a gunsmith. I'd not been gone long when I met you."

Sarge turns his horse toward the army stable. "Let's get our mounts taken care of and stay in the Prentiss House Hotel tonight."

"Best make it quick, Sarge. Annie will have my hide if she thinks I went anywhere else besides goin' to see her first."

Sarge takes Jenny's reins to lead her horse. I'm not surprised. He's taken to her like a father to a daughter, much like how my Mr. Gilmore treated Susannah, God rest his soul and hers.

Sarge straightens in his saddle. "You think Annie can make a place for Jenny?"

I stare into Jenny's eyes. "I'm sure of it."

Every corner, every street, every alley in this town holds some memory for me—some good, others not so good. I can almost smell Mrs. O'Neil's tough-as-shoe-leather rooster dumplings we were treated to while serving as city provost back in '62. That old bird was like chewing on a rubber rain slicker. But those dumplings were as tasty as Ma's back home.

I unsaddle my horse near the same stall where I found Cloud, my old mount that served me well when I was in the Rifles. Her name is still written on the wall where the clerk wrote all the horse names men could choose from during the war. I miss that old girl. I'd never buried an animal like a human before her except when I laid our dog Max to rest and said a few words over him like a preacher. It was all I could do to get the words out about Max. I'd killed him in anger. I've never wanted another dog. Cloud just went to sleep one night. There'll never be another Cloud or Max. I've not gotten attached to another animal. They die. I get more than my fair share of death being with humans.

We pass St. Paul's Catholic Church, where I spent many days thinking, praying, considering the lives of the saints, and talking with the priest. The sweetest moment in that church house was when Martha and I said our vows—vows I'm ready to get back home to. I wonder if my old friend the priest is still around. I'll see him before we leave. We need the prayers of a righteous man before we cross the Missip for Winn Parish.

We pass the recruiter's office, where I enlisted in the 1st Mississippi Mounted Rifles with Poole. I remember how strange it felt putting on the blue suit. It was the right thing to do.

Sarge backhands my chest. "The Rifles, that was a piece of work, wasn't it?"

I have to grin through the painful memory of having helped burn the factories at Bankston for General Grierson. "No doubt." My grin finds a frown, wondering what I'll add to the list of things I won't want to remember after this trip.

# CHAPTER 22

# ANNIE FANNY
# NEVER CHANGES

### 4:45 P.M., MARCH 8, 1870

*If some people were to change, life would not be the same.*

W E WALK OLD streets that I hope bring new memories—good ones for a change.

Sarge veers off through an alley. "You men go on over to Handerson's and see Annie. I'll get our rooms at the Prentiss House. Be there in just a bit."

I reach for the door handle of Handerson's Café, but the bells above it ring as Annie Fanny bursts out, arms open.

"Butter my butt and call me a biscuit. It's Lummy Tullos! What in the hell are you doin' here, brother-in-law?"

"Just thought I'd stop by and see my favorite sister-in-law."

Annie pops me on the butt. "I'm your *only* sister-in-law, you good lookin', smartass man."

I chuckle. "That makes it pretty easy." Some things don't change. Life just wouldn't be the same if they did.

"You love me, Lummy Tullos. We both know it's true. Get on in here and let me get you boys some coffee."

Ise asks, "What about me, ma'am?"

Annie laughs. "What about you, son? You're with Lummy, ain't you?"

Ise squirms. "Yes, 'um."

Annie flashes her eyes at Rainy. "And um-*umph.* That man there who looks so good in black. Fine as Cleopatra's wine."

I laugh and turn to Rainy. "I do believe it's the first time I've ever seen you red-faced, unless it was in a fight. You doin' all right over there, Rainy?"

"Shut up, Lummy. I ain't used to a woman singling me out like that."

I laugh. "Neither was I when I first got to know Annie Fanny. It ain't often I get to poke fun at a man who is so eloquent in his ways and words. You do like women, don't you, Rainy?"

"About as much as I'd like to hit you in the mouth right now. How about I stick your head in that rain barrel over there until you stop bubbling?"

I throw up my hands in surrender.

Rainy growls. "Never had much time for women. I figure the Good Lord will bring one along at the right time if I'm worthy." He's carrying a pain. I change the subject.

I lift Ise's dropped jaw back in place. "Ole Annie here used to be called Annie Fanny for the best part of her. She has a way of bringing out the most embarrassing parts of men. I'm just glad I'm not her only target these days."

Annie turns around and jiggles her bottom from side to side like a painted lady. "Ain't nothin' you ain't never seen before, Lummy, honey. You did see me bathin' in the river after the surrender."

Now I'm blushing. I try to end this line of conversation. A compliment always does the trick. "Hold on now, dear sister-in-law, I only saw your wonderfully shaped bottom by accident. Nothing else happened."

"He's tellin' the truth. Now that you boys know what to expect from me, come on in." She whispers, "Is Sarge with you?"

I nod.

Annie shakes her head with a frown. "If he's with you, nobody needs to hear what you men need to discuss. Take the back room." Back in her flamboyant voice, she announces, "I'll bring coffee and pie for everyone."

Ise brightens up. "Pie? I ain't had nary a bit in a long time."

Sarge walks up. "Best damn pie you'll ever put your mouth to, Ise. I got our rooms. Let's go inside and relax."

"You're too kind, sir." Annie kisses Sarge on the cheek and steps into Handerson's Café as Ise holds the door open. "I'll bring several kinds of pie so y'all can sample 'em all. How's that?"

Ise rubs his hands together. "Yes, ma'am."

She winks. "We'll talk about supper later."

Rainy turns to walk up the street. "Y'all go 'head. I need to see a man about some guns. Hold me a big slice of pie. Chocolate if she has it. Be back in a bit."

Ise offers his arm to Jenny, careful to be a gentleman.

Annie's wheels are turning. "Now who is this young beauty you have your heart set on, son?"

Ise's jaw drops again. He's caught, and he knows it. "I, uh—"

Annie takes Jenny by the hand. "No need to deny what everybody else already sees."

Ise hangs his head, embarrassed. We laugh, and he looks up grinning like a mule eating briars. I swear I can see Susannah in his eyes.

Sarge pats Ise on the shoulder. "We rescued young Jenny here from wicked men intending evil harm. We were wondering if you might—"

Annie butts in. "Have a place for her? Sure do. One of my servers just came down sick, and I need a pair of hands just like hers." She puts her arm around Jenny. "Come on in, young lady. We'll get you a bath and some decent clothes. You're gonna do just fine here with us."

Jenny turns to thank us, but I hold up my hand. "No need. You just make yourself at home. Annie will take care of your every need and pay you for your hard work."

Jenny drops to her knees and wraps her arms around Annie's waist. "Missus Annie. I can't thanks you 'nough."

Annie cackles. "Get up, girl. The days of black people kneelin' before white folks is over. Stand tall. Hold your head high. Poke them breasts out and wiggle that hiney. Be proud of who you are. You're special in God's eyes and ours. Let's get you cleaned up. Pretty as you are? You're gonna make my place look real good. Just watch those wanderin' hands that come in the café lookin' for somethin' we ain't sellin'."

Ise stiffens up. "Missus Annie, you won't let nobody—"

"Oh, hell no, Ise. My man Beau won't put up with any shit like that."

Jenny's eyes bulge a bit.

"Sorry, honey. I reckon if I'm askin' you to be a lady, I best act like one myself."

I wink at Annie. "You're a lady, all right, Annie. Always have been and always will be in my book. You just want to act like you're not."

Annie batts her eyes like a two dollar whorehouse hussy.

Ise can't take his eyes off Jenny, who gives him the sweetest grin.

I wave my hand in front of Ise's face and ask, "Where's Beau, Annie?"

"In Jackson on business. Not sure he'll be back before you head out."

Rainy eases in the door and takes a seat. "When do we leave?"

My eyes catch Sarge's. "Tomorrow, early."

He nods.

# CHAPTER 23

# OLD HAUNTS, BUT A NEW SPIRIT

## 8:30 P.M., MARCH 8, 1870

*Old haunts can set free a new spirit.*

**A**FTER WE'VE HAD our fill of Annie's fine food, Ise asks, "I got an old Army friend who lives just outside of town. I'll go there for the night, Sarge, if you don't mind?"

Sarge laments, "I'm sorry folks down here still frown on Negroes eating and staying where white people conduct that sort of business. Thanks for being accommodating, son. It'll keep further suspicion down."

The thought angers me, but this ain't the fight we came here for. "One day, Ise, one day it will change. I'm sorry my people ain't got their heads on straight yet. You think they would, bein' the good Bible totin', church goin' Christians they claim to be." I stop. I'm getting riled.

"I appreciate that, Lummy. We just got bigger battles to fight than this one right now."

"You're right, son. Forgive my preachin' to the choir."

"Oh no, preacher, I'd be happy to throw somethin' in the collection basket when it comes around after you rail and wail on for a while." Ise stumbles, laughing and patting his leg.

Rainy backhands my chest. "He hit the nail on the head, preacher man."

Sarge breaks up what might be the last good laugh we have once we cross the river. "Will they feed you in the morning?"

Ise nods.

"Corporal, report to the stable at six thirty sharp in the morning. I want to catch the first ferry across the river before we're noticed. That is the first one, isn't it?"

Rainy clears his throat. "Yep, Cline's Steam Ferry Boat is always on time. A least it was when I came through this way a week ago. First crossing is at seven o'clock."

Ise salutes and eases out the back door to avoid any needless suspicion from café patrons.

I reminisce for moment. "I followed those railroad tracks that start in Desoto on my way to Winn Parish. My first train ride was leaving to enlist comin' this way on those same tracks. We marched from Winnfield and caught the train at a woodcutter's station. Then, J.A. and I went the same way after Vicksburg surrendered and me again when I came back this way to go home to Choctaw County. That'll be the way to go, but weren't the railroad tracks destroyed in the war?"

Rainy smiles. "You made a beaten path easy to follow, Lummy. Not to worry. They got the tracks fixed, and trains run often now."

Sarge scratches the back of his neck. "Good, we'll get there quicker than I'd planned. Let's all get to bed early. We've a train to catch in the morning."

WE SHUFFLE TO our rooms in the Prentiss House Hotel with full bellies. This old place has seen its better days. It looks to be as old and tired as we are after the hurried ride from Choctaw County. Still, it has special meaning for me for several reasons.

Staying here in the winter of '62, I enjoyed the company of men I would later fight alongside when the Yanks came. Patrolling the streets as provost made the good citizens feel safe with Union gunboats floating in plain sight upriver and down. Fifteen men packed into each room didn't leave much room for comfort, but it did for laughs and good conversation. I find my old room and see where Edrow carved his name on the window sill. He got his nickname, Hog Fart, in this very room. That poor boy died second day of the march out of Vicksburg after the surrender.

I need to turn my thoughts somewhere else.

The best of all memories was on the hotel steps when Martha peeked out from underneath her bonnet. Her smile still makes my heart shimmer with joy. That's the one I'll hold on to now. I miss her already. This may be the only letter I'll write while I'm gone. It might be too risky sending one from Winn Parish.

Vicksburg, March 8, 1870
Dearest Martha,

*I didn't think I'd have to write letters from faraway places ever again, but here I am. We've already had an encounter with the "friends" we're soon to visit. You know where we're headed, and please continue to pray for our safe return.*

*I walked down by the river where I boarded the steamer for Memphis when I joined the Rifles back in '64. I can still see you in that pretty blue dress on the riverbank, waving. I looked up the steps of the Prentiss House Hotel when I met you the first time. My knees still get shaky at your beauty. I love you, Martha, and I will come home. This will be my last mission. It doesn't matter what Sarge, President Grant, or even the Lord Himself says, there will be no more leaving. I take back the part about the Lord. He can do with me as He wills. But I trust that He won't ask me to leave you and the children ever again.*

*Annie sends her love and hopes to visit, maybe this summer. I will write again when I arrive at our destination.*

*My love for you is eternal, Martha.*

Your loving husband,
Lummy

I seal the envelope as tears roll into my beard. In the morning, I'll drop it in the hotel post to H.P. Dotson with no return address.

# CHAPTER 24

# GOIN' WHERE NEEDS GOIN', DOIN' WHAT NEEDS DOIN'

### 5:00 A.M., MARCH 9, 1870

*It's the unexpected events that are too good to miss.*

B
REAKFAST COMES BEFORE the sun rises at Handerson's Café. Biscuits and gravy, smoked ham and fried eggs, and preserves of every berry and fruit I can think of keep our mouths closed with somber enjoyment. I study my friends quietly eating. Had our battle in Choctaw County against Captain Tom Ford been different, Poole and Old Bart would be with us now.

"What about J.A.?" Rainy asks.

"Talkin' out loud again?"

"Yep."

I tap my fork on my plate. "I wish I could stop that. Just too many days alone with Creator, I reckon." I bite into a biscuit and wash it down with good coffee. "To answer your question, though, he was by my side when we took down Dawg Smith. I'll be by his this time."

Sarge sips his coffee. "You will be. His farm is near Atlanta."

I finish chewing a bit of ham. "It is. I just hope he's all right, and his sweet family." I shudder at the thought of that man being hurt. "It's been too long since I've seen him."

Rainy comforts, "I'm sure he's fine. He'll be glad to see you."

Sarge spoons blackberry jam onto a biscuit. "He was when I was there last."

Annie eases the door open. "You boys need anythin' else?"

We shake our heads.

I take a sip of coffee. "The food couldn't be better. I don't know what we'd do without you, Annie." I gently pull her down by her dress collar and give her a peck on the lips. "I do love you, Annie, for all the right reasons."

Annie tears up. "I love you, too, Columbus Nathan Tullos, for all the best reasons." She points to Rainy and Sarge. "You men, too, and for all the right reasons. Except for my man Beau, y'all are the best God ever made from the clay, includin' that black kid with you." She dries her eyes. "Where is that young man?"

I start to say, "He stayed the night with some—"

She winks. "He ain't there now."

Sarge starts to get up. "What? Where is he? Is he all right?

Annie giggles. "Calm down. He's closer than you think. Lummy, go peek into the kitchen."

I crack the double swinging door to see Ise plant his first kiss on Jenny and say the sweetest words a man can say to a woman.

Ise is so respectful when he pulls back from the kiss. "Jenny, I don't know if I can put into words what I feel right now."

Jenny caresses his cheek. "Just say what's in your heart, sweet man."

"I loved you the minute I saw you."

Jenny smiles. "I know, Isaiah."

"How?"

"You treated me like a gentleman. And how you looked at me, not like some hungry dawg that ain't been fed in a while. Your eyes said you wanted me that day, but your heart and actions said you wanted to treat me like a lady."

"I want to marry you when I get back from this mission. I plan to retire from the Army and get a job right here in Vicksburg. My friend from the war has a place in his house buildin' business for me. He said I could start as soon as I get back."

Jenny giggles with joy. "So, what you waitin' for, boy?"

Ise furrows his eyebrows. "What do you mean?"

"Ain't you gonna ask a lady for her hand?"

Ise drops to one knee. "Miss Jenny, will you marry me? I ain't got no ring right now, but I promise I'll get you one."

Jenny pulls Ise up, wraps her arms around his neck, and pulls her feet up. "Yes, I will marry you, Isaiah."

I hate to be listening in, but this is too good to miss. I back up into Annie, Sarge, and Rainy. I grin at my friends. "What the hell?" I push open the door.

We shout, "Congratulations, you two!"

# CHAPTER 25

# A NEW CROSSING BRINGS UP OLD MEMORIES

## 7:00 A.M., MARCH 9, 1870

*Nothing like a sweetcake to make you forget your troubles—for a moment.*

A SOOTHING GLOW brightens the dark sky over the river, but I find no comfort in it. Shimmering ripples on the smooth water remind me that Creator forges ahead of me wherever I go.

We hold our horses steady as we cross the channel to Desoto, another place I can't seem to escape. Cline's Steam Ferry Boat is a far cry better than what I came across in back in '59. The boat is bigger and the ride smoother than when I chased after Susannah. If I hadn't been knocked silly by the tree that smashed my shoulder, I never would've met Annie Fanny, or Martha for that matter. I reckon things happen the way they should. All I can do is keep walking forward. My shoulder still aches from falling off my horse. That pain leads me to dream of Martha. No blue skirt to see me off this day. I'll look for that when I return home.

We dock at the ramp, and Sarge pays the ferryman. Desoto, Louisiana, gateway to my happiness and sorrow with Susannah, the good life I had and the loss of Ben and Mr. Gilmore, the battle against Dawg Smith, and losing Old Bart and Poole in Choctaw County. It's hard to know what to expect. Not much good, I suspect, if I've got this mission figured right.

I lead my horse off the ferry.

The priest from St. Paul's Catholic waits for us. "I couldn't let you men go off to battle without a word and a prayer."

We remove our hats and bow our heads.

The priest holds his arms up in the air. "The Lord said, 'Behold, I send you forth as sheep in the midst of wolves. Be ye therefore wise as serpents and harmless as doves.' God bless you men, and may His angels go before you."

I glimpse a face stealing a look from behind a wagon. "Did y'all just see—?" In a flash, the familiar face is gone. "Never mind."

Sarge mounts his horse. "See somebody you know, Lummy?"

"No, guess not."

Sarge leans over. "Keep a watchful eye open. The West-Kimbrell Gang could have spies even this far out from Winn Parish."

"I wish I'd gotten more than a glance." I watch as we walk our horses to the train tracks.

Rainy surveys the small town of Desoto. "Hmm, this might be a good place to set up a gunsmith's shop. People head west every day. If my prices are a bit lower than Vicksburg's, I could do all right selling and repairing guns. Maybe I'll come back and pick out a couple of good lots, one for a house and the other for my shop. There's more than enough business to go around. I'd be the only smithy this side of the river. What do y'all think?"

Sarge clears his throat. "If you're asking, that's your problem right there." He points at the river. "Not to rain on your parade, Rainy, but you do know Grant tried several times to dig a canal across this point?"

I scratch my head. "I'm with Sarge, Rainy. I'm not sure how long a place like this will last. You heard about the big earthquake that made this river run backwards? My uncle Silas told me about it when I was a kid. It happened about the time the Tullos's came to the Mississippi Territory in 1811. It did a lot of damage when the river changed course in lots of places. Some you couldn't recognize when it was over."

Rainy checks his saddle. "I heard it killed a bunch of folks."

Sarge cuts in. "I'll say it did. My uncle was a deckhand on a boat headed to New Orleans when the river ran backward. He said it was the damnedest thing he'd ever seen. A wave bigger than any he saw at sea rose up thirty feet higher than the riverbank. It swept them upriver a long ways. The damage was the worst parts of Revelation. Whole towns disappeared. Entire sections of land just slid under the waters."

Rainy throws his arm up in the air. "Okay, I get it. Worst place in the world to start a gunsmith business."

Sarge stretches to see upriver. "Hell, Rainy, the river's going to cut through here one day anyway. Watch what I say. Ol' Man River has a mind of his own."

Rainy pats his horse's neck. "You're right."

Sarge pays the train conductor. "Let's go, boys. Horses go in the last car."

After walking my mount up the ramp and into the car, I snicker. "Sarge, the only time I ever rode a train was in a stock car with a bunch of nasty smellin', foul mouthed, puking Rebs."

"You get the fancy treatment this trip. We're riding in the passenger car. They even serve coffee with a sweetcake as part of the deal."

"Now that's more like it. There's nothing like a sweetcake to make you forget your troubles—for a moment."

# CHAPTER 26

# BLACK COFFEE, WHITE CREAM, AND SWEET SUGAR

## 9:40 A.M., MARCH 9, 1870

*Black coffee says it best about the world when you add cream and sugar.*

ISE ASKS, "WHAT about me? What am I going to do? Negroes don't ride with white folks on trains."

Sarge pats him on the shoulder. "They have a car for black travelers. It's behind ours in front of the livestock car. I'm sorry. I don't like it either. This country still has a long way to go."

My face is hot. "One day, Ise, you watch. One of these days."

Ise winks. "Don't worry, Mistuh Lummy, we gots bigger coons to catch, you know what I mean?" His smiling eyes betray his joke. He has come to know me too well, and I laugh.

I appreciate Ise's humor in the face of injustice. He must've learned it from years of back-breaking work serving inhuman slave masters and overseers. I put those thoughts back where they came from, along with the rest I'll need later to do what needs doing. Anger can be useful controlled. I've had my fair share of learning how.

The whistle blows, and the conductor yells, "All aboard!"

We *clickety-clack* down the track at a pretty good speed. After an hour, I step to the back of our passenger car and peek through the window to make sure Ise is all right. He waves. Besides Ise, a few soldiers, several men with their wives, and a mother with two small children sit in a car not quite as fine as ours.

I find my seat, and Rainy points out the window. "That's where you ran into my camp the night those coyotes thought they had their supper lined up."

"Why do you suppose they came after me?"

Two servers enter the door to the front with trays of sweetcakes and coffee.

Rainy sniffs the air. "That coffee smells good. More than likely, disease or something killed off the rabbits and deer in this area. Who knows, but they wanted to chew on your stinking hide. One taste of you and they would've puked."

Sarge laughs. "You two ain't nothin' but a couple of wild-ass school kids who ain't got the sense God gave a mule." He's got Missip talk down just right.

A prim and proper older lady, holding her Bible for all to see across the aisle, gasps at Sarge's words. "Well, I never."

Sarge starts to apologize, but I say, "Sorry, ma'am, but his wife don't let him out much."

Sarge elbows me in the side. "Shut up." He turns to the lady. "Sorry, ma'am. I spent too much time in the Army with the likes of these shady characters. Pray to the Good Lord that I continue to improve my language."

"I will, son. That war has done damage to us all. Damn those Yankees anyway." She covers her mouth to hide a smile.

Sarge elbows me hard enough to stop me from bursting out laughing. He tips his hat to the old lady. "Yes, ma'am, damn Yankees, that's what done it."

She's not done yet, though. "And them niggahs, thinkin' they should have the same rights as a human bein's. It just ain't Christian, I tell you."

Rainy tips the black waiter who serves his coffee and sweetcake. "Lummy, was it not you who said, 'It's takes a niggah to know a niggah?'"

"Yeah I did. I've known way more white niggahs than anything else."

The server smiles, and I try not to laugh.

The old lady gasps again. "Son, what did you say?"

Rainy sips his coffee. "It's not worth repeating, ma'am. You enjoy your refreshments now."

"If my son were here, he'd take care of you." She points her boney finger at him. "He was a Captain in the Third Looseana."

Rainy's ears pin back like a mad dog ready to strike. His face softens, and he ends the conversation. "Ma'am, I'm quite sure you're not ready to attend his funeral anytime soon. But if you are, this good man here has done several eulogies in his time. If your son is anything like you, I'm confident my friend could find plenty of good words to say over his grave. Now, let it end with that." She starts to speak. "I said, good woman, this conversation is over."

I'm surprised, and not. Rainy is usually cool as a cucumber, but this old lady struck a chord with him. He looks at me and Sarge. "What?"

Sarge whispers, "Well done."

We enjoy our coffee and sweetcakes in silence. The waiter returns a few minutes later to offer seconds.

I ask, "Aren't you gonna serve the car behind us?"

"Oh, no, suh, we don't serve anythin' to black folks on dis here train."

I hand Rainy my coffee cup. "I do." I rub the agate stone in my pocket and take the tray, adding the remaining sweetcakes to it.

"Suh, please don't do that. I'll gets in all kinds of trouble."

I start for the back of the train. "Tell 'em I put a gun to your head if you have to, but this is happenin'."

Sarge hands the waiter two dollars. "That should cover it. I'll speak to your boss about it."

"Yassuh. I thanks you, suh."

I lean down to the old lady. "Wouldn't you like to wash the feet of the Lord's disciples this mornin' by helpin' me serve the least of these?"

She folds her arms in a huff. "Not in this lifetime, you horrible man."

Rainy snickers. "Nor in the next life either, ma'am."

She huffs and moves to a seat in the front of the car.

I can't help myself. "Ma'am?"

She stops.

"Have you read where the Good Lord says the first shall be last and the last shall be first?"

"How *dare* you." She turns her nose up and marches to the front.

Rainy grumbles, "I'd turn my nose up, too, if my brand of Christianity stunk like horseshit."

Sarge is laughing so hard he's bouncing up and down on his seat, though making no sound. He wipes tears from his eyes. "That's the most respectful disrespectful comment I believe I've ever heard. Well done, son."

Rainy shows his teeth. "Why, thank you, kind sir. It's not often that I receive a compliment for speaking such well-worded poetic truth."

I move things around so as not to spill anything on the tray. "Rainy, you spent way too much time with James T. Gilmore."

Rainy purses his lips. "And a damn fine man he was."

I squint as a flash of good memories race through my mind. "Yes, he was."

I get plenty of dirty looks as I carry the tray to the rear.

A well-dressed man rises to open the door leading to the back passenger car. "I appreciate what you're doing, friend. Not all of us wanted to secede from the Union, and some of us even set our slaves free before they fired on Fort Sumter."

"More coffee before I serve our black brothers and sisters?"

"Just a taste."

"Cream and sugar?"

"Please."

It hits me. "Black coffee says it best when you add white cream and sweet sugar, don't you think?" Another thing that sounds like something Mr. Gilmore would have said.

The educated man bangs his cane twice on the floor. "Damn straight. It ought to be that way with people. What Babel did to separate the races, Lincoln did to bring them back together." Several people scoff and shake their heads. "But not by himself, as I witness your actions."

As I pull the door closed, I ask, "May I speak with you when I return?"

"I'll be waiting."

# CHAPTER 27

# GOOD MEN UNABLE TO DO GOOD DEEDS

## 10:00 A.M., MARCH 9, 1870

*Good men and women must stand together, or evil will prevail.*

T HE SMILING FACES of the two children who I served each a sweet-cake strengthens my heart already weary of this mission—at least all the way to Winnfield. The light in the eyes of the adults, who reluctantly partook of the refreshments, fuels my fire. I can do this now.

Ise follows me to the car we're riding in and speaks loud so all can hear. "Thank you, suh. It's good to be treated like a human bein'."

I return the tray to the waiter, whose tears spill down his cheeks. "God bless you, suh."

As he walks to the front carrying the tray, the old woman threatens, "I'll be speaking to the conductor about this!"

The waiter cowers, trying to shuffle through the door.

Sarge walks to the front of the car and flashes his badge from underneath his jacket. "You do that, ma'am, and I'll have you put off this train. Do you understand?"

She jerks her head to look out the window.

Sarge sits back down. "There now, maybe she'll shut the hell up."

Rainy chuckles, "Can you do that?"

Sarge winks. "No, but she doesn't know that."

I elbow Sarge. "I'm goin' to speak with the gentleman in the back for a bit."

"Who is he?"

"Tell you when I get done."

The older man moves over to make room for me to sit. "And who might you be, friend?"

"Columbus Nathan Tullos from Choctaw County, Mississippi. Call me Lummy if you'd like. I lived in Winn Parish for three years before I left for the war, but I've only been back once since I left in '62."

The man checks his watch and taps his chin. "Why do I know that name? Lummy Tullos, hmmm." He turns astonished. "You're the one who—"

I whisper so as to quiet him, "Led the men who killed Dawg Smith and his gang."

"I'm happy to make your acquaintance, brother. I'm David Pierson, who—"

"Was one of the six delegates who refused to vote 'yes' at the Louisiana secession convention back in '61."

"You know you're history, sir. That will forever be my greatest achievement, I do believe." David shakes his head. "The powerful rich of Winn Parish illegally had our vote changed. For a minute, the Free State of Winn emerged, but that failed, too."

I ask, "So, you must've been friends with James T. Gilmore?"

"As good a friend as I've ever had. I spoke at his funeral." He shakes my hand. "I attended your brother Ben's funeral the next day. Two of the best men to ever grace Winn Parish."

"Thank you for sayin' that, David. Didn't you practice law in Winnfield?"

"I did, starting in 1859."

"So you know the Davises?"

"Sure do. In fact, my partner and I handled Mister Wiley's property you inherited when he passed. He was a good old soul."

"That he was."

"You did a fine job at his funeral, fine job."

"Thank you. So, you fought for the Confederacy?"

"I did. Company C, the Winn Rifles of the Third Louisiana Infantry. We were all over the place, from the battles at Oak Hills, Missourah, Elkhorn Tavern Corinth, and Iuka to Vicksburg."

"That means you were just across Glass Bayou from the Twenty-Seventh Louisiana Lunette."

"You were with the Winn Rebels? Formed up in '62?"

"Yes, I served until after the surrender. My two brothers were with the First Mississippi Light Artillery, Company C, just down the hill from y'all."

"Those men did a good job of keeping the Yanks off our left flank while we defended the Redan. Just horrible, those two mine explosions." David drifts back there. He returns and taps his cane twice on the floor. "I got exchanged after the parole and finished the war as a lieutenant-colonel. I surrendered in Shreveport May of '65. And you?"

"After the surrender at Vicksburg, I wandered back over here with a good friend to visit my wife's grave." We pass by the exact spot where J.A. and I hid under a bush and Dawg Smith nearly relieved himself on our heads. I shudder like when I hunt with Elihu on a frosty winter morning.

"Mister Davis told me you married that pretty black lady Mister Gilmore called his daughter."

"That was me. Anyway, after me and a group of former Rebs killed Dawg Smith, I went back to my home in Choctaw County to see about my family. It wasn't long that I decided to help get the twentieth star for Mississippi put back on the true flag. So, I enlisted in the First Mississippi Mounted Rifles and finished out the war fightin' for the Union with Company C."

David offers me his hand. "We all did what we believed was right."

"Why did you go through the war fightin' for the Rebs when you voted against secession?"

"I was a state's rights man to the core, and though I opposed slavery and leaving the Union, I couldn't stand to see the politicians in Washington stomp on what the Constitution says is our right. I still believe that, but like I said, I set my slaves free before the war. In fact, I sent them all to James T., who I knew would treat them as freed men and women. They're still living on his property. Your friend Mister Davis made sure of that. He holds the land in trust, and they pay the taxes. The rest of what they earn they keep for themselves. James T. Gilmore's new world came to pass just like he wanted, except for the Nightriders giving them hell, not to mention travelers heading west."

"How bad is it with these Nightriders?"

He gazes at me from under his eyebrows. He knows I know the answer to my own question. He opens his jacket to reveal two small pistols holstered under his arms. "I still have folks who don't appreciate my perspective. I'm sure you do, too."

I want to tell him that's why we're here, but I need more time to see if he's trustworthy.

David closes his coat. "After the war, I practiced law in Natchitoches." He shakes his head. "Just too much bad blood for me to stay in Winn Parish."

"I understand."

"You do know Missus Davis passed?"

That message stings my heart. "I did not. How?"

"They say it was some kind of cancer. She was a good woman, a might testy, but a good ole soul. She got a lot sweeter after Mister Gilmore and your brother died. It hit her pretty hard. I don't think she ever got over the death of your Susannah. She took to that girl after you left for the war. I was there when an old gray-headed black man buried her. What was his name?"

"Old Bart."

"Kindest old gentleman I've ever met. Funny, too. I've always been amazed at the strength and tenacity of Negroes in the midst of such injustice and abuse. And still be able to laugh off the hardship. Happy people are happy wherever they are, whatever they're doing."

"Mister Gilmore was the reason for Old Bart's happiness. But not all got the same treatment. You know that better'n I do."

"Maybe, Lummy, maybe not. My slaves were like family to us. I inherited them from my grandfather but didn't know what to do with them until I heard what James T. was doing." David sighs. "I miss that man. Did y'all have any slaves?"

"I'm thankful to say that our family in Choctaw County never owned a slave. Pa wouldn't have it. He watched how badly my grandpa treated them, you know, the whippin's, breedin' cages, and such. In some ways, we were like Mister Gilmore. If a Negro stepped onto our property, he was a slave no longer, except old gray-haired Miss Lucille. Pa kept papers on her until right before she died for her own protection, like Mister Gilmore did."

"Breeding cages, huh? I cannot imagine."

"Yeah, Pa said he was made to watch when my grandpa put a man in a cage with a woman, at least until he got bigger and refused. My grandpa would laugh and say, 'If Jefferson won't let us import 'em, we'll just have to breed 'em.' That happened at least until my uncle Silas threatened to whoop the hell out of my grandpa Willoughby."

David smiles. "I like that. Tell me about your pa not wanting to have slaves."

"Grandpa Willoughby Tullos brought seven slaves with him when he came to the Mississippi Territory back in '11. When our family moved north to Choctaw County, about the time I was born, he forced Old Miss Lucille on Pa. He said she was useless to him. Pa didn't want her, but Ma made him, saying we could take care of her in her old age. Sweetest woman I've ever known. If anybody makes it through the pearly gates, Old Miss Lucille will be first in line."

"I believe you."

I laugh. "She loved poppin' corn and always put black pepper on it."

David keeps talking, but I drift back to a time when I sat on Lucille's lap as a young boy. She'd talk to me about how good Creator was and how to see him in all things.

David taps his cane on the floor. "Lummy, did you hear me?"

I rub my eyes. "I'm sorry. I drifted off into a good old memory."

"I could see that. I was just wondering how you and Susannah came to know each other."

I don't want to do this right now. "Could we talk about somethin' else if you don't mind?"

"Sure. Some memories are best held in the heart, not on the tongue." David rubs his chin whiskers. "I hope you men are here for the reason I believe you are."

I figure I can trust David now. "I'll not speak of why we're here, but I will nod if you say it."

"West-Kimbrell Gang?"

I give a slight nod.

He says, "The Irishman Edmund Burke once wrote, 'When bad men combine, the good must associate or else they will fall, one by one, an unpitied sacrifice in a contemptible struggle.'"

"Words well-written. We aim to gather the right men and end 'a contemptible struggle.'"

David puts his chin on the head of his cane. "Your mission is safe with me. If you need any legal work done, let me be the man to handle it for you." He pulls out his wallet and hands me five hundred dollars in greenbacks.

"Sir, there ain't no need to—"

"As you can see, I'm unable to fight anymore, or I'd be with you. The wounds I received at Iuka and Vicksburg pretty much knocked me out of any more scrapping. Let this be my way of fighting alongside you."

I give him a firm handshake and return to my seat. I whisper to Sarge what David and I spoke about and the money.

I start to pull the cash from my pocket, but Sarge shakes his head. "Keep it. We'll figure out what to do with it when we get to Winn Parish."

Rainy lifts his hat up from his napping. "I know one thing we can do with part of it."

Sarge asks, "What?"

"Get that young man in the back passenger car a ring for his new bride."

Sarge elbows me. "I can't think of a better reason to spend it."

# CHAPTER 28

# RETRACING OLD STEPS

## 11:30 A.M., MARCH 9, 1870

*Traveling old paths resurrect old memories.*

S ARGE FLAGS DOWN the conductor. "We'll exit the train at the next wood and water stop. Would you kindly inform the engineer?"

The conductor nods. "I'll tell him you'll de-board your horses, too."

Soon we come to a halt. Sarge stands to stretch. "Gather up, boys. This is our stop."

David stands using his cane. "You men take care of yourselves."

I give him a firm handshake. "I'm glad we talked, David. You travelin' on to Shreveport?"

"Yes, I have court matters to attend to there. I should be back in Natchitoches in a few days. But I'll come through Atlanta soon. If not, look me up if you need me, or just come for a visit. I'd enjoy hearing more of your family stories."

"My niece, Mary, has already started writing a Tullos history. I'm guessin' it'd be like most folk's history around here."

"Ah, but they will never take the time to put theirs to paper. I want a signed copy of Mary Tullos's first book."

I chuckle. "I'll guarantee it. See you again, David."

He raises his cane and tips his hat. "Sooner than you think."

Sarge whispers, "That man could be a very useful friend."

"Already is."

As we move to the front of the car, David limps up to tap Rainy on the shoulder. He whispers into Rainy's ear, "Not many men wear all black like you. I heard about a man killed in the Indian Territory also believed to have helped Judge Jeremiah Waters leave this earth."

Rainy searches David's eyes. "Not much escapes men in your profession."

"It doesn't pay to let good information pass us by."

"What are your intentions with this information?"

"I want to congratulate that man on a job well done. The town, newspaper, and even the farmers are prospering. The man wearing black with no name is still spoken of as a hero even today. I had to offer my thanks, son, that's all."

Rainy tips his hat. "I'm trying to leave that part of my life behind."

"Take a word of wisdom from a man who knows?"

Rainy nods.

"Lay down the clothes of mourning and suit up in the clothes of a new life."

A tear sparkles in Rainy's eye. "Thank you, kind sir. I need to wear the clothes of death a little longer. Then I'll shed this snakeskin forever."

"Bless you, son."

When we step off the train, I ask Rainy, "Who is Judge Waters, and what's that about?"

Rainy cuts his eyes at me like a hawk spying a mouse in a field. "I'll tell you later."

We purposefully pass by the old lady who gave us grief earlier. She turns her nose up like a herd of stinking hogs are passing by.

In the sweetest syrupy tone possible, she leans out the window and says, "I hope y'all all go to the Devil."

Rainy whispers, "Yes, ma'am, the Devil. Being the gentleman that I am, I'll be holding the door open for you. Good day."

Sarge tips his hat, but I can't resist. I stick out my tongue and blow it at her.

She gasps and turns her head.

We walk our horses down the gangplank across the tracks to the same woodcutter's station where I once boarded a crowded train car with J.A. to go enlist in the Reb Army. The place hasn't changed much, except for a new cabin built off the tracks a hundred yards away. The same man who ran the place back then greets us, though having grayed a little. His wife sits in a rocking chair on the porch, darning a sock, while two towheads play in the yard.

The station manager's son trots up. "I'll take your horses, water and feed 'em, and brush 'em down good for a dollar a piece." That's too much to pay this far out, but it's worth it to have our horses in the best shape possible.

Sarge tosses him a five dollar gold piece. "Keep the change, young man. Check the saddles and shoes, too, and bring them when you're done."

The boy shakes like a rabbit ready to bolt. "A whole extra dollar? Yes, suh! I'll even clean the hooves." The boy races off like he's just struck gold. He has.

I backhand Sarge's shoulder. "You old softy."

"They look like they can use it. Five dollars goes a long way out here. Y'all get your legs stretched."

I look around. I'm an outlaw going after outlaws.

Sarge laughs. "Didn't you say, 'It takes a devil to catch the Devil?'"

"Talkin' out loud sure makes me an easy target, don't it?"

"Yeah, but the Lord wouldn't have it any other way."

When this is over, I'll disappear to the same Mississippi River sandbar I went to after mustering out of the 1st Mississippi Mounted Rifles. A few days to get my soul back will be good before I go home.

The train blows its whistle, spits steam, and pulls away. The woodcutter's son walks our horses across the track to a shed. I watch the train disappear. I close my eyes and can see pretty Susannah's face fading from my sight for the last time as I rushed off to war. Though life has moved on, my heart'll always have a place for Susannah.

The station manager's wife sings a melody as the kids chase each other. My mind floats to another place. A sweeter place. Home.

I can see Martha shelling purple speckled butterbeans on the front porch while Ma teaches Mary how to make her famous blackberry cobbler. Elihu and John A. tiptoe away to go fishing so Elihu can sip a little moonshine. Jasper and James gee haw the mules, breaking ground early just because they like doing it. Smells from the kitchen make my mouth water. The children laughing melt my heart. Martha's sky blue eyes soothe my soul. I want to be home.

Rainy squeezes my shoulder. "'One beautiful heart is better than a thousand beautiful faces,' William Shakespeare said. Martha's got both, you lucky dog."

"That I know, brother." I wipe a tear on my pants, and my thumb brushes against the pistol Mr. Gilmore gave me when I left for the war. I'm reminded of why I am here. Damn.

Sarge trots over like he's headed to a fire. "Boots and saddles, men. The woodcutter told me those West-Kimbrell boys are stirring up more trouble than Winn Parish can manage. What's the quickest route, Lummy?"

CHAPTER 29

# PREPARING FOR OLD WAYS

### 1:30 P.M., MARCH 9, 1870

*Some memories blow through my soul in the flash of a tornado,*
*but the damage remains.*

I MOUNT UP and situate my butt in the saddle. I'm still a bit tender from the ride to Vicksburg. I haven't been on horseback this long since I rode with the Rifles. Maybe this leg of the journey will work out the soreness.

As I pull down my hat, I catch a glimpse of the same familiar face I saw on the ferry. He's a skinny young man tugging on an ornery mule that doesn't want to leave the train car. He sees me and turns his head. I still can't remember where I've seen him.

I trot up next to Sarge. "Somebody's followin' us."

"You think?"

"I don't know, maybe I'm wrong."

"Keep a sharp eye. We've made it this far without trouble. I'd like it to stay that way."

I let Sarge, Ise, and Rainy get ahead, maybe a hundred yards. I backtrack to see if anyone is following us. I must've been mistaken. I can't let my feelings affect my thoughts too much, but they are the best sense I have when I'm in the woods, or in possible danger.

I trot to catch up. "Didn't see nobody."

Sarge gives his mount a gentle nudge with his spurs. "We're good for now."

I pop my mount's hip. "There's a place up ahead I need to pay my respects."

"Be quick."

"Come with me. You'll want to know about this."

We rein up in front of a half-burned house overgrown with weeds and saplings. I dismount and walk to the window J.A. and I sneaked up to on our way to Winn Parish after Vicksburg surrendered. A rabbit bursts out, and my pistol is out and cocked before I know I did it. I wave to the others, and they lower their weapons. It's a swamper just like the one that saved our lives the night Dawg Smith surrounded the place. Smith killed five good men who just wanted to get home after Vicksburg, like me and J.A. They didn't make it. I make the story short, lift up a prayer for those boys, and get back on my horse.

Sarge nudges his mount forward. "They say the West-Kimbrell Gang makes Dawg Smith and his outlaw home guard look like a bunch of sissy hymn singing choir boys."

I place a percussion cap on each nipple of my ten gauge shotgun and lay it across my lap. "We'll just have become pastors from on high and teach them the new way of the Lord."

Rainy eases up, checking his pistol. "Damn straight."

Sarge turns. "You all right back there, Ise?"

"Yassuh. I'm just tryin' to soak in what you men is becomin', you know, meaner than a ball of cottonmouths rollin' down a creek in the springtime. I sure wouldn't want y'all mad at me."

Sarge chuckles. "We're not mad, but we do have to conjure up anger to get through this."

"It's like this, Ise," I say. "Remember when you and the Third U.S. Colored Troops swooped down from the Franklin Baptist Church to that creek and drove them Rebs back?"

"Yassuh, I remember."

"Get that anger back. You're gonna need it. We're havin' to come from livin' for the Lord down to the depths of Hell to defeat these bastards."

"So, that's how it is?"

I hate to say it. "That's how it is. The trick's knowin' how to get your soul back from that hellish hollow place. Like you did after you fought like a demon against Wirt Adam's cavalry."

"And then?" Ise asks.

I whisper, "Get it back into Creator's arms where your soul really lives."

Rainy grumbles through the smoke of his cigar. "Just don't lose it in the fight. You might not get it back."

Ise whispers, "Sounds like you know what that's like."

Rainy shudders. "Son, you don't want to know."

We make the Dugdemona River just before midnight and cross where I removed Dawg Smith's head from his body. I touch the knife that did the deed. I'm glad Old Bart found it after I chunked it into the river. In that moment, I wanted to throw away everything associated with my anger, rage, and violence. It just wasn't to be. I shiver like a cold wind just wrapped around my heart. I can almost hear Pa say, *"Bow your neck, boy. Finish your work."*

Rainy eases his horse up. "Is this where it happened?"

"Yes."

He leans on his saddlehorn. "Some memories blow through your soul like a tornado, but the damage remains."

I take in my surroundings. "Ain't that the damn truth."

Sarge looks around. "Let's make camp near here. We'll go into town around midnight and see your Mister Davis, Lummy. Where's a good spot to rest for a couple of hours?"

"On the other side of that ridge and down a ways there's a small pasture. It'll have new grass by now. It borders the river so we can water our horses and stay out of sight."

Ise dismounts. "Is that him?" He points up into the cypress tree where Sheriff Barnett hanged Dawg Smith's headless body. The sign is blurry in the darkness. That fits.

I tie my horse to a limb and stare at Dawg Smith's sun-bleached skull. The bottom jaw is gone, but the rest sits in the tree crook facing the road. It's so white it looks to glow in the dark. The words painted on the sign can't be read for all the bullet holes. One word is clear—*Dawg*.

The skull wobbles and falls to the ground.

Ise jumps back. "Lawd help us! That ole haint done come back to get us!"

A familiar face pokes his head over the crook.

I laugh. "It's just a possum, Ise."

"Ain't just a possum. It's a sign."

Rainy squeezes my shoulder. "It is, and I know what it means."

Ise's eyes are big as saucers. "Do tell, Mistuh Rainy."

Rainy rubs his chin. "Those West-Kimbrell boys come to this very spot and worship Dawg Smith on Sundays. That possum tells me that a quiet group of men will topple the tyrants who plague this good land. Like when Dawg Smith was brought down, the boys we're after don't have long until we put them in the ground under that skull."

I purse my lips. "Maybe so, but they only worship themselves and their devilish lust for power and possession. Somebody put Dawg's skull back in place."

Ise shakes his head. "Nawsuh, I ain't touchin' it."

Rainy starts to pick up Dawg's skull, but I stop him. "No. Ise, you need to do this. This man raped and killed your sister, Susannah. Do it. That's an order."

"Yassuh." Ise wraps leaves around the skull so he doesn't have to touch the bone. He wedges it tight into the crook of the tree. "That good, Sergeant Tullos?"

"Yep, and no more Sergeant Tullos."

"Yes, sir." Ise looks at the skull, then at me. "You cut his head off with that big old knife?"

I pat the knife Pa made for me. "Sometimes love takes a man to places he'd never go to do things he never would otherwise."

Rainy nudges my shoulder. "No regrets, Lummy. Let's go rest a bit. What do you say?"

"Y'all go ahead. I'll be along. I'll cover our tracks when I come."

They disappear into a switch cane patch.

I drop to my knees, not to ask forgiveness for killing Dawg Smith, but for his soul that must be enduring torments worse than anything on earth. "Lord, if what you say in the Good Book is true, then I'm askin' a mighty big favor. You promised to remember our sins no more if we walk with Jesus. It ain't easy, not on this earth. I don't know if Dawg Smith ever gave his heart to you, but let me give it to you." I hesitate. "Even if you have to take part of whatever reward you have waitin' for me." I adjust my aching knees. "Somethin' pretty bad must've happened to men like Dawg Smith, Lester, and Captain Tom Ford to do what they did. These West-Kimbrell boys, too. They've done things that only the Devil could conjure up. I could've turned that way just as easy as them, too, had Your love not been taught to me. They didn't get that good teaching when they were little like I did. I want Dawg, Lester, Tom, and the men whose lives we're about to take to know somethin' good."

It's hard not to recount my sins right now. "They deserve no reward, but it ain't never been about deservin', right, Lord? It's about you sayin' that Jesus died for the whole world. Does that leave anybody out? Are there sins that can't be forgiven? They didn't get a proper understanding in this life. Otherwise, they wouldn't have done what they did."

I scratch my head, trying to find the right words. "This ain't easy to ask, and it'd be even harder to do, but would you consider forgiving their wrongs, Lord, and let them enjoy Heaven with you? That's all I've got to say about that, Lord. I leave it in Your hands." I wipe tears from my eyes. I look once more up at Dawg's skull. "Lord, I don't want to be here. But I'll be your man for the good of others if that's why I'm here."

As the sounds of horses walking on dry leaves disappear around the river bend, I close my eyes and take the multi-colored agate from my coat pocket. I empty my mind, chasing unwanted thoughts away. I ponder the power and wisdom of the universe captured in the wavy lines in the rock in my hand. Flowing robes of misty fog rising from the small river to surround me.

"Granny?"

*"I'm here, Grandson."*

"In this terrible place of my sin and shame?"

*"There is no sin or shame for he who gives himself for the good of another."*

"Will I have to do more terrible things?"

*"Yes, if you want it to end with you."*

"What do you mean?"

*"The Tullos family can be spared further anger, abuse, and violence if you will but sacrifice your vow."* Granny starts to fade into the fog as the sun sends its last rays through the trees. *"You will not be alone. I will be with you. And Michael will come with his mighty sword."*

I whisper, "And I will have to take life once more."

The agate glows until Granny disappears.

# CHAPTER 30

# WINNFIELD, AGAIN

## 3:00 A.M., MARCH 10, 1870

*Good and bad memories. You can't have one without the other.*
*Not in this world.*

OUR HORSES SPLASH across the shallow Dugdemona River in the cool misty darkness. It won't be long before spring rains swell this lazy stream into a boiling mass of water not unlike the Mississippi when snowmelt travels south. Many a day in Vicksburg, I watched eddies and whirlpools swirl in the big river to command the path of any unpowered, and sometimes steam powered, boat, wherever it chose to send it. That's the way my soul sits this morning—going forward with little control as to what happens next. This is all too familiar.

No moon shines tonight, just a quiet gloom that speaks too many words. Shadows remind me of the day I received the news in Mr. Gilmore's letter that Susannah had died. What I didn't know then was that he and Ben were killed not far from this very spot trying to rescue her. A hoof splash reminds me of when I saw Jasper and James down by the river. I was deep in distress about what I'd just read in Mr. Gilmore's letter when James threw a rock in the river a few feet away. Though stuck in the depths of my worst despair, I was so grateful to be reunited with my brothers. We wrestled like boys in a schoolyard that day. Good and bad—can't have one memory without the other. Not in this world.

I shiver like I just woke up with frost on my head from sleeping outside. There's no frost this morning, except in my soul. My horse looks back at me. I pat his neck and quiet my cold shivers with good thoughts of Martha and the kids. Though pain raises its ugly head like the nine-headed Hydra Hercules killed, it gives me everything I'll need to resurrect my anger when the fight comes. This time though, I have that old dragon by the tail, not the other way around. I need to pray on that more.

An owl hoots, and I remember Dan Creekwater's words about listening to the voice of the wisdom bird.

I take it as a word that I'm doing the right thing. "I'm listenin', Dan. Thanks."

Ise eases up beside me. "Who you talkin' to, Mistuh Lummy?"

"The universe, son."

"Does it talk back to you?"

"Why, she's the one who started the conversation."

"What'd she say?"

"Be ready to give everything you got because she did to get us here."

"I don't understand."

I nudge my horse. "You will. C'mon, let's go. We'll be in Winnfield in no time." I search for the brightest star and whisper, "Thanks, Granny."

A coal oil lamp shines dimly in the window at Davis's Mercantile, the signal that it's clear to come in. We hide our horses in a shed out back, careful to notice if anyone stalks the streets. It's too early for good people to be stirring, but we take no chances. Though Sarge got us mounts that don't have the U.S. brand, it's still best that we hide them for now. We'll leave before first light.

Sarge removes his jacket. "Mister Davis should be up. I telegraphed him from Vicksburg that we'd be here today."

I tap on the back door that I came in and out many times while working for Mr. Davis before the war.

The door swings open, and Mr. Davis whispers in a louder voice than we expect, "Get in here, boy, and tell me all about it." He wraps his arms around my chest and waves in the rest. "Y'all, c'mon in. Good to see you, Lummy Tullos."

"It's been too long, old friend."

We file in like good children ready for Christmas dinner. The smell of good food wafts over us like the river fog we left behind.

Mr. Davis thrusts out his hand. "Rainy Mills, it cheers my heart to see you. I need to discuss a gun order when you have a minute."

Rainy removes his hat. "Absolutely."

Mr. Davis offers his hand to Sarge. "You must the one they call Sarge?"

"Good to finally meet you, sir. I've heard so much about you, and I see that it's all true."

Mr. Davis chuckles and looks around at the rest of us. "I'm not sure if that's good or bad."

Sarge laughs out loud but covers his mouth. "It's all good, sir. I stole that line from Lummy back in the war."

Ise eases up the steps.

Mr. Davis takes his hand like he's trying to shake his arm out of the socket. "Don't be shy, son. You're family here."

Ise grins. "Yassuh. Thank you, suh."

Mr. Davis rubs his chin, looking around to see if anyone is watching, and eases the door shut. "Lummy, guess I'll have to get used to these Army boys calling me sir."

I enter the stock room and sit in a straight-back chair. "It's a hard habit to break, suh," I say, grinning. "You won't believe this, but Sarge is a lieutenant, and he made me a sergeant."

"Tell the truth and shame the Devil. I don't believe it."

Sarge laughs. "It's true, Mister Davis. This sorry ridge running, swamp jumping, river rat was the only man President Grant could find who'd take on a job like this. And just call me Sarge. I haven't gotten used to being an officer yet."

We all laugh, but Mr. Davis doesn't. "I don't envy you men. You've got a helluva fight comin'." We wait. Mr. Davis laments, "This is much worse than Dawg Smith. These boys are the worst demons Satan ever set loose. They do things no normal human bein' could even imagine."

I shoulder hug him. "Let's not think on that right now. We're hungry as a pack of coyotes chasin' a man down the railroad tracks."

Rainy grins. "And that's hungry. I know. I was there."

Ise rubs his neck. "Did that really happen, Mistuh Rainy?"

"Ask your brother-in-law over here."

I sigh. "That's a story for another time. Mistuh Davis, let's eat."

Mr. Davis buzzes around like a bumblebee bringing food from the kitchen. He pours coffee, and Rainy decides it's time to lighten the mood with one of his jokes.

"If you won't tell that story, I'll tell you—"

I swat the air with my hat. "Aw hell, this ain't gonna ruin our breakfast, is it?"

"If it does, that just means I get more biscuits."

I sip my coffee. "Go on, get it over with." I elbow Ise. "It'll be funny if Rainy tells it."

Rainy takes a deep breath. "A new wrestler appeared on the circuit and started making a name for himself by winning a few contests."

Ise squirms with excitement. "I watched several matches in Saint Looey a few years back."

Rainy holds his finger to his lips. "Let me tell it. Anyway, he'd never wrestled anyone important, but his agent got him a match with a seasoned undefeated professional they called The Hatchet."

I can't resist. "Why'd they call him that?"

Rainy holds up his hand. "They called him The Hatchet because of a trick hold he'd developed that no other wrestler could break free from. He called it the Hatchet Knot Hold, meaning, if caught, it'd take a hatchet to get you loose." He leans in. "The torches were lit around the ring for the nighttime competition. The crowd roared, and bets were made all around. The match was about to start when The Hatchet entered the ring, taunting the newcomer. 'No one has ever broken free from the Hatchet Knot Hold. No one ever will. Only a hatchet can do it!'

"The young wrestler cringed, and his manager reminded him, 'Whatever you do, don't let him get you in the Hatchet Knot Hold. It'll be over.'

"The young wrestler closed his eyes, knowing he was beaten before the match even started. The bell dinged, and they were off, circling each other like a couple of dime novel western gunfighters. The Hatchet grabbed at him this way, and the youngster escaped that way. Then, The Hatchet cornered him. The young wrestler screamed in pain as The Hatchet wrapped around him like a great snake. Locked down in the Hatchet Knot Hold, the young wrestler couldn't breathe, and things started going dark. He strained with his last bit of energy but couldn't budge against the strength of the warlord of wrestling. Sweat ran down his face as he gasped for air. All of a sudden, The Hatchet sprung from his death hold like a cat stepping on a hot stove. The young new wrestler quickly pinned The Hatchet for the count. He won!

"Newspaper reporters and bet winners flocked to the new champion, shouting, 'Nobody's ever done that before! How'd you break the Hatchet Knot Hold?'

"The young wrestler straightened up and said, 'I was just about to faint when I saw a hairy pair of man stones hanging down in front of me. With all I had left, I surged forth and bit down on 'em with all my might.' The reporters were stunned. 'That's amazing!' The young wrestler puffed out his chest and smiled. 'Yeah, it's amazing how fast you can break loose from the Hatchet Knot Hold when you bite down hard on your own stones.'"

I shake so hard laughing, coffee spills all over the table.

Ise falls out of his chair and rolls on the floor with tears in his eyes.

Sarge bursts out laughing.

Mr. Davis thanks God Mrs. Davis wasn't here.

It's a good moment. We needed it. We won't have any more like this until we've completed the mission.

Mr. Davis puts his knuckles on his hips. "I won't forget that story for a long time, Rainy." He studies the table. "That looks to be everything."

I reach for a biscuit.

Mr. Davis bows his head. "Y'all mind if we thank the Lord?"

I pull back my hand. "I should've thought of that myself."

We bow our heads around the small table covered with smokehouse ham and eggs, hot biscuits and gravy, fresh butter and molasses, and steaming coffee to wash it down with. Mr. Davis asks Ise to lead us. I'm at home for the first time since we left Choctaw County.

Ise prays in the voice of a prophet. His words remind me of my black grandfather, Old Bart.

Mr. Davis smiles. "The last time one of our black brothers prayed in this room, we were about to do a similar thing." He looks to the ceiling. "Bless you, Old Bart."

We say amen together.

Mr. Davis picks up the biscuit basket and hands it to Ise. "Fine prayer, thank you. But now, you men have too much to think about with what y'all got coming. The rest of us can do the praying while y'all go with the angels after the demons." He stops. "Keep 'em safe, Lord." We amen again and dig in.

Mr. Davis passes the ham platter to Ise. "Just figured you men might be ready for some home cooked vittles." No one speaks for stuffing their mouths.

After my first taste, I ask, "Dang, Mistuh Davis, where'd you learn to cook like this?"

"From two of the best this town ever had. My loving wife, God rest her soul, and your old friend, Mister Wiley. That man should've been a chef on a Mississippi River steamboat. He would've drawn a dinner crowd. I wrote down all his Cajun recipes before he left us. I know you've enjoyed a pot or two of his fine gumbo."

"There ain't nothin' like it. Still, I never could get used to eatin' chitlin's with him and Old Bart. Creator don't make men like them anymore."

Mr. Davis chuckles. "That's for sure. Y'all eat up now, there's plenty more on the stove. What you don't eat, take with you. I made extra for the road."

Sarge mops up gravy with a biscuit. "Thank you, sir. You are too kind."

Mr. Davis blows on his coffee. "I put together the supplies you ordered, Sarge. I got a mule and a two wheel cart to haul them to where you'll be staying."

Between bites, I ask, "South Farm?"

Mr. Davis grins. "Yes, but sorry to say, the West gang shot up the place and ran the Negroes out. They killed the men and raped the women. They just left them there to die with children scattered about crying. Terrible sight when we got there. I couldn't help it, Lummy, I cried."

I squeeze his shoulder. "Strong men always cry over such things. It's when we don't, we become like them."

Mr. Davis dries his eyes. "They bring hellfire down on good folks, working their way across the parish one farm at a time. I'm just glad they didn't burn Ben's old place down. I got those who survived relocated up at the big farm where Mister Gilmore and Sus—well, you know."

Fear seizes my heart. I ask, "Is Elzey all right?"

Mr. Davis nods and blows his nose. "Yeah, he's in good hands."

"I thought they only waylaid folks moving west. They're hittin' local farms, too?"

Mr. Davis sighs. "Just those who threaten their outlawing and complain too much."

Sarge leans back in his chair, rubbing his belly. "And they own the law?"

Mr. Davis spits. "They *are* the law."

We sip our coffee, pondering the road ahead.

Ise speaks up. "Lummy's told us about you takin' care of my people. It's about time they get a chance at a free and good life."

Rainy raps his knuckles on the table. "Damn straight."

Sarge leans in. "Mister Davis, you don't know how much your government appreciates the risk and sacrifice you're—"

"Y'all can stop all that shit." Mr. Davis throws his hand up like he's about to get his mouth washed out with soap. "If Missus Davis heard me, I'd be the worse for it."

I laugh. "Don't worry, she does."

Mr. Davis grins. "Guess I'll get my scolding tonight in my dreams. Anyway, Sarge, this ain't the first time I've helped Lummy clean up the parish."

Sarge salutes. "Forgive me, sir. This kind of work receives neither medals nor recognition. But it does offer the satisfaction that the Good Lord does win some of the time."

Ise looks to heaven. "Thank you, Lawd."

We sit quiet, remembering past battles, counting the cost of what's coming, and wondering who might not come back from this mission. I catch Ise searching my eyes. He sees the truth of my thoughts—not fear, just the fact that one of us might die in the next few days.

Ise spreads out his arms, palms up. "Lawd, you know who we is. You know why we'z here. Let us all go back home to the people we love. Protect our wives, and wives to be, the children, and good Mistuh Davis here. We're all dependin' on you, Lawd." He sighs. "Amens, Lawd." He sits up straight and smiles. "Just one more thing, Lawd. Bring Mistuh Rainy here a good woman. It's plain to see he's 'bout ready to settle down."

Rainy furrows his brow. "Now, how would you know that?"

"Mistuh Rainy, don't you know that the Lawd tells me things?"

I push back my plate and slap Mr. Davis on the shoulder. "Mister Gilmore would be proud of how you've carried on his legacy and grown it, too."

He sips his coffee. "I do what I can, when I can, but these jokers mean business. So far, I've been able to stay off their list. I'm afraid that's gonna change though. Not if, but when, they find out what I've been doing. It's just a matter of time, I'm afraid."

Sarge reassures him. "If they're moving south to north like you say, we'll stop them before they ever make it here."

Mr. Davis wrings his hands for moment. "I'm countin' on it, Sarge."

"Come with me. You'll want to know about this."

## CHAPTER 31

# AN OLD FRIEND SHOWS UP WITH A NEW NAME

### CLOSE TO DAWN, MARCH 10, 1870

*Redemption ain't a place to sit but a moment to rise from*
*and make things right.*

A S I DRAIN the last bit of coffee from my cup, someone passes a side window headed to the back of the store. "Y'all excuse me for a moment. Somebody's skulkin' around."

Everyone stands, cocking pistols.

I draw the knife Pa made me and thumb the blade. I yank the door open, grab the coat of a skinny young man, and throw him to the floor. "Speak quick and plain before I gut you like a fish."

"Please, suh, you know me. I'm Matt, Tom Poole's nephew."

I stare at him like he's already dead. I shake my head to clear my thoughts. I'm surprised at how quickly I struck without thinking. I press the owl talon into my wrist. I'm all right now.

Sarge pulls the knife back. "He's the bartender at the Bankston Hotel, Lummy, remember?"

I pull him up and dust him off. "Sorry, son. It's good to have an old friend show up with a new name." I wish Poole was here with me.

"It's all right, Mistuh Lummy. My uncle told me a little about what you went through in Vicksburg. He said it was worse'n hell."

I sheath my knife and turn to Sarge. "You still think I can do this?"

Sarge nods. "Without a doubt. You didn't kill him, did you?"

I calm myself. "Guess you're right. Anyway, Matt, you're a long ways from home. What in the hell are you doin' way out here?"

"I came to help."

"How'd you get here?"

"I borrowed my grandpa's new mule."

"How'd that go?"

"Not good at all at first. The damn thing threw me so high a bird built a nest in my ass before I hit the ground."

We laugh, and Rainy says, "Damn, I'd like to have seen that."

Matt grins. "But I kept talkin' to him, givin' sweet feed, and it wasn't long before we became best of friends."

"So, I wasn't crazy when I saw you at the river ferry and when we got off the train at the woodcutter's station. You followed us all the way here?"

Matt lifts his chin. "I did, and I can shoot and fight. At least I think I can."

Sarge sits down. "Think you can? I'm not taking on an inexperienced youngster who'll be an easy casualty of battle."

Matt purses his lips. "I'd appreciate it if you would not refer to me as a youngster. Just because my face says boy doesn't mean my heart don't say man. I'm just here to do whatever I can to help. You name it, I'll do it, but I'm stayin'."

Sarge scratches the back of his neck and looks to me. "He's sure enough got the fire."

I nod. "He does."

Sarge sighs. "All right, Matt, here's what we need you to do. First, Mister Davis, can you put him on as your new hired help? I'll reimburse you for the pay and—"

"No need for that. I'll tell people he's my nephew making his way west and just stopped in for a short time to make some money to keep going."

"That'll work fine. Matt, you can... pardon me, this is Rainy Mills and Ise."

"Good to know you men. I saw you in the Bankston Hotel, Mistuh Rainy."

"Glad you're here, son. Your uncle was of the finest sort Creator ever fashioned from the clay."

"I appreciate that. Good to know you, Ise," Matt says as he offers his hand. Ise shakes it and grins.

Sarge stands. "Matt, throw up your right hand and repeat after me."

Matt stands up straighter than a telegraph pole and looks to be twice as

thin. He repeats the oath Rainy and I took in Bankston with a solemn heart.
He reminds me of the strength and innocence I found in my friend Poole.

Sarge drops his hand, as does Matt. "I'm making you a private, and your
job will be to run messages back and forth between us and Mister Davis. You'll
take care of all telegraphing and letter mailing. You'll drive the supply cart
to South Farm with us this morning and make food runs as needed. I'm sure
other duties will come up, but that's a start."

"Why did you have me join the Army, suh?"

"So you can get paid for your service, and if something happens to you,
your family will receive government death benefits."

"Thank you, suh. I won't let you down."

"If you're anything like your uncle, I'm confident that you won't."

Mr. Davis brings Matt a plate. "Get some food in you, so"

"Thank you, suh. I haven't eaten in two days."

I sit beside him, nursing a cold cup of coffee. "Where's your mule?"

"Just outside of town in a cane break."

I hold out my cup for a warm up. "You got any weapons?"

"I have the old pistol my uncle used in the war and a shotgun stuffed
with buckshot."

"That'll do." I pat him on the back. "Eat up now. We leave in a few minutes.
I'm better now that we have a Poole with us."

Matt digs in like a hawg on slop. It's good to see him eat. And still be alive.

# CHAPTER 32

# SOUTH FARM SOLACE

## DAWN, MARCH 10, 1870

*Retracing old steps with a new spirit brings a bit of hope.*

**M**R. DAVIS PATS his cart mule on the shoulder as the first traces of light drift in from the east.

Matt checks to make sure everything is tied down tight.

"Sadie, she's a good 'un, Matt. You won't need to put the whip to her back. She'll go where you want. Just take your time, and I'll see you back here before noon tomorrow. I don't want you traveling in the dark with those damn Nightriders lurking about. I'll have food ready when you get here and your bed set up in the stock room. We'll get you working in the store right after you eat. Folks will want to know who you are."

"Thank you, suh. I'll treat your mule good. Thanks for the job and puttin' me up."

Mr. Davis winks at me and chuckles. "This ain't the first time I had to take in a scruffy lookin' Missip boy. Ain't that how y'all say Mississippi over there?"

I start to speak, but Matt cuts in with a toothy grin. "Yes, suh, if you want to say it right."

Mr. Davis backs away. "Matt, leave before daylight. If riders show up, whatever you do, don't get smart with them. They won't bother you if the wagon's empty. Play dumb and tell them you work for me."

"I will."

Mr. Davis pulls Sarge and me to the side. "If anybody stops you, you're just passing through with goods to sell and plan to take a load of salt back home for tanning hides. That's what I'll tell people. A messenger said that there'll be a noon meeting at Shiloh Baptist Church in three days. The men who'll be there have had enough of the West-Kimbrell Gang. Lummy, you know the place."

I nod.

Mr. Davis shakes Sarge's hand. "The kind of men you want will be there. I'll let them know you're here."

Sarge tips his hat. "Sounds good, and thanks for everything."

I mount up, and Mr. Davis holds my bridle. "Lummy, stop in and see J.A. after you make South Farm. He's tough, but what he went through... his wife and son—"

My heart jumps like a scared rabbit. "What happened? Are they all right? They didn't—"

"No, everyone's fine. But he needs to tell you what happened."

I breathe a sigh of relief. "I'll visit him once we get settled at South Farm."

"I'll tell you he sent his wife and son to Vicksburg two days ago after I told him you were comin'. He said some lady who is a good friend of yours would put them up until this is over."

"Yeah, that'd be my sister-in-law, Annie Handerson. That'll keep them out the West-Kimbrell Gang's reach."

Mr. Davis kicks the dirt. "Good."

"Are Dorcas and Freddy still up near Sikes?"

"They've been there ever since you left back in '63. Doing good. Tell them I said hello. I'm sure that's second on your list."

I smile and give my mount a nudge. "Be seein' you soon, Mistuh Davis, suh."

He throws a horse apple at me and laughs. His mouth straightens as he squints. "You be careful, son. I want you boys back in one piece."

"Yes sir, we will."

We take the wagon road to Prairie Home and cross Bear Creek. By early afternoon, Ben's old house on South Farm comes into view. We unload our weapons and supplies on the porch.

Ise leads our horses to the barn where Old Bart and I stayed the last time I was here.

"Let me take care of the horses, Ise. I kinda like doin' it."

"Yes, sir, go ahead."

Sarge shields his eyes, looking to the west. "Matt, Ise, let's get these supplies inside. It looks to rain tonight."

Rainy wanders off, armed to the teeth, watching every direction.

After everything is stored away and in its place, I walk through the rooms. Good memories flood my mind. The old feelings about Ben are gone. He was just a man doing the best he could with the way he was raised. I miss that boy. South Farm brings a bit of solace in the midst of the storm. I sit and stare for I'm not sure how long. Remembering.

I step into the kitchen, recognizing a familiar smell. Rainy took a couple rabbits while checking for any unwanted visitors. He's making the stew I had when I met him on my way to Winn Parish back in '59.

I take in a deep whiff. "Dang, that smells good."

Rainy stirs the pot. "You should recognize the taste. I got the recipe from old Mister Wiley years ago."

Sarge slurps in a spoonful of stew juice. "It don't get no better than this."

Rainy pours us a cup each of Elihu's muscadine wine and lifts his into the air. "Here's to good men everywhere fighting the good fight and living to tell about it."

I take a steep draw from my cup. "Amen to that."

Sarge takes his cup out on the porch and nods for me to follow.

Before I go, I pull out the pipe Dale sent me. "Rainy, could I get a taste of that fine tobacco you're totin'?" I fill the horsehead bowl and light it with a twig from the stove fire. I step into the darkness and let my eyes adjust for a second.

Sarge leans back against the log wall, sipping his wine. "I know what you have to do."

"I appreciate that. I'll leave out before daylight to see how J.A. is faring."

"That's a good idea. Should only take a day, you think?"

"I had somethin' else on my mind, too, Sarge."

"Spit it out."

"After I visit J.A., I'd like to make a quick run up to Sikes and see Dorcas, my late brother's wife, and family. You remember me talking about Ben when we were in camp at White Station?"

"Yes. He died trying to save Susannah, right?"

"That's right. I want to go see them before we start this thing. I don't know how long I'll want to stay once this is over."

"We'll need to get out as soon as we can, you understand?"

"Yes, sir, I do."

"Tell you what. Leave me a map to Shiloh Baptist Church and how long it'll take to get there. Go on to J.A.'s and up to Sikes to see your family. I'll see you at the meeting on the thirteenth."

"I appreciate it, Sarge."

"Not a problem, but promise me one thing."

"Sure."

"Stay away from people and don't go getting yourself in some scrape because of some bully."

"You know me too well, Sarge."

"I do, and we don't need you bringing any unwanted attention to who we are and why we're here. Hell, just being six foot six is noticeable enough, you long-legged, high-steppin' son of a bitch." We laugh. "Seriously though, make up your mind that you will see things you won't like. Remember that there's a bigger day coming, and soon. Can I count on you to keep a cool head and a sharp mind, son?"

"I promise, Sarge."

"That's good enough for me. How about letting me take a draw of that good southern tobacco?"

I knock out the used tobacco and ask Rainy for a refill.

Rainy hands me his tobacco pouch. "Just a word before you go to make your rounds. A Greek philosopher once said, 'Rule your mind, or it will rule you.' Horace, I think. Yes, it was Horace."

Sarge blows a smoke ring and says, "Damn, that's good." He hands the pipe back to me.

I take a deep draw. "Yeah, the tobacco and the wisdom."

A soft wind pours across the cabin porch. Ise steps out into the yard. "A storm's comin', Lummy. I can smell it."

"No, she's already here. She's been waitin' on us, and her name is Terror."

A large drop splatters on the roof.

It rains so hard the droplets splash back up half a foot off the puddles.

# CHAPTER 33

# AN OLD FRIEND
# WITH NEW PAINS

## MID-MORNING, MARCH 11, 1870

*Understanding another man's pain comes only
with havin' had the same experience.*

I MAKE BEAL Crossing as the first squirrel chatters to wake up the forest. I stay a rock's throw from the wagon road that leads to Atlanta and turn north on the trail that follows Hill Bayou.

J.A. sits on the porch steps, head in hands.

I yell, "The last time I came here, you were stretched out on that bench snorin' like a big ole lazy boar hawg."

"I'll be a suck egg mule. Lummy Tullos, didn't expect you so soon."

"But you *did* expect me?"

He grins. "Well, yeah."

"I had to come see the man who can stand straight up in a rifle pit, musket in hand, eyes open, just a snoozin' away."

"Get on up here, boy. Glad to see you."

"Good to see you, too. Just wish it was under better circumstances."

We hug like brothers, and he motions for me to sit beside him.

"Ain't that the damn truth. I was just dreamin' about my wife like I did when we were stuck in the Twenty-Seventh Looseana Lunette. Damn, I miss her and my boy somethin' fierce."

"Sarge said you sent your Mary Jane and Aaron to Annie's in Vicksburg. Good idea."

"I did. That's the hardest thing I believe I've ever done, except when we left for the war."

"What happened?"

"I was off meetin' with some cattle buyers down the road in Atlanta a week ago. I invited them out to the house for supper and to stay so they could spy out the herd the next mornin'. Excuse me a minute." J.A. rushes into the yard and throws up.

The chickens come running and peck about the chunks.

He sits back down. "Sorry 'bout that."

I wave off his apology. "Done it many times myself, brother, you know that."

"I do, and that's what I want to say. Lummy, I never fully understood your rage about Susannah dyin'. Boy, I do now." He wipes his mouth with a kerchief.

I reach down and squeeze his shoulder. "Understanding another man's pain comes with havin' had the same experience."

"I reckon so."

I ask, "How 'bout a cup of cold water with somethin' a little stronger added in to make this go a little easier?"

J.A. stands, his knees popping like a green pine log thrown on a fire. "Be back in a second."

We sip cool water laced with moonshine and listen to cattle moo.

"When did you send your family off?"

J.A. rubs his forehead. "I put them on the train for Vicksburg day before yesterday. I telegraphed Annie the day after the incident. She said for them to c'mon. Annie never forgets what somebody did for her and wants to repay the favor a hundred fold."

"They'll be safe there. Looks like you're doin' all right, J.A."

"I am, I am, thank you. We're makin' a fine livin', and life has been good until the incident."

"Can you talk about what West did?"

"It ain't easy."

"Is it ever?"

"Never."

"It'd be best to get it on out now, don't you think?"

"Yeah." J.A. looks into the forest beyond his house. "When me and the cattle buyers went to look over the herd after breakfast, West and his damn demons sneaked up to the house. They planned to rob the cattle buyers and kill us all. It's what they do."

"Had you ever had any trouble from West before?"

"Never. He generally leaves local folks alone and goes after traveling business men and folks movin' to Texas. He must be gettin' desperate."

"Must be, and damn him if he thinks he's the only one livin' in desperation. There's a bunch of folks tired of his wickedness."

"I'm right in there amongst 'em, too, now. Mary Jane said that when she told them to leave, one of 'em jumped off his horse intendin' to rape her."

"Did she recognize him, say who he was?"

J.A. glares at me like a wounded animal ready to fight. "It was that bastard John West himself. You remember him. We fought in the same damn rifle pit together. Hell, I even killed a Yank who was just about to stab his ass with a short sword."

"He didn't even thank you if I remember right."

J.A. cuts his eyes at me. "We didn't do such things for the thanks, but this is the thanks I get?" His face is turning red, and sweat beads pop out on his forehead. "My soul burns, Lummy, way down deep."

"Now you understand."

"Yeah, and like you, I can't let it go."

"That's why I'm here, brother, to walk this hellish road with you."

J.A. throws his arms up in the air. "West knew me and still came to my house to do his murderous deeds. I'm gonna kill that bastard myself!" The fiery rage I see in his eyes is what I felt just before I killed Dawg Smith. It can only be cured one way. "What a soulless bastard. I'll be damned."

I stomp my foot. "You won't be, but he already is."

J.A. stands to scream at the trees waving in the breeze. "He wanted to have his way with my wife!" He sits down hard. "They would've killed my boy Aaron just for being a witness."

I put my around the man's shoulder who has been more brother than friend. "I'm sorry." I sip my moonshine. "Give me the rest."

J.A. calms himself and takes a drink. "When Mary Jane ran back in the house, West yanked off her blouse. She made it inside and shut the door.

When he kicked the door in, Aaron had my scattergun up ready to shoot. But wouldn't you know it? That coward West sent one of his men in after Mary Jane. Aaron filled that man's shoulder with a load of squirrel shot. The blast blew him back out the door. We heard the shot and raced home, but they were already gone."

"I'm so sorry, brother. What are you gonna do?"

"What do you mean, what am I gonna do? You ignert ass, I was the one who asked Sarge to get you here."

"You knew I'd come."

"I did. Sorry, I don't mean to be so sharp. I'm just a bit messed up right now."

"It's all right. Take your time."

"I begged Sarge to bring you when he came back. He stayed at my house when he came through to size up the situation. You're here for one reason, aren't you? I wasn't sure you'd come."

"You came when I needed you. Now it's my turn to help you get back what I now have in Choctaw County."

"You did that once already, when we took down Dawg Smith."

"Who's countin', brother?"

"Nobody. Is Sarge already here, too?"

"He is, and Rainy Mills, too. A kid named Matt, who's none other than Poole's nephew, is tagging along. And you won't believe this, Susannah's brother Isaiah, who fought with the Third Colored Troops at Franklin Church, is with us. He goes by Ise. I told you about that battle when we hid out at Big Sand Rock, and you helped us get Captain Tom Ford hanged?"

"I remember. That's like a dream come true for you, ain't it?"

"Yep, he was the one who carved the words on the millstone when we raised the Ebenezer following the battle not long after we burned the factories at Bankston. I watched as he did it and didn't even know who he was."

"Ain't that somethin'?"

We sit quiet for moment. I wait for J.A. to ask.

He does. "So, what's the plan?"

"Can we talk about that later? You've got somethin' good cookin'. I can smell it."

"I do. Fried beefsteak, taters and gravy, and a pan of biscuits. How's that grab you?"

I rub my belly. "Just where it needs to."

## CHAPTER 34

# TALKIN' OVER
# OLD TIMES

8:30 P.M., MARCH 11, 1870

*An occasional smoke makes the shine of the moon a little brighter.*

WE WHILE AWAY the evening talking over old times, remembering those who didn't live to have the pleasure of reminiscing with a cup of good moonshine in their hands after a fine meal. I pull out my pipe when J.A. brings out his tobacco.

"When did you start smokin', Lummy?"

"I take a puff on occasion. Tastes pretty good after a good supper with a little moonshine."

He pours two finger's worth. "All right, I've waited long enough. What's the plan?"

"We'll meet Sarge and the local men at Shiloh Baptist Church noon on the thirteenth to hear what they want to do about this West-Kimbrell Gang."

"They want 'em dead."

"Figured as much, but we need a good plan."

"If Dawg Smith was a demon, John West is the Devil himself."

"Sarge told me most of it. How mean are they?"

He pours us another round of moonshine. "You may lose your supper."

"I want to know it all."

"It started after New Orleans fell, about the time we rode the train up to Vicksburg. This ain't the bastards who wear bedsheets and give the Negroes hell. They ain't the Ku Klux Klan."

"Sarge said as much."

"But they harass blacks on occasion to keep 'em quiet. They've murdered quite a number."

That makes me a bit worried about my son, Elzey. I put that out of my mind for now.

J.A. draws in a deep breath and blows it out. "I'll make this short as I can."

"Take your time. We got all night."

J.A. gets angry, even enraged, sobs, and cries in the telling. He recounts everything Sarge had told me but with much greater detail. About midnight, he finishes.

I wince. "Damn, I've never even heard of people doin' such things."

"I know, right?"

I touch the knife Pa made me. "They ain't no meaner than us."

"I agree, but we'll have to be the Devil himself to end this storm of terror. It's gone on too long, and there can be no mercy when we take them. Only God can offer that now."

"We'll just have to be extra careful then, won't we?"

J.A. hangs his head. "I reckon."

"One thing, J.A., we don't want anybody knowin' we're with the government on this thing."

"I was hopin' you'd come back with Sarge."

"I did, by order of President Grant himself."

"How's that?"

"Too long a story to tell tonight, but General Grierson put my name up to be a part of this mission. He remembered that me and Poole led the Yankees to burn the Bankston mills. Sarge knows I once lived in Winn Parish and looked me up. Grierson said if I do half the job here that I did on the Bankston raid, the mission will succeed."

"Hell, that's a great compliment."

"Yeah, and they made me a sergeant, too. Ain't that somethin'?"

"Damn sure is. But I ain't callin' you Sarge or salutin' your ass. I had enough of that in the army, and with your Sarge, whose now a lieutenant, I hear."

"Just call him Sarge. We're makin' out like he was one of our sergeants in the Reb Army."

J.A. stares into the sky. "When do you want to leave?"

"Before daylight."

"How long will we be gone?"

I shrug. "Don't know. Maybe a week. A month. I don't know."

"I'll hire a boy to watch the farm and keep the cows fed and watered."

"Good enough."

"We goin' to see Dorcas?"

"Yeah, I won't have time for that after the deed is done. We'll skedaddle out of the parish soon as we're finished."

J.A. stands and shakes my hand. "Good to be back with you, old friend."

"Me, too, J.A. Let's turn in to get a jump on daylight."

"I'll have the coffee ready at four o'clock."

"I'll be up and ready. Thanks."

# CHAPTER 35

# TO SIKES AND A BIT OF HOME

## MID-MORNING, MARCH 12, 1870

*Somebody once sang, "Jesus is a rock in a weary land." So is family.*

T HE VILLAGE OF Sikes sits in the northeast part of the parish. Freddy and Dorcas's farm is a bit farther on up. Ben's grave at Fellowship Baptist Church is just beyond that.

We tie our horses in front of the same store in Sikes as when I passed through after killing Dawg Smith. That was seven years ago. Sarge did say that a man six feet six ain't easily forgotten.

We ease into the store and café. A few old men sit at breakfast. The same sweet lady, who gave me directions to Dorcas's home last time, scrubs a cast iron skillet.

I whisper across the barrel and plank bar, "Some flowers get prettier the longer spring lasts."

Madison turns and gives me a big smile. "You sure made it stay spring-time a long time after taking care of Dawg Smith." She grins. "I'd know the voice of that long tall man anywhere. How's the world been treatin' you, Lummy Tullos?"

"A lot better'n the last time I passed through."

She throws a dishtowel over her shoulder and rounds the bar to give me a hug. "I don't know you, but any man who did what you did to save the parish from that demon deserves a kiss." She plants a good one on my lips and laughs. "Hope your wife don't mind."

"You don't tell on me, I won't tell on you."

Laughter erupts from the old men's table. The old one arm man who was here last time yells, "We thought we'd never see you again. Is that J.A. Killingsworth you got there with you?"

J.A. steps forward, throwing his hands up. "It is but guess I don't rate to get no good to see you kiss."

The old men howl like a pack of coyotes. "You got that right," the oldest one yells.

Madison pats her hands in the air. "You old hound dawgs go back to your salt pork, grits, and biscuits." She kisses J.A. on the cheek and batts her eyes like Annie Fanny. "Just funnin' you, J.A. How's Mary Jane?"

"Fine, fine, Madison. Thanks for asking."

The old men whisper about Dawg Smith's death.

I ask, "Madison, it's good to see you, dear, but I need to know. Is Dorcas and her family all right? I don't want any unpleasant surprises if you know what I mean."

"They're fine, Lummy. You just go on out there and enjoy seein' your sweet sister-in-law. Just know them kids have grown up tall as sweetcorn and are fillin' out right nice."

"Thanks for sayin' that."

She pulls me close and whispers, "We all know why you're here. Them West-Kimbrell boys made a dash through here not long ago to attack families. They killed a few folks, burned a few farms, and stole as much as they could carry. The men winged a few of 'em, but they all got away. Devilish bastards. Freddy and them Tullos boys gave 'em hell when they came to Dorcas's farm." She smiles knowing that would make me proud.

"That's good to hear."

"Yell out when you get close to the house. Freddy's still a bit skittish."

"I'll do that, thank you." I start for the door and grab a pouch of tobacco. I leave a gold eagle on the bar and wink.

"Thanks, Lummy. It'll be a big help." She tests the gold with a bite from her eyetooth, leans over the counter, and yells as I close the door behind me, "Don't be such a stranger. You tell Dorcas that I'll see her and the family at church on Sunday."

I tip my hat. "Yes, 'um."

The wagon road leading up to the house brings back the time Dorcas and I visited Ben's grave. There we found redemption and forgiveness, and shared it.

We stop at the edge of the clearing.

A shotgun barrel slides out an open window. "What do you want?"

A young man, about my height, steps from behind a tall pine with an aimed rifle. "He asked you, 'what do you want?' Ain't gonna ask again." The muscles in his arms ripple like water dancing in a rocky creek, and his face reminds me of someone I knew long ago.

We lift our hands. "Son, if I didn't know better, I'd swear I was talkin' to my big brother Ben, except a bit taller."

The young man lowers the rifle and steps out with a big grin. "Uncle Lummy, what in the hell are you doin' here?"

I elbow J.A. "Talks just like him, too. How do, Tarleton Wesley."

"No harm intended, but I go by Tarle now."

"Then Tarle it is."

A man with thinning hair opens the door and leans the shotgun against the wall. He walks to the edge of the porch, shielding his eyes from the sun. Dorcas's husband, Freddy, laughs. "I swear by the sun rising and the moon waning that I never expected to receive this blessin'. Get down off them nags and get up on this porch to rest your weary bones. Welcome home, brother."

I wink at J.A., and we dismount.

Tarle looks me in the eye as he takes the reins. He looks very familiar but not because he's Ben's son.

I shake his hand. "Tarle, son, you've grown." His grip is stronger than mine. I like that.

"Yes, suh." He grins. "Momma's good cookin' and Poppa Freddy's hard work, I reckon."

I take a second look. "You look like someone I ain't seen in a long time. But for the life of me, it escapes me. It'll come to me."

Tarle yells up to the house. "Mother, you might want to come out here. You ain't gonna believe this."

Dorcas walks out of the house, fixing her hair with one hand, holding a young child in the crook of her other arm. She looks to faint and grabs a post to steady herself.

"It's me, sweet sister. Lummy."

She recovers and smiles like she did when I was a kid. "Lummy Tullos, my dear brother."

I trot up to the house.

She throws out an arm to hug me and gives me a kiss on the lips. "Does my heart good to see you, brother."

"You will always be my sister." I don't want to turn her loose. I need her strength right now.

"I'm so glad you came."

"I needed to be with family, Dorcas. I haven't been gone from home very long, but—"

Dorcas smiles. "You don't miss the water 'til the well runs dry."

"I miss my family, and I'm pretty dry."

Two pretty girls, looking to be around ten or twelve, chase each other out of the house and stop short.

I look at Dorcas, then back to the girls. "No. It can't be. Is this Martha and Amanda?"

Dorcas adjusts the child sitting on her hip. "Yep, it's them. Growin' up way too fast."

"My goodness, how you've grown, girls. I mean, ladies. You're both prettier than all the flowers Creator ever made."

They look to their mother.

"Girls, this is your uncle Lummy. Martha, you may remember him visitin' us a few years ago. Amanda, maybe not."

They rush to hug me, and I scoop them up, one in each arm. "Two of the prettiest girls I ever did see. That is, just a wee tiny half-step behind your beautiful momma, but you'll catch up with her any day now."

Martha hugs my neck, and Amanda lays her head on my shoulder.

Martha kisses my cheek. "I remember you, Uncle Lummy. We're glad you're here."

Amanda jerks her head up. She stares into my eyes, and I swear she's looking into the deepest part of my soul. "You pray like God's sitting right here with us." She said those exact words after I prayed over the last supper I had with them after I killed Dawg Smith.

A good memory never comes without a bad one for me it seems. I shake off the bad. I throw my head back, laughing. "You do remember me." I set them down.

Dorcas smiles with pride and whispers, "Amanda has got that way of seein' the universe like you and Granny Thankful."

I wish I could get to know her better.

Two teenaged boys step out from behind the barn, carrying shotguns, each with three or four squirrels tied to their belts. They lean their guns against the barn and drop their squirrels.

The tallest asks the other, "Who's that?"

They trot over and look me up and down.

The youngest stands straight as a tree and offers his hand like a banker. "Are you who I think you are?"

I give a firm grip that he returns. "I believe I just might be."

"You sure look like Uncle Lummy from the way Momma described you."

The oldest peeks from underneath his hat through ruffled hair that flows to his bent shoulders. He studies me for a moment. "I know who you are. You're Uncle Lummy. I'm Elihu Allen, but I go by just Hugh."

"There ain't no doubtin' that, son. You are Elihu."

Dorcas laughs. "Yep, he has the look of your oldest brother back home."

Freddy walks down the steps. "And his ways in the woods, from what I hear. That boy lives in a hollow tree most of the time." Freddy lays his arms on his son's shoulders. "These two fine young men are proud to wear the Tullos name."

I turn loose of the younger one's hand. "And you must be Monty."

"Yes, suh, but I apologize, I don't remember you."

"That's all right, you will after we talk here in a bit." I take Freddy's hand and pull him close for a hug. "It's so good to see you, brother. Where'd he learn to talk like that? In fact, all your children speak very good English."

"We have a fine school, and the children are fast learners. Monty is becomin' the family scholar. He loves book learnin' and is already doin' some teachin' with the school marm's help. He might be a doctor or a minister someday."

Hugh smiles. "I go to school, but I'd rather be in the woods with the animals and fish."

I laugh. "Me, too."

A young girl about eight peeks out from behind Dorcas's skirt. I shield my eyes and wink at her. "You must be Mary, named after my ma."

She looks up to Dorcas. "Is that right, Momma?"

Dorcas leads her by the hand, and I kneel. "Yes, and that makes you extra special. Your grandma would be very proud to know you are named after her."

I pat Mary's shoulders. "She knows, Mary. I told her."

Little Mary turns red and tries to hide her face. She's cute as a button and twice as shy.

Tarle strides from the barn where he left our horses. It hits me. He stops at my staring. "What? I got somethin' on my face?"

"You sure do, son. You're the spittin' image of your great uncle Silas who fought at New Orleans with General Jackson."

"No foolin'?"

I lay my hand over my heart. "If there's a truth to be told, there it is."

"I wanna know all about him and... my father."

"It'd be my pleasure and privilege." I turn back to Dorcas and pull back the blanket covering the infant's face. "And who might this be?"

Dorcas bounces the child in her arms. "Little Joseph, me and Freddy's first child together."

"A fine boy. I'm so happy for you two. There's a new world on every turn if we just let Creator have his way with us."

Freddy wraps his arm around Dorcas. "Ain't that the truth, brother?"

I soak in the moment. I lay a hand each on Freddy and Dorcas's shoulders. "Somebody once sang that Jesus is a rock in a weary land. So is family."

# CHAPTER 36

# HOME AWAY FROM HOME, FOR A MOMENT

## LATE MORNING, MARCH 12, 1870

*Being home soothes the soul, even if it's not where you live.*

J.A. CLEARS HIS throat.

I squeeze my eyes shut for a second. "Sorry, brother. Y'all, this is J.A., my best friend who saved my life—and often my soul—in Vicksburg."

Freddy takes J.A.'s hand. "I believe we've met."

"We did once, at a cattle auction a year or so ago."

"That's right. I bought two of your calves to butcher for the winter. Good meat. Fine taste."

"Thanks, Freddy. There's more where that came from."

"I'll be sure to find you at the sale in the fall. Y'all come on up and take a taste of spirits." Freddy puts his arm around J.A.'s shoulder as they walk up the steps. "I might be in the market for a few cattle myself. The boys and me cleared some fine pasture land that might turn out some good beef, if they come from good stock like yours."

J.A. grins. "Sounds good. Let's talk after supper and see what we can work out."

I elbow Tarle. "There's two jugs on my horse. Fetch 'em, would you, son?"

"Only if I get to have a taste."

I shrug and look to Dorcas. "He's old enough, don't you think?"

She smiles. "I'm sure it won't be his first drink, but how could I deny him a sip of good Wood brothers' moonshine whiskey made from the sweetest water in Choctaw County, Missip?"

"Straight from Aaron Wood's Spring and stronger than a mule's kick."

Dorcas raises her eyebrow. "He can have a sip, but you make sure that other jug gets in this house. I know what's in there. Ain't nothin' better'n a cool cup of Elihu's muscadine wine."

Freddy rubs his palms together. "Can't wait. I've heard about that sweet nectar of the gods for way too long now."

Dorcas brushes her skirt down as a breeze passes by. "Y'all come eat. You can do your sippin' after supper."

J.A. nods. "You ain't gotta call me twice."

I start up the steps. I'm home.

# CHAPTER 37

# WHEN ANCESTORS ARE REBORN

## EARLY EVENING, MARCH 12, 1870

*Telling the old stories lets ancestors live again.*

FEASTING AT DORCAS'S table is like eating at home—finest food a mouth ever took in. I eat so much I can hardly get to Ben's old rocking chair afterwards. I take out my pipe and knock the bits of old tobacco out on a porch post.

Freddy yells into the house. "Tarle, get my tobacco, would you, son?"

"Yes, sir." Tarle pitches the pouch to Freddy, who hands it to me. Tarle sits on the porch steps, staring into some far off place like Ben used to do. I don't think he's much like Ben, though. He has a different way about him. But Silas? Yeah. He looks like him, walks and talks like him.

I pack the pipe and draw the string on the pouch tight. "If I'm gonna smoke this thing from time to time, guess I need to get my own tobaccy."

J.A. stuffs a wad of tobacco in his mouth. "Do that and you'll get to likin' it too much." He sits on a bench, rubbing his lower back.

I snicker. "Are you all right over there, old man?"

J.A. laughs. "No, I ate too much."

I can't help myself. "What'd you do, J.A.? Get your rump out of joint racin' to the table?"

"Shut up, Lummy. I hurt my back keepin' your long, tall, and sorry ass alive in Vicksburg."

He chuckles. We laugh.

Dorcas yells from the kitchen window. "I heard that. If you don't quit that cussin', come Sunday I'll make you boys listen to the worst preacher known to man, the angels, and the Good Lord himself."

I grimace. "Not that old Cajun preacher who did Ben's funeral?"

Freddy whispers, "Yep."

I whisper back, "Worst damn preacher ever." I yell to Dorcas, "My cussin's done for the day, church lady!"

J.A. mouths, "Church lady makes the best biscuits I believe I've ever tasted."

Freddy laughs and pats his belly. "Good food makes a man well-rounded."

I look down at mine. "Guess I'm gettin' a bit thicker, too."

J.A. spits. "Wasn't gonna say nothin'. Guess it's that good Christian livin', huh?"

I look around to see who is listening. "That and a beautiful wife who makes a man want to stay in the bed 'til noon."

Freddy smiles. "You got that right."

Dorcas sings out from the kitchen. "Freddy Hawthorne. Remember, young ears."

Freddy laughs. "Tarle's a man now, and he needs to know how much I appreciate you in every way."

"Just don't go no further on the subject."

"Yes, ma'am."

I blow tobacco smoke into the air. "Dorcas is as sweet a woman as God ever made."

Freddy sighs. "Ain't it so?"

Tarle rubs his arms. "I appreciate you saying that, Uncle Lummy."

I take another draw from my pipe. "You'll want to marry one just like her. Take your time. She'll be worth the wait."

"I'll remember that, and Freddy, thanks for treating my mother so well. You make her happy."

"Son, I meant every word I said when we took our vows. It ain't just about what happens in the bed that makes for a good marriage. That's a very small part of it. There's a whole lot more."

I relight my pipe. "Tarle, a good woman is to be cherished and loved for who she is, not for what she can give you. The first time I saw Martha at the

Prentiss House Hotel? I felt what Adam did when he got his first glimpse of Eve. Do you remember what I said, J.A.?"

"You said, 'My goodness, would you look at that?'"

Tarle grins. "That must've been somethin'."

I lean back in my chair. "It was, son." I can see her now in my mind—in that blue skirt she wore when I left Vicksburg on a steamboat for Memphis to fight with the Rifles. Then, beholdin' her slender body when light showed through her sheer nightgown the night before we left out on this mission stirs my soul and body.

J.A. elbows me. "That must've been a sight."

I squeeze my eyes tight, embarrassed. "Talking out loud again?"

J.A. nods. "Yep."

Tarle grins. "I've noticed that about you, Uncle Lummy. I remember Pa sayin' you did that a lot because you talk to the Lord that way in the woods."

"He was right. I'm just glad I didn't say with my mouth what all I was seein' in my mind. Otherwise, you boys would've all had, how'd Pa say it... a bad case of the red rooster?" We laugh.

Dorcas isn't laughing, though. "You just wait until I meet your Martha, Lummy, I'm gonna—"

I throw up my hands in surrender. "I'm out. I'm done."

Dorcas steps out on the porch. "You better be, little brother."

I try to recover and do a fine job of it, I believe. "But that aside, Tarle, there's nothin' better than lovin' a wife who loves you back for who you are, not what she tries to make you be." I take another draw from my pipe.

J.A. smiles, but in a sad way. "Ain't that the truth."

I see the hurt in his eyes. "We'll get her home soon enough, brother."

"It's just... I miss her somethin' fierce."

I hang my head to avoid a tear. "I miss Martha, too. Let's get our minds on somethin' else."

J.A. wipes a tear. "That'd be good."

Tarle shields his eyes from the setting sun. "Tell us about Uncle Silas and General Andrew Jackson."

I draw and exhale the sweet tobacco smoke. "All right." I start with my grandpa Willoughy and his brother Temple moving from Georgia to the Mississippi Territory. "Grandpa Willoughby was a hard man with a mean streak. I'm sure that's where my pa and us Tullos boys get it. That and hatin' bullies. Willoughby had slaves, but Pa didn't go for that. It was a point of contention between 'em. In fact, Uncle Silas, son of Temple and Grandpa Willoughby's brother, almost came to blows with Grandpa Willoughby over how badly he treated his slaves. That's a story for another time." I relight my pipe. "J.A., you'll appreciate this. Grandpa Willoughby recorded the first cattle brand in Marion County, Mississippi. That's the only good thing I remember Pa tellin' me about him."

J.A. snickers. "Do tell."

I tell Tarle the stories Uncle Silas told me when he and his wife, Martha, Grandpa Temple, and Granny Thankful came for a visit when I was ten years old. I lay it on thick about Silas being Captain Sam Dale's sidekick and running around the Mississippi Territory during the Creek War.

"In May of '14, Silas enlisted in the 13th Mississippi Regiment Militia under George Nixon. He was only eighteen. Like a lot of the men, Silas got called up just two days before the New Orleans fight. Silas fought the British black troops who tried to flank the Americans in a cypress swamp. The West Indians got pushed back. Uncle Silas said it was a terrible day. Only good thing about it was, besides the Americans beatin' the britches off the British, he got back his childhood Negro friend, Henry, but not as a slave."

I talk about Uncle Silas's fight with Mike Fink at Natchez, his marrying Martha Carney, and the rest of his life lived too short. "Uncle Silas was a man to admire. Granny Thankful said I'm a lot like him." I squint. "So are you, Tarle."

"Thanks, Uncle Lummy. Telling the old stories lets ancestors live again."

"They get reborn all over in the retellin', over and over. Lord willin', and I live through the next few days, I'll finish tellin' them all to your cousin, Mary, who's writin' them down. That'd be somethin'. Tullos family stories put to paper. Maybe they'll end up a book someday." Tarle wants to ask, but I beat him to the punch. "Will stories about Dawg Smith, Vicksburg, and what we're about to do be in there? They will."

J.A. says, "Good, people need to know the truth."

Freddy chimes in, "Like the Lord said, 'The truth will set you free.'"

Tarle stands to stretch. "Uncle Lummy, would you walk with me to the barn. I need to talk private like about that very thing."

"What thing?"

"Being set free."

CHAPTER 38

# THE TULLOS WAY

## AFTER DARK, MARCH 12, 1870

*If a man is to truly become himself, he must be free to
find the story of his ancestors and go from there.*

I GRAB THE moonshine jug and pour two cups half-full. I hand one to
Tarle and nod for us to ease over to the barn.

Freddy gets up. "J.A., how 'bout you and me gettin' a taste of the grape?"

J.A. slaps him on the shoulder. "Lead on, brother."

I put a foot up on a fence rail, and Tarle does the same. I take a deep swal-
low and let it slide down my throat. The burn is good.

Tarle takes a sip and coughs but gets it down. He swirls the remainder
around in his cup. "I don't think I'll ever get used to this stuff."

"Try your uncle Elihu's muscadine wine. It goes down easier and will be
more to your liking."

We enjoy the silence.

I drain my cup and set it on the top of a fence post. "Gotta know where
you've been, to know where you are, to know where you're goin', I always say."

Tarle takes another sip and coughs. "You're right, and sometimes you have
to follow the tracks of those who know the way."

"Wise words from a young man."

"I gotta request, Uncle Lummy. We know why you're here. Mother and
Freddy won't be having it, so I decided to ask you first."

"You want to go with me after the West-Kimbrell Gang?"

"How'd you know?"

"You're a Tullos, ain't you?"

"It's that easy to tell?"

"Just that easy." We let those words soak in. "You haven't talked to your folks yet?"

"No, sir, but I think Mother knows."

"Tell me why you want to go."

"They killed my best friend, Eb."

"What's Eb short for?"

"Ebenezer."

How fitting. "Your friend was black, wasn't he?"

"Yes." Tarle whimpers for a moment. He grits his teeth and kicks the fence rail, breaking it half in two. "They killed him down on Mistuh Gilmore's old South Farm."

"I'm sorry. So, what do you want, son?"

"Make them pay."

"Do you want revenge or reckonin'?"

"Ain't it the same?"

"No, there's a big difference."

Tarle leans in. "How so?"

"Revenge turns into murder, which can lead to more killin'. Reckonin' is settin' things straight, makin' things right and equal again. Then, you walk away and try not to look back."

"You mean justice."

"Right."

Tarle picks up the two broken fence rails. "Revenge is in my heart, but reckoning is what needs to happen. I want justice for my friend, and I have to help. Do you understand?"

I chuckle. "Yeah, I do." I stare at the broken fence rails in Tarle's hands. "It's like that. Your friendship with Eb was broken, but not by your hand. You must set things right but not keep breakin' fence rails, you understand?"

"Yes, sir, I do. I can't carry what happened to Eb and what's about to happen with me the rest of my life."

"You've got a good head on your shoulders, son. Make sure you use it."

"Will you back me up when I ask the folks about going with you and J.A.?"

I stare into his eyes long enough to make him uncomfortable.

He looks away.

"That, you cannot do, Tarle."

Tarle looks back and doesn't blink. "It's tough staring back. Your eyes are turning into the Devil's eyes."

"You have to become the Devil himself to survive. You cannot look away. When you step too close to a cottonmouth, do you look around or up in the trees? You keep your eyes on him. You have to look the Devil dead in the eye and let him know you ain't backin' down."

Tarle doesn't break eye contact. "I can do that."

I squint and study him. "You better, or you'll be dead." I soften a bit. "I believe you can."

"So, you'll go with me when I ask?"

"If you promise me one thing."

"Anything."

"That you'll do as I say, when I say."

Tarle straightens his shirt collar and stiffens. "I will obey every word you say, Uncle Lummy."

"If you don't, I'll kick your ass and send you home. Understood?"

"Yes, sir."

"Then, let's go."

"Now?"

"No time better than right now. Besides, we leave before sunup."

# CHAPTER 39

# ASKING FOR WHAT I DON'T WANT

## NIGHT, MARCH 12, 1870

*A boy starts to become a man when he puts on his father's boots.*

DORCAS STANDS, KNOCKING her chair over. "No way am I gonna let Tarle go with y'all."

Freddy gently pulls her back down. "Just hear Tarle out, dear."

I lay my hand on Dorcas's arm. "He's no boy, Dorcas. Not anymore."

Dorcas cries, "He's *my* boy!"

Tarle consoles, "I always will be, Mother, but please understand what I need to do. They murdered Eb."

"Just like your wild ass father, rushin' off to get killed, and for what?"

"Mother, you know why Pa went off that day."

Dorcas lays her head down. "I'm so sorry, Lummy, I didn't mean—"

"You have every right to be upset, but Tarle has to do what he has to do."

"And his mother has to live with whatever happens. Freddy, what am I gonna do?"

"What you always do, dear. You'll pray and be ready to welcome him home."

Dorcas squeezes my arm. "You'll bring my boy home?"

"He'll never be out of my sight."

"J.A.?"

"Ma'am, if he's with us, we can teach him how to do the Lord's work right and deal with his soul after it's over."

Dorcas shakes her head. "You're right. But we've had too many leave us too soon. I won't survive if my Tarle doesn't come home."

I turn to Tarle. "Maybe you should think about stayin' home."

"My mind's made up. I'm almost twenty-two and born a Tullos in Missip. Nobody's gonna stop me from doin' what needs doin'. They killed my best friend, and they're gonna pay." Tarle is well-built in form and soul. "If you leave me, I'll sneak off and find my own way. Either way, I'm goin'." Just like Matt Poole. I'd do the same. Heck, I did.

Dorcas wipes her eyes and stuffs the kerchief in her apron pocket. "All right then. You do what your uncle Lummy says and keep your head down. If you don't have to be in the fight, don't. And you make sure you—"

Tarle wraps his arms around his mother. "It'll be all right, Mother. Trust the One who's sending us, and trust the ones I'm going with."

"I will, son. I'll be prayin' every minute of the day until you get back."

"Uncle Lummy, what gun should I take?"

Dorcas drops her head on the table.

Freddy rubs her shoulders.

I nod to Tarle. "Let's talk about that in a minute. Go pack a change of clothes, get your huntin' knife, and sack us up some food if you don't mind."

Tarle walks away slump shouldered. He's not happy he's made his mother sad, but he's doing what he has to do. I went through the same thing with Ma, Susannah, and Martha when it came time for me to leave. I left too many times when I wanted to stay. It's the part I hate the most about all of this.

When Tarle gets to the other side of the dogtrot, I try to comfort Dorcas. "I'll keep him by my side the entire time, Dorcas. I promise you. Better he goes with us than him showin' up when I don't expect it."

Dorcas dries her eyes. "You're right. He needs to do this. Hell, if I was a man and didn't have these children, I'd be goin' with you." She props her elbows on the table. "He's had so many questions about his father's death. I don't have the answer except that Tullos men won't stand for bullyin', and Lord knows what they do if family is hurt in the process."

I rub her forearm. "Grandpa Temple said that goes all the way back even before Cloud, who came from Scotland in the sixteen hundreds. Our way of seein' the world started with the people painted blue who danced naked around the fire in the deep woods and left carvings on stones scattered about the countryside. They shed blood to keep the Romans out. They succeeded. That blood runs thick in Tullos folk. It has to be satisfied, or we ain't fit to live with."

"That I do know."

"A boy starts to become a man when he puts on his father's boots, even if they don't fit yet."

Dorcas sighs. "He's already started fillin' those boots."

Tarle brings his things and sets them by the door. "I'm ready."

Dorcas turns her head. "God will protect him, won't he?"

J.A. leans in like when we aimed our rifles at the Yanks attacking the 27th Louisiana Lunette in Vicksburg and growls like a bear. "We will make sure."

Tarle stands wide-eyed, not knowing what to say.

There's nothing to be said.

"You're a Tullos, ain't you?"

# CHAPTER 40

# THE BETTER PART
# OF MEMORIES

## BEFORE DAYLIGHT, MARCH 13, 1870

*Sometimes remembering only the better part of memories just won't do.*

A BITING WIND tries to steal the last bit of dawn as the sun's spring warmth chases the chill away. The talk Tarle and I'll have will add to the cool brisk air. Tarle needs to know his father. Besides his mother, I knew him best.

J.A. knows Tarle wants to talk. He prods his horse. "I'm gonna ease on up the road a bit and do some thinkin' if y'all don't mind."

Tarle asks, "Just how good a friend is J.A., Uncle Lummy?"

"Good enough to die for."

"Y'all fought in the war together, but did you have a close friend like him growing up in Choctaw County?" He's fishing now.

"I did. His name was Thomas Poole. We just called him Poole. The Good Book says, 'There is a friend who sticketh closer than a brother.' I've been blessed to have had two."

Dan Creekwater, Annie Fanny, Mr. Wiley, Mr. and Mrs. Davis, Mr. Gilmore, Old Bart, and Rainy Mills come to mind. Creator has always given me good friends—friends willing to die for me. Some did. I need to count my blessings more, as Granny used to say.

Tarle glances over. "Is Poole still in Choctaw County?"

I look straight ahead. "Yeah, he's buried there."

"I'm sorry, I didn't—"

"It's all right. You'll get to meet his nephew, Matt. He came with us."

"Really?"

"Yeah, and for the same reasons you're coming with us."

Tarle ponders my words. Here comes the question. "My pa wasn't a very good brother, was he?"

"Ben was difficult to be around, but he was always there when I needed him most. You want the truth?"

"With no sugar thrown on it."

"All right, then. Your pa wasn't treated very well by our father. None of us were. Don't get me wrong, we loved our pa, but he had a mean streak in him that got out of control sometimes."

Tarle cuts in. "And he took it out on y'all."

"In the worst kind of way sometimes. You've got to understand, most folks raise their children like they tame farm animals. They break an animal's spirit with a whip, or whatever they can get their hands on at the time, to train them into somethin' useful. Problem is that don't work on some children. Your pa and me were children made with feelin's that could be hurt pretty easy. That didn't go well with bein' told we weren't worth anythin' and got whipped if we talked back or did somethin' wrong."

"So, Grandpa Archy did that?"

"He did. But as I grew older, I realized that our pa got it worse than we did, and he was only doin' the best he knew how."

"I remember Grandpa Archy. I was little, but I remember him rocking me on the front porch. He was talkin' to some people, I don't remember who, and pointing at his chest."

"He was showing them where the doctor said he had a cancer that couldn't be cured. That wasn't too long before he died. I'm glad you have that memory. It's one to keep. Your grandpa softened up as he grew older. We all do in time. He even realized his wrongs, but it was too late. And so would your pa, had he lived. But the damage was done, and there was no makin' it right in our lives. Me, my brothers, and our sister Rebecca dealt with it the best we could. Most of us left early because our pa acted like he didn't want us around."

"How'd it all end up?"

"I was one of the fortunate ones. Pa and I made peace before I left to come here. Said he was sorry, and I accepted his apology. Pa changed there at the last." I ponder that a moment. "You know, Tarle, I had to let him change. If I didn't, who would I be, and how could I expect somebody to let me change when my time of enlightenment comes?"

"I never thought of it that way."

"Me, either, until I got older. Wisdom is a wonderful thing if you gain it and use it."

"Did my pa make peace with Grandpa Archy?"

We pass the general store in Sikes. I search every shadow and corner hoping no one is out before daylight. Except for Madison rattling pots and pans in the Sikes Store kitchen, it's quiet.

I shift in my saddle. "He didn't. That was one of his biggest regrets and the reason for his drinking. His pain could never be healed."

"Tell me about Pa. Mother only tells us the better parts of who he was."

"Why do you want to know?"

"So I can choose to be the best parts of him. I know about his drinking."

"He drank, sometimes too much, but it never interfered with his work. He always worked hard, sometimes too hard, but provided well for his family."

"Ma speaks about how hard he worked for us. He died when I was fourteen. But I also remember his rage and meanness."

"I will say that he was better than our pa when it came to controllin' his temper."

"But it was his mouth that did the most damage."

"It was the same with our pa. Ben became everything he hated about your grandpa Archy. The moonshine just made it worse. That, and your grandpa dying before they made peace. I sat with him the night he read the letter from Ma about Pa dyin'. He cried like a baby."

"So, you made peace with Grandpa Archy. Why didn't Pa?"

"I did, but remember, y'all left Choctaw County several years before I did. Your grandpa, what's the word, had mellowed?"

"That's the word."

"Your grandpa hadn't changed before your ma and pa left Choctaw County."

"That's too bad."

"It is. Things might have been different." I ponder that a minute. "I loved your brother and enjoyed workin' with him. In fact, workin', huntin', and fishin' were the best times we had together. That, and cuttin' up in church every chance we got, even as adults. We never had a problem doin' any of that stuff until Ben picked up the jug. Then, things went straight to hell."

"Did y'all ever fight?"

"Not after we grow'd up. We came close, though. Be careful about the jug, Tarle—"

"I won't. Too many bad memories. And besides, Freddy has been different toward us."

"That's easy to see, and who's to say that your father didn't give his life for another so you kids could have what you needed in Freddy to grow up?"

"Freddy came along at just the right time."

"Let's just remember the best parts of your pa, what do you say?"

"Sounds good."

We prod our horses into a trot and catch up with J.A. at Royal and skirt the small village. We pass Smithtown without seeing a soul and cross Piney Woods Creek where Ben and I used to fish after church service. We slow our mounts to a walk when the Shiloh Baptist Church roof comes into view.

"J.A., we're early. Mind if Tarle and me visit Mistuh Gilmore's old home place? And you know what else."

"Y'all go ahead. I'll wait on Sarge, Rainy, and Matt to get here. See you in a bit."

I tip my hat and spur my horse. "C'mon, Tarle."

# CHAPTER 41

# RUNNING TOWARD PAIN

## MID-MORNING, MARCH 13, 1870

*Sometimes it's tough to tell if you're runnin' from somethin' or straight at it.*

O LD FEELINGS SLITHER out of the pit I'd stuffed them into. A thousand thoughts race through my head, and I make my horse run. Tarle tries to keep up as I duck and dodge tree limbs on the old deer path shortcut I used when I worked for Mr. Gilmore. I dig my heels into my horse. I can't tell if I'm running to something or away from it. I want to be somewhere else. I want to be home. I want to be with Martha.

I skid my horse up to the remains of the house Mr. Gilmore built, where I saw Susannah for the first time after leaving Choctaw County. My mind races—the fight, the flames of the burning house, the smell of smoke, the heat, Dawg Smith's devilish laugh, Susannah screaming. I fall off my horse. I'm up like a cat as quick as I hit the ground, knife in hand ready to kill.

Horse hooves come at a run. I grab the reins and raise my knife to stab—

"Uncle Lummy, it's me!"

"Ben, is that you?" I drop the knife, and I shake my head.

Tarle dismounts and brings a canteen. He splashes water on my face.

For a moment, I realize where I am and who I'm with. Footsteps sneak through the brush, and I jerk my pistol. "To arms!" I don't know why I said that. Guess I heard it too many times at Vicksburg when we thought the Yankees were coming.

Tarle draws a pistol Freddy had given him. "Uncle Lummy, what do I do?"

"Do what I do, Ben."

A few old men and boys ease out of a thicket with pitchforks, axe handles, and a couple of old muskets. I'm too weak to get up.

Tarle holsters his pistol and throws up his hands. "It's me, Tarle Tullos, from Sikes. My pa was Ben, a friend of Mistuh Gilmore. My best friend was Eb."

An old graying gentleman speaks up. "We'z sorry, but we just know'd y'all be dem Nightriders a'comin' in here fast. We was gonna fight 'em or die tryin'."

I take a sip of water and calm down. My waking dream, or whatever the hell you call it, passes, and I stand to dust off my clothes. "No, suh, we ain't Nightriders or with John West. But we came here for just that reason though. Their day is over, and we aim to see it through."

The old man dances. "Glory be, it's da Year of Jubilee when all God's chil'ren go free!"

An old woman steps from behind the crowd of men. "You know'd my grandson, Ebenezer?"

Tarle kicks the dirt. "Yes, 'um, I did. We spent many a day hunting and fishing together. We just didn't let on about our friendship, as much as I hated that. We didn't want the West gang to find out and bring terror down on you good folks or my family either. Eb was my best friend."

The old woman cries for a moment, then lifts her head high. In perfect English, she yells, "O Lord, protect these good men who will bring your wrath down upon those wicked Nightriders. Let them terrorize the terrorists! Send Michael, the Protector of Your People, to lead them into battle. Your goodness will win over evil, for You are our great Creator, and You will not let your people fail." She faints, and a couple of men catch her before she hits the ground.

Tarle leans over. "She was a house servant at a big plantation over in Alabama for years before Mistuh Gilmore won her in a card game. Eb told me so."

"But how'd she know what we're up to?"

Tarle shrugs. "He said she was some kind of seer."

I whisper, "She's one to listen to and take her words to heart."

# CHAPTER 42

# SITTING
# WITH SUSANNAH

## LATE MORNING, MARCH 13, 1870

*Eternity separates only for a time for those meant to be together.*

T HE OLD MAN hands his pitchfork to a boy beside him. "Come with us and have a bite. You got a meetin' here in a bit, but you can take time for a salt pork biscuit."

Tarle tips his hat and ties off the horses. "We appreciate it, sir."

The old man motions for us to follow. We walk a familiar path, past where Mr. Gilmore and I had buried the money that I shared with Old Bart after killing Dawg Smith. The old man leads us through a small patch of woods to a clearing where ten or more cabins stand with children playing everywhere. The sound of their laughter makes me homesick, but I'm one day closer to being home.

Women and children wander out. Built from local trees, the cabins stand strong and proud like the people who built them. The older women and men whisper and point at me. Their eyes widen, and their mouths drop open. They rush to hug and kiss me, telling how much they appreciate me and how sad they still are that Susannah passed. I hug them all and throw some of the young children into the air and catch and cuddle them.

Tarle smiles. "These are your people, Uncle Lummy."

I gather as many of the kids as I can lift them up. "Ain't it so?" I'm thinking, with Elzey here somewhere, more than he knows.

Tarle grins. "And another day closer to these people being free of those damned Nightriders."

"Talkin' out loud?"

"Mother told me you do that on occasion."

"It's just a habit, sometimes good, sometimes bad."

"I appreciate how you talk to the Lord. It's like he's always with us."

"He is, and I need Him to be right now. Go ahead and get your food. I'll be along in a bit."

The old man points. "You know where to go, and you need to sit a spell, son. I'll check on you in a bit." He nods and waves. "Go on now, you don't have a lot of time."

There's something familiar about the gentleness of this old man.

I tip my hat and take a shortcut through the woods to the place where Susannah rests. I'm not sure about this, but I have to visit and talk with my first love. The place has grown up a bit, but her grave is neatly kept with all sorts of offerings laid about—old flowers and pictures from catalogs, handmade crosses and carved animals, cups and bowls, spoons and forks, dolls' heads and other children's toys, a knife and a razor, medicine bottles, and a mirror. I'm not sure what these offerings mean but surely something good.

Mr. Davis had had a porcelain angel set on top of her stone. Someone painted the angel's white skin dark brown and the eyes black. A beautiful black angel.

Susannah.

I look away, then back. I can't keep my eyes from staring into the angel's eyes that capture my soul. I drop to my knees. All that surrounds me fades, except the small angel statue. I grip the agate stone that Granny gave me. I want Granny with me. I squeeze my eyelids tight.

The sound of trickling water in a crystal clear stream sings a heavenly tune. As it draws closer, I tremble. A voice behind me whispers, *"Do not be afraid, boy, she comes to give you strength."*

I turn to see Granny disappear in a wisp of smoky flowing robes.

*"Lummy, darling, I'm here."*

I jerk my head back around, and Susannah, glowing like the sun, stands still, tall, and as beautiful as I have ever seen her. "It's you. It's really you."

*"It is. I will be with you until your work is complete. Then, I shall see you on*

*that great day when you and I will forever run through fields of green under skies of always blue."*

"But I don't want you to go away. I need your guidance still."

*"She will guide you to the place of peace only she can provide. You know this."*

I hang my head. "I do. Martha has been a gift sent by Creator."

Susannah smiles. *"That I asked for on your behalf. Enjoy the gifts of Creator. Your time in this place is almost over."*

"Is what I'm doin' right, Susannah?"

*"You know the answer to your question. They stand all around you."*

I see Seth, Mr. Allrice, Momma Sophie, Old Bart, and all murdered by slavers, masters, overseers, and Nightriders.

The multitude stands still, but tall and straight. They all say in one voice, *"It is for right that you do this thing."*

And they disappear in a misty fog.

*"Lummy,"* Susannah whispers, *"it is for love you have come to this place. It is for love that Creator will keep you and yours safe. But one very dear to you will fall. Have no fear, his name is already written in the Book. Mourn for me no longer and live as Creator has blessed you—freedom from all that has hindered your happiness."*

"What about the memories, the war dreams I have? Granny said they will get worse."

*"They will, in time, so live Creator's will as he lays it before you. Know this. You will be cared for in the same manner you cared for others. I must go now. I leave you a token of the eternity that separates only a short time for those meant to be together."*

Susannah disappears, as does the great throng surrounding me. A gentle breeze sweeps past, and I catch a glimpse of Granny's flowing robes rising into the sky.

A multicolored feather floats from the heavens and lands at my knees. I place it in the band on my hat. "I am not alone."

A voice behind me whispers, "No, you're not."

I turn, unsure of what or who I'll find. "How long have you been standing there, Tarle?"

"Long enough to know that you loved Susannah with everything you have in you."

I lay my head in my hands. "She was the love my life, and now she says I'll not see her again until I meet her on the other side."

"That's something to look forward to. That and your wife back home, who Susannah must be pleased that you now have."

"Susannah freed me to love another a long time ago, but my love for her is eternal."

"And that's a good thing."

"It is." I point at the objects scattered about. "What's this?"

"Eb said people put those items on graves to keep the dead where they are so they won't come back amongst the living."

"So that the livin' don't get scared and the dead stay in their better place on the other side?"

"I reckon so." Tarle has something on his mind. "Tell me again the story of how my pa died? I need that picture in my head for what we're about to do."

I understand why he asks. "It ain't pretty. Are you sure, son?"

"I am."

"Be mindful that these words can take your heart. Do not let them take your soul." I tell him the story from start to finish. One minute he tears up, in the next, he clenches his fists.

I finish, and he wipes the tears from his eyes. "You all right?"

"I am, and don't worry about me. I don't have the rage you and Pa had to deal with."

"Then you're ready to bring the kind of justice that Tullos men won't stand by and not make happen. It just ain't our way. It is because of the love I had for Susannah that your pa is buried in Friendship Baptist Church graveyard. His sacrifice gave life to many others."

Tarle lays a cedar branch by the stone. "Here lies the woman my pa died trying to save. I want to be like him."

"Ben is proud of you, son."

We sit with our backs against a pine tree and eat a salt pork biscuit. We walk back to the clearing so I can address the crowd of freed men and women. I can't get Elzey off my mind.

The old man brings our horses and smiles. "I knows you gots to make your plans and all, but could you and your friends come back here after your meetin'? We plannin' somethin' special for you good men of God."

I look at Tarle, and he shrugs. "Okay by me."

I whisper in the old man's ear, "There's somethin' else I'll want to do when I come back."

"Yassuh, I knows what that is. He'll be here when you get back."

I shake the old man's hand. "Then I'll wait till then."

I can't wait to see my son, Elzey.

"That'd be wise. Might I say a prayer over you fine angels as you make your plans?"

"Sure. Just know that I consider myself a dark angel in need of much mercy and grace."

The old man stares into my eyes with the fire of Michael's flaming sword. "Sometimes it's the heart of the darkest angel whose light shines the brightest. It's because he knows he needs his Creator." He looks to the sky. "Let me say a word of prayer."

We remove our hats.

The old man calls to the Lord, "Wait on the Lord and be of good courage. Expect Him to come. He will strengthen thine heart. Wait, I say, on the Lord, and hope for and expect the Lord. Amen."

"Thank you. What is your name, suh?"

"Nathaniel, but folks just call me Old Nate."

"I knew an Old Bart who used to live in these parts. He was my black grandfather. Did you know him?"

"I knew him but not well. We got separated when he was sold when we was just boys. I didn't come to these parts until after the war. I don't think he knew I was still alive."

"How'd you know him? Was he an acquaintance, kin, or a friend?"

"Son, he was my brother."

# CHAPTER 43

# THE MEETING AT SHILOH BAPTIST CHURCH

## NOON, MARCH 13, 1870

*An evil man seeketh only rebellion; therefore a cruel*
*messenger shall be sent against him.*
*—Proverbs 17:11*

WE TIE OUR horses to a hitching post in the shade of a great old oak. It reminds me of the tree Pa sat under after a good day's work. There's even an old straight back chair leaning against the trunk just like Pa's. It's a good memory. I need one right now. I wonder what dreams and visions the sitter has had in this sacred place. I can almost see Mr. Gilmore there, pondering secrets of the universe. But Rainy sits there now with his hat pulled down over his face, snoring.

I kick the chair, and Rainy flails around, trying not to fall out of his seat. Tarle laughs.

"Damn you, Lummy, I was dreaming about a woman the Lord said he will send me. You kicked the chair just before I could see her face."

I don't take such dreamings lightly. "If she's the one, brother, it will be revealed. Why are you out here anyway? You should be inside listenin'—"

"Aw, I don't care anything about listening to a sermon. Besides, I was waiting for you two to show up. I figure that's my cue to show my face, when things start to happen. I've never been much for pew sitting, but I do listen to the Lord when he speaks, especially in a dream."

"That's what I like most about you, Rainy. Let's get inside and see what the fuss is all about."

As I walk up the steps, I remember good times attending church services with Ben, Dorcas, and the children. I can almost hear Mr. Gilmore's hearty "amens" after Ben had taken a visiting preacher to task on some sermon point he'd disagreed with.

I stop and listen. The speaker rails on about how the West-Kimbrell Gang has brought hell to earth for way too long. It's David Pierson, the lawyer I met on the train.

I open both doors at once. Rainy and I walk in, side by side, just as David quotes a scripture. Tarle trails in behind us.

"And God said in the Proverbs—" David swallows hard when he see us. "Yes, yes, God said, 'An evil man seeketh only rebellion. Therefore a cruel messenger shall be sent against him.'" His jaw drops, and everyone in the room turns to see us enter the building.

A familiar man with a thick beard announces, "If it ain't the death angel himself and his servant dressed in black. Hellfire and damnation has come for the West-Kimbrell boys."

No one moves. We look around to find an empty pew.

Rainy snickers. "Some of these folks look as out of place in church as a mule in a parlor."

I elbow him. "Just like you and me, brother."

David Pierson raps his brass handled cane on the speaker's stand. He nods as I remove my hat. "As the Good Book says, 'Be not forgetful to entertain strangers... for thereby some have entertained angels unawares.'"

Sheriff Barnett rises "And those angels are amongst us now."

Rainy leans over. "Don't think I've ever been called that before."

I bump him with my shoulder. "I'm sure of it."

Sheriff Barnett laughs. "There's all kinds of angels, son. Thanks for coming, Lummy. Rainy and Tarle, you, too. We need organizing like when we took down Dawg Smith. But first, listen to Jim Maybin, recently returned from his visit with Governor Warmoth in New Orleans."

I start for an empty pew near the back behind Sarge, Ise, and Matt. Tarle sits and slides down, and Rainy follows him. Before I can sit, the room grows quiet as midnight in a graveyard. One man stands to shake my hand, then another, and another, until over half the men crowd around me to offer solemn welcomes.

A man dressed in homespun and long hair gasps. "You're the one we gave the silver badge to back in '63, ain't you?"

I hold up the honorary badge. "My friends here with me are your servants to right the wrongs that still plague this land. Some of you remember me, but I ask that you call me by the name Handerson. I still have family in these parts, and I don't want any harm to come to them because of me. The rest of these men you will only know by their first names. Rainy, Ise, Matt, and Sarge, and of course, you know J.A. After we hear from Mistuh Maybin, Sarge has a few words for you before you make a plan."

They nod and return to their seats.

J.A. pats me on the back. "We couldn't do this without you, Lummy."

# CHAPTER 44

# WHEN THE GOVERNOR CAN'T, GOOD MEN WILL

### 12:15 P.M., MARCH 13, 1870

*Being set free to go as a far as necessary removes all limitations.*

JIM MAYBIN, A stocky man, walks with a limp to the front with a small satchel. David Pierson stands beside him.

J.A. leans over. "I know Jim. He got shot in the leg at Port Hudson. He reminds me of you. He ain't afraid of nothin'."

Tarle whispers, "He's a good man. He and Freddy do business together. Freddy says there ain't a more honest man."

I rub my chin. "That's good. From the looks of things, I believe we may have the best Winn Parish has to offer."

Jim lays the satchel on the pulpit. "I'll make this short, 'cause I ain't runnin' for office and ain't lookin' for no collection." A few men snicker, but a mood of uncertainty shrouds the room. "Y'all know I did my duty for God and the Confederate States of America. When the war ended, I swore an oath to the flag my father fought under during the Mexican War. That being said, we ain't fighting each other no more. No, we're fighting Satan and his band of demons, the West-Kimbrell Gang. You must know that I've got nothing for this weak ass government that can't even protect itself, much less our homes and families. When me and a few others decided we'd had enough, I knew the U.S. Army Major General Rousseau wouldn't lift a finger to help us. So, I decided to go straight to the Governor of Louisiana, the honorable Henry Clay Warmoth.

"I gave him a detailed account of all that's transpired these past few years and named John West and Laws Kimbrell as the leaders. I was received with great interest on his part, but to put it to you straight, his hands are tied. Congress won't let him raise a militia, and without that, he could do little to quell the reign of terror sweeping Louisiana. Yes, I was disappointed, but not discouraged from completing my mission. I asked the governor if there was anything I could do.

"He replied, 'I never said this, but here's what you need to do. Go back to Winn Parish, gather up a posse, and hunt down West and the entire clan.' I was a bit shocked, and at first resisted his suggestion, until I realized there was no other way. I argued that the carpetbagger court officials would charge us with murder if we did his bidding. The governor smiled and offered the support available to him." Maybin thrusts the satchel into the air.

Sarge whispers, "I know what's in that satchel. They can deal with the devil and still come out as righteous angels."

One man stands. "What about the real law? Won't we get hanged for killin' these bastards?"

Sarge bears down on the man holding his hat in his hand. "Some people worry so much about doing the wrong thing that they never do the right thing. Don't let that be you, friend."

Maybin opens his satchel and holds up a thick stack of papers. "Signed and sealed pardons for all men who'll join us in ridding the earth of the West-Kimbrell Gang."

The men throw up a cheer.

Maybin pats the air to quiet them. "His exact words were these as he signed each pardon. 'You can go as far as necessary. You have complete executive clemency in your hand.'"

Sarge whispers again, "You boys won't need to have one of those. We're covered by Grant's executive order, and we'll be out of here quicker'n shit through a goose when the deed is done."

Maybin steps down. "I'm done, except you should all know I'll guard these papers with my life and make them be available as soon as we take those bastards down."

# CHAPTER 45

# WHEN IT GETS PERSONAL, IT GETS UGLY

## 12:30 P.M., MARCH 13, 1870

*Some things you gotta put your whole heart into,*
*otherwise you'll lose it.*

**D**AVID PIERSON CALLS the meeting to order again. "Before we greet our guests, Jim Maybin just told me we need to hear from Dan Dean, recently from Texas, where he's been hiding from West. Give him your ear."

Some of the men bristle at Dean's introduction, knowing he's been party to some of the gang's wickedness and about his friendship with Laws Kimbrell.

Dean, a man of few words, wastes no time. "Let me get straight at it. I've done wrong, but I'm here trying to make amends and help bring that bastard West down. West wanted to show me how I could make some easy money. I arrived at the appointed time to find the glass peddler, Dutch Jones, bound and gagged, sitting on a stone that covered one of West's death wells."

J.A. growls, "Them boys dug cisterns to throw dead bodies into. Sons of bitches, anyway."

Dean points at J.A. "That's exactly what they planned to do. When I challenged West about killin' Jones, Laws Kimbrell pointed his gun at me, intendin' to shoot me 'cause I wasn't goin' along with it and bein' a witness. West saved me because he thought I'd join the gang. Laws put a bullet in poor ole Dutch's head and chunked him down the well. I couldn't believe it, but they let me go. I didn't tell nobody about what I'd seen, not even my parents. John West realized he'd made a mistake and tried to lure me into a meeting so he could kill me. I disappeared. Can I have some water, please?"

Ise leans over. "That man's shakin' like a possum shittin' a peach pit."

I want to laugh, but it's really not funny what Dan Dean has gone through.

Dean drinks the entire dipper of water, swallowing hard. "I'm a man who wants the same thing as you—a wife, children, home, and a farm."

When he says those words, killing Dawg Smith flashes through my mind. I press the owl claw into my wrist. It helps.

"If I was to ever have those things, I'd have to come home. Fearing West would eventually find me, and him having outlaw friends in East Texas, I decided to come back. West sent several letters inviting me back for a sit down. The last one was written in blood. Whose I don't know, but he sketched a coffin at the bottom of the letter."

Several men gasp and curse.

"Before I could contact Jim Maybin to join what you're doin' here today, one of West's men came to my father's house and said West wanted to have a few words with me. They already knew I was back. There was no escapin' the situation. I went to the old Peck Gin where we were supposed to meet. Knowin' that the Prison Well, as they called it, wasn't far away, I figured they'd hold me there until they decided what to do with me. As I rode up to the gin, I figured West still wanted me in the gang when I wasn't shot by a sniper."

David Pierson accidently drops his cane, and Dean ducks like he's been shot at. David apologizes. "Son, it's all right, take your time."

Dean grasps the podium like he'll break it. "I got off my horse, and West said, 'Dan, let's settle our differences. You need me, and I need you.' He stepped to the side, and a woman with a baby sat cowering by the gin wall. I couldn't help but show my anguish, and in a blink, West shot her dead. What happened next, I—" Dean cries and drops to a knee.

J.A. rushes to the front and comforts the man. "Tell it all. We need to hear it. We need the rage. A good friend of mine taught me that."

Sarge whispers, "And that right there is why J.A. needs to lead this bunch."

Dan straightens up and wipes his face. "All right, you asked for it. After he shot the woman dead, West turned to me and said, 'Look, I've fooled with you long enough. Take that baby by its dress, knock its brains out, and we'll be even. And you'll live!' That cut my heart in two. I screamed, 'I'll see you in hell first. Kill your own babies. Then go teach your Sunday school.'" Dean swallowed hard. "West grabbed the baby and dashed its head against a gin post, dropped it beside the dead mother, and turned to me with with both guns drawn."

Men curse, some men stand and shout, and some cry like babies.

Rainy speaks up. "'All cruelty springs from weakness,' the philosopher Seneca once said."

Dean agrees and draws in a deep breath, having let out the evil story he's been holding for too long. It's like he's breathing in fresh air for the first time in a long time.

Tarle asks Rainy, "What does that mean?"

Rainy quips, "To be kind in this world, you must make an effort to possses qualities above the average man—strength of character, self-mastery, aware-ness, and courage. Cruelty shows up in a person who has not those qualities."

Tarle whispers, "I need to spend more time with you."

Rainy grins. "That can be arranged."

The men quell their outrage and settle back into their seats.

"The showdown was on, and you'd think I was dead in the water, but West was so mad he couldn't shoot worth a shit. He shot my hat off, but I gave the bastard a new part in his hair. He fired all of his rounds and had blood all in his eyes. I should'a shot his ass, but for some reason I didn't. Laws Kimbrell did nothing, and I rode away. But that was only the first gunfight. I stopped by my father's house, told him all that happened, and he advised me to go see Sheriff Joe Adams. Before I could, West and his men rode up. A second gunfight broke out, but they retreated. Makin' sure my family was all right, I left for Winnfield. I decided on the way that Sheriff Adams was in cahoots with West, so that'd do me no good. I figured to join Jim Maybin here and help recruit anyone willin' to fight the Nightriders." With that, Dan Dean sits down.

David Pierson taps his cane hard on the floor. "So, before some of you men get too riled up at Dan, know that he's a changed man, willing to sacrifice himself to help us clean out the West-Kimbrell gang." He turns to me and nods.

I return the favor.

# CHAPTER 46

# WHEN TALKIN'
# LEADS TO KILLIN'

## 12:40 P.M., MARCH 13, 1870

*I don't talk much, but when I do, it's usually with my hands. Bloody hands.*

"LUMMY TULLOS, IT'S good that the man who relieved Dawg Smith of his head is here to help us defeat the West-Kimbrell Gang. Would you say a few words before we discuss our plan?"

I nod. "This morning, young Tarle here, who y'all know as Benny Frank's son, and I were reminded of why we came to help. My first wife lays cold in the ground because of ruffians like those we'll go after soon. The men you seek have but a few days to live. They don't know that yet, but soon they will. All I ask is that we get the killin' done quick and go back to our families, farms, and businesses where we belong. Don't let Satan infect you with the same love of killin' and lust for blood as them. If you do, you'll become just like them. Know the truth of why we have to do this. We're goin' on a wolf hunt, and we will have to kill. We do this to protect innocent lives—your wives and sweethearts, children, and property. And to give our Negro brothers and sisters their new found right to... what are the words, David?"

"Life, liberty, and the pursuit of happiness."

Sheriff Barnett adds, "And justice for all."

"Yeah, the things all Americans are promised. So that you know who we are, this is Sarge, who I rode with during the war with the First Mississippi Mounted Rifles." Sarge salutes. "The one dressed in black is Rainy. You might have done some gun buying or repair business with him. Our black brother here is Ise, short for Isaiah. He's Susannah's brother and a seasoned soldier who fought for the blue in the war. Matt, the tall and lean one, is the nephew of my other best friend who died doin' the same thing we're about to do here, but in Choctaw County, Missip. J.A. you know as one of the finest citizens in the parish. We are here to help you save Winn Parish, and by God, we will. I'll speak the words of a great man who I follow in the newspaper. 'If there is no struggle, there is no progress.' Frederick Douglas said that." I let those words sink in. "I don't talk much, but when I do, I talk with my hands. Bloody hands." I sit down.

The silence is thick enough to cut with a knife. The man with the thick black beard who spoke earlier and looks like he's plowed with a mule all of his life stands. "You don't remember me, Lummy, but I worked on Mistuh Gilmore's farm with you and Ben back in '59 and '60."

I strain to see his face through a thick beard and long hair. "Mose Cockersham? It's been too long, old friend. Good to see your face, or at least what little I can see."

Everyone laughs.

Mose chuckles. "Yeah, my wife has about had enough of this rug. I'll shave it off after this."

"You went off to war and—"

"I enlisted in '61 but got wounded early on. I came home and healed up pretty quick. I was there when you preached Mistuh Wiley's funeral." Mose stands and addresses the crowd. "I worked alongside this man long enough to know he's trustworthy and willin' to lay his life down for other people. And from what I remember about how he handled that mangy Dawg Smith, Lummy should lead us. I was there."

Several men clap, and some stomp their feet, shouting, "Here, here!"

Another man jumps up. "I was with you, Lummy, when you lopped off Dawg's head. I was the one who stuck his head on a pike and raised it up for all to see."

My stomach sickens picturing Dawg Smith's skull in the tree, remembering the gurgling sound he made as I sliced through his neck and the popping sounds his neck made as I twisted his head off. A war dream's coming on.

Sarge presses the owl talon into my wrist. It works.

"You okay?" He stands to pull off his coat and addresses the crowd. "I've led men in battle off and on for thirty years now, starting with the Mexican War. You're good men, and you'll have to live here long after we leave. Lummy leading this fine group of men would be good, but he can't. It must be one of you." Sarge looks around at the crowd of twenty-five men or so. "Before we move forward with our plan, is there anyone in this room you men don't recognize?" They look around at each man.

David Pierson reports, "No, we know every man here. Why?"

"Because what I'm about to tell you must stay in this room, and we can't afford to have any spies amongst us."

The men take a moment to double-check.

Sarge moves to the speaker's podium. "We come with the authority of the United States government. We're a special squad of soldiers sent here to help you succeed in defeating the West-Kimberell Gang without anyone knowing we're U.S. Army. That can never get out, understood?"

The men nod in agreement.

"I tell you this so you're clear about our intentions. It's true that Lummy led you against Dawg Smith, and he did the same against Captain Tom Ford in his own home county in Mississippi. But you need a leader from among you who'll rise to the occasion, a man you can trust, who knows you men, can form a plan, and lead you. We're here to assist you, not lead you."

The men scratch their heads and look around.

David Pierson stares at J.A., who hangs his head trying to hide. He knows where this is going.

David taps his cane on the floor twice. "There is a man among us who recently had a terrible experience at the hands of the West-Kimbrell Gang. They slapped his wife around and hurt his young son. Fortunately, nothing more was done and nothing taken that cannot be replaced."

Mose raises his hand like a schoolboy with a question for the teacher. "That's J.A. Killingsworth. He should lead us."

The men turn to J.A., who lifts his head with pursed lips. I haven't seen fire in his eyes like this since we were in Choctaw County last.

I whisper, "J.A."

He jerks around like a rabid coyote ready to strike. "What?"

"You are the man to bring down the West Gang. Think about how they man-handled your wife, hurt your son, and havin' to send them away. Damn boy! They almost raped—"

J.A. slaps my face. Hard. "Don't you ever say—"

He snatches his hand back as fast as he struck me. "I'm sorry, Lummy. I didn't mean to go that far."

"Don't forget that I did the same to you when you told me I needed to lead the men against Dawg Smith."

"You did, and I understand why now," he says, laying his forehead on the back of the pew in front of him. "We're much more alike than I ever knew."

"And that's a good thing, brother."

Men wait and wonder if J.A. will step up to the task. Some mumble, some grumble. David Pierson looks around, and his eyes land on mine. I nod that it's the moment.

David clears his throat. "We'll do this democratically. Who'll nominate J.A. Killingsworth to be leader of this army set on ridding Winn Parish of the West-Kimbrell Gang?"

I start to raise my hand, but Sarge shakes his head. "It has to be one of them."

Tarle rises. "I may be young, but my pa died fightin' the same kind of devils as these. I have a right to be a part of this. I nominate J.A. to be the leader."

Several men second his motion.

David raises his right hand. "All in favor, say 'aye.'"

The room resounds unanimously in favor of J.A. becoming the leader of the group.

J.A. looks out the window.

I lean over. "I'll be by your side the whole way. I led then. You lead now, old friend."

J.A. watches a crow fly by. He turns with watery eyes. "My life just flew away. I won't survive this, Lummy."

"You don't know that." I clench the back of the pew in front of me.

"I feel it in my bones and know it in my soul. I'll die in this battle."

"I won't let that happen." I look up at the ceiling and back at him. "God is on our side."

J.A. grins sadly. "You know that ain't true better'n I do, Lummy. God left our fightin' ass ways a long time ago like when we were in Vicksburg. There never was any gray or blue, just innocent men killin' each other for somebody else's greed. There's nothin' more than just livin' and dyin' with the hope that we lived well and did the right thing."

We stare into each other's eyes for what seems like an eternity.

He removes his jacket and whispers, "All right, dammit. Tell 'em I'll do it."

Rainy leans in and squeezes J.A.'s shoulder. "Atreides once said, 'A great man doesn't seek to lead. He's called to it, and he answers.' J.A., you are that great man in this place today."

J.A. grins. "And Leonidas did not survive Thermopolaye, like Gunnard told us in Vicksburg."

I stare into the eyes of the man I count as my best friend on earth. I rise. "J.A. Killingsworth will lead us, and by God, we will follow him."

The men cheer, chanting, "J.A., J.A."

# CHAPTER 47

# WHEN THE DEVIL LEARNS THE PLAN, HE RUNS

## 1:00 P.M., MARCH 13, 1870

*The Devil always sends his best spies to church.*

J.A. RISES WITH the fiery eyes of a demon. He fires a pistol shot through the roof. He spits bitterness out like a mouthful of sour wine. "And by God, I will lead you, dammit!"

Sarge waves J.A. to the front. He steadies himself as he approaches the speaker's stand, ready to make a plan. He sits on the front pew to gather his thoughts.

Sheriff Barnett holds up his hand. "Before J.A. begins, and first of all, good to see you again, Lummy, a hearty welcome to you other men." He steps to the front. "J.A., you are a man to be as feared as you are admired. Thank you for putting your hands to the plow." He leans his elbows on the podium. "Men, I want this all to be clear to you. No real law exists in Winn Parish, especially after John West illegally had me voted out and put in his own man. Their devilment has turned so evil the Federal government placed us under martial law. Whether you like President Grant or not, by his order and my request, he sent these special men to aid us in bringing law and order back to Winn Parish, and to the entire length of the road from Natchez to Texas. Listen to what Sarge and J.A. have to say."

Barnett sits next to J.A. He takes out as little book and records what's happening. I'm reminded of Gunnard at Vicksburg and Mary back home, recording history for ages to come.

Sarge rises. "Let's take a break. If you need to visit the latrine or smoke, do it now. We'll gather back up in five minutes."

A man in the back pulls down his hat and sneaks out the back, trying to hide his face.

I elbow Rainy. "I know him. C'mon, we can't let him slip away."

Rainy and I dash out a side door just in time stop the man who's spurring his horse without mercy. I drag him off out of the saddle.

He yells, "I ain't done nothin' wrong."

I jerk him up as Rainy holsters his pistol. "Yeah, but you were on your way to doin' wrong, John Duncan."

Rainy snatches a small revolver from Duncan's belt. "You got any more weapons on you?"

Duncan shakes his head. "That's all."

Rainy finds a hidden knife. He backhands Duncan. "That's all, huh? I'll kill you where—"

I step between Rainy and Duncan. "Where were you headed in such an all fired hurry? To see John West?"

Duncan spits. "I ain't sayin' shit, you carpetbaggin' son of a bitch."

Rainy lays Duncan's knife to his throat. "Talk, or I'll cut you up for catfish bait, understand?"

I push the knife in Rainy's hand away. He steps back.

Duncan shudders. "You can't prove nothin'."

I press my hand against his chest. "Do I need to?"

David Pierson hobbles out, leaning on Sheriff Barnett's shoulder.

Without turning, I ask, "Sheriff, do you know this man?"

"I do, and if my suspicions are correct, Duncan's spying for West."

"I ain't doin' no such thing. Let me go."

I place the knife Pa made for me against his throat, drawing a thin red line. "That ain't happenin', John. What'd you do after the war, turn outlaw?"

Duncan grins. "No worse than you bein' a turncoat, Tullos."

Sarge steps in but doesn't take my knife from Duncan's throat. "Tell us what you know."

Duncan spits and says nothing.

Tarle shouts. "Duncan cheated Freddy in a hawg buyin' deal last fall."

He barks, "I did no such thing, you—"

Tarle kicks Duncan's shin—hard. "That son of bitch would rather climb a tree and tell a lie than stand on the ground and tell the truth."

Duncan cries out in pain more from the knife cutting him than the kick. "I ain't tellin' you a damn thing."

Sarges asks, "Where's West and Kimbrell right now?"

Duncan grins. "I don't remember."

Rainy, in his cool manner, offers, "'If you tell the truth, you don't have to remember anything,' Mark Twain once said."

"I don't know."

Sarge growls. *"Liar!"*

Duncan spits again. "Even if I did, I wouldn't tell you bastards. John West is the greatest patriot who ever fought for the stars and bars."

Rainy snaps his fingers. "There it is. 'The truth has no defense against a fool determined to believe a lie.' Mark Twain also said that."

The hair on the back of my neck stands up. Rage clutches my heart. I draw the knife tighter on Duncan's throat. "Talk or die."

Duncan whimpers. "You don't know what he's capable of, Lummy. He'll—"

A cold shiver races up and down my spine. "Yeah, but you know what *I'm* capable of." I relax the knife. "You saw what I did to Dawg Smith with this same knife." Mercy has no place in my heart right now. "You want your head on a pike, too?"

Sheriff Barnett pulls my hand back, and blood trickles down Duncan's neck. "C'mon, son, we've got him now."

I slip the blade back into its sheath. I want to kill and cry in the same moment. I press the owl claw into my wrist.

Sheriff Barnett handcuffs Duncan and chuckles, "He'll talk soon enough. Sarge, by the authority of President Grant and recognizing your military rank, I take this prisoner into custody to hold until your mission is completed."

Sarge spreads his feet and stiffens. "Done. Chain him to that tree over there so he can't hear a word of our plan."

Two men take log chains from their wagons and wrap Duncan up so tight he can hardly breathe.

He sits on the ground, gritting his teeth and cursing. "These chains won't hold me. West will come get me. He's smart. He'll figure it out. We're the righteous ones. We're on God's side. Y'all are all the evil ones, with your Yankee niggah lovin' ways. You're damned to hell already and don't even know it."

Rainy lights a smoke and shares a bit of wisdom with Duncan. "You may be right. We're all damned to hell for what we will do here. Following a man like West and calling what you have done—murdering, robbing, raping, and even bashing an infant's head against a barn post—righteous? You have deceived your own mind. A man once said, 'When you can only see the depravity of another and not your own, you're already damned.'"

Duncan's eyes blaze red. "Then we'll all be in hell together."

"Yeah, but you'll go before us."

I spit at Duncan's feet. "If I had my way, I'd put your head next to Dawg Smith's skull down on the Dugdemona River."

"Yeah, you're good at that, ain't you, preacher?"

I grab his hair and yank back his head. "It'd be so easy, Duncan."

"Do it, you niggah lovin' bastard."

Susannah screaming while being raped seizes my mind. I snatch my knife from its sheath, drop to my knees in front of Duncan, and rear back to slash his throat. Someone grabs my arm.

"Lummy, don't!" It's Ise. "Don't do it, brother-in-law. You is better'n this."

I stare into John Duncan's eyes and can see down deep into his soul. There's nothing there except hate. I relax and sheath my knife. I get up and kick dust at Duncan. "Your time is short."

He laughs like a giggling idiot. "You ain't gonna do shit."

"Soon, John. It'll be soon."

Duncan's laughing falls flat. "Y'all better let me go. John West will kill all of ya. You wait and see." He looks around for any sympathy he can get. There's none to be had. "I should've killed you after we took Dawg Smith down. I'll get you, Lummy Tullos."

Ise puts his arm around my shoulder. "Keep walkin', Lummy. He ain't worth killin'."

J.A. kicks Duncan's boot. "You won't live long enough to get the chance."

Rainy lights up a smoke. "Truth is always well said."

# CHAPTER 48

# THE PLAN

## 1:25 P.M., MARCH 13, 1870

*Good men doing the right thing ain't always pretty.*

DAVID PIERSON RAPS his cane on the floor. "Here, here, men. Get seated. It's time to begin."

Sheriff Barnett raises his hand. "As you can see, this is serious business. Be watchful for spies amongst us. Sarge, please proceed."

Sarge stands behind the podium where I heard many a bad sermon. This one may be the worst yet for what we have to do. It ain't the speaker, but the message he's delivering.

Sarge stiffens as if at attention. "Let me say this at the outset. If harm comes to any of my men by your hand, or you give any aid to the enemy, I'll have you hanged. If you run, I will hunt you down like a rabid dog. That being said, I need you to take an oath to hold this mission in secret until it's completed and that you will do as instructed by those in authority over you."

Men nod and whisper among themselves.

"If you cannot, you will be held in custody until we've done our work." No one speaks up. "And if you betray us, the men with me and I have the authority to shoot you down where you stand. Do you understand?"

They all nod.

"Hold up your right hands and repeat after me."

I repeat the words of the oath again just to remind myself that I'm here only to do the work of saving lives. The sorry part of that is I have to end lives to save lives.

Sarge finishes saying the oath. "That's good, men. You can lower your hands now. I'm not here to lead this meeting, just to make sure we stay civil and get our plan together. You will follow orders given you by the men under my command, Lummy first, and the others under him. Do you understand? To ensure that the government will not be seen as having anything to do with what happens, we will operate in the shadows. J.A., will you come forward?"

J.A. starts to get up, but I pull him back down. I whisper, "These men trust you more than anyone else in this room, including me. You live here. I don't. They will follow you."

"I can't do it by myself."

I squeeze J.A.'s arm. "You don't have to. I'll walk every step of the way with you, brother. Me and Sarge will hold your arms up like Aaron and Hur did for Moses when they fought the Amalekites. They defeated them, and we will defeat John West. We'll do it together."

He snickers. "I did get to slap your face, didn't I?"

I rub my jaw, grinning. "You did, you dirty, rotten sack of fish guts." I cover my mouth.

J.A. stands. "With the help and strength of the Good Lord and you fightin' men, we will end the West-Kimbrell Gang."

David Pierson shouts above the congratulatory noise, "Here, here, we have a new Joshua amongst us. The Promised Land is just beyond the Dugdemona River. The walls of Jericho will fall once again."

J.A. looks to the heavens and whispers, "They will fall down and crush John West's sorry Canaanite head." He takes a deep breath and grips the speaker's stand. "The date for the reckoning is April seventeenth, Easter Sunday. We'll meet at Clem Wilson's farm at nine a.m. sharp. Be early. Here's what we believe will work."

I whisper to Sarge, "On that Sunday, there'll be men who'll die but never be raised."

# CHAPTER 49

# CELEBRATING
# THE DEAD

## 3:00 P.M., MARCH 13, 1870

*It's in the deed that ends all deeds that a soul will be purified.*

THE MEETING IS over, and our small band makes its way through the pines to the clearing where Mr. Gilmore's house once stood. Sawhorse tables are set up covered with foods and sweets of every kind. My mouth waters just looking at it all.

The people of this small hamlet greet us with open arms and smiling faces. Old Nate stands. "All is ready. Come to the feast in your honor."

Young men take our horses, and ladies guide us to special seats. I don't know how to act with all of this attention. None of us do.

Old Nate pats the air with his palms to quiet the crowd. "Brothers and sisters, we're here to send these good men off with full bellies and on the wings of your good prayers. They are family. Let us treat them as such." He steps over to Ise and lays a hand on his shoulder. "You may not know, but this man is Susannah's own brother." The crowd claps and cheers. Old Nate raises his hand. "Quiet down, now, as he leads us in the blessin' over these good vittles."

We all remove our hats as Ise stands. He leans over and whispers to me, "I ain't never led no prayer in front of so many people."

I take his arm. "Just talk to Creator like you're talkin' to me."

He straightens up. "Y'all bow your heads as we all pray together."

Ise prays a fine prayer, one Mr. Gilmore and Susannah would both be proud to hear. What am I saying? They do.

Ise finishes. "And all the good folks of this community and my God-fearin' brothers in arms say together, A-a-amen."

Old Nate stands. "Thank you, Brother Ise, for that fine prayer. We're also gathered to honor some of God's children who, though we may not see them, are with us here today."

*Susannah?* I snatch my head around, looking. There she is, behind Old Nate with Old Bart and a young man I don't recognize.

Tarle leans over. "That's my best friend Ebenezer, Uncle Lummy."

I blink. "What?"

Tarle grins. "Didn't think you were the only one with the sight, did you?"

"I'll be—"

"Yeah, Mother told me about yours when I told her about my experiences. So, can you see the others who just arrived?"

I look again. "Mistuh Gilmore, Missus Davis, Mistuh Wiley, and Ben." I want to jump out of my seat, but Tarle catches me before I rise.

"They're all here, Uncle Lummy, just on the other side of the thin veil."

Peace and comfort fill my heart like a warm blanket in wintertime. I now know I can do whatever it takes because Creator brought them here.

"You can, Uncle Lummy, and you will."

Granny steps from behind the heavenly crowd and in the sound of trickling spring waters says, *"You must do the deed that ends all deeds. In this, your soul will be purified."*

Tarle grabs my arm. "What did she say?"

"That I'll kill John West when the time comes... and that there will be a great loss."

# CHAPTER 50

# MEETING THE SON I ALWAYS WANTED BUT CAN'T HAVE

## 3:30 P.M., MARCH 13, 1870

*There's no greater joy than to be reunited with ones
you love dearly, but who've been so far away.*

O NE BY ONE, the good folks of this small village come forward and share their remembrances of those who now live on the other side of the thin veil.

Old Nate says another prayer and offers to those who have been harassed by the Nightriders to come forward and share what happened. He pulls a chair up beside mine. "Y'all know that it ain't just been them folks movin' west who've been hurt by the West-Kimbrell Gang."

A middle-aged man and his wife stand up, their young son standing in his chair beside them. The child looks too familiar.

I start to get up. "That's—"

Old Nate holds me down with the grip of a vise. "In a bit, Lummy."

"Elzey?"

"It is, son, and you'll visit with them in a minute." Old Nate's gentleness reminds me so much of Old Bart. "Lummy, we told Elzey that his uncle was comin' for a visit. We thought it best to handle it that way for now."

A lump as big as a wad of tobacco sticks in my throat. "I understand."

Joshua hugs Sudie Mae and lays his hand on Elzey's shoulder. "It's by the hand of the Good Lord that I am here today. But y'all ain't never seen a black man run so fast as this child did when them haints with the hoods came chasin' after me. They hounded me all the way from the Dugdemona to Shiloh church house. I dove behind a grave marker thinkin' maybe the good church

goin' haints buried there would protect me from the Devil's haints chasin' me."
Everybody laughs. He shakes his finger in the air. "But white folks don't know
how'z we been trained to run faster'n the Devil himself from bein' chased by
lions back in the old country."

The small crowd laughs. Some dance and shout.

Joshua points at me, and everything stops. "But that ain't the only white
folks dey is. Just like the biggest slaver in Missip once was a black man livin'
down in Natchez, the man whose land we live on now freed the most slaves
of any white man I know, Mistuh Gilmore."

Everybody claps and cheers.

Joshua pats the air to quiet the crowd, still pointing at me. "And these good
men have come to keep us free." He winks at Old Nate. "You talk to Lummy?"

"I did, and he's good with it."

"Elzey Tullos, son, I want you to meet a very special man. He's come all
this way to see you." He sets Elzey on the ground, and the family walks to my
chair. I rise to greet them.

Sudie Mae leans down to Elzey, who hides half of his face behind her
skirt. "Elzey, this is your uncle Lummy, who loves you very much. He lives
in Mississippi. He has come all this way just to make sure you stay safe, get to
go to school, and have what all children deserve to have."

I reach to shake his hand. He smiles at me, and I swear I'm looking into
Susannah's eyes. I fight back the tears. The crowd claps, and the feast begins.

Elzey looks me up and down. "Are you like Goliath in the Bible?"

I laugh. "Only in size, son."

*Son.* I'm speaking to my son, Elzey Burk Tullos.

"Did you know my father?"

"I did, a long time ago. He loved you dearly. Still does."

"What happened to him?"

I want to cry. I bite my lip. "He needed to go away so he could become a
stronger man."

"Will I see him again, Uncle Lummy?"

"I guarantee it, son."

His puzzled look turns into a big smile. "You're Tarle's uncle, too?"

"I am."

"Eb was his best friend." Elzey wipes a tear. "He was mine, too."

Tarle reaches to hug Elzey. "How 'bout I be your new best friend? You do know I'm you're cousin, too, don't you?"

"Momma said as much. She said your pa was Uncle Lummy's brother."

Tarle grins. "That's right."

Elzey studies Tarle for a moment. "I'd like you to be my new best friend."

Tarle sticks out his hand. "Let's shake on it."

Elzey looks back at me. "Uncle Lummy, can I sit by you and Tarle?"

My heart swells to burst. "You sure can. But first, meet your other uncle here today. This is your uncle Isaiah. But just call him Uncle Ise."

Ise shakes Elzey's hand. "I'm your momma's brother."

"Did you know my momma?"

"I'm sorry to say that I didn't. We got separated when we were little, and—"

Elzey points to the sky. "You'll get to see my momma in heaven like I will one day."

Ise hugs little Elzey. "That I will, nephew."

I can't keep my eyes off of my son. He listens to the horrible stories told by those who have been chased, whipped, robbed, and raped by the Nightriders. I hate that he has to hear this.

Elzey looks at me with eyes the same color as mine—hazel. He feels my anger and rage mounting. He presses the owl talon into my wrist. "Does this help, Uncle Lummy?"

"It does. It keeps my mind where it needs to be. How did you know to do that?"

"An old lady in a rainbow dress told me."

I can't believe my ears. "You see her very often?"

"In my dreams, except when I saw her with the others behind Old Nate a few minutes ago."

I look at Tarle.

He shrugs and smiles. "It *does* run in the family."

Elzey plays with the owl talon. "Who gave it to you?"

"An old Choctaw warrior named Dan Creekwater."

He chuckles. "Dan Creekwater. Dan Creekwater. That's a funny name."

"Indians do have interesting names, but I like it, don't you?"

He grins. "I do." He looks over at Joshua and Sudie Mae. "Would it be all right if I go back and sit with my momma and daddy?"

"Sure, son, but I want to give you somethin' first." I pull the gator necklace from my pocket and put it around his neck. "You wear this, okay? It will protect you from monsters."

Elzey rolls the tooth between his fingers. "You're giving me this?"

"Yes. An alligator almost got me a long time ago, but a captain on a steamboat didn't let him and gave me this necklace. He said it would protect me." I straighten the chain and lay the gator tooth over his heart. "Now it will protect you, so wear it every day."

Elzey's eyes grin bigger than his mouth. "I will, I will." He dashes over to his parents and tells them all about it.

They nod and mouth, "Thank you."

I mouth back, "Thank you for lovin' my son."

Those visiting from the other side slip back through the thin veil one by one.

Susannah turns. *"Lummy, I love you."*

# CHAPTER 51

# LEAVING WHEN I DON'T WANT TO BUT HAVE TO

## SUNSET, MARCH 13, 1870

*Sacrifice is required for people to be free.*

S ARGE QUIETS THE crowd. "We must leave now, but I speak for all of us when I say thank you. You have treated us better than we deserve. Don't forget to say a word to the Good Lord for us. Y'all stay close to home for a few days, at least until you get the news."

"What news?" Elzey asks.

Old Nate rises. "That the day of the Lord's deliverance has come."

Elzey runs to throw his arms around my neck and squeezes with all of his might. "Uncle Lummy, my momma said you won't get to come back on the day of deliverance. She said I need to tell you goodbye now."

"She's right. I love you, and I'm so proud of who you are. You are always in my heart, and I will never, ever forget you. You are my son, too."

"I am?"

"Always will be. You will have many fathers to guide you. Listen to your momma and daddy, Old Nate, and the other good people who want the best for you."

"And Granny?"

I tear up, but try to keep it together for both our sakes'. "You listen to her most of all. No one speaks with Creator's voice better than her."

Elzey grins. "Can I come to your house one day?"

"I'd like that, Elzey."

Elzey grabs the gator tooth and holds it up. "I'll always remember you."

His eyes change from hazel to a swirl of rainbow colors.

I pull the agate Granny gave me from my pocket. It glows to match Elzey's eyes. On the path that leads to her grave, Susannah waves and fades into the shadows.

I startle when Sarge barks, "Boots and saddles men, mount up."

I hug Elzey once more, and he skips away, happy as a puppy. I slip Joshua a small bag of coins.

He doesn't want to take it, but I make him.

"Joshua, Elzey is where he should be, and I'm more'n grateful for you raisin' him." Elzey chases other children around the bonfire. "He's so smart, gentle, and respectful."

Sudie Mae cozies up to Joshua. "We promised he would get a good education and be taught of the Lord."

"You've done that better'n I ever could."

We watch Elzey play and laugh. Leaving Elzey is almost as hard as when I left Susannah and Martha to go fight. A rainbow mist forms on the path to Susannah's grave. *Granny.*

The sound of a trickling stream floods my soul. *"Because of your love and selfless sacrifice, your son will become everything you were supposed to be. His life will be filled with peace and love. You have made it so."*

Joshua squeezes my arm. "Lummy, where'd you go just now?"

I smile. "Not very far, but now I'm back."

Sudie Mae wraps her arms around my waist and buries her head in my chest. "Will we see you again, brother?"

"Probably not. When it's over, we'll disappear like we were never here."

Joshua takes my hand. "How will we know if you're all right?"

I squint. "When you hear it."

Old Nate surrounds us all with a hug. "God bless you, son. May Saint Michael, the Protector of God's People, come to lead you and your men."

I tip my hat and smile. "He's already here."

# CHAPTER 52

# A QUIET ROAD
# TO DESTRUCTION

## SATURDAY, NOON, APRIL 16, 1870

*History ain't only facts. It's a story to be reckoned with.*

I**T'S TAKEN ALL** month, but we're set. The word went out, and scores of men responded—farmers, backwoodsmen, store clerks—all prepared to do what needs doing. They worked from Friday on through day and night Saturday to prepare for the great "cleanup fight" to come. All are armed to the teeth with shotguns, rifles, pistols, and plenty of ammunition. Some carry short swords leftover from the war. They'll gather at Clem Wilson's farm at nine o'clock tomorrow morning. Our small band will meet West with the intention of joining his gang. That should give us an advantage when the fighting starts if our ruse works.

Our five-man army has managed to stay in the shadows. We're also armed for battle. I have Ben's sawed off ten gauge shotgun across my saddle, my .44 caliber Colt Dragoon pistol, and the knife Pa made me, sharp as a razor. Mostly though, I carry no fear. Only contempt for a man who rapes, murders, plunders, and even kills a crying infant. I shudder this warm morning from fear—fear of what I'm capable of doing when fear can't be found in my soul.

ATLANTA. THE TOWN that has cried out the loudest against John West and his gang of bastard outlaws has had enough. West is unaware of our plan to eliminate his gang. Jim Maybin reported that since Dan Dean returned from hiding in Texas, he's been recruiting men for the coming battle. West wants Dean killed because he witnessed Laws Kimbrell murder Dutch Jones. We'll tell West we have Dean in custody. He should count us as an ally then.

As we travel the Winnfield-Alexandria Road, I ponder what's about to transpire. Too bad we'll take the West-Kimbrell Gang down on Easter Sunday. We'll put people under the dirt on the same day Jesus walked out of the tomb. Satan thought he had Jesus dead to rights. But that was only Saturday. The Accuser never expected what happened on Sunday. The greatest fooler of men got fooled. And that Bible-toting fool John West thinks he can hide behind being a Sunday school teacher and song leader at the Methodist Church in Atlanta. He's forgotten that the Lord once said, 'You will know the truth, and the truth shall set you free.' John West will soon know the truth, and Winn Parish will be resurrected and set free once and for all. But first, I have to befriend my old comrade again, no matter how rotten of a soul he has.

Our small band rides into town, checking every alley and what could lie behind every tree. J.A. is on my left. He's well-known and liked by the townspeople. The only trouble he's had with West was recently. J.A. holds that anger at bay. Behind him is Ise, who will play the part of J.A.'s "boy." Sarge has let his scruffiness grow to the point that Rainy won't ride near him because of his foul smell. That's good cover, though. And Rainy? Rainy is just Rainy, and that'll do.

We left Matt at South Farm. He's waiting with fresh horses and food to speed us on our way when we're done. I keep Tarle close. That's my only fear. If something happens to him, I'd never be able to face Dorcas.

"Lord, protect my nephew at the cost of my life."

Tarle whispers, "God's got us, Uncle Lummy."

I snatch my head around. "Stay behind me and do what I say."

"Yes, sir, I will."

Tarle is too starry-eyed about all of this. Any young man would be, being a part of something greater than himself. Yeah, right. It's what got Granville and Hog Fart killed at Vicksburg.

I've got to stay calm when I meet West and Kimbrell. The anger in my heart that has saved me so many times can't overrule my mind. That's not easy, but I once escaped a snake pit filled with dead and dying Yankee soldiers at Vicksburg.

"If I got out of that pit, I'll get out of this one. Thank you, Creator, for cooling the rage and clearing my head."

The difference? I didn't choose falling into the pit in Vicksburg. This time, I'm jumping into the middle of it.

# CHAPTER 53

# THE SIT DOWN

## SATURDAY, 1:30 P.M., APRIL 16, 1870

*Daniel got thrown into a pit, and the Lord shut the lions' mouths.*

I TIE MY horse to a hitching post outside Collier's Store and Saloon. West and his boys are here.

Rainy whispers, "The Lord allowed Daniel to be thrown into the den of lions, and it was He who shut the mouths of the beasts."

Ise pats his mount's neck. "Thank you, Lawd."

Sarge gathers us in a circle out of view. "Lummy, would you say a word?"

My anger is hot. My face is red. My hands grip the hitching post. I pray just one sentence. "Lord, give us strength to send these demons back to hell from whence they came."

All whisper, "Amen."

West and Kimbrell are inside with a number of men. Our show of force should even the odds if they decide to fight. It would either be their last or ours.

I take the doorknob in hand. "Remember, we're here to befriend them, not take them down. We want to get them all at the same time." I turn the knob. "Tarle?"

"Keep my head down and mouth shut."

"Good. Let's go have a drink with these ruffians."

Rainy growls. "We gotta take whatever shit these bastards shovel at us."

A store clerk squints as we file in like the roughshod characters we want to portray. The store is well-stocked with canned goods, candies, cloth, dishes, tools—everything needed to keep house and farm.

West, his back to the wall, sits with six men who turn our way as we ease up to the bar for a drink.

Laws Kimbrell brandishes his yellow teeth in a grin I'd like slap off his face. "Who's that?"

West swirls whiskey in his glass. "Just a bunch of sister boys who part their hair in the middle and squat to piss." The men laugh. "I'm guessin' they're nothin' but a bunch of niggah lovin' Yankee bastards who don't know they're dead already."

We don't acknowledge West's taunts.

Sarge gives me a look of confidence that I need to not just go ahead and kill them right now.

We ignore his insults until West decides to address us directly. He studies each of us for any clue as to who we are. He stands, and we place our hands on our pistols.

The clerk ducks behind the counter. "Don't want no trouble in here. Please take it outside."

West steps out from behind the table and shields his eyes. "Hellfire and damnation if that ain't who I think it is?"

I don't turn around. "Maybe. Depends on who you think I am." I do look a bit ragged with my scraggly beard and unkempt hair stuffed under my hat. But that's how he would remember me in the rifle pits at Vicksburg.

"Is that you, Tullos?"

"Depends on who's askin'."

"You remember me, you self-righteous, preachin' son of a bitch. I'm John West." He looks around and grins at his men. "We fought together with the Twenty-Seventh Louisiana Volunteer Infantry, Company F, but you—"

"Yeah, I remember you. You sorry ass, no good, shit shoveler. Worst damn soldier in the whole Rebel army."

"That's what I always liked about you, a preacher one minute and a hell-raiser in the next."

"Where we've been and what we've done, it takes a little of both, don't you think?"

West scratches his chin. "I'd have to agree with that."

I watch his every move. "Good, we're gettin' off on the right foot."

"I'm not sure I like it that you're here."

I say nothing.

"So, tell me Tullos, why are you here?"

I turn to face him with one hand on my pistol and the other on the knife Pa made me. "If you've already decided that you won't like the answer, why ask the question?"

West laughs, but irritation laces his voice. "So I can stir your ass up. You forget I saw that holy rage you conjured up in the Twenty-Seventh Louisiana Lunette when the Yanks came up the hill."

"Then you should already know that I'm not easily shaken, not by the likes of you. How did fillin' in that trench for that Yankee on the march out of Vicksburg go?"

"About like you and chicken shit J.A. there runnin' off into the night."

I take it up a notch. "Okay, West. Let's find out who's chickenshit and who ain't. How 'bout you and me steppin'—"

Sarge grabs my arm, playing his part in this dangerous game. "Settle down, son. Don't forget why we're here."

West flips a gold dollar on the table. "No need to get testy. I'm just foolin' with you. Let me buy you a drink, for old time's sake. That includes your friends there."

I take my hat off as the clerk pours five glasses of bourbon. "Long as you don't try throwing us down one of your wells when we're done. We will not go easy."

West's eyes burn right through me.

I shrug and throw back the whiskey as if the whole world knows about West's devil dealings.

He wants to ask what I know but takes a different approach. "So, what are you doin' here, Tullos?"

I backhand J.A.'s chest and laugh like the whiskey is already taking effect. "I got people over in Tullos town just west of here. Ain't seen 'em since I left for the war. I needed to get away from the farm to get some fresh air and find some easy money. Thought I'd pay 'em a visit."

West downs his whiskey. "Easy money, you say?"

I avoid the question and try to lighten the mood a bit. "But I had to come talk old times with my old friend, J.A., and drink moonshine whiskey. You do remember J.A., don't you?"

"I do, but who are these other men?"

"Deadbeats who want some easy money, too. Ain't been easy makin' a livin' after the war."

West hisses like a snake. "And what about you, Killingsworth? You just jawing with Tullos for a spell, or you got something else on your mind?"

"I tend my own business and keep my mouth shut. But you already know that, don't you?"

West studies J.A. for what seems like an eternity. "Yeah, I do, now that you mention it."

J.A. bristles at not being able to kill West for trying to rape and murder his wife.

Laws Kimbrell taunts J.A. "Hey, that your niggah standin' there behind you, Killingsworth?"

J.A. can't resist. "The only niggahs I know of in this parish happen to be painted white. But yeah, he works for me. Seems he got away before certain bandits killed the folks he was traveling west with. They happened to disappear into the darkness. Ain't it amazin' how people just seem to do that around here."

Laws Kimbrell sits up with his hand on his pistol. "You best leave before I kick your ass down the road."

J.A. doesn't blink. "You get to feelin' froggy, you sorry bastard, go ahead and jump."

West's men bristle up, but he throws up his hand up to hold them off.

J.A. plays his part perfectly.

West rubs his neck. He's visibly uncomfortable. We know about his devil dealings. He tries to regain control of the conversation. "You fight for the niggahs wearing a blue suit, too, Killingsworth?"

J.A. snaps with a grin. "Hell, no, I didn't fight for no lyin' ass government who said they wanted all men free but didn't make slavery illegal in Washington, D.C. until a year after the war started. I ain't never wanted no darkies. When the Confederate States government said that any man owning twenty or more slaves was exempt from fightin', it was time for me to go home and let gray and blue just kill each other off."

West leans in. "Rich man's war and a poor man's fight?"

J.A. stares at Laws. "I came home to mind my own business. You'll do well to do the same."

Laws throws up his hands in surrender and snickers. "Shit, you're all right, J.A., and besides, you ain't worth killin', Killingsworth."

We all laugh, and J.A. fakes a chuckle. The boy should've been an actor in a traveling show.

West returns to business. "You want some easy money, too, Killingsworth?"

"The cattle business ain't been too good lately. I got a good reputation. No one'll suspect me. I'll do anything to keep my farm. Even if I have to live up to my name, you understand?"

West and his men snicker.

He likes an audience, that much is clear.

West signals for another whiskey. "Get your Killingsworth, is that it? What about that thing that happened at your farm a while back. Surely you know—"

J.A. leans in. "What I know is that I'll kill every one of you mangy sons of bitches and throw your asses down your own death wells if you ever try somethin' like that again, understood?" He eases the old short sword from his belt that he found when we escaped Vicksburg and thumbs the blade. He licks the bit of blood. "That is, one piece at a time."

"Just the kind of soldier I'm lookin' for. We can always use another good man." West figures if he can keep us close, he'll know our every move. Then he'll use us and dispose of us anytime he chooses.

Laws Kimbrell laughs. "Good man. Yeah, right."

J.A. slides his short sword back in his belt. "Laws Kimbrell, you and me will have a discussion some time soon."

Laws spits and turns his head. "I'll be ready."

West studies Sarge. "Don't I know you?"

Sarge doesn't blink. "If you did, I would've killed you already. I fought for the Yankees but went over to the right side. No more stars and stripes ever. Only the stars and bars suit me."

West doesn't seem satisfied. "Lummy, ain't that the man who talked you into swallowin' the yellow dawg and joinin' the Yankees?"

I'm a little shocked that he knows that, but I keep my poker face. "Yeah, I took the oath, but it didn't take me and Sarge long to figure out how to rob the Yankees blind. We—"

Sarge butts in. "It was easy pickings, like that saddlebag you bastards took off Lieutenant Butts a few years back."

West frowns, but I continue. "We figured out how to keep the signup bounty by enlisting men who never showed up, you understand."

West starts to speak, but I beat him to the punch. It's a tactic I use to level the playing field and get my opponent off balance.

"I can vouch for Sarge." I sip my whiskey. "He's done his share of givin' the Yankees hell."

We pull up chairs like we're old friends and sit down cool as buttermilk in the springhouse.

West turns to Rainy. "Haven't seen you in some time. Where've you been?"

"Here and there, trying to make a dollar."

West leans in. "Word is you put your father under the dirt at Skullyville in the Indian Territory some years back."

Rainy turns with a grin. "Well, you know just about everything that goes on, don't you?"

"I try to."

"That bastard Ratliff was no father of mine. We'll both be better off if you leave that alone."

West slaps the table and looks at me, grinning. "I always liked Rainy." He glares at him. "I've got to know who I'm workin' with when my neck is at stake. You understand?"

Rainy leans back so the two Army Colts he's packing are visible. "I understand a lot, John West. More than you probably think. You figure on it getting your neck stretched anytime soon?"

"Not in Winn Parish—or anywhere else, for that matter." West taps the table with his right index fingernail. "I also heard about a man dressed in black who disappeared about as fast as he showed up in Bossier Parish. Seems they found a dead judge lying on the floor about the same time. You know anything about that?"

Rainy pulls a cigar from his coat pocket and lights it. "I will tell you that I do not."

West trims his nails with a pocketknife. "You should've joined us a long time ago, Rainy."

Rainy shrugs and blows a perfect smoke ring that travels right to Laws Kimbrell's nose.

Laws swats at the smoke and snaps, "You got any guns for sale? We could use some Henry repeaters everybody thinks are God's gift to the shootin' man."

"Fresh out, Laws. That's why I'm here, to gather some cash to get my business going again. I lost my poke in a Mississippi riverboat card game in Natchez a while back."

Laws barks, "You got some kind of other deal going I need to know about, Tullos? You took Dawg Smith's gang down for killin' your niggah wife."

He's fishing for information.

I press the owl claw into my wrist. "And do tell, what do you think that could be?"

Laws sneaks his hand down his side to his pistol.

I pull my pistol quicker than a cottonmouth strike. "Go ahead, Laws. Do it. Do it, and I'll blow a hole through you so big West'll be able to throw an apple through it."

Laws turns to West. "We don't need these bastards. Let's—"

I take a chance. "We came here to do business, but I can see who the sister boys are in this room."

Rainy and the rest of our group snicker but never take their eyes off of West's men.

"And as for you, Laws Kimbrell, you better go on to hell now before I send you there."

Laws jerks up like he's about to pounce on me like a bobcat on a bird.

West pulls him back down. "Settle down, Laws, he's just yanking your rope like we did him. He's just returning the favor. Back to business. What do you want, Tullos?"

"I told you once. We want to make some of that easy money you got floatin' around. We know Yankee law ain't worth spit in these parts. I figure you got the rest tied up nice and pretty like a birthday present. So, what's it gonna be? We get in on the take or start our own business?"

West bristles. That's a threat he hadn't counted on. He knows I have kin who could help me get started and give him a run for his money. His eyes offer a sinister gleam that would make Dawg Smith's look like an innocent child's. "I might be interested in helping you out, one old soldier to another."

I almost shudder, but I contain myself.

West asks, "Have you seen John Duncan since you've been back?" He's trying to make me slip up. "He disappeared like a haint about the time y'all came to Winn Parish a month ago."

I don't blink. "Sounds like you got eyes and ears most everywhere."

West picks his teeth with his pocketknife. "We know our business."

I laugh. "But you don't know where John Duncan is?"

West squints. "He'll turn up."

I chance stirring the pot. "Maybe Duncan swung over to the Yankee government side. They'd pay good money for information about your ass." I just signed Duncan's death warrant.

West studies me for a moment. "That's good to know, Tullos, that's real good, 'cause folks around here don't go in for them Yankee carpet baggin' sons of bitches."

"You gotta be careful whose eyes you see through and whose voice you listen to."

West nods to one of his men. "Find Duncan. You know what to do."

The man exits out the back door, checking the rounds in his pistol.

I entice West with a chance at glory. "Like Sarge said, we heard about y'all relievin' Lieutenant Butts of a payroll back in '66. How much was it?"

West bristles. "I had nothin' to do with that. I just—"

"Oh, didn't you? An apostle once said, 'Have I become your enemy by tellin' you the truth?'"

Laws puffs out his chest. "Twenty-seven hundred cash dollars."

West slaps Laws's chest hard but laughs to play it off. "Yeah, twenty-seven hundred dollars the niggahs didn't get." His demeanor changes from playful to dead serious.

The cat's out of the bag. They just confessed to Lieutenant Butt's murder. Sarge heard it. So did the rest of us—as witnesses.

West looks at me, then at J.A., realizing we're gaining the upper hand in this conversation. "Enough of this shit. What do you two want, Tullos? I'm tired of your gassin'."

"I want to know what I'm gettin' myself into."

"You'll get the easiest money you'll ever make. And ain't a damn soul who'll do anything about it."

I slap the table. "How do I know you're tellin' the truth?"

West spits a stream of tobacco into a spittoon. "If I tell you a chicken dips snuff, you can lift up its wing and find a jar of snuff."

"I'll hold you to it, John West."

West stuffs tobacco into his mouth. "You gotta prove yourself first, Tullos."

"I ain't gotta prove shit, West."

"All right, no need to get riled up. How do I know I can trust you?"

I play my card. "A smart man always requires proof. What if I said we have in custody the man you want the most?"

West grins like possum. "You have Dan Dean?"

I nod. "I can put him anywhere you want him."

"No, that's quite all right. Hold onto him for now."

"We've got him tied up tighter'n a bull's ass at fly time."

West elbows Laws. "We'll capture his family and bring them here tomorrow morning. Tell him I'll negotiate their release if he comes in peaceably."

I check with the others. They nod. "We can do that. Call me Handerson from now on. I don't want this comin' back on my family."

"We can do that." West pours whiskey all around, eyeing me like he's still unsure if he's going to kill me or enlist me into his gang.

I stare back just as cold and lean up a bit to let him know I'm not afraid.

Sarge, J.A., Ise, and Tarle all sit on dead ready to brawl if I give the signal.

I hope West doesn't provoke a fight. This isn't the time. Not yet. We want the West-Kimbrell Gang together when the bullets start to fly.

West raises a glass and toasts, "All right, Handerson, you're in. Our plan happens tomorrow."

# CHAPTER 54

# PUTTING OUT
# THE BAIT

## 2:00 P.M., APRIL 16, 1870

*Even the best laid plans could lay the planner in the grave.*

WEST LOWERS HIS glass and smiles. "Have Dan Dean at the Methodist Church by ten o'clock."

I have to ask. "What's the plan at the church?"

"Trust me, Tullos. You're gonna like it."

"Trust is like trying to hold water in your hand."

"You don't trust me, Handerson?" He's playing with me now.

"It's not that I don't trust *you.*" I turn and glare at Laws. "I just don't trust who you trust."

Kimbrell shows fear for the first time. I'm getting between him and West, and he doesn't like it. Trying to regain his place, Laws barks, "That's all he'll tell you for now."

West searches my eyes for any slip up.

I shrug and drain the last few drops of whiskey. "We can live with that, can't we, boys?"

All nod without a word.

"What guarantee do I have we'll be legal?"

"You don't understand, Handerson. I am the law here. I've been Justice of the Peace for some time and have a warrant sworn out for Dan Dean and ten blank warrants prepared for anyone I choose to name."

Rainy relights his cigar. "And who would that be?"

"Any damn person I please, gun dealer. No more questions. I'm in charge, so you gotta trust me first. Then, maybe I'll trust you." West lays his hand on his pistol.

I do the same.

Rainy nods as he rolls a silver dollar between his fingers. "Sure, West, whatever suits you."

"That's the spirit. You men go on back to where you're stayin' for the night, and I'll see you, Handerson, at Sunday meetin' in the morning." When we get up to leave, West laughs. "Don't forget your Bibles, boys. I'm teachin' class tomorrow."

We fake snickers.

Sarge pulls the door behind us. "That'll be the last time he shames the Lord in church."

## CHAPTER 55

# THE NIGHT BEFORE
# THE FIGHT

### DUSK, APRIL 16, 1870

*Sometimes the heart of the darkest angel shines the brightest light.*

THE SUN HAS set on South Farm and so have my hopes of doing anything other than what is in the stars above. Though I don't believe in fate, some things happen without a choice. My heart grows cold, but my skin is on fire. My thoughts take me down roads I never wanted to travel again. And my soul? Empty.

Matt's prepared a fine meal, and we eat like there's no tomorrow. There might not be for some of us. We step out on the porch. Rainy lights a cigar, and J.A. offers me tobacco for my pipe. Tonight I smoke.

The song of a whippoorwill breaks through the oaks to smooth my aching soul. A shooting star flashes green across the sky in the direction of Atlanta, a sign that St. Michael goes before us to prepare the way. I'm just hoping so, I reckon.

We walk out to where Ise has a fire going with makeshift seats in a circle. Ise and Tarle have become friends and talk while sharpening their knives.

I sit on a barrel and warm my hands. "A bit chilly tonight, ain't it?"

No one speaks. Matt serves coffee like he did at the Bankston Hotel. He's outdone himself on this trip. Sarge was smart for keeping him around. Satisfied everyone's cared for, Matt takes a long slurp of coffee like a calf sucking on his momma's teat.

Sarge laughs. "Dang, boy, sounds like you hung on to your momma's titty a little too long."

Matt spills his coffee laughing. No one else laughs.

Sarge sits back. "Y'all are awful quiet tonight."

Rainy blows three smoke rings in a row. Someone has to break the ice to get us prepared for the coming storm of terror. "Lummy, you never told us about Lester."

"Yeah, that's one I'd like to forget."

J.A. whittles a piece of cedar. "Yeah, but we need that story to remind us why we're fightin' and what it takes to survive. Your stories helped save us all at Vicksburg."

Tarle stops sharpening his knife. "I need to hear it, Uncle Lummy."

I cringe at the thought of resurrecting those memories—even more so that my young nephew will hear me tell them. But I do, anyway, talking about how Lester bullied me for years.

Ise covers his mouth as he laughs. "So, what'd you do?"

I stand to stretch my back. "I got bigger." Everyone laughs.

Rainy flicks the ash from his cigar. "That's for damn sure."

J.A. sips his coffee. "Peas and cornpone, taters and gravy, biscuits and butter, fried deer meat and catfish, blackberry cobbler, and—"

Sarge chuckles. "Sure as hell worked."

Tarle stands to measure himself against my height. "Six foot six?"

"That's what they tell me." I step beside him. "Hell, boy, I'm only half a head taller'n you."

Tarle grins with pride. "Just like Uncle Silas who fought at the Battle of New Orelans?"

"You favor him. I got to see him a couple times, once just before he passed. I was ten. That's when he told me his stories."

Tarle sits down. "The ones cousin Mary in Choctaw County is writin' down for the family?"

"Yes." I tell how Lester laughed and jeered when Susannah was taken by Mister Gilmore in a cardgame in Bucksnort, about picking up Kneehigh over my head and slamming him down on hardpan street in Bankston, and later killing Lester when he attacked Ma and the girls. That's more history than anybody should have to remember.

I look over at Ise, whose eyes are big as saucers. I tell a few more stories but figure that's enough for now. I finish with a funny.

"I had a mark on my back that drew bullies to me like flies to the shit pile." It didn't work. Nobody laughs. I didn't think it was that funny either.

Ise isn't satisfied with my answer to his question about bullies. "There has to be somethin' else besides you gettin' bigger that made you strong enough to fight them demons. This ain't gonna be like fightin' in the Army. I need to know what you did, so's I can be ready tomorrow."

I jerk the knife Pa made me from its sheath and thumb the blade. A thin red line appears, and I put my thumb to my mouth to stop the bleeding. "Gettin' bigger wasn't it at all. A large man doesn't make a big man. How big a man is never determines who he is or how he handles bullies. Many a giant has fallen like a lightning struck, rotten ass hickory tree in the forest, and no one even took notice."

Ise eyes my knife. "So, what then?"

I grin at the flickering campfire. "I lost my fear." I pick up a smoldering stick that stings the fire out of my fingers but not the fear out of my soul.

Ise sits up, wondering what I'll do next.

I throw the glowing stick back into the fire.

Rainy leans forward. "Sometimes the heart of the darkest angel shines the brightest light."

Sarge draws his coat closer. "And that angel does the most good for the most people."

I rub my fingers together, experiencing the pain once again. "There comes a time when the soul becomes like stone, and pain is put to the side for what must be done."

Ise asks, "How'd you get over your fear, Lummy?"

"Yeah, about that. When I was eleven years old, my ma and me went to pick an old couple's kitchen garden who couldn't do it themselves. We went inside to visit, and Ma took longer than I wanted to listen, so I went outside to play with their dog, like I'd done many times before. He was a cur, but he was big. We ran and played and had a great time. Ma finished her visitin' and called for me to come help her. We finished pickin' and brought the vegetables to the house. We laid them on a table where the old couple could get to them. They'd gone with our preacher to town for supplies. I'd just slapped the reins on the mule to get the wagon rolling when Ma said she'd left her bonnet inside the house.

"I hopped off the wagon and petted the dog as I trotted inside. As I shut the door behind me on the way out, the dog attacked me, biting my wrist as I fended him off. He bit my side as I scrambled up into the wagon, but not before slipping and bumping my head on the wagon wheel. A goose egg knot swole up on my head faster than I could rub it. Ma was crying. I was shaking and mad as a hornet. I couldn't figure out why he attacked me."

Ise shudders like he just stepped out into a frosty night. "I would'a fell out and gave up."

I stir the fire with a long branch. "My pa came to me after Ma patched me up. He said, 'Son, your ma's afraid that what happened today is gonna change you, knowin' you've got a soft heart.' It was my best moment with him. He asked, 'Lummy, how do you feel about what happened?' I answered, 'Like I trusted a good friend but was tricked and beaten up by a bully, like Lester at school.' Pa said, 'Son, there's two ways you can go. Let it defeat you and always cower to bullies. Or, learn to defend yourself.' He left the room so I could think."

Ise asks, "What about the dog?"

"The dog did what the dog was supposed to do—be a dog. From then on, I knew what to expect and prepared myself for what a dog might do. It's the same with bullies. Bullies do what bullies do. So, I prepare to defend myself at all times."

Ise squints. "And you lost your fear by—"

"By decidin' I'd be as mean as I needed to be at all times, ready for whatever came at me."

Rainy shifts to a more comfortable position. "Hence, it takes a devil to whip the Devil."

I snap my head around. "I ain't proud of the things I've done, Rainy." I walk away from the fire. I stop at the barn where Old Bart and I stayed when we fought Dawg Smith.

Pain strikes my forehead like someone popped me with a hammer. I want to puke. Dawg Smith's eyes bulge as I slice his neck with the knife Pa made me. His throat gurgles as it fills with blood. I press the owl claw Dan gave me into my wrist until it bleeds. It doesn't work. They all come back to me. The beatings Pa gave me, the anger when I cut Ben with the same knife, Captain Tom Ford taunting me and the sound of his neck snapping when they hanged him, the eyes of the sailor I shot off the gunboat the night the Yankees ran the batteries at Vicksburg, the last words of friends I hold dear—Mr. Allrice, Poole, Old Bart—and Seth hanging from the tree on our farm, his cabin burning in the dark night. I'm angry and weak as a wilted leaf. I collapse to my hands and knees.

J.A rushes over. "It's all right, Lummy. It's all right."

Sarge brings whiskey.

I swish it around in my mouth and spit it out. I clear my throat. "The memories that kept me alive at Vicksburg and with the Mounted Rifles are destroying me now. Poole and Old Bart dying... oh, hell, I can't do this. Conjuring up the Devil's anger don't work no more." I puke.

J.A. comforts me. "You're alive because of those deeds. Lives have been saved, property has been protected, and the right flag flies in the wind over Mississippi because of those deeds."

I cry. "What about Seth, Mistuh Allrice and Momma Sophie, Poole, and Old Bart? Susannah?"

J.A. whispers, "They knew the possibilities but didn't turn away from the path set before them. Will you?"

I shake my head and touch the handle of the knife that took off Dawg's head. "I won't turn away from what the Lord has called me to do, dammit."

J.A. squeezes my arm. "Lummy, I've known you for some years and fought by your side. I'm better for it. You are who you are, in this place, in this moment, because of those deeds."

I suck in a deep breath. "It's time."

Rainy hands me a cup of shine. "Can't sing, can't dance, so we best go do this."

I drink it all. "Morning will come soon enough. We better get some rest."

# CHAPTER 56

# DAYTIME STORMS ARE THE WORST

## BEFORE DAWN, EASTER SUNDAY, APRIL 17, 1870

*Daytime storms are the worst. You can see death coming.*

**M**ORNING COMES TOO soon, but the last bit of darkness gives me comfort. I wander away from the house. I whisper to the stars, "I gotta keep myself together."

I wring my hands. I shiver from the damp air, but I shudder from the ice in my soul. I press the owl claw into my wrist. I puncture the skin. I put the small wound to my mouth. Blood. I'm tired of tasting blood.

Granny whispers in the breeze wisping through the pines, *"If you stand fast for a right and just reason, you will stand alone like a great old oak. A good friend with whom I speak from time to time says, 'If you fall to the ground, fall like a seed, you'll sprout—'"*

I'm aggravated. "To do what, Granny? Fall again, again, and again?"

Granny's eyes glow like fire, swirling like the agate she gave me.

"I'm sorry, Granny, I'm just so tired in my soul."

*"You've always known that you were given a special work, Grandson, and that the risk is great."*

"This West is the worst I've ever encountered."

*"You must defeat him, but the cost will be great."*

"The cost is *already* too much. Do I need to repeat the names of those—"

Granny steps from the shadows. *"They are where Creator wants them."*

"There's a lot at stake with Martha and the kids. I can't see what's comin'. I must know—"

Granny flashes like a lightning bug. *"What will happen tomorrow?"*

"Will I die, Granny?"

*"Who knows that but the Lord of the Universe? Even Creator chooses not to know at times."*

"What about my wife and children?"

*"You worry about that which has yet to happen."*

"Who will take care of them if I'm killed?"

*"You trusted Creator when you left your son."*

I hang my head. "He's in good hands."

*"And you believe you made that happen?"*

"I don't."

*"Never forget that your granny knows the woes of the living. I understand worry."*

"But I could be dead."

*"Yes, but not your story."*

"How do you know that?"

*"You know mine, don't you?"*

"I do."

*"You want to know about my father?"*

"Yes. If I die, who would remember me? I'd be forgotten."

*"Have you forgotten your niece, Mary, who pens the story?"*

"I just don't know if I can do this."

*"You would not be the first to give the supreme sacrifice. You must know this. Ask my father, the captain."*

"That's all fine, well, and good, but where would that leave my family?"

*"In the hands of the One who gave them life in the first place."* Granny wisps away like the smoke of our cookfire.

I look to the sky. "Damn, it's hard to trust you, Creator."

Granny speaks from pine needles brushing against tree bark. *"I heard that, Grandson."*

I press the agate close to my cheek. It's warm. The rattling of pans startles me. I put the agate back in my pocket and walk back to the cookfire.

Rainy pours himself and me a cup of coffee, while Matt rolls out biscuit dough and cuts circles with an empty bean can.

Rainy looks to the east. "If the sun decided not to shine this day, we'd all be better for it. Some things are best done in the shadows of a dark moon."

Ise pokes his head up. "Is coffee ready yet?"

Rainy throws a stick at him. "Roll over, sleeping beauty. You need all the rest you can get."

He snickers. "Just wake me when the biscuits are done."

Matt lays strips of salt pork in the frying pan. The sizzle sounds good, and the smell is inviting. But I have no appetite.

Rainy nods for me to walk with him. In the kindest voice I've ever heard him speak, Rainy whispers, "Your granny's voice is gentle as a breeze through pine needles."

"She's always with me, good and bad, through thick and thin. She walks with Creator like no one I've ever known."

"She said your story won't die."

"Why does she even bother with me?"

"She knows your heart, brother."

"But ain't it the heart of a demon?"

Rainy grabs my jacket and jerks me close. The fire in his eyes glares as bright as Granny's did a moment ago. He catches himself and relaxes. He straightens my coat and smiles like a big brother who wants to hug me and beat me to death at the same time.

"Wait. How'd you hear Granny talkin'?"

Rainy's stare penetrates the deepest part of my soul. "I've been hearing her speak since I was a kid. She's my kin, too."

I rub my head. "Why haven't you told me before now?"

"I didn't know until I heard her voice speaking to you just now."

"You mean we're kin?"

"Kind of. Granny Thankful and her sister Anna were daughters of Captain James Mills. They married your grandpa Willoughby and great uncle Temple, who you call your real grandpa."

"That's right, but how'd you—?"

"When I left Captain Tom Ford hanging in Choctaw County, I went to Natchez to find out about my people."

I scratch my head. "I never knew anything about the Mills people. I'm not sure Pa did, either. He never spoke of them."

"It appears Captain Mills started off as a lieutenant but was killed some time after he became a captain in the 10th North Carolina."

"None of my people talked about that, except for Uncle Silas who fought at New Orleans with Andy Jackson. He once mentioned that we had somebody who died in the Revolution."

"That's him, I bet."

"Grandpa Temple *did* say they had land and a grist mill in North Carolina before they moved to Georgia. That's where two Tullos brothers married Mills sisters. I'd like to know more about Captain Mills." Mary will be excited about this. "Amazing, Uncle Silas didn't even know his own mother's maiden name."

Rainy shrugs. "Guess they didn't discuss such things back then."

I drain the last of my coffee and pitch the dregs into the grass. "So, what'd you mean by kinda sorta bein' kin?"

"Remember me telling you my real father's name was Thomas Mills? The devil who raped my mother murdered him."

"Yeah, I do."

"I've made peace with all of that. But I did get the blessing of my father's spirit the preacher at the Natchez orphanage said."

"And Granny?"

"I call her Granny, but she's my grandpa's sister. She came to me after I killed Ratliff and confirmed it. She said, *'Blood doesn't make people kin. Souls do.'*" Rainy takes out a smooth river stone the size of a quail egg that's clear as a crystal. "She said this rock would remind me to keep a clear eye and keep my life going in the right direction." He holds it up to the sunlight breaking through the trees. "Funny thing, she gave it to me just before I crossed the Mississippi River to find my father. Not long after, I met you the night the coyotes chased you."

I hold up my agate. "She gave me this."

It hits us both at the same time. Without thinking, we embrace like I did with Jasper and James when they found me down by the Mississippi in Vicksburg back in '62.

Rainy pushes me back, holding my shoulders. "After all this time, how could we not—"

"Granny knew the right time to reveal that truth."

Rainy bear hugs me again. "You're the only kin I got, boy." He whimpers just a little. "I've never had any family around."

We realize what we're doing and break away like two schoolboys who put a frog in the teacher's desk and act like they didn't do it.

Ise rises up. "What's all the commotion? Can't get no sleep 'round here with all that yappin' about devils and dark angels, captains, and such. Y'all makin' me scare't over here."

We playfully say at the same time, "Shut up, Ise."

He laughs, then ducks and covers his head, expecting a stick to come sailing in his direction.

Matt pours Ise a cup of coffee. "Get on over here, Ise, before you talk yourself right out of gettin' any of these biscuits. They'll be done in a bit."

Ise grins. "No, suh, I can't be missin' out on dem der catheads. You cook gooder'n my maw, and my backbone done stuck to muh ribs. Cans I'za pleaz has one uh dem biskits, dear suh? I knows theys got to be gooder'n grits."

Matt hums a hymn as he pulls pieces of salt pork from the iron skillet.

Sarge strolls into camp, having visited a nearby tree for his morning constitutional. "Those biscuits are good enough to make a rabbit slap a hound."

I shake my head. "Ain't none of y'all right in the head. Where's Tarle?"

Rainy nods in the direction of the barn. "Reliving old times, I reckon."

Matt yells, "Tarle, breakfast's 'bout done."

Tarle starts walking back but stops like somebody called his name. He shakes his head and comes our way.

CHAPTER 57

# PREPARING
# FOR BATTLE

## DAWN, EASTER SUNDAY, APRIL 17, 1870

*Prayers don't always calm a storm, but they can get you through one.*

ISE SPREADS HIS arms like a duck cupping its wings to land. "Let's leave on a prayer."

I look at Sarge. Sarge looks at Rainy. Rainy looks at J.A. who looks at me. We're surprised that Ise has stepped up to take the lead like this.

I remove my hat. "That'd be good right about now, Ise."

We shuffle to form a circle with heads bowed. Ise takes out a small piece of paper. It's obvious he's taken time to prepare.

Ise studies the words, then lifts his eyes to the heavens. "Lord, today is special. Easter day should be a time of resurrectin', but I believe it will be a time of layin' evil men down. There'll be men left in the tomb today until you decide, O Lord, what to do with them. You knows how much I care for my brothers here, for who they is, and what they be willin' to sacrifice for your work of savin' souls from evil men. So, I'm callin' on you, Lord. Your servant David said in a Psalm, 'The Lord is my light and my salvation, so who am I gonna fear? The Lord is the strength of my life. Of whom shall I be afraid?' So, we're askin' for your help, O Lord, in our time of desperation and need. The man who killed the giant Goliath says again, 'I will lift up mine eyes unto the hills, from whence cometh my help,' yes, 'My help cometh from the Lord who made both heaven and earth.' Send that help to go before us, Lord. Saint Michael, the Archangel, defend us in battle. Be our protection against the wickedness and the snares of the Devil. May God rebuke him, we humbly pray. And do thou, O Prince of the Heavenly Host, by the power of God, thrust into hell Satan and all evil spirits who wander through the world seeking the ruin of souls. Amen."

We soak in the words.

Ise fidgets around. "That's all I got. I hope I didn't go too long."

Sarge nods and squeezes his shoulder. "Fine prayer, son. You remind me of another preacher."

Ise gives me a toothy grin. "That there's a compliment I'll take, Sarge."

Rainy backhands Ise in the chest with a smile. "Hell, I thought we were going to have to take up a collection to get you to shut up. Good words, Ise. Good words."

I pat Ise's shoulder. "You done good, son. We're all prayed up now. You got that Saint Michael prayer from the priest at St. Paul's Catholic Church in Vicksburg, didn't you?" I straighten his coat. "You'll do well to spend time with that good man."

"I'll go see him jest soon as we get free from here, and take Jenny wid me."

We all laugh and offer our congratulations to Ise—until we notice J.A. isn't joining in.

He lifts his head. "Brothers, my time is up today."

Nobody says anything. Sarge starts to speak, but I shake my head. We just leave it alone. There's a sense that comes over a man when he believes his life is over. There were men in Vicksburg who knew when their time was up.

This is not like Doc Simpson, who stood up and took a Yankee bullet to head at Vicksburg after his wife sent him in a letter to say she had left him. No, those men wanted to live, go home to their families. But they just knew their days were up.

J.A. knows. And Granny said as much.

# CHAPTER 58

# SUNDAY AIN'T FOR CHURCH THIS MORNING

### 6:00 A.M., EASTER SUNDAY, APRIL 17, 1870

*We're not gettin' all dressed, but we do have some place to go.*

S ARGE FINISHES TIGHTENING his saddle. "No fancy dressing for church service this morning, unless it's for a funeral, boys."

Rainy stuffs his gun cleaning kit back into his saddlebag. "I'm always dressed for it."

J.A. asks, "What was West talkin' about, you killin' your father and somethin' about a judge, if you don't mind me askin', Rainy?"

Rainy studies the pinkish clouds lighting up from the sun peeking over the horizon. "It was a day not unlike this one when I killed the man who raped my mother and murdered my daddy." He turns to J.A. "But it was a cloudless day when I killed the judge who allowed it to happen."

Matt yells, "Y'all come eat." He's cooked up salt pork, a pot of grits, and biscuits golden brown. "I don't have eggs, but Mistuh Davis sent this fine pear syrup, if you like."

I don't want to eat, but I need to. It'll be a long day.

Matt hums "Amazing Grace," and Ise sings the words. We gather weapons and mount up. I take a long look around at the farm where I worked several seasons with Ben and Dorcas. I won't come back here.

A stray cat sneaks from the barn where Old Bart and I stayed before we took down Dawg Smith and his outlaw Home Guard. The cat twitches his tail with eyes fastened on a squirrel chiseling a nut at the base of a big hickory. *You won't catch that squirrel. And West, you won't catch this one.*

# CHAPTER 59

# THE DEVIL GOES TO CHURCH, TOO

## 9:50 A.M., EASTER SUNDAY, APRIL 17, 1870

*The Great Deceiver goes to church, too. But not to praise the Lord.*

WE MEET DAN Dean on the road leading a group of men three hundred yards from the Methodist Church.

"Lummy, you won't believe it. The West-Kimbrell Gang walked into the church house like they were going to Bible study and took my family. Lec Ingram and the Collins brothers came in with Colt .44s cocked and warrants in hand."

I beat Sarge to the punch. "Where'd they take 'em?"

"To Collier's Store and Saloon. A lady on her way to church said West pointed to the stairway, and they rushed them into the hall above the store. But my pa, Abel, stood up to West and challenged what he was doin'.

"West, in his devilish sweet and mild voice, said, 'Mistuh Dean, we only want Dan. He's a fugitive. Tell us where he is, and you'll save us a lot of trouble.' Pa said he didn't know where I was, and West knew this all along but acted like my pa was lyin'. He shoved my ma and pa, sayin', 'Get 'em upstairs, and make it quick. Tie 'em up.' Then he sent the Collins brothers and Ingram to arrest a few more folks. They're with my parents in that upstairs room."

Sarge rubs his chin. "Anything else?"

Dan sobs but collects himself. "Yeah, town people have gathered around the store, wondering what's happening."

"That's good and bad. Good that we will be able to count on their help but bad that some might get hurt."

Rainy blows a smoke ring. "It's not uncommon to get bit when you put a rabid dog down."

Dan cries. "I should've just given myself up to 'em. But I—"

Sarge snaps, "Would be dead. We'll get your folks back."

"But West will convince the good citizens that he and Kimbrell will take them to court in Natchitoches, but he'll fake them trying to escape and kill 'em all. Oh Lord, what have I done?"

"Exactly what you should've done. You've set our plan into motion. The West-Kimbrell Gang is going down today, dammit! How many men you got?"

"These twelve, and there'll be more comin' where I spread the word."

"Good." Sarge is nervous. He hadn't counted on West taking hostages.

A whistle comes from the church house. One of West's men waves him in for Bible study. West dusts off, straightens his jacket, and removes his hat before entering, Bible in hand.

I can't help myself. "What a brazen son of a bitch West is."

Sarge leans over and whispers, "I'm not sure what to do now."

"I do." I tap my horse with my boot heels and ride to the church.

Sarge whispers, "Lummy…."

I pat the air with my hand. "Just watch for my signal."

Sarge growls. "Damn."

# CHAPTER 60

# GOIN' TO CHURCH WITH THE DEVIL

## 10:05 A.M., EASTER SUNDAY, APRIL 17, 1870

*"And no marvel; for Satan himself is transformed into an angel of light. Therefore it is no great thing if his ministers also be transformed as the ministers of righteousness; whose end shall be according to their works."*
*—Paul, the Apostle*

I TIE MY horse to a tree a few yards from the building. I dust off my clothes and remove my hat as I enter the whitewashed clapboard church house. Sweet voices sing "Rock of Ages." But wait. It can't be. West, with eyes closed and arms lifted, leads the congregational singing. What gall. I sit before he finishes.

West moves to the speaker's podium and flips pages in his Bible, searching for the place from which he'll teach class. He adjusts his glasses and looks up when I clear my throat. The look on his face is worth his weight in gold. At first he scowls but turns that into a grin.

"It seems we have a visitor on this great and glorious resurrection morning. Welcome, friend. We're just about to start Bible study."

That's the last thing I want to be called by West—*friend.*

I sit in a pew in the back with easy access to the door. From there it would be only five good running strides if I had to make for my horse in a hurry.

West breaks into a demonish smile. "Would you be so kind as to grace us with your name, sir?"

"Handerson."

"Thank you, Mistuh Handerson. Would we be having the pleasure of anyone else accompanying you on your visit today?"

"I *do* have a traveling companion, but he's not of the church-going persuasion. He tends to seek peace for his soul with spirits elsewhere. He found a suitable meeting hall in Collier's Store and Saloon."

A few snickers erupt from men who probably frequent the bar but whose wives elbow them back into holy submission.

West tries to keep his smile, but he's unsure of my meaning. "We will pray for his soul and his wicked habits."

"Not to worry, he'll soon be in good hands."

That's what West wanted to hear. He gives a slight wink, and I nod. He takes on a cheery tone. "If you have your Bibles, turn to the Book of Matthew, chapter twenty-six, starting with verse number two." The small crowd flips the pages to the assigned text. West compliments them. "Listen to that. Sounds like angels wings fluttering with every page turned in the Good Book."

I'm thinking, yeah, the same angel wings that'll soon pick your ass up by the shoulders and carry you to Hell. You won't be so sweet spirited then.

West holds his Bible high in the air. "Ye know that after two days is the feast of the Passover and the Son of man is betrayed and to be crucified." He begins there and teaches a rather fine lesson on the resurrection of Jesus and the gratefulness we should have for his willingness to die to save us from our sins. After talking with Granny Thankful a few hours ago, is this a prophecy about what's fixing to happen? I shake off the shudder that tries to seize my soul. Any other time, I'd appreciate the speaker's words. Not today. If Satan can masquerade as an angel of light, so can his ministers. In fact, I want to scream, "How can you teach God's Word after having thrown hundreds, maybe even a thousand, murdered people into wells all over the countryside?" I don't. But I do something else, though.

West declares, "And when Christ took on the sins of the world, his Holy Father turned his back on his dying son. God is truth. God is pure. He cannot look upon sin. Jesus died alone with no comfort and—"

I raise my hand with my index finger pointing to the roof. "Hold on just a moment. Did you say God the Father abandoned his only begotten in the time of his greatest need?"

West leans in. "That's what Scriptures teaches."

"As you see it, Mistuh West. Doesn't mean your word is gospel."

West tries to recover. "Well, I—"

"The word states that God will remember our sins no more. It seems to me he can't forget 'em if he can't see 'em. No, I believe God the Father was the closest he'd ever come to God the Son when Jesus bore every sin of every human being for all time. No, he looked straight at His Son when Jesus said, 'It is accomplished,' because it was at that very moment the sins of the world were forgiven."

West smirks. "What about when Jesus said, 'My God, my God, why hast thou forsaken me?"

"I'm glad you asked. So, I'll ask *you* a question. If it was you, with nails in your hands and feet, the flesh ripped from your back by the lash, and blood dripping from a crown of thorns wedged onto your head, wouldn't you be wondering where your daddy was? I do believe the Lord also says, 'I will never leave thee, nor forsake thee.'"

West remains silent. Church members nod and whisper, agreeing.

"Jesus is God, but he chose to be just as human as you and me. Best to let him stay that way, don't you think?" My soul burns with anger now, and West sees it.

"You *do* know your Scripture, sir."

"Not so well as you will know it soon, I think."

"I'm not sure of your meaning, stranger."

"There are no strangers in the house of the Lord. For do we not all seek the Lord's face together in this house of worship?"

West cringes for the first time since I saw him cower in Vicksburg when the Yankees attacked. I can't help myself. The last time I had this much fun in church was when Ben gave that Cajun preacher hell at Shiloh Baptist Church years ago.

"For the Lord says through the Psalmist, 'When thou saidst, Seek ye my face, my heart said unto thee, Thy face, Lord, I will seek.' Maybe more preachers should seek the Lord's face and look to their own sin before they call others to change."

West closes his Bible, saying, "I believe that's all the time we have for today.

I leave you with this admonition. Good Christians, leave this place loving God with your whole hearts and your neighbors as yourselves."

I rise at the closing song, "My Hope is Built on Nothing Else," staring West down, never blinking.

West gives me a furrowed brow look, and I wink. He relaxes the tension in his face.

At the start of the closing prayer, West ducks out a side door. He's headed back to Collier's. He'll be expecting me to bring Dan Dean there.

But I won't be there.

# CHAPTER 61

# IT BEGINS

## 11:45 A.M., EASTER SUNDAY, APRIL 17, 1870

*You may not get what you want, but you will always get what's coming to you.*

OUR BAND OF demon-hunters watch from a nearby thicket as West paces back and forth in front of Collier's Store and Saloon. He wrings his hands, waiting for me to hand Dan Dean over to him. When I don't show up, West takes a youth named Lige from his stash of prisoners in the hall above the store and forces him into the woods within earshot of our position. He pelts him with questions about Dean's whereabouts.

Lige stands stiff as a cypress plank and stutters, "But, but—I don't, don't know where he is!"

West waves his arm. "Have you seen him or a man named Handerson?"

Lige shakes head, tears streaming down his cheeks. "Please, suh, don't hurt me. Please!"

"Hurt you,"—West laughs—"why, if you don't help me find Dan Dean, I'm leaving you in these here woods for the possums."

Lige cowers like a whipped pup. "B-but honest, I—I d-don't know. He could be anywhere, on either side of town, hidden in a th-thicket or a hollow like a wild animal."

West shouts, "Yeah, and you have a pretty fair idea where that thicket or hollow is. Now quit stallin', or I'm putting a bullet plumb through you."

"I—I don't know for sure," Liges whimpers. "B-but more'n likely he's hi-din' out 'tween h-here and the Killingsworth farm. You know he and J.A. are friends. Th-that's all I know."

One of West's lead gunmen swats the air. "This kid don't know shit."

West turns with his pistol drawn. "Let's go the Killingsworth place and find that bastard. If Dean gets to the law in Nachitoches before we get these prisoners on the road to the jail there and kill 'em all, we'll all be had."

Collins throws up his hands. "I'm with you, boss."

West and Collins put Lige back with the other prisoners above the store and ride off.

We sit still until they're out of sight.

Dan squints with a hint of fear in his eyes. "They have my folks."

Sarge leans on his saddlehorn. "We know."

"So, what are you gonna do?"

I break in. "I think we're makin' this up as we go along."

We sneak into the empty building across the street from Collier's Store and Saloon to wait for West's return.

# CHAPTER 62

# EASTER SUNDAY MASSACRE

12:15 P.M., EASTER SUNDAY, APRIL 17, 1870

*Death and resurrection. It takes both for new life to begin.*

WITH WEST GONE, the crowd of onlookers grows, as do the number of men who want to join the takedown. Several young men step up on the porch of the building where we're hiding. The oldest says, "Dan Dean ought to be told. His whole family is in there." Another agrees. "He's hidin' close by. He'll have some guns, too."

Dan starts to open the door, but Sarge stops him. "What are you doing?"

"I know these men. They'll help." Dan waves for the leader to come inside. He motions for the others to keep talking as if nothing has changed. Dan asks, "John Patten, what're you doin' here?"

Patten bear hugs Dan. "Good to see you, Uncle Dan. We thought you was hidin' out in the pine woods or, at worst, West kilt you by now." He straightens up and announces, "They got your family in there. Me and my friends are here to take back the store and free the prisoners."

I whisper to J.A., "Some young men with brave ambitions but no plan and no weapons."

He grins. "A lot like us when we left Winnfield to enlist."

Sarge takes charge. "Let's get moving. Patten, who's the youngest?"

"Jesse," Patten answers.

"Get him."

Patten waves in Jesse.

Sarge grasps the boy's shoulder. "How old are you?"

"Thirteen next month, sir."

"How good are you on a horse?"

Jesse smiles. "I won the five mile town race last Fourth of July."

Sarge smiles. "Good. I want you to ride hard and tell everyone you trust what's about to happen. Tell them to bring arms and meet us here quick as they can, you understand?"

"Yes, sir, I do."

"Get going, and be careful."

Jesse nods and slips out the back so as not to be seen by the guards who stand in front of the store waiting for West's return.

I follow him. "Jesse, take my horse. He's a good 'un." I reach in my coat pocket. "Here, take this." It's the derringer I took from the bully who disrespected Susannah's sister, Ruth, in the Bankston Hotel.

He stares at the small but lethal weapon. "Thanks, Mistuh. Can I know your name?"

"How good are you at keepin' secrets?"

"As good as I can ride this horse and better."

"I'm Lummy Tullos, but call me Handerson because, as they say, I was never here."

He blinks twice. "My daddy knows you."

"And who would that be?"

"Mose Cockersham. He said y'all worked together a long time ago on Mistuh Gilmore's place and that you and him—"

"Took down Dawg back in '63." I hand him the silver badge the good folks of Winn Parish gave me after it was over. "That's right, he was there."

Jesse nods. "He'd be here now with us except West's men beat him up when he chastised them for takin' what they wanted from Davis's Store. They made me watch, and I had to haul him to the Doc's in our wagon."

I take Jesse by the shoulders. "Mistuh Davis is all right, ain't he? Tell me he's okay."

"Yes, sir, he's fine. They didn't do nothin' to him except rob him blind right in front of his face. My pa took an axe handle to 'em, but they wuz too many."

"Is Mose gonna be all right?"

"Yes, suh. He's bruised up pretty good, and the doc says he's got some cracked ribs but nothin' my old pa won't come back from in time to get seed in the ground."

"You best get goin', and don't run my horse flat out, just steady. Give him only a hat full of water at every other stop. Keep the pocket pistol handy and show 'em the badge if anybody needs proof of what you're sayin'." I slap the horse's butt. "I expect you to bring my horse and my stuff back."

He tips his hat and gallops away.

I walk back inside to find West's guards have gone into the saloon for drinks. "Perfect. They'll lose their edge gettin' liquored up." I notice the young men are gone. "Where'd those boys go, Sarge?"

"They're like hunting dogs let out of the pen. I couldn't hold them here. They said they had to go do something."

Rainy snorts, drops his cigar, and grounds it out with his boot. "Yeah, something foolish."

# CHAPTER 63

# WHEN BOYS BECOME MEN

## 1:10 P.M., EASTER SUNDAY, APRIL 17, 1870

*Youth ain't always wasted on the young.*

JESSE RETURNS, WALKING my horse down the street to a warehouse at the edge of the village. He nods as he leads my mount through the double doors.

Sarge scratches his head. "What's he doing?"

I grimace. "Beats the hell out of me, Sarge."

Rainy jumps up. "Look! There they come. Looks to be ten or twelve boys, and Patten's leadin' them."

J.A. shields his eyes. "They've got shotguns and pistols."

Ise grins. "Them boys mean business."

Tarle starts out the door to join them.

I snatch him back by the coat collar.

"Those are my friends, Uncle Lummy. If they're gonna take on Laws Kimbrell and the rest of West's men at the saloon, I'm gonna help 'em."

"My ass, you are. You promised to do what I say."

Tarle wrestles his jacket collar out of my hand. "Yes, sir, I did. But I sure as hell don't like it."

Sarge pats the air with his hands. "You'll get your turn, son. Just hold on a bit. Let's see what your friends are up to."

We watch the boys march to Collier's Store and Saloon like good soldiers. They make a considerable amount of noise, and the crowd regathers near the store where Laws Kimbrell arrived earlier to supervise guarding the prisoners above the store. A man wearing his Sunday best and glasses trots down the hill to intercept the small army of young men.

J.A. squints. "That's Professor George, their schoolmaster. Maybe he can talk some sense into them."

Tarle laughs. "I doubt it."

We overhear every word they banter back and forth.

Professor George stands between the boys and the store. "Now wait a minute, Patten, boys. This is all very good, but it's dangerous."

"Somebody's got to do it," Patten cuts in. "The old men won't do a damn thing to free those prisoners."

"You go in there like this, you'll be shot down."

Jesse barks, "They can't kill all of us, we—"

Professor George sighs. "You boys know Laws Kimbrell is a gunfighter." That didn't deter the boys in the least. "All right, I'm your schoolmaster, so listen to me now. I have an idea of how we can work this out a safer way." The boys gather around like a flock of turkeys ready to peck a pile of corn. "Jesse, I want you...."

Sarge looks at me. "Oh, hell, I better—"

I grab his arm. "No, I'll go." I hand Tarle my shotgun. "Be ready to use it if I call."

He nods.

I claw my long hair closer to my bearded cheeks, lower my hat to shield my face, tuck my chin into my chest, and ease out the door.

# CHAPTER 64

# SCHOOLMASTER
# AND GENERAL

## 1:20 P.M., EASTER SUNDAY, APRIL 17, 1870

*Being a professor ain't only about teaching history. It's livin' it, too.*

I CAN'T BELIEVE my eyes. These boys follow their schoolmaster to Collier's Store and Saloon like a general leading an army expecting to be victorious—calm, cool, and collected.

I slip into the crowd and shuffle to a shadowed corner. My pistol's primed, and my knife's ready to be unsheathed in a moment's notice. I whisper, "The nerve of these boys and their schoolmaster. We should've had them at Vicksburg." I can see Granville's face. "Hell, we did."

The boys scatter around the room, looking at items as if they intend to buy. Drinks in hand and laughing, the Nightriders don't give them a second look.

The storekeeper polishes glasses as he looks over the boys who are now in position. The signal having been given, the boys draw their guns to cover the Nightriders.

Patten shouts, "Put up your hands, all of you!"

Laws Kimbrell laughs with the others until they look around at all the pistol barrels pointed at them. It's as if they see these young men for the first time and as boys no more.

Kimbrell is visibly shaken. "What's the matter here—you kids gone crazy?"

"No time for talk, Kimbrell," Patten barks. "Turn around, all of you. Put your guns on the counter."

Laws gets up, but the sound of pistols cocking float around the room. "Now look here—what do you want?"

Professor George walks in. "Do as the boys say,"—he aims his shotgun at Laws's head—"and no foolishness, you understand?"

Laws and the rest of the guards look this way, then that. They have no choice but to do what these crazy-eyed boys demand.

Laws grits his teeth and spouts venom. "You're makin' an awful mistake, you rotten little sons of whores." He flashes his reddened eyes from one boy to the next. "Mark my word, all of you!"

The boys step forward, disregarding Laws's contempt.

Patten, cool as the center seed of a watermelon, says, "Don't be worryin' about all that. Turn around and do as you're told, Nightrider."

Laws and his men grudgingly drop their weapons on the store counter, and the boys herd the Nightriders out the door and into the street, where a wall of shotguns, old war muskets, pistols, and clubs hem them in.

One boy, holding an old flintlock that looks old enough to have been used by Uncle Silas at the Battle of New Orleans, yells, "Let's finish the job. March 'em over to the road."

Jesse shouts, "Yeah! Give 'em some of what they've been givin'."

They start to shove their prisoners toward the road when Dan Dean steps out of the abandoned building with Sarge and the rest of our small band.

"Wait a minute!"

All eyes of the crowd turn to Dan. He takes charge. "Get some rope from the store. Tie these men up and take them upstairs."

Jesse grumbles. "Shit, I want to kill these bastards for hurtin' my pa."

Sarge takes Jesse by the sleeve. "Let Dan take care of this."

Dan takes a key from Laws Kimbrell's pocket and marches West's men up the stairs. I duck in behind them, hat pulled down low. Dan unlocks the door and shoves the Nightriders inside. He cuts the ropes binding his parents and those of the other prisoners.

As he frees his brothers, he says, "I left guns and ammunition in Missus Peace's orchard, just inside the fence. Get over there and arm yourselves."

Most of the men who had been held hostage either arm themselves or take off on mounts to gather more recruits for the coming battle.

Dan spits at Laws Kimbrell. "You men still here, tie these bastards to the rafters. This is goin' to be a fight to the finish, and we'll end these demons' lives soon as we get West."

Sarge slips in the door unnoticed and stands by me. "This is exactly how I hoped this would go. A local boy taking charge."

Dan turns to Professor George. "I have a plan, and I need your help. Can you find me a hunter's horn? Not a powder horn, but one I can blow a call the Nightriders will recognize. Then we'll capture 'em all like a seine net catchin' shad."

Professor George trots to his desk and produces a horn. "I keep one handy to round up the boys from recess."

Dan walks over to Sarge and me. "I know their signal. Let's go out on the stairway balcony. That should be a good place to give the call." He blasts several long blows with the horn and a few shorter ones one after the other. He repeats the same calls two more times and says, "That ought'a bring 'em in."

# CHAPTER 65

# WAITIN' ON THE DEVIL TO APPEAR

## 1:30 P.M., EASTER SUNDAY, APRIL 17, 1870

*When good men do something, the world changes.*

SARGE INQUIRES, "HOW many men do you have?"

Dean smiles. "Seventy-five good men showed up at Clem Wilson's farm by nine o'clock this morning. They're coming from all over."

J.A. checks the rounds in his pistol. "Looks like your horn blowin' trick worked, for both good men and bad. West must be on his way here now."

I see a dust cloud in the distance. "Find your places, men. Here they come."

Dan Dean shields his eyes. "No, that's the men from Clem Wilson's farm."

Tarle gasps. "Hell, that's a damn army."

I cut my eyes at him. He knows to curb his cussin'.

Townspeople cheer when the posse arrives. The young men who took Laws Kimbrell and West's men into custody jeer. "It's about time!"

Jim Maybin, Clem Wilson, and the rest file into Collier's Store and Saloon.

Maybin asks, "Where's Kimbrell and the others?"

Dean answers, "Upstairs, tied up."

Maybin's sidekick, John Barr, yells, "What are we waiting for?"

Dean explains his hornblowing strategy and that he recognizes some of West's men already in the crowd.

Maybin leans in. "So, how can we tell the difference?"

I step up. "West gave me the gang's password."

Maybin turns to Sarge. "Let's get this thing done. I say we—"

Dean holds his hands up. "Let's wait a bit. Let's see if West himself comes in."

Everyone agrees and spreads out in the crowd, taking notice of West's men who have already arrived and are mingling around. They have no idea of the trap being set for them.

TWO HOURS PASS, and no West.

Sarge asks Dean, "Could he have been warned?"

Dean grimaces. "It'll be a damn shame if we don't get West. No matter how many of his men we capture or kill today, he can always get more."

Rainy lights a smoke. "That would not be good."

Sarge takes Dan Dean by the arm. "We can't wait." He turns to me. "What's the password, Lummy? Let's round these bastards up."

I share the password with Dean. He eases through the crowd speaking to the men he knows are part of the West-Kimbrell Gang.

I stay within earshot. When Dean whispers, "The clover is blooming," and an outlaw responds, "Spring is here," I mark the man as a Nightrider.

Dean instructs the men to assemble at the stairwell leading to where Laws Kimbrell and his men are held prisoner. He whispers, "We're gonna break in and set 'em free."

Dean wanders through the crowd, gathering the Nightriders who never question or protest his order. They nod and do as they are told, never suspecting a thing. They stand around, smoking and laughing, waiting for Dean to lead them upstairs.

Eight Nightriders gather under the stairwell to free Kimbrell and his men. Dean gives the signal, and before they can pull pistols, twenty shotguns and rifles are aimed at their heads. The Nightriders jerk around, this way and that, expecting Dean to get the drop on these crazy clerks and farmers. Tricked completely, the Nightriders drop their guns and knives and throw their hands in the air.

John Barr barks, "Put your hands down. We'll kill the first man who moves." He turns to Dean. "Cut Kimbrell and his men upstairs loose and bring 'em down here."

Sarge whispers to our small band, "This is working out just perfect. These men have stepped up and taken the bull by the horns."

Tarle whispers, "Yeah, but we don't have West."

I assure him, "He's comin', just watch and see."

# CHAPTER 66

# EXECUTION, ROMAN STYLE

## 2:00 P.M., EASTER SUNDAY, APRIL 17, 1870

*The Romans gave Jesus a mock trial and executed him.*
*These men don't even get a trial.*

SAM BARR TAKES charge and hustles the Nightriders to where the crowd awaits. We follow at a short distance.

Dan Dean leans against a post. "Damn if I ain't worn smooth out. I could fall asleep leanin' on this post right here."

I laugh and shake my head. "I know a man who slept standin' straight up in the rifle pits at Vicksburg."

J.A. grins. "Shut up, Lummy. I wasn't the only—"

Barr finishes talkin' with the others and holds up his hands to get the crowd's attention. "These murderers have been harassing us a long time. Murdering and stealing is their business. We aim to deal with them today and clean up this country. I want some law-abiding citizens with some guts and good eyesight each to take one of these coyotes as his personal responsibility. I want men who will shoot these coyotes and who are able to hit that coyote when he shoots. No man is to get away. Is that clear? All who figure they can do this job raise up your guns."

Rainy snickers. "I've shot coyotes before if you but remember?"

The pain of what's about to happen to these Nightriders grabs my soul. My stomach aches. I shake. Heat in my face brings sweatdrops.

Sarge presses the owl claw into my wrist.

I come back. "Thank you."

A few men raise their guns. Barr is disappointed.

Tarle rants, "Why won't they step up? I'll do it if they ain't willin'.'" He raises my ten gauge shotgun.

I yank his arm down. "This ain't for us to do. Give 'em a minute. They'll come through."

Barr confers with Maybin and Dean, then turns to the crowd. "All right, I want two men with a shotgun for each Nightrider. One will have a full load of buckshot and the other just powder and wadding. This'll relieve you of moral and legal responsibility. Jim Maybin has pardons signed by Governor Warmoth for all men willing to do their duty for home and family."

Men talk among themselves, and in just a few moments twenty-two men raise their guns into the air. Barr has his executioners.

Dean asks, "What about West?"

"What *about* West? Let's get these men in the ground and worry with him later."

"Gotcha." Dean had been the first volunteer to be in on the firing squad and has no problem leading the townsmen who drag the Nightriders to their fate in a field south of Atlanta, between the town and the woods.

Rainy whispers, "At least Romans gave Jesus a mock trial before they executed him. These men don't even get a trial."

"They don't deserve one."

Sarge says, "Rainy, Tarle, and J.A., you stay here with these men who'll remain at the store in case West shows up. Lummy, Ise, you're with me. Let's go."

Tarle shakes his head. "I want to go witness this." He starts out to follow Sarge and Ise.

I pull him back. "You'll be able to see it fine from here. Anyway, I need you here in case West shows up." That satisfies him for the moment. I follow Sarge and Ise, trailing behind the band of executioners and Nightriders.

The clouds part like Jesus coming back for the faithful as Barr yells, "You Nightriders line up, and you executioners aim straight and true. I don't want any buckshot hittin' anybody but these bastards." Each man is handed a shotgun not knowing if his is loaded with buckshot or not.

Laws Kimbrell looks around, expecting West any minute to swoop in like a hawk to rescue his Nightriders.

He doesn't.

Laws breaks the silence in this place of death. "Ain't it customary in these cases to grant the condemned a last request?"

Dean and Barr look at each other.

Barr answers, "If you have somethin' to say, get on with it. We don't have a lot of time."

"Dean, I served in the war with you, did you many favors in service and out. Is this how you repay me?"

No one knew Laws kept West from killing Dean.

Kimbrell doesn't tell much, but he does say, "All I want is for you to return the favor, friend."

Dan Dean drops his head. "It's too late, Laws, you know I can't."

Kimbrell steps out of line and lets out a string of words unfit for the roughest of men, blaming Dan for his being in this predicament and that he ought to be in line with the eleven about to meet their Maker.

But to no avail.

Kimbrell says, "If I'm to be shot without a trial, I want Dan Dean to take the first shot."

Dean looks around at the crowd. "I'm always happy to oblige a friend. If it's all right with everybody, I will fire the first shot at him."

The crowd that followed the death march from town roars with approval.

Barr barks, "You men who are condemned, turn with your backs facing your executioners. On the count of three, you can run for your lives."

Sarge looks at me. "What in the hell?"

I shrug. "I guess we'll be able to say they were trying to escape."

Sarge stomps his foot. "Lummy, soon as the guns fire, I want you to run back to town in case West has showed up."

Barr raises his right hand. "Three, two, *one!*"

The Nightriders run like their asses are on fire.

Primers pop, and shotgun blasts roar across the field.

Bodies drop like rocks.

It's done.

Sarge nods to me. "Glad that's over with. Now go!"

I set out in a dead out run for town. Tarle is there. I can't let anything happen to him.

West is coming.

# CHAPTER 67

# WHEN DEMONS ARE REMINDED OF HELL

## 2:30 P.M., EASTER SUNDAY, APRIL 17, 1870

*The Devil is once again defeated on resurrection day.*

I WORK MY way through the crowd in town to find West and his gunhand Collins yelling, "What's going on here? What's the meaning of this? My prisoners have been released. Where are my men?"

"You'll soon find out," J.A. says.

I pull him back. "Let's stay out of this."

Men rush in with rifles and shotguns. West and Collins pull guns and knives to fight. The townsmen disarm the leader of the Nightriders, but not before West slashes Tarle's shoulder.

I scream, *"Tarle!"*

He slips through the crowd. "Sorry, Uncle Lummy, but I had to—" He faints from blood loss.

I catch him before he hits the dirt. "Rainy, get him to a doctor, will you?" With the help of a couple of men, they carry him to Collier's Store and Saloon. I pick up my ten gauge shotgun and check the primers on the rabbit ears.

West spits. "I hope he's dyin', Handerson. I cut his ass good and—"

I hand J.A. the shotgun and pull the knife Pa made for me. I start for West. It's the first time I see fear in his eyes.

J.A. grabs my jacket and presses on my arm to lower the knife. "The doc's already on his way. Tarle will be fine. He'll get sewed up in no time." He hands me my shotgun. "You need to see this through the right way, Lummy. After all, he was our—"

"Comrade at arms, and he deserves a clean death?" I snatch the ten-gauge from his hand. "What am I sayin'? Shit, he deserves to be slow-roasted over a fire."

J.A. presses the owl claw into my wrist. "Stay with me, Lummy."

West laughs like a coyote yelping. "Handerson, shit. Everybody? This is that niggah lovin' bastard, Lummy Tullos." He stares at me with eyes of the Devil. "You helped set this up, Tullos. If I get free from all of this, I'm gonna skin your ass alive. Then I'm gonna cut that little bastard half-breed child of yours up, piece by piece, for catfish bait."

I reply in the calmness of a man resigned to death. "You won't."

West's eyes turn from a hellish glare to a mindless stare. "What was all that shootin' about?"

Dan Dean trots up with Sarge. "You mean, you don't know?"

West grits his teeth. *"You!* Laws should'a let me gun you down."

Dan kicks the dirt. "You can tell him that yourself."

West grows pale. "You mean, he's—"

"Yeah, along with ten other men of your hellish horde."

Sarge asks, "What's next?"

Dan studies West and Collins, making them sweat the silence. "March them over yonder." He points to the field where Laws Kimbrell and the rest of the Nightriders lie dead.

West screams, "No! No! No!"

Dan turns to Sarge. "In a few minutes, this thing will be over."

A cheer erupts from the crowd.

West and Collins jerk their heads this way and that.

West cries, "You're making a terrible mistake." He looks around the crowd, trying to find a sympathetic face. None is to be found. "You're obstructing justice. That's agin' the law."

Sam Barr walks up from the field of death where West and Collins will soon be taken. "We'll take a chance on that. Let's get moving. The executioners are waitin' over yonder."

West starts throwing out secret hand signals to friends, church members, and acquaintances in the crowd, in a frantic appeal for help. All turn away.

Dan's father, Abel Dean, shouts, "You should've thought of brotherhood when you stuffed all those good and innocent folks into your wells of the dead."

Barr and Dean shove West and Collins down the street toward the field where the executioners await their second round of delivering justice.

I walk beside West, who leans over to whisper, "Tullos, help me escape. Come on, now, we fought in the trenches together. Don't that mean anything to you?"

"Not a damn thing. I should've shot you when the Yankees attacked. Lots of lives would have been saved."

West rubs his shoulder on mine. "Listen to me, Tullos. You're a practical man. I have thirty thousand dollars in gold in a strongbox hidden at my farm. It's all yours if you get me out of this."

I act as if I'm interested. "That's an interesting proposition."

West pants. "Ain't it so? You'd be a rich man." The sound of his voice reminds me of Dawg Smith's venomous hiss. "I don't care how you do it, just so I get away."

I nod, giving West a glimmer of hope. "You best go on to hell now before I send you there."

Rainy whispers, "And you know the way. Your father the Devil waits for you."

West barks, "You'll get yours, Tullos. You, too, gun dealer. I still have friends who'll avenge my death." He winks at Laws Kimbrell's younger brother, Tom, who talked his way out of being executed along with the other Nightriders minutes ago.

Tom gives a slight nod.

West laughs hysterically.

Sarge slaps West on the back of the head. "Not before you get yours. And by the way, if that gold is where you say it is, it'll be found, and we'll distribute it to families of those you raped, murdered, and plundered. You can bet on that."

West growls like a wounded animal. He breaks free and rushes over to a group of women from his church. "Pray that I escape. I have a wife and daughters." He looks them each in the eye, hoping.

No one prays.

West looks around and grabs an old branding iron leaning against a hitching post. He jumps up on a nearby stump and raises the branding iron to bring it down on my head.

J.A. rushes West, who swings the iron and catches J.A. in the temple. J.A. falls and crawls around on the ground like a turtle making for water, blood gushing from a head wound.

West gloats. "How do you like that, Tullos? I just killed your best friend."

I say nothing.

West laughs and spits. "You ain't no better'n me, Tullos. Bein' a preacher don't make you right. Never did, you self-righteous son of a bitch. You've done just as much wrong as I did and more. And you're fixin' to do it again."

I check the caps on my ten gauge shotgun and without looking up say, "I do just enough wrong to keep the wrong people away."

West continues ranting, "I should've shot you in the back of the head when you talked about puttin' the twentieth star for Mississippi back on the Union flag. Damn turncoat."

Satisfied my weapon is in order, I bring the shotgun to my shoulder. "You missed your chance, John." I start shaking, and not from old memories. It's from seeing J.A. taken down to the ground, Tarle slashed, and the man who did it stands before me glaring and grinning. I know what I have to do. I look from Sarge to Ise to Rainy.

They nod in approval.

It has to be me. Granny said as much. I have no feeling about it.

West takes advantage of the lull and yells at the crowd, "Listen to me! Give me three days, and I'll open your eyes...."

I raise my shotgun and level it at his head. I cock the rabbit ears. "No one will ever know what you'll have to show them, West. No one."

West turns and closes his eyes. "Mercy, please, I—"

"Where no mercy has been given, none should be expected." I aim at his neck. I pull both triggers.

Smoke blankets the street like Mississippi River fog.

As a gust of wind clears the smoke away, Rainy announces. "I believe it was Adam Smith who once said, 'Mercy to the guilty is cruelty to the innocent.'"

The crowd falls silent. Women gasp, men cringe, and children hide behind their mothers' skirts.

West's body stands in place, quivering like the Yank did at Vicksburg who caught the grenade. Almost severed from his frame, his head falls over, still attached by a patch of skin. His once arrogant, murdering body crumples to the ground and flops around like a fish thrown up on a creekbank.

No one moves. We watch until life slips away from his carcass.

On the ground lies John West—Bible class teacher, choir leader, church superintendent, lodge member, Justice of the Peace—murderer of the innocent.

It is accomplished.

# CHAPTER 68

# SOMETIMES THE BEST OF US HAS TO LEAVE

## 2:45 P.M., EASTER SUNDAY, APRIL 17, 1870

*When the Devil loses, he always takes a few down with him.*

WEST'S COMPANION, ARTHUR Collins, lights out like a rabbit but doesn't get ten feet before guns open fire, Rainy and Tarle among the shooters.

Tarle turns with the grin of a madman but drops the pistol borrowed from Rainy. He cries.

I bark at Rainy, "I thought you took him to—"

Rainy gives me a penetrating look. "The boy—I mean, this *man*—made his decision. It's done."

Tarle looks pale as fresh milk. "I wish I hadn't done it now, Uncle Lummy."

I check his shoulder. "I know, son."

He nods and dries his eyes.

"Rainy, will you?"

Rainy takes Tarle by the arm. "I've got him. Come on, son, go with me." He whispers to me, "He just kept on sayin', 'This is for my pa, this is for my pa.'" He sees the hurt in my eyes for what Tarle did. "You'll have to light out quick. I'll talk him through this, I promise."

"Thanks. You're the one to do it. I couldn't, even if I'd still be around."

Rainy squeezes my shoulder. "Don't forget, I'm his uncle, too. And kin takes care of kin."

I nod and hug Tarle, who is still in shock at what he's done. "It's all right, son. You did the just and right thing."

Tarle squints. "My bullet hit him square in the back." He pukes but waves off my help. "I'm all right, but I ain't never gonna do that again. Ever." He grins, and I know he's all right.

"Now get your ass back in there to let the doctor finish up, or I'll—"

Rainy laughs. "We're going, Uncle Lummy, we're going."

I wish Tarle had been spared doing that. But who knows? He may be bein' prepared for somethin' worse comin' down the road.

Sarge yanks on my coat. "C'mon, I'm getting you out of this street." He takes the shotgun from my hand and gives it to Ise. "We're already known by the good citizens of Atlanta town more'n I'd hoped." As we slip through the crowd, he whispers, "You should carry no guilt for killing John West."

"I don't have to be guilty to feel guilty." I press the owl claw deep into my flesh. Blood drips from my wrist.

Sarge pulls my hand back. "It's all right, son, you're doing good."

Then it hits me. "J.A.!" I rush to where I remember him falling after West smashed his head.

Several people kneel, tending his head wound. One man binds a lady's scarf around his head to help stop the bleeding. We rush J.A. into the store, where Tarle sits with the Doc, who's tying off the last stitch.

Tarle smiles. "I'm okay, Uncle Lummy. I'll be able to tell my grandchildren how I got cut by John West when we—" He leaps from his chair. "What happened to J.A.?"

Ise cries for a moment. "West got him in the head with a cattle brand."

The doctor pulls the scarf from J.A.'s head. He examines the wound. He shakes his head and mouths, "There's nothing I can do. Best make the most of the time you have left."

J.A. winces and looks up at me. "I told you it was my time, didn't I?"

I can't help it. I cry.

"Don't cry for me, brother. Heaven's waitin' on me. Don't bury me facing east, but west. I don't need to see Jesus coming. I want to be pointed in the right direction so I can get up and go with him." J.A. takes my hand. "Just make sure Mary Jane and Aaron are taken care of." He turns to Rainy. "I've been noticin' somethin' about you, Rainy Mills."

Rainy wads up the scarf, knowing there's nothing left to be done. "Pray tell, what is that, my dear brother?"

"You're a good man, whether you believe that or not."

Rainy tucks his chin into his chest. "You don't know the things that I've done. I—"

"I know you well enough. I don't have much time, so I'll say it straight. You've wanted to settle down and open a gunshop." J.A. touches his head and grimaces. "Rainy, marry my wife, Mary Jane. Be a father to my son, Aaron. Lummy, tell them both what I'm sayin'. Will you?"

I can't speak, so I nod, tears dripping.

Rainy backs up. "I'm not fit for such a fine woman of God. She wouldn't have me."

J.A. coughs and spits blood. "She'll have you if Lummy tells her that's my wish." He pulls the wedding band from his finger and places it in Rainy's hand. "She thinks highly of you, and my son will come to respect and love you as a father. Do this for me, please. Let me leave this earth knowing my family is in good hands."

Rainy nods and lays his hand on J.A.'s arm. "I'll do my best."

"That's all I ask, Rainy. That, and one other thing."

"Sure, anything."

"Bury the dark past that has imprisoned your soul for too long."

Rainy stares at J.A. He removes his black shirt and holds it up like he's looking at it for the last time. He hands it to me. "I will wear black no longer. Lay it on John West's corpse when they chunk him in the hellish hole that will be his grave. Lay it on his chest so he'll be wearing it when he meets my father's murderer and my mother's rapist, John Ratliff."

I take the shirt from him and stuff it into my coat pocket. "Done."

J.A. raises his hand like he's reaching for the door. "Lummy, guess who's comin' to get me?"

"Who is it, brother?"

"Susannah, with her arms outstretched. Is that you, Ben, Mistuh Gilmore? Hey, it's Old Bart and Poole. My goodness, it's good to—"

With that, J.A. closes his eyes to open them no more on this earth.

And I wail uncontrollably.

Everyone leaves me alone.

I wipe my eyes and see Granny Thankful walking through the door behind J.A.'s spirit, surrounded by all of our friends who came to welcome him through the thin veil.

Rainy offers comfort. "A famous writer once said, 'The boundaries which divide life from death are at best shadowy and vague. Who shall say where the one ends, and where the other begins?'"

I straighten up. "That I believe."

Granny gives me a nod and a wink. She disappears into a mist I believe that only I can see. My heart wants to burst with grief, but my soul settles in peace for my friend.

Rainy pats my shoulder. "I hope Granny comes for me like that when my time comes."

I grin. "She will, cousin. I guarantee you she will."

Tarle says, "I know who that was."

I smile. "Yes, you do, son."

Tarle checks his stitches. "She's my great grandmother."

Rainy sighs. "She is, Tarle, and you will see her again."

I rub Tarle's head like I did when he was but a boy. "No doubt."

# CHAPTER 69

# NOT ONLY THE FAITHFUL GET RAISED FROM THE DEAD

## LATE AFTERNOON, EASTER SUNDAY, APRIL 17, 1870

*A fitting finish for such a fine churchman.*

D AN DEAN WALKS into Collier's Store and Saloon and throws a twenty-cent piece on the bar for a strong drink. He turns with his back to the counter. "What a mess we've gotta clean up."

Rainy nods for the barkeep to bring a bottle and some glasses. "Henry Adams once said, 'It is always good men who do the most harm in the world.'"

"Ain't that the damn truth. If there were no West or Kimbrell men in the world, good law-abidin' citizens wouldn't resort to violence." The clerk hands Dean a whiskey, and he throws it back like an old hand. He's not and gags for a moment. It's comical at first, and he laughs but chokes a little. His face turns sour.

No sooner than Dean clears his throat and sets his shot glass down, two men burst in the door.

Jim Maybin is right behind them. "I have bad news. These two dumb ass boys, with absolutely nothing else to do but guard the Nightriders' dead bodies, have something to tell you." They hesitate. "Go on, you ignorant fools."

The eldest of the two, who couldn't be more than seventeen, stutters and stammers. He can hardly get the words out he's so ashamed of himself. "A-all of a-a-a sudden, Laws Kimbrell and another man g-g-got up and runned off."

Rainy spits. "How in the world did that happen?"

Dean yells, "What in the *hell* were you doing?"

"We thought they was all dead. So, after you left, we stood our guns up beside a tree and sat on a log to rest and smoke for a spell. Then when we heard a noise, we looked around and saw Kimbrell and this other man tearin' up the ground headin' for the woods. Laws went south, but the other fellow swung over to the east a bit."

Maybin is beside himself. "And before you could get your guns they were out of sight?"

The boy whimpers, "That's right. I'm sorry, they all seemed dead to us."

Maybin kicks a chair. "Shitfire and damnation. You can't trust two boys to do a one man job." He turns to Dean. "I thought you examined the bodies."

Dan Dean holds up his hands. "John Barr and I did, but we didn't kick them over or anything like that. Our minds were still on catchin' John West. Whilst we were standin' there, we heard a commotion in town and headed back, figuring we might be needed. There was just too damn much going on, Jim."

Maybin relents. "You're right. Sorry for yelling."

Sarge steps up to get things back on the right track. "Sounds like Laws Kimbrell headed straight for the Harrisburg Road and his folks' place."

Dean squints. "Yeah, and if his brother Tom got him a horse, they're already in the wind."

Sarge steps up. "Where to, you think?"

Dean shakes his head. "Texas. If so, forget it. You won't find 'em. He's got kin there."

Rainy taps his foot. "Let's find that younger brother of his. What's his name, Tom?"

One of the young guards speaks up, "I'm not sure you'll find him, either. When we came in town yellin' about Laws escaping, Tom grabbed two horses and sped off."

Dean looks at me with one eyebrow raised. "Didn't you tell us that it takes a devil to catch the Devil, Lummy?"

"And we caught him." He's enticing me to help find Laws Kimbrell. It won't work.

Rainy lifts his glass for a toast. "To good men appearing in the midst of evil and doing what what was needed. May the Lord rob us of feelings that may harm our souls."

Everyone lifts his glass, and we say together, "Amen."

Sarge sticks out his hand to Jim Maybin. "It's been a pleasure working with you, sir, even if it borders on evil. We need to leave Winn Parish, and soon."

I offer my hand to Dean and Maybin. "I did say those words, and you will catch West's partner. But like Sarge, I'm done. It's time for us to disappear."

Maybin and Dean shake our hands all around.

The store clerk hands us food and a couple of jugs for the trip.

Sarge says as we gather around J.A.'s body, "We've done enough, boys. Let's get J.A. home and leave from there."

Local men wrap the body in a new blanket and carry it to a wagon.

Sarge waves Dean over. "You think you got a chance of finding those Kimbrell brothers?"

Dan shakes his head. "We've got men all looking for them now, but I do believe they got smooth away. They know this country better'n anybody, and Texas is a big place."

With that, Sarge orders, "Boots and saddles, men."

We gather our things and file out behind the men carrying J.A.'s body.

Out of a corner steps a young boy with his hand out. It's Jesse Cockersham, my friend Mose's son, who made the gallant twenty-two mile ride to round up men willing to fight. He also helped capture Laws and the Nightriders in this very saloon.

"Mistuh Tullos, thank you for belivin' in me when I wasn't sure I could do the job y'all asked me to do. But here's your pocket pistol and silver badge like I promised. Both of 'em gave me courage. Your horse is outside. He's a good 'un like you said."

I put the derringer into my pocket but hold the badge in my hand. I rub its face with my thumb and read the inscription one last time. I place it in his hand and close it up. "This is yours. Always remember to do the right and just thing for everybody, not just when it suits you."

He looks to swell up like a bullfrog ready to belch out a croak. "I don't know what to say. Thank you, Mistuh Lummy. I can't wait to tell my pa about this."

I squeeze his shoulder. "You tell him I said he couldn't have a better son.

You take care of your pa. You only get one, and he's a good 'un." I step out into the street where death ruled the day.

Men have already removed West's body, but the blood stain remains.

Dan Dean walks up from a group of men gathered around the wagon. "We took West's body away. Families of the rest of the Nightriders came and claimed their bodies for burial."

Sarge asks, "So, they've all been properly identified?"

Maybin cuts in. "They have, and I have pardons ready for the executioners. Don't think I'll even have to use them, though."

I ask, "What'd you do with West's body?"

Dean scoffs. "We should've let the damn crows and buzzards eat his ass right here in the street for all to see."

Maybin grins. "We sent his carcass to a potter's field without benefit of sermon, song, or prayer. The men pitched that black shirt on West's carcass and covered him with clods."

Rainy spits. "A fitting finish for such a fine churchman."

Mr. Davis rides up. "Got here as quick as I could. You boys all right? Did J.A. get hurt bad? I sent a message to Mary Jane. How's he—"

I nod to the back of the wagon.

Mr. Davis peers at J.A.'s body and squeezes his eyes shut. He wipes his face with both hands like ants are crawling all over it.

Grief does that to a man. You can't rid yourself of it, and it's inescapable. You just let it be what it is.

Mr. Davis straightens his clothes and tightens his belt. "I'll come with you. Mary Jane's gonna need some help."

Our little funeral procession takes a slow and sorrowful road to J.A.'s house. I don't look forward to laying my brother in the ground.

# CHAPTER 70

# RESURRECTION BRINGS NEW LIFE

## NOON, APRIL 22, 1870

*"Greater love hath no man than this, that a man lay
down his life for his friends."*
—Paul, the Apostle

MARY JANE AND young Aaron make it home in two days. It's an amazing and terrible world in which we live. What once took a week to travel now can be done in a couple of days by rail and stagecoach. Mary Jane's eyes are red, but Aaron looks to be holding up pretty well. The death of his father hasn't set in just yet, I'm sure, and he's trying to care for his mournful mother.

The undertaker has already taken care of J.A.'s body. Mary Jane asked me to say words over J.A. before we leave. Ise and Matt dug a grave on a hill behind the house early this morning. Mary Jane and I sit on the front porch—without a word between us.

She takes in a deep breath. "I know what you're gonna say, Lummy. Like Dorcas, I can't run the farm and raise Aaron without a good father." Mary Jane sniffles. "He was the best. What am I gonna do?"

I put my arm around her. "J.A. would want you to thrive, not just survive, dear sister."

"I can't stay here. I'd see him on every turn. I have too many memories here." She sighs and runs her hands through her hair. "Maybe we'll sell out and move to Winnfield. You know, make a new start."

"You don't have to stay here. Resurrection brings new life. Creator provides what and who we need at just the right time." We sit silent for a moment. "Before J.A. closed his eyes, he asked me to tell you that—"

Mary Jane pats me on the knee. "I should consider a certain man wearing black who would make a fine husband and father?"

I sit back, surprised. "How'd you know?"

She smiles. "J.A. came to me in a dream last night and told me as much. He released me to love another."

I kiss her forehead. "Susannah did the same for me. It will take time to grieve and heal, but Rainy's decided to open a gun shop in Winnfield. Mistuh Davis will find you a good place to live as you find peace again."

Mary Jane wipes her eyes with a kerchief. "In time, I could get to know Mistuh Mills."

I laugh. "It is a bit awkward courting at our age, but you'll do fine. You sweet ladies just seem to know how to snare a man."

Mary Jane swats my shoulder. "Why, Lummy Tullos, I never—"

I cover up like she's about to take a switch to me. "If you haven't already, you will soon." I take her hand. "Rainy has been alone a long time. He'll need to get used to the idea of marriage for the first time. He's a good man and has complimented you and J.A. on your love and friendship as husband and wife several times. He was learnin' by watchin' y'all."

"I'll have to think on all of that later, Lummy."

"I understand. Let Mistuh Davis help you with the sale of the farm. He's the most honest man I know, and he will get you top dollar for the land, house, and cattle."

Mary Jane smiles through her tears. "You were J.A.'s true brother, Lummy Tullos, and the best friend he ever had. I will never forget you—ever."

"Let's go say goodbye to J.A. Just for now, that is."

# CHAPTER 71

# CAMPING BY THE TRACKS

## EVENING, APRIL 27, 1870

*Time spent to turn loose of the bad is done by sitting with good company.*

A LONE COYOTE howls into the darkness to remind his friends they are not alone. I have my friends here, and I am not alone.

I break the silence. "It's a might strange to not have Rainy with us tonight, Sarge."

"I bet so. This is where you two met the first time, right?"

"It is. Thanks for lettin' us ride horses back to Vicksburg. It gives a man time to get his heart aimed back in the right direction."

Ise grins and asks, "Is this where the coyotes almost caught 'cha?"

I laugh. "The very same place." Memories flood my mind like a spring gullywasher. I push them away to think on Martha. "But right now, I've got my mind on an angel in a blue dress."

Sarge laughs. "I know you do. I don't care what mine will be wearing when I get home."

Matt asks, "Sarge, what will you do after this?"

Sarge throws a stick into the fire. "It's time to retire from this man's army. Maybe I'll go to making and repairing shoes."

I'm shocked. "You, a cobbler? My great grandfather Cloud Tullos did that when he came to Virginia from Scotland. I'll be a mule's uncle. Never imagined you'd do that for a livin'."

Sarge crosses his feet in front of the fire. "Yep, I'm looking for peace and quiet, being with my kids, and loving up on a sweet lady who waits for me."

I grin. "That's good, Sarge, that's real good. It's about damn time."
Sarge laughs. "Ain't that the truth."

# CHAPTER 72

# VICKSBURG, HAVEN OF PEACE

## 1:00 P.M., APRIL 29, 1870

*Can pain and joy be had in the same place?*

THE STARS AND stripes flap in the wind over the Warren County Courthouse in Vicksburg. I find the twentieth star for Mississippi. I count back a couple of stars. Louisiana.

"Thank you, Creator."

No sooner does the ferry touch the Vicksburg river bank than Ise bounds away like a deer spooked off of his bed in wintertime. "I'll see y'all in a bit."

Sarge nods for me to look up Crawford Street.

Martha is running down the side of the Prentiss House Hotel wearing that same blue dress she wore when I left with the 1st Mississippi Rifles back in '64. She never looked so good.

Sarge slaps me on the back. "Go see her, son. Matt and I will take care of our mounts."

Martha and I rush together so hard we almost knock each other down. I drop down and wrap my arm around her legs just below her bottom and lift her high. She clutches my face with both hands and kisses me like there's no tomorrow. I'm in heaven.

I set her down and place my hands on her shoulders. I look her up and down like it's the first time I've ever seen her. "My goodness, would you look at that?"

Martha blushes and grins like a young schoolgirl kissed for the first time. She jumps up and grabs my neck, hanging on for dear life. I close my eyes, thanking Creator for his greatest of all blessings. I open them, and I'm shocked to see Susannah standing on the riverbank, smiling like the day we married. Behind her in robes of the rainbow, Granny's hands lay on Susannah's shoulders.

"I thought I wouldn't see—"

Granny smiles. *"Creator has been known to change his mind. You needed to see her."*

They wave and disappear.

My day is complete.

# CHAPTER 73

# GOING HOME NEVER SOUNDED SO GOOD

### 5:00 P.M., APRIL 29, 1870

*Somebody once wrote, 'Cast me not away from thy presence;*
*and take not thy Holy Spirit from me.' He must've done some bad things, too.*

MARTHA AND I sit in the back room of Handerson's Café.

"I can't go home just yet, dear wife."

"You need time to get your soul back?"

"I'd like to go to the sandbar for a few days."

Martha grins. "We will *all* be better if you do."

"So, you're good with it?"

"I am, if you're careful."

"I will be."

Martha looks weary. "Can you go tomorrow? I'm ready to go home."

"I'll leave come first light."

"Back in a couple of days?"

"That should do it."

"I'll pack food."

I shake my head. "Just water, please. I want the pain of hunger to remind me of what I need to focus on. I need to go to the desert like Jesus did."

Martha slips her arm under mine and pulls me close. "You watch out for Satan. He comes when you least expect him."

I pat her hand. "I do know that."

"What if you have one of your war dreams?"

I point to the owl claw bracelet Dan Creekwater gave me. "This kept my head goin' in the right direction several times while I was away."

Martha grabs my wrist and blinks. "Lummy, what have you done to your-self? There's scars and fresh holes."

"What I had to do to stay sane." I rub my wrist. "It works."

Martha takes my arm and kisses my wrist. "I'll get some medicine. We don't want that gettin' infected." She starts to get up.

The door bursts open, and it's none other than Annie Fanny. "Lummy, honey, back safe and sound!"

She sits in my lap and kisses me like only she can.

Martha pushes Annie back. "All right, Annie, get back before Lummy gets to likin' it too much."

Annie sticks her tongue out at her sister.

I shrug. "She is your sister, you know?"

Martha laughs. "And I can't do a damn thing with her."

Annie hops up and shakes her behind in my face. "Good thing Beau showed up when he did or you'd be mine, Lummy Tullos." She rushes out the door.

I shake my head. "That woman will never change."

Martha lays her head on my shoulder. "We don't want her to, either. She loves you, Lummy, for bein' the brother she never had but deserved."

"I love her, too. She makes me laugh. And kisses good, too." I throw my shoulder up waiting for Martha's slap.

"Lummy Tullos, talk about somebody I can't do nothin' with. I—"

"I love you, and you alone, Martha, my dear."

"I'm just glad you're back, and I want you all to myself, that's all."

"Let me go to the sandbar and sit with Creator, and a better man will come back to you."

Annie bursts in the door again, this time with Ise and Jenny. Matt and Sarge bring trays of of pie and coffee. Beau holds the door open for the priest from St. Paul's Catholic.

I stand. "What's this?"

Annie grins. "Ise and Jenny are jumpin' the broom. Right here and now."

I take Martha's hand as we stand.

The priest talks through the words that bind husband and wife together. It's a solemn occasion, but a joyful one as well.

The priest asks, "Do you have rings?"

Ise turns to Sarge, who hands him a small gold band.

Jenny is embarrassed. "In all the excitement, I forgot to get you a ring."

Martha steps up. "We didn't." She takes a tarnished, scratched up brass ring from her skirt pocket. "Lummy's momma sent this to you when she found out you two were gettin' hitched. Thanks, Annie, for lettin' us know."

I stare at the ring. "Pa's wedding ring?"

Martha nods. "You all right with that?"

"I can't think of a better way to have his legacy live on."

Vows are taken, rings are placed, the pronouncement is given, and Ise kisses Jenny.

We shout and cheer for what Creator has done.

# CHAPTER 74

# A FAMILIAR PLACE BRINGS BACK A FAMILIAR SOUL

## 6:00 A.M., APRIL 30, 1870

*You must go to the place that knows you the best to get back what's been lost.*

THERE'S JUST ONE place I can go. It's the safest, unsafe place I know—the sandbar.

I paddle a pirougue Beau let me borrow downstream to the same sandbar I visited after mustering out of the 1st Mississippi Mounted Rifles. What wisdom will I gain this time? What pains will I turn loose in that place of healing?

I ease up to the edge and pull my boat far up the sandy bank. "I can't live with what I've done. I'm so sorry, Creator. At least Elzey won't grow up with a father like me."

Granny whispers in the breeze, *"The first to apologize is the bravest. The first to forgive is the strongest. The first to forget is the happiest."*

"But Granny, how do I forget?"

*"You don't. But those you saved will."*

"Well, ain't that a kick in the head?"

*"It is if you're a stubborn ass, like those who came before you."*

"So, keep lookin' ahead and not behind?"

*"Bring your memories with you, for the road you must travel now will be even more difficult."*

"So, there's another fight, another battle, another war?"

*"Only the one within your soul, Grandson."*

"I can't do this."

*"You will not be alone, even in your worst times."*

"You mean when I die?"

*"He will come to you when it matters the most."*

"Who? Who will come?"

Granny smiles and disappears.

I make camp and stare out across the long sandbar. I remove my clothes to shed all traces of the man I've been these past few weeks. The owl claw bracelet Dan gave me remains. There's not a soul on the river. That's good. I need to find mine again.

I wander along the river's edge. Gentle waves ebb and flow, back and forth, reminding me that all things come and go. I spy a rock bed and walk across the warm sand to look for one to take with me. Searching for agates always clears my mind and brings needed peace.

I look up at the sun and back to the rocks. Every agate in the bed glows like a star in the night sky, each a different color. I'm weak and strong at the same time. The agates rise and swirl around me like a flock of birds. I sit to watch. They stop circling and drop to surround me.

"My protection. Damn, that means a test is coming."

Granny's voice shimmers across the waters. *"Yes, if you are to be the man you wish to be—the man you were intended to be—the man Creator formed from dust and filled with his spirit."*

I want to cuss, but I best not. I look into the sky. "This will not be easy, will it?"

Granny snickers. *"Has it ever been? Life's disasters separate those who love you for who you are from those who love you because you are what they want you to be."*

I pick up an agate that captures my soul and hold it tight.

One word comes from the sky. *"Swim."*

I see a tiny sandbar with a lone willow standing tall. Without thinking, I walk to the edge of the river, clutching the agate, and say, "All right, then!"

I wade into the stream and swim to the small island. The current is strong but not strong enough. I dodge a tree that rolls up and out of the river like the one that injured my shoulder back in '59. I'm getting tired and turn over on my back to swim. It gives some relief.

Without warning, an eddy rises from beneath me, and a large whirlpool forms to suck me down. John West's laugh echoes in my ears as I struggle to swim away. I'm being pulled under like when I was drawn in to take Dawg Smith's head from his body. I'm flailing now. My legs twist this way and that in the swirl. I can't do anything. I lose control. I go down. And down.

I grab one last deep breath before I'm sucked under. I thrash. I'm losing my mind. I have to hold on, but there's nothing to hold on to.

A voice in the water speaks, *"You have everything you need to hold on, Grandson. Give yourself to the cleansing waters so that you may have a clearer understanding of your coming trials."*

The whirlpool takes me deeper and deeper, but I trust Granny. I'm running out of air. Things grow dark. I ball up like a roly poly and clutch the agate for dear life. The river twister takes me where it pleases. I—

When I come to, I lay on the sandy shore of the small island.

Granny sits in the shade of the lone willow.

I puke up river water and roll over on my back. "Granny, what was that all about?"

*"You now know the extent of the troubles you shall face."*

"My war dreams?"

*"Yes. You must know the darkness to live in the light. Do you understand this?"*

"I do."

*"Good. I will always be with you."*

Granny disappears.

# CHAPTER 75

# IN SEARCH OF
# MY SOUL... AGAIN

## 3:00 P.M., APRIL 30, 1870

*Being alone with the Great Alone is never lonely.*

THE SWIM BACK to the riverbank is much easier. "Thanks, Creator." I'm exhausted—from the swim and the whirlpool, from war dreams and killing. I sit on the sandy bank for what seems like hours. A steamer pumps its way upriver near the opposite bank. The captain steps out of the tower and waves.

I wave back and whisper, "There ain't no escapin' human bein's these days." I'm glad when the boat rounds the bend out of sight.

A breeze caresses willow leaves, and an occasional water bird squawks to break the silence. Those are welcome sounds.

Clouds amble by. "Creator, will you send my friends from the other side to come help me when I have the war dreams? I can't do it alone."

Out of the rock bed, Granny rises and walks to the log where I sit. She places an agate in my hand. It glows. It's the most beautiful one yet. *"Your sickness is the price you must pay to help heal the world and to ensure your eyes are always on Creator. Did you not receive the message of the living water?"*

"*You* sent the whirlpool?"

*"Not me."*

"Then who?"

Granny grows brighter, shakes her head. *"Do you not know the answer to that question even now?"*

"Why would Creator put me in danger like that?"

*"No one made you step into the water."*

I hang my head. "Somebody did." I'm confused. "Goin' down in that whirl-pool was like when the war dreams spin me around into places I hate and can't escape. When I woke up on the island, it's like when I come back to myself but don't remember where I had been."

*"Your true and best self led you to find the redemption you seek."*

"Redemption from what?"

*"Everything you hold against yourself."*

"That seems like an odd way to deal with my war dreams—being reminded of them by the very things that cause them."

Granny smiles. *"Creator does have His ways, Grandson."*

Now I understand. The war dreams will continue to remind me that I should carry guilt no longer.

*"You* do *understand. The wisdom of the owl will see you through."*

"The claw Dan Creekwater gave me has saved me several times already."

*"Creator imparts wisdom to all of His children. Only those who are truly His does He use to bless the universe."*

The agate in my hand sparkles when she says the word "universe."

And I am blessed.

# CHAPTER 76

# NEVER THE TWAIN SHALL MEET. BUT WE DID

### DAWN, MAY 2, 1870

*When you cannot see, you listen.*

THOUGH I WANT to stay, I need to go. I dress after a last dip in the river and load my few belongings into the pirougue. I shove off into a fog that's almost too thick to see the end of my boat. And it's a small boat. Granny whispers, *"Let the cloud in your mind be cleared by the light in your soul. She will bring the light to the dark place you wish to leave."*

"Martha."

The gentle thumping of a steamboat creeps around the bend. I can't tell how close it is. I paddle for the shore as fast as I can, but the river holds me in place. I'm fighting the current, but I'm not going anywhere. As the sun bursts through the fog, the front of a barge looms large above me. There's just one thing I can do. Stop wrestling the power of the river and paddle straight into the main stream.

It shoots me out into the channel like a bullet. The wake from the barge swamps my pirougue. I start to swim when a hook grabs the back of my shirt and hoists me up onto the steamer deck. My boat disappears under the silty waters. Beau's pirougue is gone. I shake the water from my hair to see the face of a man whose picture is in newspapers—a thick mustache with wild, wavy hair dancing in the wind.

"You're Mark Twain, aren't you?"

"It's nice to be recognized, although I'd rather no one on this boat know who I am. Just call me Samuel if you don't mind."

"Why?"

"So I can relax. I'm on my way to be married and want one last taste of freedom." Twain chuckles and points to my wedding band. "You understand?"

"Marrying my wife was the best thing I've ever done to be set free."

Twain rubs his chin. "I'll have to ponder that for a bit, son." He throws out a hand to pull me up, and I take it. "Who might you be?"

"Columbus Nathan Tullos, but my friends call me Lummy."

"Count me as a friend, Lummy Tullos. You headed to Memphis?"

"No, suh, just up to Vicksburg. I spent a couple of days on that last big sandbar you passed. I needed to get my soul back."

"Sounds like you need to go to church."

I laugh. "I didn't expect that comin' from you. Not from what I've read."

"You're a reader?"

"I am, and one who finds Creator on a sandbar easier than in four walls of a church house."

"So, you think for yourself?"

"It's gotten me into a bit of trouble from time to time, but yes." We walk to the rail overlooking the water. "I wonder what it was like to have seen Jesus walking on the water."

Twain snickers. "I've never seen anything like that, but I did walk along the shore of the Sea of Gallilee where that was supposed to have happened. It doesn't even compare to our Lake Tahoe. Not terribly inspiring if you ask me."

"Your writing inspires the world. I read where you went to what they call the Holy Land."

"Do you not think it is? Holy, I mean?"

"I tend to believe any place God touches is holy land."

"What about a battlefield?"

I bristle at having to field such a question. "We look to be about the same age. Were you ever on a battlefield in a fight?"

"I volunteered to join a Rebel unit, but it was disbanded in two weeks. I left to work for my brother in the Nevada Territory. But to answer your question, no, I can't say that I have, but—"

"If you had, you would know that the field is always holy because Creator made it, but the battle man brings to it makes it unholy."

"That's a perspective I can agree with. The most holy thing I experienced on that trip was meeting my wife-to-be." He smooths his mustache. "But lest we become too cynical about the human race, man has made some progress."

"Ask the men who fought at Vicksburg if they agree with you."

"Hmmm, I hadn't thought of that."

I laugh and change the subject. "So is Jim Smiley still racing that frog, Dan'l Webster?"

Twain laughs. "You read that story?"

"I did, and it was a good'n. I bet that old frog is still puking up squirrel shot."

Twain chuckles. "And Jim Smiley never got his forty dollars."

We laugh and watch a large log float by.

Twain asks, "Why did you leave organized religion?"

"I realized I was with the wrong crowd." I wink. "After all, bad company *does* corrupt good morals."

Twain snickers. "Well said, my friend."

"Truthfully though, I like goin' with my family to church to sing, pray with the saints, hear Scripture read, and worship with folks I care about. But the railings of a preacher? That I can and will do without."

"Why, too many rules?"

"Rules are for those who need them. Like it says in the Good Book, a man can know Creator just by what we're looking at right now."

"I believe William Blake once said, 'Make your own rules or be a slave to another man's.'"

"I'll not be slave to another man's interpretation of anything, especially not about Creator."

"Hmmm, interesting. You sound a little angry."

"No, just fed up with men who claim authority over souls, and to quote my brother Ben, 'Who ain't got the sense to know whether to scratch their watches or wind their asses.'"

Twain laughs so hard he almost flips over the rail into the river.

I grab his jacket and hold on.

He straightens up, wiping tears. "I ain't heard anything that hilarious since the last time I wrote something funny."

"Maybe I should write a book?"

"I believe you should, my friend, or at the very least, have someone write about you."

My niece Mary is doing just that.

"MISTUH TWAIN, IT has been a pleasure."

"No, Lummy Tullos, the pleasure has been all mine."

"Thanks for saving my hide back there."

Twain waves off my gratitude.

I offer, "If you have the time, I'd be happy to buy your dinner and treat you to the best pie on the Mississippi River. It's just up the street. Handerson's Café. I guarantee you will enjoy the food and leave having a new character for one of your stories after you meet my sister-in-law, Annie Fanny."

"Sounds magnificent, but I must tearfully decline. Tears shed over the laughter that will bring me to tears that I'm going miss. The boat leaves in an hour, and I have letters to mail, telegrams to send, and a few articles to get sent off. Deadlines. It's always those damn deadlines." Twain takes my hand. "But I will remember you, Lummy Tullos."

"Best wishes on your upcoming weddin'."

Mark Twain waves as he races up the street.

I go to Handerson's Café. I want to hold my Martha.

CHAPTER 77

# NO MORE WARS

## SEPTEMBER 1880

*A letter from a friend makes for the best writing never published.*

AT DUSK, JASPER walks up the steps of our dogtrot cabin. I already know the news he brings. He sits quiet for a long time. He fidgets and turns to me. "Ma just passed."

"I'm glad she's finally at rest." We sit in silence.

Jasper rocks in his chair. "You thinkin' we should bury her tomorrow?"

I don't want to answer, but there's no avoiding it. "Yeah, maybe an hour before sunset?"

Jasper gets up, hugs me, and says, "We'll bring her here mid-afternoon, if that's okay."

"That'll be fine."

I look off into the field where Pa used to sit. He's leaning back in his straightback chair against the great oak after a hard day's work. Ma sits in his lap with her head on his shoulder.

James passed last year. He just wasn't the same after Ruth died of pneumonia two winters ago. He turned to the moonshine for comfort and spoke often of how he regretted deserting the Army on the march to Tupelo. His military trial in Mobile shamed him to no end. The shine finally laid him in the grave.

Elihu was found sitting against an old cedar near Phoenix Creek back last spring. A copperhead finally got him. He never could resist stomping a venomous snake's head. This one got the better of him. The venom must've hit his heart so fast his leg didn't even swell up. He just went to sleep smiling with his eyes open, staring into the forest he loved so dearly. I will miss his serenades from atop Tullos Cemetery Hill.

I smile at Jasper. "It's just you and me now, brother. We're the last of the family who settled here."

Jasper wipes a tear. "We've had good lives, and there's still more to enjoy if we just 'bow our necks' like Pa used to say."

We laugh.

"It's the way of things, death coming for us all but never knowing who or when it will be."

Jasper squeezes my arm. "We have good wives and children, Lummy. Ma and Pa, and all the rest, would tell us to get on about livin' life to the fullest."

"They would, without a doubt."

Mary, now a beautiful woman of letters who serves as the school marm near Bywy Creek, rides up in a carriage. "Am I too late? Is Aunt Mary gone?"

Jasper whimpers. "She is. Martha and Isabell are caring for her body at my house. They'll need some time."

Mary starts to step down from her carriage. "Uncle Jasper, may I—"

"Yes, child, go on ahead. But be careful, it's almost dark. Plan to stay with us tonight."

"Thank you. I will." She taps the back of her mule with the reins.

I stand. "Hold up, Mary. I have somethin' for you." I hand an envelope thick with folded papers up to her.

"What's this?" She reads the return address. "This is from Rainy Mills?"

"Yep. It's his story you wanted for your book. He wrote it all down. I read it. Hope you don't mind. I added a few details he forgot or didn't know about I think will help."

Mary hops off the wagon and hugs me. "Uncle Lummy, you're the best."

"So are you, my little dear."

She stares into my eyes. I can see the swirls of an agate that tells me she has sight into the wave of the universe.

I blink. "Best get going, Mary, it's gettin' late."

Jasper asks, "How is ole Rainy doin'?"

"He sent a letter along with his story. He, Mary Jane, and Aaron are doin' quite well. His gunshop has become the place to go for repair and purchasing firearms. Heck, J.A.'s boy, Aaron, has taken a liking to the gun trade."

"That's good. I'm happy for Rainy. He's a good 'un."

"That he is."

I step to the edge of the porch and stare into the growing darkness. A small light floats and flickers up on the hill where so many of our family rest from the troubles of this world. I still have mine, and I can't seem to shake them. I need a change, but I don't know what I need.

I read the last words of Rainy's letter again.

*In the words of the great emperor and philosopher of Rome, Marcus Aurelius, 'Think of yourself as dead. You have lived your life. Now take what's left and live it properly.'*

## CHAPTER 78

# SAYIN' GOODBYE CAN TAKE A WHILE

## LATE FALL, THE TULLOS FARM, 1885

*Sometimes you have to leave a place to continue loving it.*
*But not before you're ready.*

I TAKE A long, good look across the Tullos farm. "I do love this place. Always have. But I can't live here no more, Jasper. I've tried. Too much death. Too much loss. Too many bad memories. I need a fresh start. And besides, I've got that wandering foot again."

Jasper rubs his brow. "I understand. Just know, you helped save us all, and I—"

"Enough. I don't need to hear all that."

"What you need to hear, brother, is that I hate you had to become somebody else to fight somebody else's battles so we all could enjoy our time here on earth. You were the gentlest of us all. You hated the anger, the violence, and abuse. But you had to use it to stay alive. Nobody fought any harder or rougher than you did at Vicksburg, against Dawg Smith, Lester, Captain Tom Ford, and that John West outlaw. You couldn't have done it any other way. Or would you, given the choice?"

I shake my head. "Don't think I could have."

"It's just who you are. You've told me too many times about Granny Thankful always being there to walk with you and guide your steps. The Lord doesn't allow that unless he's behind it all. She'll be there for you now." He stops. "Sorry, didn't mean to preach."

I laugh. "That's all right, I've done enough preachin' in my time."

"That's for damn sure."

"Did you get the farm split up and my part sold?"

"I did." He hands me a roll of greenbacks thick as an axe handle tied up tight with twine. He puts his hands behind his head. "Is paper money okay?"

I stuff the roll into my coat pocket. "Spends just as good as gold or silver, I reckon. Were J.J. and Uriah Miller okay with the deal?"

Jasper nods. "And said if we ever wanted to buy it back, they'd be open to that."

"You?"

"Yeah, I am. Ain't no way I can keep up the whole farm by myself, even with my children helpin'. 'Sides, they got other things on their minds than farmin'. I'm good with that."

I take in the view of the farm. "This is such a lovely, peaceful place."

"Ain't it so? Where will you go?"

"As far as this money will take me. Texas. Maybe the Indian Territory. I don't know just yet. I'll just wander for a while until my soul settles down. I'll find a peaceful little town where no one knows me." I stretch my leg out, and it pops like a stick breaking. "That may take a while."

"So, you might settle somewhere?"

I laugh. "Seems I can live anywhere because I don't belong anywhere."

Jasper smiles. "Think you can take care of yourself? You ain't gettin' younger, you know."

"I believe I can. Yeah, with Martha gone and her children off livin' their own lives, I only have Delaware and Rose. With them attending the women's school over in Columbus, I don't have much need to keep house. Be all right if they come to your place on their breaks from school?"

Jasper squeezes my arm. "Hell, they're me and Isabell's daughters, anyway, you know that."

"You don't know how much I appreciate it."

"We'll treat 'em like our own."

"You always have. Thank you." I glance up the hill at the Tullos cemetery. "With Martha and Ma gone to the other side, I need a change of scenery, as they say."

Jasper laughs. "Brother, you've had enough scenery changes for all of us."

I gaze out over the farm. "We had a good life here growin' up, didn't we?"

"Yeah, we did."

"You gonna stay here, Jasper?"

"Got nowhere else I want to go. Like Grandpa Temple used to say when we were little, 'We were Celts of the moving and settling kind.' I'm of the settling kind, brother."

"Yeah, and I'm of the wandering kind."

Jasper points at me. "You were always more like the blue-painted people who danced naked around the fire in the old country."

"I'd rather live that way any day than be mashed like a tater under somebody else's fist."

Jasper fidgets, wanting to ask a question he knows I don't want to answer. "What about—"

"Elzey?"

"Yeah, you gonna go see him?"

I rub the back of my neck. "Not sure yet."

"He'd be what, twenty-two, twenty-three?"

"Twenty-three next month."

We sit quiet for a while.

Jasper changes the subject. "You'll write, won't you?"

"Yeah, I'll write to you and Martha up on the hill in the cemetery. Would you read my letters to her, if you don't think that's too crazy?"

"Not at all, brother. Glad to do it."

Through the leafy pines, a single moon beam catches the edge of the simple marble stone I set for Martha after she passed. The glistening blinks, reminding me of Martha's eyelashes fluttering over sky blue eyes the first time we met on the steps of the Prentise House Hotel. That memory still takes my breath away. It seems like a thousand years ago.

The pine needles shift in the wind, and a moon beam catches the agate I left on top of her marker. It glows like the sun itself. A wispy cloud drifts across the little cemetery up on the hill. It stops, and Granny Thankful appears with a grin and waves, the signal that she will always watch over our people.

I walk back inside and sit alone in the dark. Firelight flickering keeps me company. I look around at the old cabin the Tullos family built so long ago. Despite all the hell I've been through, I've had a good life here in Choctaw County. But I need to go. Somewhere. Else.

But right now, I'm tired. So very tired.

"I'll just rest a bit."

I ponder leaving the Tullos farm. Again. Leaving Choctaw County. Again. For good, this time.

"This may take a little gettin' used to."

I close my eyes, praying for a good dream.

# CHAPTER 79

# GOING WHERE
# I DON'T KNOW WHERE

## MID-MORNING, SATURDAY, JULY 29, 1886

*Sometimes your feet do the thinking when your mind can't.*

ARIDER TROTS down the road that leads to our old dogtrot cabin. It's Matt Poole. He ties off his mount and hands me a message. "What's this?"

"Don't know, but its marked Special Delivery. The new Postmaster asked if I would bring it out to you when I told him I was headed to Columbus. I didn't mind."

"Thank you, Matt. Can you sit a spell? I don't have any of Elihu's fine muscadine wine, but if you'd like a taste of good Wood brothers' moonshine, I believe I could scare up a jar."

"That sounds good, Uncle Lummy, but I'm on my way to a friend's weddin'. I best keep goin'."

"Anybody I know?"

"Don't think so. He's the grandson of some fellow named Nehemiah."

"Kneehigh?"

"They do call him that."

"Will he be there?"

"Don't think so. My friend mentioned that he's out in Kansas someplace called Fort Leavenworth. He went to work at some new place for soldiers from the war who don't have any other place to go if they're disabled or old. It sounds like a good thing, but that's all I know."

"Well, I'll be. Kneehigh." I cringe at the memory of picking him up over my head and slamming him down on the hardpan street in Bankston so many years ago.

"Sorry, Uncle Lummy, but I better get goin'."

I shake his hand. "Don't forget to think of your Uncle Tom Poole from time to time."

Matt grins. "I think about that great man every day. I'll stop by and put flowers on his grave next time I pass through Greensborough."

"Rainy once told me a saying from some philosopher named Pericles. 'What you leave behind is not what is engraved in stone monuments, but what is woven into the lives of others.'"

"My uncle's life is woven into mine, and I'm the better man for it."

"Don't be a stranger, Matt."

He tips his hat and grins.

I watch until he makes the turn onto the main road. Poole and I had many good times growing up together.

For the first time maybe ever, I'm alone.

I look to the sky. "Creator?"

Granny's voice wisps like wind through a cane break, *"Remember what Creator said, Grandson."*

"I will neither leave nor forsake you." I look down at the letter in my hand. "It's addressed to me, but the return address says... Winn Parish?" My heart leaps. "Who's writin' me from Winn Parish?"

# CHAPTER 80

# IT NEVER ENDS

## NEAR NOON, SATURDAY, JULY 29, 1886

*Some letters are as bad as the taste of chicken and dumplin's is good.*

JASPER EASES OFF his wagon with a pot of something that smells good.

"Chicken and dumplin's?" I smile at the wonderful gift.

"Just like Ma used to make. Isabell thought you might like a batch."

"You'll thank her for me, won't you?"

Jasper sets the pot on the stove and returns, stretching. "It seems I get stiffer these days. Doc told me the day I sit down, I'll stay down. Arthritis, or some fool thing like that."

I say nothing, holding the crumpled letter in my hand.

Jasper finally says, "All right, out with it, Lummy."

I hand him the letter. "You remember me telling you about fightin' the West-Kimbrell Gang in Winn Parish back in '70?"

"I do. What's this?"

"Read it first, then I'll tell you."

*Atlanta, Winn Parish, July 20, 1886*
*Lummy Handerson,*

*I have not forgotten the treachery you measured out on our family. The reckoning is coming for you and yours.*

*No friend of yours,*
*T.K.*

Jasper hands back the letter. "Who is T.K., and what's this about?"

I give Jasper the short version of that story again and finish by saying, "So, you see, Tom Kimbrell helped his older brother, Laws, escape. John West and Laws led the West-Kimbrell Gang. Laws and Tom disappeared into Texas after the Easter Sunday massacre. Laws later got hanged for murder, but Tom talked his way out of it like he did in Winn Parish the day we executed the gang."

"So, this is that Tom Kimbrell?"

"Who else could it be?"

"But you used Handerson as a fake name like you did when you helped the Yankees burn Wesson's Mills. That's the name he uses—"

I wince at that painful memory. "Yeah, but I see now that was a mistake. Kimbrell knows my real name. He was there when I told West to use Handerson instead of Tullos. Kimbrell's just using it to get at me." I crumple the letter again. "Tom Kimbrell wrote this, I just know it. Don't think trouble will find its way to Vicksburg, but I'll get word to Annie Fanny and Ise, just in case. No, I'm pretty sure I know who he's after—Tarle for sure, maybe Elzey."

"Some grudges last a long time."

I spit. "The fire that burns the slowest burns the hottest."

"What are you gonna do?"

I stare down at the initials T.K. I look up, tears dripping. "I can't do it, Jasper. I just don't have it in me anymore. The war dreams come every other day. I'm old, and my hands shake. Old age plays hell on an old man." We laugh for a moment. "I can't do it, but—"

Jasper leans in. "But what?"

"I know who can."

A TALE OF TWO COLORS

# COUNTED NOT
## among the DEAD

A SHORT STORY

# THE STORY OF
# MARION TULLOS

"**M**Y SISTER'S IN there! Get her out! Please!"
Men and women rushed from every direction to make a water bucket line as the volunteer firemen ran their wagon too close to the flames. They fell back from the heat, choking and coughing from inhaling heavy smoke. A loud crack. An ear-splitting pop. The cupola gave way and crashed into the center of the burning ruins of the Marion County, Mississippi, courthouse.

Ashes of all the important papers—land deeds, censuses, births and marriage records—floated up into the night sky like so many lightning bugs in summertime. The recorded life of families who pioneered our county vanished in a blue hot blaze. It was all by design. Big leather books smoldered in the ashes, along with my uncle, Silas. And with him, my big sister, Marion.

I cried. I screamed. I finally fainted into the arms of the volunteer firemen who held me back. I woke to the sheriff addressing the crowd. Not a stick of the courthouse was left standing.

"The war's been over, but carpetbaggers and scalawags have been burnin' down courthouses everywhere. No account men with no breeding who steal good folks' property while the government turns a blind eye. Sadly, we lost more than our county's records tonight. Two of our fine citizens died in the fire—Mexican War veteran, Silas Tullos, and his lovely niece, Marion. Silas guarded our courthouse every night. His last words when I saw him earlier tonight were, 'I fought at San Jacinto with Gen'l Sam Houston, and I'll keep them thievin' carpetbaggers away!' I've got a good idea who caused this calamity. I'll be leadin' a posse come first light."

Truth be told, the sheriff didn't know who'd done it. I didn't, either, and I didn't know what to do, not until I heard a whisper when I stepped into Uncle Silas's old house at the edge of town where we lived.

"Sissy, that you?"

I shrunk back, never having seen a ghost before. I squeaked out, "Yeah."

"It's me, Marion."

"You're alive!" I hugged her and didn't want to let go.

She finally peeled me from her body. "Anyone think I'm alive?"

"No, they think you burned up with Uncle Silas with nothing left to bury."

"Good. Then I can do what needs doin'. You can't charge a woman with a crime if she's dead. When it's done, we'll come back. I won't be counted among the dead."

"Sheriff's leading a posse in the morning."

"Does he know who did it?"

"Do you?"

Marion didn't say, but she knew—a preacher, a voodoo witch, and the ringleader—a beady-eyed carpetbagger who you knew lay awake every night scheming like the Good Book says.

"When are you leaving?"

"Soon as I get packed."

"I'll be coming with you."

"Good. Throw some bacon and beans in a flour sack. I want to get a jump on the posse."

We sneaked west out of town, smelling of smoke—and vengeance.

SLEET PELTED MARION'S face like buckshot, but she didn't flinch. No unexpected early spring ice storm could stop her. "They ain't gettin' away with it. Not by a long shot. I'll catch 'em come hell or high water. I'd just as soon go ahead and catch hell first, then get baptized again in the Mississippi River on the way back through—whether I need it or not." She let out a little chuckle—a rare event.

"You'll catch hell all right. That pistol toting carpetbagger is no fancy pants dandy dude. Aren't you scared?"

"I'm more scared of what I'll do when I find that low down skunk. Besides, they won't be expectin' me. I'm dead, remember?"

"For what you're planning, you better get them sins washed off. If we make it back, that is. You do know a preacher has to do the dunking or it won't take."

"No scalawag preacher is ever gonna touch me again. Besides, the Bible never says who has to do the immersin'."

Marion read her Bible religiously and could hold her own arguing scripture with any preacher foolish enough to try her on. I wouldn't dare, even though I had more schooling.

Marion sniffed. "Ol' preacher took up with that voodoo witch when I worked in Natchez. I know where they're headed."

"Where?"

"To Hell after I'm done with them but west to the Indian Territory first. Out there, outlaws who want to get lost won't be found. They won't get that far, though."

My horse shivered and snorted, shaking the ice from her mane.

Marion patted her horse's neck. "Ain't that somethin'? A scalawag preacher, voodoo witch, and a thievin' Yankee carpetbagger conspiring to burn down the county courthouse to get rich. Beats anything I've ever seen!"

I shivered worse than my horse. "I can't believe Uncle Silas is gone. They don't make them any better."

"Ole witch tried to kill him just before he went to work at the courthouse last night. Took the little pension money he'd squirreled away in a snuff jar and left her pet cottonmouth in his bed."

"No! I thought she came just to help out an old veteran, keeping house and such."

"And offerin' a little 'comfort' now and again. I warned him, but he wouldn't listen. He did yesterday afternoon, though, when her cotton-mouth's fang caught his thumb. It swelled up bigger'n a cucumber. 'Don't hurt so bad,' he said when I brought his supper to the courthouse. Those were the last words he ever spoke to me." Marion wiped a tear. "That snake-bite won't go unanswered."

HER NAME WAS Marion. I don't know if they named my big sister after the county when Ma and Pa came to Lott's Bluff or if the county was named after her. History is often written by those who spin the best fairytales. Either way, she had the spirit of the Swamp Fox they now claimed inspired the name. She was the prettiest girl in the county—too pretty to stay in the orphanage they put us in when our folks died.

Marion sneaked to my bed one night. "I'll come back." She slipped away into the darkness. I had no idea where she went. Not until Uncle Silas came for us when he moved to Mississippi from Georgia. That seems so long ago.

"HOW DO YOU do that?"

"Do what?"

"Go on like you're not freezing your hind end off."

Marion said nothing. Cold blustery wind never seemed to bother her. Nothing did.

My hair was frozen to my hat.

Marion muttered under her breath, "Hadn't been for Uncle Silas snatchin' me up by the hair of my head and gettin' me out of that 'den of iniquity' in Natchez, I'd already be counted among the dead."

"I didn't know, honest I didn't."

"Some things you do because it's the right thing to do. Some things you do because you don't have a choice. And some things you choose to do to make a wrong right."

"Uncle Silas saved you?"

"Wasn't like a knight in shinin' armor in some storybook if that's what you're thinkin'. He knifed a man to get me out of there. Then he came for you. Said he couldn't leave you with a child violatin' preacher in that orphanage. No more'n he left me to rot in Natchez."

"He wasn't our real uncle, was he?"

"Closest thing to an uncle we'll ever have. Pa saved his life in the war. Guess Uncle Silas was payin' him back by takin' care of us." A tear sparkled on her cheek. "He taught me how to be human again." She brushed away the tear. "Now hush up! I'm tired of talkin'."

Marion didn't mean anything by her harsh words. She had a good heart. Working in a house of ill repute made her hard. Uncle Silas murdered made her dangerous. The only sweetness she had left was in what she was doing now—avenging Uncle Silas's death and caring for me.

There'd be no sweetness, though, when she caught up to his killers.

WE REACHED THE Homochitto River as the sleet let up—but the cold didn't.

"Aren't we taking the ferry?"

"Strip down to your drawers. Now!"

I tied my clothes to my horse's saddle. "I can't swim very well."

"Great, then I'll have four deaths on my head."

I had nothing to say to that.

Marion waded out into the swollen current and yelled, "Grab your mare's tail and follow me. I've got her reins."

Midway across, my hands slipped. I yelled, but there was nothing Marion could do.

I crawled out on the sandy bank a quarter mile downstream and limped my way upriver. "Why didn't you come after me?"

"You're here now."

"I could've drowned!"

"I taught you how to swim, didn't I?"

"Yeah."

"Then there it is. Knew you'd make it. Besides, I knew you'd need a fire when you got here. Get under this tarp and strip off them wet rags. Take this blanket I've been warmin' for you."

I thought my teeth would chatter right out of my head. The blanket and fire felt good but not my feelings. It wasn't Marion's fault I was swept away. Neither was Uncle Silas's death her fault or Ma and Pa's for that matter. But she took it that way.

I didn't know how to start, but I did. "Marion?"

She didn't look up from drying off two shiny pistols. "Yeah?"

I didn't ask where she got them. "When will you stop taking responsibility for things not yours? Those robbers killed Ma and Pa, not you."

"I might as well have. I hid, too scared to move. They butchered Ma and Pa. I'll never get that out of my head."

"You were only seven."

"Old enough to pull a trigger!"

"Going after Uncle Silas's killers won't fix that."

Marion handed me a steaming cup of coffee. "No, I can't fix that. But I will fix this." She threw a stick on the fire. "Enough! Put on these old work clothes. We don't want to be seen as two women traveling alone. Open a can of beans and then get some rest. I want to make the Rodney ferry tomorrow before dark. We leave before daylight."

THE SUN SET in the west as we crossed the Mississippi River. The ferryman said three ragged characters traveling fast crossed not four hours earlier.

Marion handed him an extra dollar.

At dusk, we sneaked up to the edge of a nothing little Louisiana town named Waterproof. The ferryman told us a steamboat captain named the place when he saw an early settler standing on the last piece of dry ground surrounded by floodwaters—hence, Waterproof.

I expected fire and brimstone to rain down from heaven any minute for the wickedness I saw there—drunks lying in the street, scantily clad women calling after every man, and gamblers looking to separate anyone from his money.

"I didn't know such places existed."

Marion snickered like one of Satan's minions. "You've never been to Natchez, have you?"

I understood then. Marion knew how to fight evil—become more evil than the demons she wanted dead.

The town proper seemed deserted except for the fancy wooden building lit up at the other end of the muddy street. Men brandishing shotguns guarded the doors.

Marion pointed. "There. Let's hide the horses around back." She handed me a pistol. "When I say shoot, you shoot but not before."

No one noticed us with our hats pulled down when we took a table in a corner. It was that kind of place. A large pit commanded the center of the room, and men placed bets as women caressed their bodies, hoping to cash in on some of their winnings.

Marion and I peeked over into the pit. Several rattlesnakes hissed, angry at being poked.

A crusty old timer holding up a silver dollar cackled, "Here comes the Voodoo Queen!"

She swung her hips from side to side, carrying a caged raccoon high in the air.

"Place your bets, boys. My 'coon against five deadly serpents."

The carpetbagger took bets as the scalawag preacher counted money.

Marion whispered, "Stay here. Fire every bullet you got when I say."

I felt for the pistol as Marion made her way around the ring.

The voodoo witch's eyes rolled up into the back of her head. "May the gods of my ancestors fill this masked warrior with power to defeat Satan's slithering dragons."

Just as the voodoo witch opened the raccoon's cage, Marion shoved her into the pit. Rattlers latched onto her from every angle. She screamed.

Marion shoved the flailing raccoon into the carpetbagger's face.

He flopped around on the floor, his eyes torn from their sockets.

The preacher ran to the bat wings with Marion hard on his heels.

Just before she exited, Marion smashed a coal oil lamp in the corner where the carpetbagger lay moaning, and she yelled, "Shoot!"

I fired every round I had into the ceiling. I ducked through the smoky blaze and scrambling crowd after Marion.

The carpetbagger ran out of the saloon, covered in flames, clawing at his eyes.

I gasped for air, looking for Marion.

She was holding the preacher's head underwater in a horse trough across the street.

"Touch me again, will you, Preacher?" She let him up for a breath. "Any last words?"

"Please, I ain't ready to die! I need to repent!"

"No time left for repentin'! This baptism will just have to do!" Marion held him under until no more bubbles came up. "In the name of the Father, Son, and the Holy Ghost, I say amen!" She let go and collapsed.

I threw a double handful of water on her face, and she jumped up ready to fight. "It's done, Marion. Let's go."

In the noise and confusion of the fire, we walked our horses out of town, unnoticed, back to the ferry and camped for the night.

The deed was done, but absolution was in short supply. We crossed the peaceful easy flowing big muddy river at sunrise.

A young preacher stood on a stump near water's edge, speaking words of mercy and grace to a small crowd. "Ain't nothin' you've done too long, or too bad, that God won't forgive your every wrong."

Marion handed me her reins and hopped off her horse. She looked up at the preacher. "Is it true, what you're sayin?"

"Every word."

"Then I'm ready."

The preacher hurled himself into the air, arms raised to heaven. "Hallelujah! Witness God resurrect this soul from a grave of sin and give her new life!"

Marion shucked her boots and walked into the silty stream, holding the preacher's hand. She turned and smiled at me for the first time in a long time. "Told you I wouldn't be counted among the dead."

ANTHONY WOOD grew up in historic Natchez, Mississippi, fueling a life-long love of history. Not long after high school, he lived and worked in Alaska for several years. He returned to the South and ministered for nearly three decades among the poor, homeless, and incarcerated. Leading an effort that planted five urban churches inspired him to co-author *Up Close and Personal: Embracing the Poor* about his work in Memphis, Tennessee. He also authored a number of articles and stories about inner city ministry.

Anthony is a member of Turner's Battery, a Civil War re-enactment group, the Civil War Roundtable of Arkansas, and serves as President of the White County Creative Writers group. His short stories and poetry have won multiple awards and have been published in *Saddlebag Dispatches, The Vault of Terror,* and *The Avocet: A Journal of Nature Poetry.* One of those stories, "Not So Long in the Tooth," won a Will Rogers Medallion in the Best Western Short Fiction category for 2021. Anthony is also the Arkansas Writers' Hall of Fame inductee for 2024.

When not writing, Anthony enjoys roaming and researching historical sites, camping and kayaking on the Mississippi River, and being with family. Anthony, and his wife, Lisa, live in Arkansas.